Honey

ALSO BY VICTOR LODATO

Edgar and Lucy

Mathilda Savitch

Honey

a novel

Victor Lodato

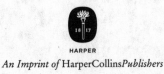

HARPER

An Imprint of HarperCollins*Publishers*

HONEY. Copyright © 2024 by Victor Lodato. All rights reserved. Printed in the United States of America. No part of this book may be used or reproduced in any manner whatsoever without written permission except in the case of brief quotations embodied in critical articles and reviews. For information, address HarperCollins Publishers, 195 Broadway, New York, NY 10007.

HarperCollins books may be purchased for educational, business, or sales promotional use. For information, please email the Special Markets Department at SPsales@harpercollins.com.

FIRST EDITION

Photograph by Ton Kung/Shutterstock, Inc.

Library of Congress Cataloging-in-Publication Data has been applied for.

ISBN 978-0-06-330961-6

24 25 26 27 28 LBC 5 4 3 2 1

for Chris

and for the women in my family,
the warriors, who protected me

It is beautiful to be in love. It is also beautiful to be alone.

—OSHO

Bodies have their own light, which they consume to live; they burn, they are not lit from the outside.

—EGON SCHIELE

Part One

1 One Hundred Dresses

In the tub, Honey lifted a varnished toe—Sunset Peach—to turn on the tap. She'd been soaking for nearly half an hour but didn't feel ready to get out. A bath soothed the mind, as well as the lines on the face; one emerged not only calmer but a few years younger.

As the heat bloomed again, she sank into the remaining scum of bubbles. Her breasts floated at the surface like so much curdled pudding, and in her ears she could hear her blood. The candlelight, an attempt to evoke a spa-like atmosphere, now just seemed depressing. And there was something funereal about the creeping scent of roses. Honey glared at the ceiling.

What had happened earlier today with her grandnephew continued to vex her. She shifted her weight and groaned. Sometimes her life seemed absurd—a far-fetched movie pitch. How could a woman who collected rare Japanese porcelain, and who was so well versed in the spiritual teachings of Osho and Yogananda, also know where three bodies were buried in the state of New Jersey?

And she wasn't talking cemeteries. She was talking the unmarked graves of so-called missing persons. Rush jobs, with garden shovels and plastic tarps. One of these bodies was quite close, in fact—just a few miles away, behind her nephew's house, the house that had once belonged to her father, the Great Pietro. It was the house in which she'd been born.

Let us bow our heads and pray, the priest used to say, in that old stone church with its leering, overdressed saints. Let us, indeed, thought Honey. Her father and brother, and possibly even her mother, had purchased first-class tickets to Hell.

Not that Honey believed in such a place. But she could easily imagine it; she could see the flames and the pitchforks, a storybook from her childhood. The fact that it was imaginary was irrelevant. The imagination was surely all that mattered after death.

Despite these irksome thoughts, Honey scrubbed her elbows with the loofa, emulating a technique she'd once read Joan Crawford had used: counterclockwise, in fierce determined circles. It was no doubt meant to be symbolic, a slap in the face of time. Honey approved. At her age— eighty plus a dash of salt—she had every right to whatever Hollywood arrogance she could muster in the war against oblivion and ruin.

As she extended her leg to turn off the hot water, she got a cramp in her foot. Her painted toes clenched and separated like some sort of prehistoric bird. The pain was horrid. Perhaps she'd get Dominic to give her a foot rub after dinner. That is, if she didn't croak first, right here in this wretched tub.

Honey wasn't usually prone to such maudlin thoughts, and she blamed Michael for her current state of mind. Her waif of a grandnephew had stopped by earlier. He had to be in his mid-twenties by now, but he still lived with his parents, in that dreadful house. Honey barely knew the boy; she'd long been out of touch with her relatives. Even after moving back to New Jersey, she'd made no real effort to see them. Similarly, her grandnephew had come to visit only once before, when he'd been short on money. And why had he come today? Well, bingo!

"I know you have it, Aunt Honey." He'd brandished his cunning dimples without shame. The kid was a looker, disarmingly pretty. "I'm family," he beseeched at one point, trying to bribe her Italian heart. He was flirtatious for the most part, but then suddenly he'd become quite agitated, and while pacing to and fro had knocked into a side table. A porcelain vase decorated with snakes and flowers had fallen to the floor and shattered. Honey had bought it years ago, in Paris.

They'd both stared at the wreckage for several seconds, during which time Honey awaited an apology. But Michael hadn't offered one. "That alone is probably worth more than I'm asking for. A few hundred dollars is nothing to you."

"You're absolutely right," she'd replied. "But my problem is what you might be using this money for." Honey suspected gambling or drugs. She told him she could sniff out vice better than a border collie.

At which point the boy proved to be a clever negotiator. "You weren't a saint, Aunt Honey. I've heard stories."

"Have you, my dear? Do tell."

But Michael stayed mum, offering only a gentle shrug. He'd even blushed a little, proving he was human. When he spoke again, suggesting that the two of them might be more alike than she realized, Honey had capitulated. "Fine. Just don't tell your father."

As she walked away to the bedroom to get her checkbook, she'd had to suppress a smile. Because it was true enough—she hadn't been a saint. In her youth she'd occasionally ventured beyond the pale. At Bryn Mawr she'd experimented with drugs, mostly psychedelics. And of course she'd done a little cocaine in the seventies. Who hadn't?

Obviously, she didn't mention any of this to her grandnephew. She just wanted to hand over the money and get him to go. And it was true, she did have plenty—all of it her own. From her family she'd inherited nothing.

"A check?" he said, when she returned to the living room. "What am I supposed to do with a check? It's *Sunday*."

"Can your passions not wait a day?" she asked. "Besides, I don't keep that much cash in the house." She was a fabulous liar.

"Give me less then. Give me what you have."

Goodness, it sounded like a stickup. Honey was old-fashioned, in certain ways, and the lack of *please* irritated her. *Please* give me what you have. Simply that, and she would have handed over the cash without argument.

By this point Michael was jitting around the room again, tugging on a frond of his shaggy, unkempt hair—blonder than Honey recalled and nearly as long as a girl's. As he paced, she studied him more closely. He wasn't very clean, and his eyes were so dark with fatigue that he seemed to be wearing makeup. The thinness of his limbs, the chaotic stomping—something wasn't right. His ripped shirt fell to his knees and looked more like a dress.

"What's going on, Michael? What's the problem?"

"Nothing's going on." He stuffed the check into his pocket.

"Why don't you sit with me for a bit? We'll talk."

But apparently this suggestion was something to sneer at. When he picked up a framed photo of Honey in her youth and said, "Well, weren't *you* the bomb," she suspected he was making fun of her.

Still, she'd pushed on civilly. "I haven't seen your father in a while. How is he?"

"My father's an animal."

Honey couldn't argue with this assessment, but in an attempt to be politic she said, "We all are, darling."

When she offered to make the boy a cup of tea, he seemed amenable. But then she mentioned his father again, and he snapped. "I have to go!"

Marching away, he banged into another table—this time it seemed on purpose. A lamp tottered (cloisonné, expensive). Honey lunged to catch it before it fell.

She was so relieved by her success that it took her a few seconds to realize that Michael was gone. Peering out the front window, she saw him getting into his car—his father's old Beemer. It was filled with junk—boxes and clothing and what appeared to be a guitar. Was the boy living in the damn vehicle? Honey gestured for him to come back, but he paid her no mind—and when he pulled out of the driveway it was with such force that he left black lines on the pavement.

* * *

In the tub, she managed a few deep breaths. Hadn't she learned it was useless to attempt conversation with her family? Her parents and brother were dead, and while they'd never been easy, this new generation seemed worse, in that they lacked even the pretense of civility.

A pity there wasn't a niece or a grandniece to balance out the testosterone. But her brother had produced only a boy, and that boy had begotten more of the same. And though Honey was generally quite adept in dealing with men, this expertise didn't seem to apply to those with whom she shared her blood.

Maybe because all of these men had a bit of her father in them, and that was a territory Honey still stumbled through. She'd loved her father desperately. She'd detested him. It was as simple as that.

Perhaps the real problem was that Michael resembled her father physically—to the point of being uncanny. The blond hair, the valiant blade of his nose. The more Honey thought about it, the more it upset her—

and she wondered why she'd come back to New Jersey at all, after spending so much time away.

When her brother, Enzo, was killed, she'd made a vow never to return. Nearly half her life had been spent in Los Angeles—her home up until a year and a half ago. Even after college, when she'd lived in New York City, it was as if she'd lived on the other side of the globe. Her parents had rarely visited—her brother only once. Honey had returned the favor by coming home infrequently. At a certain point she'd stopped visiting at Christmas. No doubt she'd broken her mother's heart.

But she was different from her parents, her brother—or so she'd always told herself. At seventeen she'd left home because she wanted another kind of life. Of course, the rest of them had taken this as an insult. This wanting of other things was just not done. Her choice to go away to school had elicited a chorus of whys and what fors. There were so many men interested in her, her mother had never ceased to remind her. "Everything you need is right here." The message was disgustingly clear: marriage trumped education.

But Honey hadn't wanted a husband back then. She was too curious, too hungry—both of these things a sign of her perversity. *Orgoglio*, her mother called her—arrogant. And Honey chose not to argue, since this word also meant self-respect.

Even her beloved brother had informed her that she didn't know her place. Her duty, apparently, was to stay home, give the family more children, contribute to the welfare of the animal, the beast that was the Fazzinga family. When she'd left for Bryn Mawr, it was at the height of her father's power. After a long history of poverty in the broken ankle of the old country, the Fazzingas had finally, in their adopted homeland, achieved a considerable degree of wealth. They were respected in New Jersey. And feared.

"Ilaria," her father had said to her on the day she was leaving for college—trying to claim her by invoking her given name—"I know you come back." "Of course I will," she told him, shaking in his presence, as she often did. He'd kissed her gravely, his terrifying mustache scouring her cheek as he slipped her a roll of bills. Nearly two thousand dollars—a fortune back then. Honey had thanked him and put it in her purse. Later, on the train, when she pulled out the green wad fastened by a blood-red rubber band, she wondered: Was it a gift? A bribe?

But what was he buying? Her silence? Her love? She'd considered throwing the money out the window, but she wasn't stupid. She could use it to buy a hundred dresses. A new life would require new costumes, new disguises.

Philadelphia. Bryn Mawr. How she'd adored those names as a girl. They'd seemed part of a superior language, one in which there existed a word that did not exist in her father's house. *Freedom.*

Perhaps it was her grandnephew's anger that disturbed her most of all—so much like her father's. The way the boy had barged into the house, demanding things. The living, the dead—for a moment, the story had blurred.

I know you come back. Over sixty years ago it was, but she could still hear her father's voice. Still feel the grip of his hand, so tight it had made her knuckles crack.

*   *   *

Honey closed her eyes and quietly recited a mantra she'd learned years ago in Varanasi. The exact translation escaped her, but it had something to do with dispelling the mind's impurities. She rolled through it twice, with limited success. As she climbed from the tub—no easy task—she considered the sobering fact that, eventually, she might need to have one of those dreadful support rails installed.

Limping across the floor to work out her kink, she gave a quick glance to her form in the full-length mirror. She'd stayed in the bath too long. She was pink and puckered and sweating like a butcher.

After blowing out the candles and flicking on the lights in the adjoining room, she put a towel down on her grooming chair and sat before the vanity. A peculiar woman stared back at her.

"Shall we begin?" they said, in unison.

There was still an hour and a half before her date with Dominic—but she'd need every minute to make herself presentable. She was not the kind of woman, like so many these days, who left the house in sweat-pants and flip-flops, with those ghastly plastic clips in their hair.

Besides, she didn't consider it an imposition to fuss with her appearance. The formalities of attire, of maquillage, of proper grooming, it was a pleasure for Honey, a project akin to art. And though she always employed certain signature motifs, the paintings were never the same. She allowed her moods to influence the sweep of her hair, the cut of the clothes, and especially the colors—not only of the garments but of the makeup. The fleshy peach slathered on her toes no longer seemed appropriate for her current state of mind, but it was far too late to consider a fresh pedicure.

Anyway, Dominic liked this particular shade. He said it reminded him of coral he'd once seen in South Korea during the war. The night he'd told Honey this, inspired by the madeleine of her nail polish, she hoped he might dive down and kiss her toes. Mr. Hal, a lover from her youth, had often done that, and she'd found the sensation quite pleasurable.

But Dominic was rather old-school. Which was fine. She actually liked how proper he was, especially considering what a rascal he'd been in his youth. Honey was not blind to the absurdity of her affair—dating a man who'd once been the kind of boy she'd spurned, as a girl.

And despite the lack of toe kissing, Nicky was a good lover, in his slow-motion, workhorse sort of way. Honey did not for one second take this friendship lightly. It was a wonder to her that she'd finally found a man with whom she'd happily spend the rest of her life.

Of course, such romanticism had a limited sweep, considering the fact that Honey had—what?—maybe five, ten years remaining. Dominic, who was older, probably less.

She'd met him—*re-met* him—a year or so ago, at Florence Fini's funeral. Florence had been a girlhood chum, an excellent seamstress who'd made Honey a number of dresses. Wonderful things that still fit her. And though they were old, these garments hadn't lost their youth. Florence was a genius and had stitched something eternal into her creations. Honey planned on wearing one tonight, maybe the green silk with the marigold cuffs. Accompanied, perhaps, by a thin orange ribbon in her hair, which she was thinking of doing *au chignon*.

Dabbing some geranium oil on her neck, Honey felt a pang of hunger. A welcome thing, because she and Nicky were dining at Dante's. Honey adored the place, even though it was considered out of fashion, with its red velvet walls and penguin waitstaff. There was still a coat check and a restroom attendant. And if one wanted some privacy, there was a bank of cozy mahogany booths, each with its own dim, secret-keeping lamp. The light, coming through a tortoise-shell shade, was the color of bourbon.

The place, to Honey's mind, was not out of fashion at all. It was the world that was out of joint, most people in such a rush they failed to see the beauty of lost time.

✳   ✳   ✳

In the living room, when she saw the porcelain shards on the floor, she was confused. Hadn't she cleaned them up after her grandnephew had left? She got out the dustpan and the broom, collected the pieces, and deposited them in the trash bin in the kitchen.

But then it seemed wrong to just toss them out like that, among coffee grounds and carrot tops. She dug the shards back out and laid them on a tea towel. Someone very skillful had made this vase; even in pieces, it was beautiful—so much so that it seemed to possess a soul.

Again, the bodies came to mind. And the sense that maybe she'd come back to New Jersey for *them*. As if they were children that must be put to bed. Somehow, she had to finish things. Make amends. For a long time Honey had considered herself blameless; but now it seemed possible that she, too, had booked a first-class ticket to Hell.

She leaned against the sink, feeling woozy. When the room stopped spinning, she wrapped the fragments in the towel and put them in a drawer. And then she called Dominic and told him not to pick her up. Dante's was only ten blocks away. She'd rather walk, she told him.

"Are you all right?" he asked.

"Fine, I'm fine. I'll see you there at seven."

Besides, it was spring, almost warm, and she could glimpse, just out the window, a slow breeze ringing the bells of rhododendron.

The air would do her good.

2 Dante's

Maybe it was more than ten blocks. Or possibly she'd made a wrong turn. Honey glanced around, humming. She wasn't worried. She knew this town like the wrinkles on the back of her hand.

Of course, a lot of things had changed. At the northwest corner of Pickens and Garfield, for instance, Mrs. Collucci's bakery had vanished. Instead there was a shop that appeared to be selling only baseball caps—the items displayed on metal spikes, like barbarian trophy heads.

Honey walked on, her pace not exactly brisk. She'd been forced to take her cane tonight. An unfortunate accessory, but she made it work with the counterintuitive audacity of sling-back pumps—the sharp click of her heels trumping the dull thud of the rubber-tipped cane.

As she turned right on La Rosa, she spotted Mabel's. The bar had opened just over a year ago, not long after Honey's return to Ferryfield. Several young men were standing outside, chatting and smoking. She could tell, simply from the motion of their cigarettes, that these men had style. They moved the glowing sticks emphatically, as if to illustrate the twin swans of suffering and love—every gesture rightly indicating that the story was epic, and that it was best told with some degree of irony. Honey smiled. She'd always admired the gays. Yes, Mabel's was *that* kind of bar.

As she got closer, she saw that the patrons were not, perhaps, as young as she'd first thought. But the good grooming and posture, the well-tended bodies, all played to the men's favor. Masters of trompe l'oeil, they generated the *aura* of youth.

Of course, their clothes were a bit disappointing. They were all dressed the same, in oxfords and chinos and dull brown shoes. Plus, those assembly-line haircuts, like soldiers off to war. It had been so much richer, the sartorial choices of these men, in Honey's old neighborhood in the city—especially in the seventies and eighties. Such marvels of hats and scarves and studs. Oh, and those skin-tight jeans; fearless, the way they'd once displayed their weapons.

For they had been weapons back then. So much style and hope and brilliance, so much beauty, had been murdered by that dreadful disease. Honey was glad the worst of it was over—at least for most of them. In many ways, she had to respect their new reserve. They wanted to seem like anyone. Well, they *were* anyone now. It was progress in some ways, in some ways a loss.

But it was their battle, and she had no right to judge. As she approached the men, she waved. A few waved back. Nearly all of them looked at her with astonishment. Perhaps, thought Honey, she reminded them of their heritage.

"Good evening, gentlemen."

"Well, look at you," one said.

"Yes, look at me," she replied. She even offered the boys a slow turn, heels and cane—*click, click, thud*—to show them the back of the dress, which had a lovely chevron-shaped plunge, bordered with the same brilliant marigold as the cuffs.

One of the men raised his glass to her, and she in turn nodded cordially. When he held open the little gate to the outdoor area, Honey was touched.

"Oh, I'd love to join you, boys, but I have a date."

"Wow," the man said. "Can I be you when I grow up?"

Honey laughed, feeling strangely flushed, and suddenly so much better. "Darling, you've made my night." She reached out and squeezed his hand.

He squeezed it back.

A little thing, but at the same time not.

In another life, she thought, I might have made a decent mother.

*　*　*

As she approached Dante's, Honey could smell the red sauce, the delicate herbaceous green beside the more buoyant thrust of the tomatoes. Then came the pungent rush of perfectly charred meat, the tang of garlic, the eye-closing perfume of melting cheese. And above all of this, like bumblebees trailing pollen, was the golden flower of the olive oil.

Could she really smell these things? She was still a few doors away, so possibly she was having an olfactory hallucination brought on by hunger. She was absolutely starving. That nonsense with Michael had given her a touch of agita, and she'd gone without lunch.

Honey was happy to finally be here, at a restaurant one could trust. As a child, she'd dined at Dante's with her family—and then later with various boyfriends. Even during her time in New York, she'd occasionally come home just to eat here. Sometimes she met her mother for lunch, and they would share a tower of frutti di mare. Dante's never disappointed. For a moment she stood before the crackling neon sign and the big oak doors that were, to those who knew the place, the entrance to paradise.

Goodness, hunger made one nostalgic! Or was that true only for Italians? And then nostalgia led to sentimentality. A spiritual mentor had once advised her to beware of such things. Nostalgia was a lying serpent.

But even as Honey felt it tightening around her neck, she didn't brush it away. Its tongue was forked, wasn't it? Half of it spoke the truth. Because Dante's *was* a sacred place. I mean, for God's sake, look.

Just outside the door, a basket sat on a small table. It was filled with chanterelles, the first of the season. Their convoluted shape reminded Honey of a hat she'd once worn in the sixties.

During her walk, she'd already decided what to have for dinner: sautéed rapini, followed by the branzino with lemon and capers. But that was out of the question now. She'd be a fool not to order risotto ai funghi, or perhaps pasta al profumo di funghi.

Well, definitely *something* funghi.

She was reaching for the door when she felt the hand on her shoulder. And then the kiss on the back of her neck.

Dominic.

She turned and was pleased to see him dressed in the pale violet shirt she'd given him for his birthday. His hair, gray but still thick, was pushed back with that dreadful cream of his that smelled like diesel. Oh, he was a lovely man, and she did not revise that opinion even as he opened his mouth and the Mack truck of his accent hit her in the face.

"Don't you look bew-ti-ful?"

* * *

"Fanooks," he said later, with disgust, when Honey mentioned Mabel's. They were sitting in one of the mahogany booths, snug as two corpses in a casket, a bottle of blood between them. Dominic had already imbibed quite a bit.

Fanook. It was a word her brother had used, too—a degradation from her father's day, when it had been *finocchio.* Fennel. Maybe because such men were soft and sweet. Or maybe it had something to do with the fact that fennel seeds were once thrown at homosexuals burned at the stake, to help reduce the stench.

Honey chose not to discuss etymology with Dominic. Instead, she extended her hand and put it over his. "Darling. I have lived near these men, and I've had many friends among them, and I find it intolerable—"

"I'm just saying, if I ever had a son like that—"

"Well, you don't have a son, dear, do you?"

Immediately Dominic's expression changed, and Honey was sorry for her words. Nicky's dead wife, Mary, had never had *any* children, and Honey could see from the sadness on her friend's face that this hadn't been a choice but rather a decree of fate.

"Let's not argue." She poured him some wine. "But please try to be a bit more open-minded."

He took a deep gulp and nodded. "It's just the way I was brought up."

"Yes, I know. It's a liability for all of us."

Honey was already tipsy from a half glass of Barolo, but she poured herself a splash more. To hell with her blood sugar—she needed a buzz tonight.

"If you want to speak about distasteful men, let's talk about my grandnephew Michael."

Sipping faster than was her habit, Honey proceeded to tell the entire story, from barge-in to broken vessel. The restaurant's walls began to spin. Where was their goddamned soup? She'd pass out soon if she didn't get some sustenance. "And then he just took off in a huff. You should see the tread marks on my driveway."

"Sounds like he's on dope," Dominic said.

"That's what I thought." Honey set down her glass a bit too firmly. "It doesn't matter. I don't even know why I'm telling you all this."

"It's your family. Makes sense you'd be worried."

Honey harrumphed. "I'm not really *worried*. I just don't understand why he doesn't ask his father for money. Corrado has plenty. Enzo left him very comfortable. And Corrado does a good business, I'm sure."

"Well"—Dominic's voice grew hushed as he looked out to the dining room to make sure no one was listening—"Corrado's not exactly the nicest guy."

"That's true. You know, they keep inviting me over for the holidays."

"You should go. They *are* family."

That dreadful word again. Honey shrugged. "I'd rather be with you."

Dominic sucked down the last of his wine. "The holidays are hard for me."

Something to do with the dead wife, Honey suspected. Mary had been quite religious—though Dominic, as far as Honey could tell, was not a believer. Still, God or no God, there was no escape from the mystery of loss. Dominic was looking pale suddenly, despite the three glasses of blood. Honey was about to suggest he eat some bread when Signor Tarantelli, the owner, appeared at the table.

He shook Dominic's hand and then kissed Honey's. With a slight bow in her direction, he apologized for the delay with the food. He sounded as if he'd just stepped off the boat from Sicily, though it was all an act—he'd been in the States since he was a child. "We are very busy tonight. The soup is coming any moment. And I give you the wine on the house."

"That's not necessary," said Honey.

"Please, allow me," Signor Tarantelli pleaded—again with a slight bow. "In fact, I bring you another bottle."

His request was so insistent—what could Honey say? She nodded. "Grazie mille."

When the owner walked away, Dominic was smiling and seemed to be suppressing a laugh.

"What?"

"Nothing," he said. "They're still afraid of you."

"*Afraid* of me? What is that supposed to mean? Signor Tarantelli is a friend. I've been coming here for more than seventy years."

"And your father before you."

"I don't know what you're talking about."

"I'm just saying, he remembers the old days."

Honey, with an irritated flourish, broke off a chunk of focaccia and dipped it in a pool of olive oil. "Sometimes kindness can just be kindness."

"I suppose. I thought you didn't eat bread."

"I don't. But I'm starving! And what are you saying, exactly—that Tarantelli thinks I'm going to pull out a gun and shoot someone if he doesn't bring my soup?"

Dominic couldn't hold it back now; he laughed loudly. "I'd love to see it." His lips were absolutely purple.

"You're drunk, darling. And the past is the past."

Dominic rolled his eyes, as if to say *maybe*.

Honey handed him some focaccia and said, "Eat, old man."

What irked her were not his insinuations, but that he could read her mind. If that's what love was, she wanted no part of it.

A woman needed her privacy, more than a man did. For a long time, it had been all a woman had. Honey had worked her whole life to build her territory, a world that was hers alone. She would let no man take away her inner life.

But look at the old fool. He continued to stare at her, with those moony eyes and that ravenous smile. *Three shits to the wind*, as her mother would say, ruining a good American expression with her Neapolitan tongue.

When she reached out to take away Dominic's wineglass, he grabbed her finger like a toddler.

"I love you, Honey."

"Is that what your silly stare is all about?" She told him he looked like a five-year-old. "An adorable one, but still."

"You know, when I was a kid," he said, "I always thought you were inapproachable. I used to think . . ."

Oh, here we go, thought Honey. The snake had bitten Dominic, too. Sooner or later, everyone, especially at their age, succumbed to nostalgia. And wine just made it worse.

Besides, Honey knew exactly what Dominic was going to say. *When I was younger, I thought you were the most beautiful girl in the world. You looked like a movie star. I knew you'd never consider a slob like me.* Well, she'd just have to let the man get it off his chest. And if he was going to profess adoration, she would at least adopt the proper pose. Turning her head slightly to the left (her right profile was superior), she lowered her eyes and said, "Tell me. What did you use to think when you were younger?"

"I don't know." Dominic's speech was slightly slurred. "I just thought if I could have someone like you, I'd be able to make something out of my life."

"But you *have* made something, Nicky. Your business with the—what do you call them?"

"Rivets?"

"Yes, it was quite successful, wasn't it? And you had a long, happy marriage."

He nodded tentatively, indulging her indulgence. She saw that there was no reason to lie.

"Well, most unions," she allowed, "are rarely what the lovers hope for."

"We were never really lovers, Mary and me."

"I see." The man wanted comfort, apparently. "Well, you know, I looked at you, too, when I was younger. When you were looking the other way, of course."

Dominic blinked, in a slightly distracted way.

"But why even pursue this line of thinking?" Honey continued. "I was not available back then. So we can just lay those old fantasies to rest. *What we might have been.* We just have to make do with what we can salvage now, at such a late hour."

Dominic didn't seem to comprehend what she was saying. He remained in a fog for several seconds more, but then regained his focus and took her hand.

Honey patted his arm. She also made an effort to stop rambling inanities—to simply meet Dominic's silence with her own. Hand in hand, waiting on the soup.

He looked different suddenly, perhaps different from how she'd ever seen him. A hopeful sadness on his face that almost frightened her.

Because what did she have to give him, really? She had nothing. And, at their age, wasn't it foolish to mimic the sentiments of youth? More than foolish, it was pathetic.

"Let me show you something." Dominic reached into his pocket and removed his wallet. He pulled out a bill.

No, it was a newspaper clipping. He unfolded the thing and handed it to her. Immediately she felt the tears spring to her eyes.

Honey Fazzinga and Florence Fini Win This Year's Singer
Sewing Competition. A dress to die for, in midnight blue!

Honey kept her head down, a wincing smile to hold back the emotion. She didn't dare look up at the man before her, the charming galoot who'd saved this ridiculous clipping. With her head lowered, she had no choice but to read on.

Watch out, Dior! These two girls have made a dress that Singer
thinks is the snazziest thing since sun on the French Riviera.
With sequins like this, your boyfriend might need sunglasses.

Honey could not distinguish her laughter from her tears. She wiped her eyes.

"We won a goddamned sewing machine, you know. I gave it to Florie."

"I remember seeing you in that dress."

"It was a good dress."

Honey looked again at the photograph that went with the article.

In black and white, a much-younger version of herself stood tall and proud, modeling the blue dress with its eccentric web of sequins, a glistening collar of tiny crystal beads. Beside her, Florence slumped meekly in nothing but a smock, a cloth measuring tape in one hand and in the other what appeared to be a wrinkled map but was surely the pattern. The photo had been taken outside—but where was it, exactly? Maybe in Florence's backyard. On the right side of the image you could see the branches of a tree and beyond that what looked like a small vegetable garden.

"It was Florie's design," she said to Dominic. "I just suggested the beads. It was wrong of me to take any credit."

The photo was blurry and there was a crease from the fold across her dead friend's neck. The ink was so faded that both their faces were no more defined than the man in the moon. But Honey could clearly recognize herself and Florence on that lawn, playing their parts perfectly. Rich girl, poor girl—Honey in velvet heels and Florie in matronly black loafers. They'd both been seventeen.

Honey studied the blur of her former countenance.

"That girl no longer exists," she said.

And Dominic said, "I'm sitting with her."

Refolding the clipping, Honey was gentle. When she held out the paper toward Dominic, his eyes were glassy, too.

"Willow marrow," he said, slurring his words, and somewhat out of breath.

Honey looked at him quizzically. "Excuse me?"

He coughed and reached for her glass of wine, and after finishing what was left he tried again.

"Will you marry me?"

Honey paused for only a second before replying. "In what life? This one? Or"—pointing toward the clipping—"that one there?"

But Dominic seemed to be in no mood for irony. He grabbed her hand again, this time with a strength that defied his age. The pressure was so insistent that Honey found herself blushing.

And then babbling.

"Well, as you can see, darling, there's not much room down there." She wiggled the fingers on her left hand—every one occupied by a semi-precious hard-candy ring. "Pity I don't have a free digit."

Dominic only smiled, undoing her.

"Marry me," he said again.

Honey's cheeks felt in need of a fire hose.

In contrast, Nicky seemed absolutely placid. His face had the look of stone, and he was squeezing her hand even tighter. When he said her name again, in abbreviated spurts—"Hon, Hon, Hon"—she wondered if he were about to scold her. But then his smile returned, though it was strangely crooked now. Clearly, he'd had too much wine.

"Dominic, stop—you're hurting my hand."

He tilted his head, like a cat playing cute.

And then he was doing more than just tilting his head; he seemed to be falling.

"Nicky?"

When he dropped below the sightline of the table, it had the feeling of a prank.

"Very funny," she said. "Fine, fine, *yes*, I'll marry you—is that what you want to hear? Now stop please and don't be stupid. *Dominic*." She could hear her voice rising; somewhere above her it cried out like a crow.

Honey worked her way out of the booth and walked around to the other side. Dominic lay there mute, with bluish saliva draining from his mouth.

"Help!" screamed Honey.

When a busboy rushed over, she told him to call an ambulance. Behind her she could hear Signor Tarantelli addressing the other patrons. "Don't worry, people, it's not the food. They haven't eaten yet."

Oh, if only she *had* brought a gun! She turned and glared at the insipid man. "Get us some water, Tarantelli. A bag of ice." Honey had no idea what she would do with either of these things, but it was somehow calming to give orders. The shimmering tin ceiling was suddenly teeming with ghosts.

Not yet, she prayed.

When she looked again at Dominic, in the lavender shirt, with his powerful old hands and that awful stained mouth, she felt completely unhinged—and though it was difficult, due to the cramp in her leg, she squeezed into Nicky's side of the booth and leaned down to slap his face.

"Did you not hear me, you stupid fool? *I said yes.*"

3 A Serious Blue

At the wake, she wore a dark-blue suit, knowing she'd be judged for black. The *other woman* did not wear black, unless of course she wished to challenge the family, the wife—vying for the dead man's loyalty in the world to come, or, even worse, vying for whatever resources remained in this one. Black meant war, while blue could be seen as humility, as deference—old-world rules Honey felt it best to abide by. There were a few women of her generation present— women who knew Honey, knew her past. Some of these women had been friends of Mary's, Dominic's rightful other half. Honey sat at the back of the room, planning to wait until the others paid their respects before paying her own.

Of course, such deference wasn't really necessary. Technically, she was not the other woman. Mary had been dead for several years before Honey took up with Dominic. But that wouldn't matter in the least to the die-hard Catholics in the room.

Besides, she had been the other woman once before in this town. Twice, actually. Brief affairs during summers home from college. Most of the girls she'd left behind had married early, their young husbands far from ready to give up their hungers. Honey had acted impulsively. Luckily, neither of the men she'd slept with—nor the wives she'd betrayed— were present now; all, in fact, were dead.

Still, there were others in the room who would be quick to judge. Angela Carini, in particular. "Little bitch with a big mouth," Honey used to call her. The freakishly tiny woman had exposed Honey's affair with Pio Fini—Florence's husband. Once the beans were spilled, Florence never made Honey another dress. Angela professed to be Florie's friend, but she had only broken the woman's heart by blabbing. Angela had a cold soul, despite the burning crucifix around her neck.

But, seeing how the woman was clearly in failing health (at the funeral parlor she was dragging around a portable oxygen tank), Honey felt no animosity. Only sadness.

Of course that didn't stop the animosity from flowing in her own direction. Despite the solemnity of the proceedings, Honey's presence occasioned certain kinds of whispers and petty shakes of pious heads.

No matter. It was enough for Honey to know that her dark-blue suit was as heavy with grief as any widow's black. It was a serious blue, one that had the *feel* of black. Darker than a midnight blue. More militant. Vivienne Westwood, circa 1980s, sleekly cut, with a few errant angles that were Honey's only bid toward power.

Now and then she could feel the eyes on her, furtive disdainful glances—but whenever she caught them, the women looked away.

Afraid of you. Dominic's words came back.

And then, to make things worse, her nephew Corrado showed up, along with one of his sons—not Michael but the other boy, Peter, named after Honey's father. The wives came, too.

What business did they have here? They were not friends of Dominic's. When she asked why they'd come, Corrado put on a show of being confused by her question.

"We're here for you, Aunt Honey."

Perhaps they were worried she wouldn't leave them her money. *Act nice to her*, she could imagine Corrado telling his family. *She's loaded.* Perhaps that's what the holiday invitations were all about.

"How did you even *hear* about Dominic?" she asked.

"It happened at Dante's on a Sunday night. Kinda hard *not* to hear about it."

She could smell Corrado's cologne, something expensive surely—but he'd put on too much. A pet peeve of Honey's, the way people wore their scents, dousing themselves in it like so much gravy. Only a lover, Honey had always felt, should be able to know the truth of one's perfume. Others should think they've imagined it, or perhaps confused the scent for an emanation of the wearer's soul.

Honey recalled how much Dominic liked the geranium oil she used. The first time he detected it, they were lying naked in bed. He said it smelled like roses and pepper. "Which about sums you up," he added, kissing her neck.

Oh, but this terrible musk coming from her nephew—the odor pompous and somewhat fecal. He was standing far too close, overpowering Honey's memories. More than anything, she wanted to get out of this ghastly room, go home, take a bath, drink some wine, fall asleep.

"I appreciate you thinking of me," she told her nephew, "but there was really no need for you to come."

"Like I said, we wanted to."

Corrado put his arm around her, and Honey felt something tighten—her heart, her breath. Such intimacy was not appropriate. Not only did this man not know Dominic Sparra, he also did not know *her*—the story of her life, the complicated path that had taken her away from this town and then, at such a late hour, back to it. Her nephew, despite being her brother's son, was a stranger, and his encompassing arm only made her feel more alone. Still, a touch was a touch, and Honey started to cry. Oh, for heaven's sake, why hadn't she worn a veil? She'd actually considered it—but when she tried one on at home, it seemed a little too much, the veil with the suit. A little too *beekeeper*.

Honey bit her lip but for the life of her could not stop crying.

"It's okay," Corrado crooned.

His wife came over next, and then his son and *that* wife. The four of them surrounded her, patting her arm, one by one, as if she were some creature in a petting zoo.

"I'm fine. I'm fine. Thank you all so much."

Honey could see Angela Carini looking over from across the room, as well as some of the other women. She knew what they were thinking: that Honey was still part of the family—that she still benefited from the money, the connections, the corruption. The truth was, she hardly knew what Corrado was up to these days.

Well, she knew a little. That the business had moved on from garbage to recycling. Apparently it was wide-open territory, where one could make a killing. The greening of the mob. Ha! Honey should write a book.

But even this jest in her head was quickly silenced. It was an old silence, one that had been instilled in her since childhood. One did not speak of these things.

Even to say to Angela Carini and these other women, *I'm not involved with them anymore, not involved with that world*, would only be to admit that such a world existed. And the game had always been to pretend that it didn't. It was as strict as any religion, one in which you associated only with your kind, and where it was forbidden to speak of certain rites and rituals. Besides, the more she protested to these women, denied her associations, the more she'd be seen as either a fool or the exact thing she was trying to convince them she wasn't: a criminal.

Corrado's hairy, scented hand remained on her arm. The rest of his family stayed close too, hovering, in a way that was both protective and threatening. Though Honey didn't really know these people very well, she considered them no different from the earlier versions she'd run from.

It was never the corruption she minded, or even the greed. Those things were everywhere—the way of the world. What Honey abhorred was the violence. Violence that they somehow believed could not stain them.

Senza infamia e senza lode, her father had said. Without blame or praise.

Only God can judge, but He doesn't judge. He forgives. That was her mother.

Honey had heard that things had changed a bit since the old days. The violence apparently was not what it had once been. Still, it hadn't vanished—she was certain of that. Even if Corrado hadn't killed anyone, he was no doubt an expert in intimidation and threats. The breaking of bones, surely, would never go out of fashion; it would remain as common as salt on the table. *My father is an animal*, to quote the man's own son.

"You know, I saw Michael the other day," she said to Corrado.

Immediately he let go of her arm, and his wife looked nervously in his direction.

"So, what's wrong with him?" asked Honey. "He seemed very distraught."

"Nothing's wrong with him," Corrado said sharply. "What did he say to you?"

"Michael's just," the wife cut in breathlessly, "he's just a little confused." Corrado glared at her, and she fell silent.

When Honey glanced at the other son, Peter, she detected a subtle sneer of disgust.

Now she was curious. She asked the boy if he was close to his brother.

But Peter only grunted and excused himself, mumbling, "I gotta pee."

Honey turned away from his crudeness and caught a glimpse of the coffin. She immediately came to her senses, remembering what was important. Not Corrado, not Michael, but the lifeless man at the front of the room, whose cold hand she wished to hold one last time. "Thank you for coming," she said to her family, "but I must pay my respects."

"Of course, of course." It was the wife—Rita? Rina? Honey couldn't remember her name. The woman was smiling awkwardly, brushing her fingers against her husband's arm. "Corrado, let her go."

Let her go? As if it was his decision, as if he held all the power. It's what they all thought, these men.

"Goodbye," she said to him.

"Aunt Honey, listen—we really would like you to come to dinner sometime. Fourth of July, maybe? We're doing a big thing in the yard."

"Let me think about it, dear. Parties are hard for me, at my age."

Corrado nodded. And then, as if to torment her, he kissed her, in the old way, on both cheeks.

*   *   *

At the front of the room, Honey knelt before the casket. The pain in her knees, stark evidence of life, only increased the gulf between her and the body before her.

This business of saying goodbye was always dreadful—but, as the years went on, it got a little less so. When she was younger, such final encounters with beloved bodies had wrecked her. She'd completely lost it at her mother's wake.

But now there was no need for such a torrential fuss. Honey would be leaving soon herself. And so with Dominic it was less an *arrivederci* than an *a presto*: see you soon.

Though how or where she would see him remained a mystery. Honey liked to imagine there were certain energies, delicate strands of light that in the chilly vastness of eternity would become entangled again. She'd had a vision once, in her twenties, while standing near the edge of a cliff, her own soul unraveled by LSD. She'd seen them everywhere, those strands of light, and she knew they were the emblems of the dead.

Of course, in such a form, she and Dominic might not remember each other's names. Possibly language became irrelevant. What were names, anyway? No more than candy wrappers.

Still, as she peered down at what was possibly the last man who would love her, Honey was frightened. What if he didn't remember her at all?

From her purse she took out the small vial of geranium oil and rubbed a drop on Dominic's cheek—a sailor's wife sending her man off to sea, keeping him safe and true with a scented handkerchief. And then she kissed him.

Behind her, she could hear a few whispers, as well as a gasp that was clearly generated by Angela Carini's oxygen-deprived lungs. Honey ignored the peanut gallery and straightened Dominic's collar. He was wearing not the lavender shirt but a white one that had gone slightly gray. The dark serge suit was not one of his best. She wondered who had dressed him. Why hadn't they put him in the Brioni she'd helped him pick out? Suddenly she was crying again.

Strands of light? Reunions of energy? It was a theory she'd held to all her life, but now it seemed preposterous. What was more likely was that she'd never see this darling man again.

*   *   *

She stood at the side of the room, by a bank of candles—like those in a church, except without a coin slot. Kneeling down before the coffin and then standing again had used up a considerable amount of energy, and she was hiding by the candles mainly to collect herself before making her exit.

"She's definitely had some work done," someone whispered.

"And look at what she's wearing."

Old people! thought Honey. The deaf ones were the worst—they imagined everyone else was deaf, too.

Or perhaps the women intended her to hear their jibes.

Honey would have liked to have turned and said, "Yes, this suit was made by Vivienne Westwood. You know Vivienne, don't you?—she designed those wonderful outfits for the Sex Pistols." And as for her face, she'd inform them that she had indeed had some work done—quite a lot. And so what? She was not ashamed of it.

But when Honey turned, she said nothing. She merely nodded at the women.

Angela Carini nodded back.

Oh, the poor thing looked terrible. Silver hair as insubstantial as smoke, and those plastic tubes running into her nose. Honey found herself approaching the creature. "How are you, dear?"

Again, Angela nodded, her whole body trembling slightly. MS, perhaps. Or Parkinson's.

"So strange that we were girls once, isn't it?" Honey said. The question contained no malice, simply wonder.

Angela's only reply, though, was more nodding, more trembling.

Honey wished to say something else, to offer some kindness or innocuous reminiscence, but a few of the other women were glaring now.

"Well, take care, ladies." Honey held up her hand in a gesture of peace, and as she walked away she heard Angela's voice, a deep breathless hiss.

"Bitch."

* * *

Outside, Honey decided she was too tired to walk and opted for an Uber. Her driver was a woman around fifty, in a stretchy glitter-encrusted T-shirt, her hair in pigtails. *Mutton dressed as lamb*, thought Honey. Why certain women insisted on doing themselves up like children was beyond comprehension. It only made them look deranged.

"You can sit up front," the woman offered, but Honey, feeling vulnerable and wanting privacy, squeezed into the rear. The tiny blue hatchback was basically a lawn mower pretending to be a car. But at least it was clean, and the woman silent, though her driving was a bit sloppy. She seemed preoccupied with other things—stealthily pressing M&M's

into her mouth, frenetically tapping on a small computer screen attached to the dash, checking her phone.

And then she made a right on Redneck Avenue, which was not the most direct route. The poor woman seemed to be under the control of her computer, unaware that it was misleading her. Honey didn't speak up. The long way home was fine. The evening ahead would be interminable, crowded with regrets. Sleep would not come easily.

Now and then the driver eyed Honey in the rearview mirror and flashed a smile. It took a surprising amount of effort to flash one in return. Honey longed for the dark glass barrier inside a limousine. She'd been chauffeured in quite a few of them, during her younger days with Mr. Hal. And she'd often taken town cars in Los Angeles, where she'd lived for nearly forty years.

California. For Honey, the word always came in song, chirped by Joni Mitchell. There was still a bit of the folk song out there in Cali. The wide-open hearts of everyone, like messy bedrooms presented without shame. The whole innocent immorality of the place. Honey had loved L.A. enough to think she would spend her final years there.

But then her two dearest friends, Lara and Suzanne, had died within a year of each other. Lara, at sixty-nine, of breast cancer. Suzanne, only in her fifties, by her own hand. Powerful women, both. Honey, who'd worked for an auction house, had consulted with these ladies about their acquisitions. Paintings and fine objects, Honey's area of expertise. Quickly Lara and Suzanne had evolved from clients to become two of the greatest intimates of Honey's life.

In the fog that followed their passing, an alien thought had emerged: *Go back home.* Lonely, retired, Honey lost all sense of time and place. She roamed around her town house, perseverating on other deaths—her mother, her brother. Plus, there was a feeling of unfinished business with her father. And it seemed that the only way to grapple with his ghost was to revisit the graveyard of her youth. If she could just sort a few things out, even if only inside her heart, then she'd be free to join Lara and Suzanne. By which she meant, free to die. She'd even signed up for something called the Final Exit Network, since the Hemlock Society was no longer in business. When Honey moved back to New Jersey, she was acting more from grief than reason.

And now here she was, grieving again, and alone. As she looked out the window of the little Uber, there was still so much that was familiar. Certain buildings returned her gaze, their time-softened brick taking on the indignity of flesh.

"You really should make a left at the next corner," she said to the driver.

The woman pointed to her screen. "It tells me to go straight."

Honey leaned back, giving up, as the car sailed blindly forward, navigated by the unknowable mind of the computer. There was little traffic, and they zoomed with merciful quickness past several land mines of memory. Enders Alley, where Honey had received her first French kiss. Prospect Avenue, where she'd lost a diamond bracelet. Bergen Street, where, on a dare, she'd stolen a pair of pantyhose.

Oh, and there was Cressida Drive, where Florence Fini had lived, and where her family still did. Honey had met the grandson and daughter-in-law at Florie's funeral. The boy was an absolute angel, an albino who'd not had an easy life. Next week, if she was feeling better, maybe she'd pay them a visit.

"Beautiful weather," the driver said.

"Yes," agreed Honey. "It's lovely." The crape myrtles were in bloom, the dogwoods. Asters and daylilies. Chummy clusters of purple hyacinth. Baffling that it could still be spring, after what had happened.

The car turned left on Hawthorn—they were getting close. "One minute to landing," Honey said.

The woman gestured toward her screen. "It says two."

"Does it?" Honey was ready for this magical mystery tour to be over. When she got home, she'd take a Valium. That and a glass of Viognier would put her down for a few hours.

As for the two minutes predicted by the oracle, they passed in surreal slowness. When the car finally pulled onto Honey's street, her sigh of relief was short-lived. Parked on her lawn there was a paneled station wagon, under whose wheels lay the crown of a small tree—the flowering cherry Honey had planted when she purchased the property. Standing beside the station wagon was a young woman in mustard-colored overalls. She stood with her hands on her hips, facing the flattened tree as if she were angry with it.

"Oh, brother," the driver said. "Looks like your day ain't over yet."

Honey was tempted to ask the woman to keep driving. Instead, she doled out a tip and stepped from the car. Immediately, the girl on the lawn turned around and grimaced at Honey.

"I think I killed it. I heard it snap."

Honey recognized the murderess as the tenant from next door, a recent addition to the neighborhood. She was a large girl, with massive uncontained breasts. The overalls didn't help.

"I hope you weren't too attached to it," the girl said. "I mean, I'll replace it and everything. Was it expensive? I'm Joss, by the way—Jocelyn—I don't think we've met."

Honey tried unsuccessfully to speak.

"And please don't call the police," the girl plowed on. "I'm sure we can work this out privately. Because I really can't deal with the police right now. I just got the most awful text. In fact, I was reading it when your tree just, like, *jumped* in front of me. I mean, not that I'm blaming the tree. I'm just saying."

"I have no idea *what* you're saying, darling. Why don't you move your car and we'll deal with this tomorrow—all right?"

"Okay, because I'm still sorta reeling from the news. I mean, I knew it was coming, but can you imagine breaking up with someone by *texting* them?"

"Maybe it was the only way he thought he could get a word in."

"Very funny. Okay, I'll shut up and move my car."

"That would be splendid. Now, if you'll excuse me . . ." Honey turned and headed toward the house.

"What's your name?" the girl called out.

"Gina Lollobrigida."

"Wait—that's familiar. Are you that famous writer? Oh my God, I think I've read your books."

Honey made a mental note to feign deafness in the future. She waved graciously at the fat girl and slammed the door.

She's in a house—not hers. Nothing's familiar. She's looking through drawers, cupboards, searching for clues. When she picks up a vase in the living room, someone rushes in and snaps her photo. As the flash goes off, she awakens, though not in her own bed. The man with the camera is lying beside her. Together they go outside, where a car is waiting—a Cadillac. The man opens the back door and she hops in. Her mother is driving.

"È lei?" asks Honey. *Is it you?*

"Touch my hair," her mother says.

Honey does and, with a jolt, wakes up—this time, for real.

*   *   *

Ever since her early thirties, when she was in the thrall of Dr. Klein-erman, a shriveled, chain-smoking Freudian on East Seventy-Seventh Street, Honey has kept a dream journal. She reaches for it now and jots a few things down—whatever fragments she can recall, whatever associations come.

> *Vase – Michael.*
> *Silver hair – not Mother's. Angela's.*
> *Cadillac – Father.*

Maybe the car with Richie Verona, she thinks—the drive to the Pine Barrens. But she doesn't write this down, since what happened that day is best forgotten. Her father at the wheel, smiling, saying, "I'm not angry, I just want to talk." Honey can recall the feeling of doom. Richie was worried too, asking, "Why are we driving so far?"

Honey's mind turns left, then right, working its way through a maze. For a moment, she can't separate the imagined from the real, the dream from the facts. It seems that someone—she can't remember who—is dead.

And then, from this half dream, half life, she falls back asleep.

* * *

Later, in the dark, she peered at the clock—the red dots between the numbers merciless as the eyes of a demon. Barely an hour had passed.

Honey got up, clicked on a lamp, and took stock of herself in the mirror. The blue suit, which she'd neglected to take off, was hopelessly wrinkled. On the floor, her chestnut wig lay in a dark swirl, like a drowsing housecat, while her real hair appeared to be sending signals into outer space; it looked absolutely psychotic. As she tried to tame it, a wave of vertigo struck—not altogether unpleasant. She must have taken a Valium.

Using the wall for support, she made her way to the closet, a room almost as large as the bedroom. Inside there were more closets—subclosets—and inside these were drawers and shelves and various other cubbyholes. It was brilliantly designed, and had played no small part in Honey's decision to buy this house, which unfortunately wasn't in the best neighborhood.

After removing the Vivienne Westwood, she put on her favorite dressing gown, a pale-yellow full-length that had once matched her hair. The gown was heartbreakingly soft. Wearing it was like wearing water.

Marveling at the lack of pain in her leg, Honey decided to take another Valium. She floated toward the kitchen, where the bottle was beside the sink, next to the newspaper clipping Dominic had shown her at Dante's.

Once more, she studied the photograph—this time with reading glasses—and saw that she'd been mistaken earlier. The photo had not been taken in Florence's backyard, but in her own. Honey recognized it by the religious statue in the vegetable garden, the one her mother had placed there, in lieu of a scarecrow.

How odd, that she could be smiling for the camera—absolutely beaming—when behind her, somewhere just beyond her mother's garden, a man lay buried. It was not something Honey could ponder for long, and her thoughts stumbled back to the tragedy at hand: Dominic.

The way they'd taken him out of the restaurant in that awful collapsible stretcher. How they'd slammed the door of the ambulance in her face, the rude paramedic telling Honey she was too old to accompany them. Ridiculous—like the inverse of a roller coaster at Disneyland. *No one over eighty permitted on this ride.*

Dominic had died on that ride. Died alone, with strangers.

Dominic Sparra. Honey said the name out loud. The brutishness of the given name, followed by the little bird of the surname. Never again would this man touch her. Never again would she put her hands through that marvelous hair. Honey's tears fell hot, like blood.

She was frightened, too. For the last year and a half, she'd avoided her family, postponing all plans to face the past. She'd been preoccupied by love, and that love had protected her. Now she was on her own, not to mention wounded. Even if she did nothing to set things straight, the past would see her weakness, and it would come to reclaim her.

Honey crumpled the newspaper clipping and stuffed it in a drawer— though perhaps she ought to burn it, like incriminating evidence. Instead, she got some wine from the fridge and poured a generous glass. But before she could take a sip there was a knock on the front door. And then, not two seconds later, the doorbell. Honey knew exactly who it was. Valium always increased her psychic abilities.

It was Michael, her grandnephew, back for more money. Honey regretted being callous with him, but still, this was unacceptable—coming by at ten o'clock at night. She opened the door, ready to scold him, but was silenced by what she saw: the fat girl who'd killed the cherry tree, grinning maniacally, with an enormous plate of brownies in one hand and a gallon of milk in the other.

"Hi, Gina. I saw your light on, so I assumed you weren't sleeping. Anyway, these are for you." She held out the confections, dusty-looking squares the color of cow dung. "Just out of the oven!"

Honey was aghast but found herself reaching out to accept them.

The girl stood there, shifting her weight from one leg to the other, as if she had to urinate. "I just felt it was the least I could do."

"Very kind of you, dear. I'll have one for breakfast. Well, good night." Honey moved to close the door.

"Wait! Don't forget the milk."

Honey took it; the damn thing weighed as much as a baby.

"It expires tomorrow—just so you know. But you can usually get a few more days out of it. Expiration dates are really just a scare tactic."

Honey nodded and attempted once again to close the door, but the eight-pound jug threw her off balance. She tottered to the left.

"*Whoa.*" The girl swooped in and caught her. "You don't want to get chocolate all over your nice white carpet. That can't be easy to keep clean. Here, let me help you to the couch."

"I'm fine," said Honey.

But, really, she wasn't. The two Valiums made her feel as if she were about to levitate. She allowed herself to be led to the sofa, and when she was settled there she decided to take a gracious approach in dismissing the girl.

"Well, you've gone beyond the call of duty. I would say that we're even now, in regard to the tree. So I encourage you to go home, my dear, and consider yourself free of any obligation to the old lady next door."

The girl nodded and stared at her.

"I really like your robe. Is it silk?"

Honey detested small talk, and gave only a curt smile in reply.

"I always thought silk was really cool. But then I heard they, like, throw the worms in boiling water, you know, to kill them, and I just thought, *Eww.*"

Possibly the girl was insane—or possibly, like Michael, she was on some kind of drug, whatever it was that they all liked now. Speed, of some variety. *Going fast*—wasn't that the expression?

"And then the other thing I wonder," the girl said, "is does the silk come out of their mouths or out of their *butts*?"

A rhetorical question, perhaps—but Honey couldn't let it pass. She would not want anyone, even a lunatic, to think she'd wear a garment made from worm poo. "I'm fairly certain it comes from their mouths."

"Well, that's a relief." The girl picked up the milk. "I'll just put this in the fridge, and then I'll get out of your hair."

"Thank you. I've had a very trying day."

"That makes two of us!"

Honey could hear the intruder in the kitchen, rearranging things in the refrigerator. "Looks like you were just about to have some wine. Do you want me to bring your glass?"

This girl was relentless. *Get out!* Honey screamed in her head.

Her body, though, reacted differently. Suddenly she couldn't swallow, and it seemed to take some effort even to breathe. She closed her eyes and said, "Yes, please."

Half an hour later the girl was still there, sitting on the lounge chair opposite the sofa, well into her third brownie. The bottle of Viognier was nearly gone—a shared effort.

"And he really wasn't *that* good-looking, he was actually pretty unattractive, but there was an emotional connection, you know—so his body wasn't *pivotal.*"

The girl was still talking about the boyfriend.

Honey had said little over the past half hour, drifting in and out of sleep—a sleep that undoubtedly, when it reached its deepest, would be littered with troubling things. And so the girl, in some ways, was a distraction, a delay, keeping Honey from a darker fate. Annoyance—though annoying—was better than existential terror.

Also, to be honest, it was fascinating watching the girl—who was probably in her twenties but sometimes, depending on the angle of her face, looked either fourteen or forty. She was still in those atrocious mustard-colored overalls, and her black hair was twisted into an enormous braid that resembled an overcooked baguette. Her brown eyes were disarmingly large, bulging and almost perfectly round. Through the fog of Valium and Viognier, it was rather like watching a cartoon. The girl's gestures, overblown and stagey, suggested a game of charades. Her voice was high-pitched and breathy; even her laugh had a small-animal squeak to it. The sound kept startling Honey awake.

"So, Gina, tell me more about *you.*"

"What did you call me?"

"Isn't your name Gina?"

Honey had a vague recollection of being snarky with the girl, when they'd first met. "I believe I may have been joking with you, earlier."

"Oh. So you're not that famous writer?" The girl sounded disappointed.

"Darling, I don't believe Gina Lollobrigida is a writer."

"I think you're wrong, actually. I'm pretty sure I've read her books."

"Be that as it may. I am not she."

"Who are you then?" The girl said this with some attitude, as if the fact that she was no longer in the presence of a celebrity released her from any need to be civil.

"My name is Honey. Honey Fasinga."

Whenever possible, Honey liked to introduce herself fully—especially since she'd made the effort, in her thirties, to legally change her name from Fazzinga to Fasinga. The *s* simplified things, as well as providing distance, she felt, from her family.

"So, is that, like, a Dutch name?" the girl asked. "Though you sound sort of British—or, like, *New* England maybe? Anyway, I can tell you're not from around here."

"Au contraire. I was born and bred in this very town."

"Get out. Really? Why do you talk like that then?"

"Like what?" Honey said defensively, though she was completely aware of her affectations. Of course, she considered it more of a vocal *style*, almost another kind of dress—and one she'd worn for so long it was now inseparable from who she was. When she'd first run into Dominic again, he'd said, "So that's how you talk now? Very fancy." *The Voice*, he called it. If she ever pushed it too far, when tipsy or trying to be emphatic, he would outright laugh at her—though never meanly. He said he could listen to her all day.

"I lost my accent many years ago," Honey told the girl. "I've lived in many places."

The girl squinted, as if trying to better understand who she was dealing with.

"So, it's *Honey*, is it?"

Honey mirrored back the squint. "So, it's *Jocelyn*, is it?"

Suddenly they both laughed—the girl spitting a little as she leaned forward to pour the last of the wine. Then abruptly her laughter stopped and she adopted a serious tone. "So, *Honey*, I wonder what else you're lying to me about."

Honey felt her heart lurch. Had someone *sent* the girl here? Honey had been followed before—though everyone, even Dr. Kleinerman, had said she was imagining it.

"It's getting late, dear. I think it's time for you to go."

The girl's face dropped. "Oh—okay. Well, it was really nice meeting you. And thanks for letting me talk about, you know, The Asshole. I would've gone crazy tonight if I was by myself—probably gone online and made some really bad decisions."

"Do you buy a lot of clothing on the internet?" asked Honey.

"What? No. I was talking about, you know, a hookup or something. I don't know why I keep trying."

"We're animals," said Honey. "It's what we do."

"Yeah, I guess. Sometimes, though, I just feel really stupid. Like I'm the only one who didn't get the fact sheet or whatever."

Honey saw now that she'd overreacted; there was nothing to be frightened of. What sat before her was simply a lonely girl—and clearly one with more than a little self-loathing.

"Darling. I have *always* had the fact sheet, and let me tell you, it doesn't help one bit. Facts are not what you have to master. *Illusion* is the only hope."

The girl blinked. Obviously she didn't get it.

"Ignore me," Honey said. "I believe I'm drunk."

"Me too. Wow."

They were both quiet then. A slumping Jocelyn stared at the floor, giving Honey an opportunity to study the girl more closely. Unpainted nails bitten to shreds; hairy forearms crusted with a few withered Band-Aids; abysmal posture.

She was no beauty, certainly—though she did have *something*. But it was something most men would never see, especially nowadays. Once upon a time, a man might have prized this girl for her tubbiness, that pale dimpled skin. Her face had something of a Flemish painting about it. Even the cheeks flaring with rosacea seemed a kind of bravery against a very cold world.

Suddenly the girl reminded Honey of herself. Not that she'd ever been fat; in fact, she'd always been a twig. And, unlike this girl, she'd always known how to dress. Still—why not be honest?—Honey had never really been a beauty. Not a natural one, anyway.

Yes, she'd fooled many men in her life, men who thought she was the most beautiful thing since spun gold. And while Honey never squandered the glow of their adoration, she was not so deranged as to disallow another version of herself—all the bony bits, the sharp angles, the less than perfect nose, even after the surgery. Still, there were plenty of tricks at a girl's disposal. The way the hair lay against one's face, the way one shaded one's cheeks—it was all so important.

Such things, of course, were the least of her charms; Honey's greatest vanity, perhaps, was her mind. She knew she was smart, and she'd always been able to talk circles around a man. Which worked for a while, but then often backfired. A clever woman was suspect, dangerous.

As Honey sipped the dregs of her wine, she was unsure how to evict the slovenly girl in the lounge chair. The silence between them lingered, though strangely it was not uncomfortable. Actually, it was a relief to just sit with someone and not talk, to dwell companionably in the damn puzzle of it all. Honey had spent nights like this with Dominic. He'd never been afraid of silence—which, in a man, seemed to imply that he wasn't afraid of love.

"Are you all right?" the girl said. "Oh my God, are you crying?"

"It seems that I am." Honey wiped her eyes with a chocolate-smeared napkin. "Merely a minor attack, I assure you."

"Is it about the tree? You know, I really am sorry about that."

"Yes. Well, I suppose I was rather attached to it."

"I promise I'll replace it."

"You will do nothing of the sort. Now come on, get up." It was time for this evening to be over. Honey clapped her hands, not only to rouse the girl but to shoo away her own insipid emotion.

"Up, up!" Honey stood, to illustrate how it was done. Apparently the only way to get the girl out of the house was to treat her like a child.

"Now I want you to go home and go straight to bed—and no nonsense on the computer."

The girl rose dutifully, then pointed to the plate of brownies. "Would you mind if I took a couple of those home with me?"

How vulgar, thought Honey. One should never reclaim a gift. But at the same time, the girl's honesty was refreshing.

"Just leave me one, darling. For breakfast."

"You won't be able to eat just one. I'll leave you two."

"Very generous of you. No, no—no hugs necessary. Off you go."

*　*　*

Honey peered out the window to make sure the girl wasn't still lurking. The lamppost was lit, illuminating the cherry blossoms on the lawn. In the glare they looked more red than pink—a botanical crime scene. By tomorrow the blossoms would be brown and shriveled.

The funeral was tomorrow.

Honey wasn't sure she'd be up to it. Besides, she'd already said good-bye. And if there was anything more she wished to say to Nicky, she would say it from the privacy of her own heart, and not in the presence of vicious old women.

And, really, why subject herself to a depressing ceremony when she could stay at home, giddy with Valium, and have a more intimate chat with her dead boyfriend?

"You wouldn't believe the night I just had," she said to him now, as if he were standing beside her. *Worm poo*, she thought, and laughed.

It was all right to laugh, wasn't it?

Nicky, of all people, would not want her to languish.

5   Too Cool to Live

Honey woke to a jack-in-the-box sun and the scent of pre-programmed coffee. A movie set of a morning, for those who could appreciate it. Honey, unfortunately, couldn't. She had a splitting headache. The adjective was not used lightly—her head felt half in this world and half in another.

In the living room she saw the empty wine bottle, the leftover brownies, and threw both in the trash. Ever since she'd learned that Corrado had gone into recycling, she saw no reason to separate out glass and plastic and paper. No doubt her nephew's company simply dumped these things in the ocean or shoved them into a stinking hole.

Entering the kitchen, she shielded her eyes. The sun had overtaken this room as well, doing a Donna Reed on the yellow wallpaper. Honey wasn't buying it. Everything seemed fraudulent and cheap. And the drip coffee was far too weak; it would do nothing for her headache. After closing the curtains, she brewed a more potent mud with her stovetop Bialetti, and then slowly sipped two cups while pretending to eat a banana. She still had no appetite.

In the shower she made the water extra-hot, scalding herself like a penitent nun. Afterward, she powdered, painted, and poofed, and then slipped on the black Versace dress with its mournful blouson sleeves. Over her chestnut wig she laid a mantilla of black lace, finely wrought and crowded with spidery flowers.

It seemed she was going to a funeral, after all.

* * *

Honey's leg was free of cramps, so she opted to take her own car, a pearlescent Lexus she had on lease. Nicky was to be buried at Hillside Cemetery, where his wife and parents were. Honey's people were there too, along with Joey Ramone and William Carlos Williams. Hillside was quite the eclectic dinner party—not a place, it seemed, where one could get much sleep.

Honey, on the other hand, had overslept disastrously. Too late for the mass at St. Margaret's, she drove straight to the cemetery. Hillside was huge, though, and she wasn't sure of the location of Nicky's interment. There was a funeral party not far from the main entrance, but when Honey approached she didn't recognize a soul, and the casket was disturbingly small.

On higher ground, another crowd was gathered. As she drove up the hill, familiar faces and silhouettes came into view—Angela Carini easily pegged by her diminutive frame and the bright blue oxygen stroller.

Honey couldn't bear getting any closer. She parked the Lexus halfway up the hill and stood on a patch of lawn, watching the ceremony from a good ten meters away. She kept her distance not because of her unapologetic widow's weeds or fear of Angela's hiss. Honey's reserve had more to do with not wanting to see a body being lowered into the ground—that implacable, irreversible gesture.

While she understood that a dead body was merely a shell whose essence had fled, this knowledge provided little solace. What use were spiritual truths when pitted against primary fears born in childhood? The man buried in the garden, behind her parents' house, remained the dark note, the double bass, in Honey's metaphysical symphony.

She leaned against a tree—a massive oak whose high branches made a sound like the ocean, a constant swishing that drowned out the drone of the priest. For a moment the holy man seemed to be looking directly at her, and Honey slipped around to the back of the tree. She felt like one of those photographers who used to come to her family's funerals—reporters or Feds, lurking in the distance, gawking and snapping. She scanned the crowd, to make sure her nephew wasn't there. When a text pinged on her phone, it startled her.

Just wanted to say hey. What are you up to???

Dominic was the only person who texted her—so who the hell was this?

The phone pinged again.

This is Joss by the way. Your neighbor!

Honey was horrified. No doubt she'd made a fool of herself last night, crying on the couch, wearing no wig. And how on earth had the girl gotten this number? Honey swiped and deleted the message.

When she looked back at the mourners, they were already dispersing. As Honey stepped toward the car, a woman lifted her arm in greeting. And then this woman, who Honey didn't recognize, began to make her way down the hill. Oh, for Christ's sake—what venom now?

Honey stood up straight. Verticality, she'd always felt, was one of the central pillars of elegance. Plus, a straight spine protected you; it was a kind of armor.

The closer the stranger came, the more the face grew familiar; still, Honey couldn't place it. A slim gal around forty, smartly dressed, prematurely gray. Her step was lively, though, almost sprightly.

"Are you a friend of my uncle's?" the woman asked.

"Yes."

"You're not Honey, by any chance, are you?"

"As a matter of fact, I am. And you are?"

"Oh, I'm sorry"—she extended her hand. "I'm Linda, Dominic's niece. His sister's granddaughter."

Yes, of course. Honey understood why the face looked familiar. It had those wide Sparra cheeks, the acorn-shaped eyes.

The woman smiled. There was no venom.

Honey chided herself for her defensiveness. "It's very nice to meet you," she said, shaking the woman's hand. "I remember your grandmother Peg."

Honey hadn't known Nicky's sister well, but recalled that she'd lost a finger in that dreadful commercial laundry where a lot of the poorer girls had worked.

"I was hoping to see you at the wake," the woman said. "Were you there?"

"I left early. Why did you want to see me?"

"Oh, I don't know—my uncle mentioned you a few times."

Honey rather doubted that. "Did he?"

"Yeah, we talked pretty often. On the phone mostly. I live in Boston now."

The woman paused, though obviously there was something she wanted to say. Honey waited, expecting the worst.

Linda shook her head, troubled by something. "My uncle was never really a happy man. I shouldn't say this, but I don't think he and Aunt Mary were a great match. He was pretty depressed for a long time—I don't know if you knew that."

Honey didn't. She nodded vaguely and let the woman continue.

"And then, I don't know, he just seemed very different after he started seeing you—and so, yeah, I just wanted to say that. I think you made him happy."

Honey felt her breath stop. "Did he tell you that?"

"Not in so many words, but . . . it was pretty obvious."

There was really no way to absorb such information. It was simply too much. Not to mention useless. When grace arrived too late, it only brought tears. Honey felt it best to change the subject.

"So you were close to your uncle?"

"Yeah. He was always so nice, you know. Maybe because he and Aunt Mary didn't have any kids. And then after my parents died, we started talking more often. He called me almost every Monday."

And Honey thought he'd been watching football.

Fascinating, how certain people continued to grow richer, even after they died. Because here was a side of Dominic Honey hadn't known. She pictured her manly man calling this gray-haired niece to chat about life and love. On Linda's hands there were two rings: one gold, one silver, both ambiguous.

"Are you married, dear?"

"Divorced."

"Well, you're still quite young. You'll meet someone, I'm sure."

Linda rolled her eyes, unconvinced.

Honey wanted to shake the girl. Did she not understand that, at forty, she was still a child? She still had a million chances left. Well, maybe not a million, but certainly quite a few. She had time on her side. And the gray hair was only in streaks, it could easily be dyed.

"Linda! Are you coming?" someone shouted.

"Be right there!" Linda shouted back. "My brother," she explained to Honey. "Listen, do you want to join us for the repast?"

"Oh, I didn't know there was going to be one."

"Yeah. We're all going to a restaurant back in Ferryfield."

"Not Dante's?"

"Oh God, no. Bazzarelli's."

Honey knew the place. A working-class establishment, more of a pizza joint. "I imagine a lot of Mary's relatives will be there."

"Yes, but that's fine. No one cares."

The girl was an innocent, and of another generation. She didn't understand that it was absolutely *not* fine for Honey to be there.

"Thank you, dear, but I don't think I'm up to it."

"Are you sure?"

"Quite sure. Very sweet of you, though, to invite me. Your uncle really was a wonderful man."

Linda nodded. Her tears came swiftly, and were wiped away in the same fashion.

"You know," she said to Honey, "you're not that old, either. I mean, I know you're younger than my uncle. And so I hope the same for you."

"What's that?"

"Just saying, I hope you meet someone too."

What a peculiar thought. Honey had never even considered it. She was eighty-two, for heaven's sake.

"I mean it," Linda persisted. "He would have wanted you to be happy."

Honey did her best to smile. "Thank you, dear. Now go enjoy your pizza." She patted the woman's cheek. "I feel quite certain that your uncle would have wanted you to be happy, too."

Linda nodded. "Lucky us."

Honey laughed, touched by the way the woman had so deftly joined sarcasm to the God's honest truth. To be loved by the dead—it was definitely a pickle.

* * *

She took her time in leaving, driving around the little lanes of the cemetery, many of which had quaint designations such as "Star" and "Flower." Honey's parents and brother were in a pink granite mausoleum, near a splendid grove of evergreens. Not far away was another tomb, with the name CROKER chiseled into the stone. One would be a fool not to appreciate the pun. *Laugh at life, laugh at death*, as Osho said.

At the Fazzinga gravesite Honey didn't get out of the car; she simply stared at the pompous pink monument through the window of the Lexus. It looked absolutely Napoleonic, with scrolls and wreaths and bas-relief columns. Inside, there was still plenty of room for additional tenants. No doubt her father imagined that his children would be more prolific in regard to offspring. But Enzo had had only the one son, and of course Honey had denied her father completely. *Denied*—that was her father's word.

Corrado and his wife, their boys—perhaps they'd take the remaining shelves in the tomb. Honey had no interest in claiming one for herself. What she wanted was to be cremated, have her ashes scattered near a small lake in southern France where she'd spent some time with Mr. Hal. Either that, or at Point Lobos, out in California. Of course, she had no idea who she'd ask to do the scattering. After death, she'd probably be kidnapped, interred against her will inside the ghastly pink palace.

She drove on, toward the Jewish part of the cemetery—and here she did get out of the car. It would be a sin not to pay a visit to the grave of Jeff Hyman, aka Joey Ramone. Not that Honey had ever been a fan of the Ramones. By the time punk had reached its apex, Honey was nearly forty. But as she liked to stay au courant, she'd poked her nose in at the periphery of the scene. The music grated, but the style of the musicians intrigued her—the way they'd made a uniform entirely from scraps and scuffs. She'd seen the band only once, at Max's Kansas City. Joey Ramone had walked stiffly onto the stage, a homely kid with a bulbous schnoz and beanpole legs. But as soon as he started to hop around and sing in that sweet voice rife with snarls and barks, he completely transformed himself.

Atop his grave, there was a lot of loving detritus. Fans had left stones and sunglasses, a rusty horseshoe, even a hypodermic needle. There was a small silver banner on which someone had hand-stitched an epitaph: *Too Cool to Live.*

As for the grave of William Carlos Williams, Honey chose not to pay her respects, though she certainly agreed with the man. So much really did depend upon the red wheelbarrow.

Though perhaps that was no longer true. Perhaps that was another world, one in which poetry was possible. A world like the one her great-grandparents had lived in—olive trees, chickens, a fertile patch of dirt.

But then history happened. Wars. Betrayals. The chickens died, the olive trees were burned. Everyone grew hungry and, finally, when they couldn't take it anymore, they put up their fists. The weak became the strong, some of them even punching their way to America.

And here we are, thought Honey, driving away from the cemetery. *Here we are.*

* * *

It was early afternoon and there wasn't much traffic. Maybe she'd stop by that good bakery that was near the cemetery and pick up some biscotti. The place used the perfect amount of anise seed, the cookies neither florid nor bland, but delicately medicinal.

When Honey spotted the bakery, though, she drove right past it. A nice idea, but to be honest she still had no interest in food. Driving was what she wanted, not cookies. The pleasure and power and autonomy of it. She sailed through the green lights, and even through several yellow. Honey had always had a heavy foot.

She sped toward Ferryfield, taking side streets she hadn't been on in years. Perhaps she was testing her memory. She still knew Bergen County well, despite the starkening of its architectural profile. The streets, for the most part, were the same old streets. Castle Terrace, Bloomfield Avenue, the corner of Chubb and Chester. Honey ticked off the names, like boys on a dance card.

She made a right turn onto Lefters Boulevard, just because she could. A few blocks later she swung around a confusing new roundabout and ended up on Robby Road, once a respectable area, though it seemed to have fallen into disrepair. Most of the large houses had been subdivided into apartments, the sidewalks cracked and cluttered with litter.

Around the corner, on Sutter, there was a convenience store where there should have been a fruit stand, and then Honey found herself on a street with no houses or even businesses. Behind a chain-link fence there were piles of sand and various drowsing machines—backhoes and bulldozers. Two pedestrians with identical halting gaits were rushing somewhere, perhaps late to an appointment with their podiatrist. Or, more likely, a liquor store. A stout woman in a short dress loitered by the side of the road. Another woman was wearing what looked like a hospital gown; in the glare of the sun, it was hard to be certain.

A car was honking behind Honey, and as she sped up she glanced at the woman in the flimsy gown. It wasn't a woman, though—it was a boy with long hair. He looked an awful lot like Michael. Honey wanted to stop, but there were at least three cars behind her now and nowhere to pull over. She decided to make the next right and then go around the block. If the boy was, in fact, her grandnephew, she might at least offer to drive him home.

The street Honey turned on was not one she was familiar with. Warehouses of some sort—gray brick and metal doors. The road went on for a long time, like a road in a dream, and when she reached the end there was only a concrete wall. *Oh, for heaven's sake.* It was a goddamned alley.

The only escape was to back out. Keeping her eye on the little movie screen that showed what was behind the vehicle, Honey proceeded slowly. The Lexus was large, and the street narrow; it was like backing a tractor out of a soda straw.

When a man appeared on the rearview screen, Honey jammed on the brakes and waited for him to move. But the idiot just stood there, with a baseball cap jammed low on his head. And then another man, also in a baseball cap, was knocking on her window, saying something Honey couldn't comprehend. Possibly she was on private property.

"I'm going," she said, making an apologetic gesture.

The man replied with a gesture of his own—a sudden lifting of his right hand. Honey had never realized before how much the barrel of a gun resembled a camera lens. Unfortunately, the man did not say "Cheese," but rather, "Get the fuck out of the car!"

Honey knew that wouldn't be a wise move. She continued backing up, despite the fact that the second man was still standing behind the vehicle. She drove slowly, wishing only to frighten him. But he didn't seem frightened at all. In fact, he began to bang on the trunk like a deranged monkey. Honey retaliated by pressing ferociously on the horn.

"Stop!" shouted the man at the window, knocking the gun so hard against the glass Honey was sure it would break.

Think, she commanded herself. In the back seat she had her cane. If necessary, she could use it to strike the men's faces, or, better still, jam it between their legs. Go for the balls, her brother had taught her.

Instead, she reached for her phone. Strangely, her first thought was not to call the police but to call Corrado. But then it was too late to call anyone at all. The window shattered, and a hand reached through the void, undoing the locks. The door flew open, and Honey was dragged from the car. The man with the gun shoved her.

"*Stupid cunt.*"

Honey was on the ground now, one of her knees bleeding. When she looked up, the two men were in the Lexus, and then without even glancing at her they backed out of the alley, the tires screeching.

She attempted to stand, only to collapse again. The Versace was torn; a dark petal of fabric dangled from one of the blouson sleeves. The street was suddenly quiet, the sun impossibly bright, exposing every detail in the filthy alley. Candy wrappers and broken bottles. A discarded sandwich covered with ants. The reek of something worse.

There'd always been too much ugliness in the world; even as a child it had caused Honey an almost physical pain. Again she tried to stand, but it was no good. She only scraped her knee further against some gravel.

Serves you right, she could hear her mother saying. *Orgoglio, arrogant. Girls like you, they always fall.*

6   Richie Verona

This is when he comes—when she's tired, when she's weak. She's still kneeling in the alley. The street tilts, the buildings spin, the past oozes through the cracks: *here* and *there* at the same time. At her age, *there* is never far.

She'd always loved his name. Richie Verona. A name for a crooner, or a movie star born to play thugs. He was almost too handsome. Black hair dark as mussel shells. The tanned, veined hands of a laborer, which he was. Hands he'd used with such gentleness at first—but that was merely an act, a pair of gloves. The hands, unsheathed, were stronger than her entire body.

Now they would call it rape, though that word wasn't used as much when she was a girl. And she did *know* the boy. Considered him a friend. She had, of her own will, gone to his house.

Why does her mind always play it like this? As if she was the one who'd done something wrong. Maybe it's the same for all women. Taught to find the fault in themselves first, before assigning blame to others.

But that's not the point. She's not looking to find fault. Nor to assign blame. She's simply looking at the facts—or perhaps they're looking at her.

Take a breath, she thinks. *Take your time.* Lying in the street, she has all the time in the world. She refuses to knock on one of those metal warehouse doors, degrade herself further. She'll just wait here, let her mind wander. Who cares if the men come back? She isn't afraid to die. She really isn't.

In fact, it's what she wants.

Though at the moment she's growing younger. What was she—fifteen, sixteen? She was on the debating team, in the French club—though with Richie she played dumb. She can't recall if she ever told him *No*, if she'd used that exact word.

Because that was a crucial point, wasn't it? That word was proof of a girl's innocence. Without it, the judges might say that her whimpers had been misinterpreted. They might say it was sometimes difficult for a man to know for certain. A woman's moans of distress could easily be confused for moans of ecstasy, of desire.

Would they really dare to say such things?

Darling, wake up, look at the news.

But I tried to push him away, she would say in her own defense.

In some ways, she was in awe of his power. That is not to say she enjoyed it. She was—and let this be clear—terrified.

They'd gone for a walk in VanDervoort Park. The swans were out on the pond, and that had felt lucky. Sitting on two swivel stools afterward, they'd eaten ice cream. She thought Richie's choice of rum raisin sophisticated. Later, in the car, he pulled out a silver flask. She'd taken a sip—disgusting but invigorating, like mouthwash. His parents weren't home, he said. *We could play some records.*

She knew it was a line, she wasn't stupid. She intended to kiss him. She'd even let him touch her breasts. Because she finally had them. Yes, she remembers now, she was fifteen, feeling very grown-up to have a date with an older boy. Richie was almost nineteen, not a boy at all.

The attack, the act itself, is blurry. What she recalls is this: that they were lying the wrong way on his bed, and that throughout the wrestling match she caught glimpses of the Yankees pennant pinned to Richie's headboard. When she turned her face to the side to escape his breath, she saw that the bedroom door was open. She kept picturing his parents coming home—how they'd see her like this, and how embarrassed she'd be. Ashamed for something she had no say in.

She remembers arriving at the house—so much smaller than her own, the furnishings like things you'd expect to see lying by a curb. The table legs scratched as if by rats, and the couch cushions worn to threads. Everything, of course, was spotless. Without that, it would have been intolerable. She understands now what a snob she was.

On a shelf in Richie's living room stood a statue of the Virgin Mary, though it looked like something you'd win at the San Gennaro Festival. Chalky plaster, badly painted. And to put it in the living room was tacky.

None of this mattered, though. Even then, she knew that beauty was a kind of wealth—and the boy, in this regard, was loaded. His beauty was certainly greater than her own. Maybe because his was effortless, unguarded, even ragged—what, ironically, in a girl might be called slovenly. He was wearing unpleated khakis, a wrinkled oxford, while she was dolled up in a gingham pinafore and a white blouse with daisies on the sleeves. This was before the era of Florence, when her mother had ruled the closet.

She'd told her parents she was meeting some girlfriends. Her parents wouldn't have approved of Richie. And she understood that. In the long run it could never work out. A boy like that, from the sooty side of the tracks. Still, she was curious.

Richie's house smelled of garlic. A clothesline strung up in the middle of the kitchen. Yet even as she privately turned up her nose at the boy's native habitat, she was smiling like a fool. Not entirely phony; she was genuinely fascinated by Richie. And he did make her swoon, nearly to sickness.

As for their conversation at his house, she recalls only the inessential. How she asked for a glass of water and how he apologized for the clouds. "Air in the pipes," he explained. When he handed her the water, it looked like a glass of milk.

Afterward, when her dress was torn and she was crying, he began to talk loudly, as if to distract her.

"Did you see the autograph?" He pointed toward the blue-and-white pennant on the headboard. "Joe DiMaggio."

Honey's father hated Joe DiMaggio. *A fucking Sicilian*, he called him.

Driving her home, Richie offered the flask again, but she refused. The whole way, she said nothing—she wasn't even crying anymore—so she didn't appreciate it when he told her, rather sharply, not to make a big deal of it. The quieter she was, the angrier he grew, and finally, when she was stepping from the car silent as a cat, he told her to keep her stupid mouth shut. Told her not to be a cunt about it.

It was the first time she'd ever heard that word; she thought he meant a tiny pig, a runt or something. She said a prayer before going into the house, and when she heard her parents in the kitchen she ran straight to her room. Took a bath and then a shower, surprised to find so many bruises on her body. Strangely they didn't hurt at all, as if someone had painted them on. Or maybe she was numb.

As she was drying her hair, her mother appeared. "Where have you been? What happened?" The ruined dress was on the floor. Honey had wrapped a towel around herself, but her mother pulled it away. When she saw the bruises, she made the sign of the cross.

"Please don't tell him," begged Honey.

"Tell who? Your father? Do you think I'm stupid?"

They stared at each other, breathing heavily. They both knew what her father was capable of.

"Come on, get into bed." Her mother pulled the covers over her body. "Thank God he didn't touch your face. No one sees nothing."

Yet somehow her father did see. Somehow he found out.

He didn't seem upset, though. He even invited Richie to the house—and what he said to the boy shocked her: *You're going to marry my daughter, yes?* A terrifying smile on the Great Pietro's face, as he bullied the hapless couple into something neither of them wanted.

Honey remembers the drive in the Cadillac, she and Richie and her father. "We'll have a picnic," her father said at one point, gesturing toward some trees at the side of the road.

But when Honey looks, there are no trees. She's back in the alley, her knee still bleeding. No cars, no breeze. Time, it seems, has stopped.

Eventually one of the metal doors creaks open and a man steps out. He's dressed completely in white—a baker or an angel.

Honey wipes her face, adjusts her wig. When the stranger reaches for her hand, she gives it to him.

What choice does she have?

A re you all right?" the man in white asked her. "Can you walk?"
        "Dear boy," she said, "I learned the art when I was eight
        months old."

"Okay, well, I still think you should lean on me."

"And where, exactly, are we going?"

"Just out of the street. We can go inside." He pointed to the metal
door he'd just walked out of. He smelled like pine sap, a whiff of tobacco. All in all, quite pleasant. "This isn't the best area," he said.

"Tell me about it. Two bastards just stole my car."

"Did you call the police?"

"My phone is in the vehicle."

When the man offered to call for her, she said she'd prefer a cigarette
first.

"Sure." He patted his pocket. "I'll have to roll it, though."

"All the better." Honey hadn't had a smoke in years, and now it would
be an honest reunion, sans the contrivance of a filter.

As they crossed the alley, their arms were linked archaically, hooked
at the elbow. The lake near Bryn Mawr, the cobbled lanes, came to mind.
Strolling with a boy in flannel or tweed.

"I'm really not injured," Honey protested, though she didn't pull away.

When they walked through the metal door and he flicked on the
light, she wondered if this angelically clad man did, perhaps, have a di-
vine purpose. They stood in a huge white room, completely empty. Con-
fusingly bright.

"I just painted it," he said.

Then she saw the ladder, the tubs of primer. These mundanities were
calming. The bars on the windows were simply bars, not the Pearly
Gates.

"I thought for a second I might be dead," she said.

He set up a folding chair and helped her down. "I'm pretty sure they don't allow high heels in heaven. You would have had to check those at the door."

"These are Louboutins, darling. I would never have given them up."

"Can't say I blame you. They're pretty swank."

"And, just to be accurate, they are not high heels; they are kittens."

"I'll take your word on that," the man said, with a solemn nod that did little to disguise his mirth.

He seemed to be in his late twenties, not much older than her grandnephews—but he was another species entirely. Honey sat on the little chair and watched as he took the pouch of tobacco from his pocket; watched as he rolled the paper and sealed it with a lick. It felt, perhaps, a tad too intimate. Honey glanced at the spotless walls, the molded edges.

"I like an empty white room," she said. "It helps one think."

He handed her the cigarette, then lit it. "It has to be the right white, of course."

"Of course," she agreed. "But I think you've rather hit it. What would you call this shade? Seashell? Or maybe Old Lace?"

He smiled at her. "It's actually called Crisp Linen."

"Ha, perfect," she said, blowing smoke toward the ceiling. And though she wished to say more (there was always more cleverness up her sleeve), she only stared at the smoke as it disappeared into the emptiness. She held a regal pose, feeling confident her mask was back in place.

The problem was her hands. They would not stop shaking.

"It's okay," the man said. "You're okay now."

*　*　*

He did everything required of a gentleman. He gave her a glass of water, a clean wet cloth to dab her knee. He phoned the police, and when they arrived he stood beside her while she spoke with them. Honey was mortified not to be able to recall her license-plate number; the officers probably thought her dotty. "I'm a bit jangled," she told them. "I'll call it in later, if I may."

"That's fine. But we'd like you to come down to the station and look at some mug shots. We can take you in the cruiser."

"Oh, no, I couldn't possibly come now. I'm much too tired. Let's do it tomorrow," she said, as if planning a coffee date.

Quite a pair, these cops—one as round and solid as an unripe peach, the other the human equivalent of a swizzle stick.

They asked more questions. Luckily she was able to remember her name and address, her age. From the latter, she shaved off her standard five years—a modest deduction, since everyone said she could pass for a woman in her sixties. She whispered the fraudulent number to the cops, not wanting the young man to hear. Then she gave the make and model of the vehicle, both of which the larger officer relayed by radio—no doubt initiating a search. Honey barely listened.

The truth was, she really didn't care about the car. Such things were easily replaced. Besides, she knew that in situations like this cars did not just miraculously reappear. No doubt at that very moment the Lexus was being quickly and doggedly dismantled—probably not unlike that clip she'd seen on the Nature Channel, a time-lapse of insects devouring a leaf. By the end, nothing remained but a latticework of veins. The car, too, was surely a skeleton by now.

Either that or deposited whole into the belly of a cargo ship destined for Croatia. Her father had once been involved in something like that.

Still, the policemen stood there hopefully with their little electronic pads, trying to help. Honey didn't want the poor men to feel irrelevant. People's sense of value often came from their jobs.

"What else can I tell you, boys?"

"Your description of the thieves was a little vague," the thin one said. "Can you be more specific than"—he glanced at his pad—*"white, with baseball caps*? What age would you say they were?"

"Honestly, to me, they looked like children. I would say somewhere between twelve and twenty."

The officers nodded slowly, and Honey sensed their impatience.

"I guess you can't tell us anything more about the weapon, either?"

"Oh, actually, yes." Relieved to finally have something to offer these men, Honey neglected to censor herself. "It was fairly small. Semi-automatic. Nine millimeter. And definitely a Glock."

One officer scribbled, while the other stared at Honey with his mouth hanging open. "And how do you know so much about guns?"

"Television, dear. I watch a lot of that *Law & Order*." Which wasn't really true; she'd seen the silly program only once or twice. Her knowledge about the gun had more to do with the fact that she had a similar one at home. Hers was a nicer color, though. Desert White, it was called. The hooligans had had a more conventional shade: Sniper Gray. She recalled the ghastly name from the catalog.

Honey had purchased the pistol years ago, for protection. Of course, when she'd brought it with her to New Jersey, her motives were more complicated. The first few weeks she was home, she was an absolute mess, and she'd kept the gun close. Now she couldn't even remember where she put the damn thing. Probably it was still somewhere in her bedroom, drowsing in the back of a drawer, unloaded. Well, she assumed it was. She'd better check.

"I really must rest now," she told the officers.

"Do you need medical attention?"

Honey looked down at her ripped sleeve. "The dress needs more help than I do."

"You said you hurt your leg?"

"It's nothing a dog couldn't fix with a single lick. Of course, I don't have a dog. I live alone. I've lived alone for many years."

Why was she babbling?

"I really must go," she insisted.

"Do you need a ride?" the burly one asked. "Or we can call you a cab."

"Obviously I need a ride," Honey replied peevishly.

"I can take her," the man in white said. Honey had forgotten he was there.

"Were you a witness, sir?"

"No, I found her afterward."

"He's what we used to call a Johnny-on-the-spot," Honey explained. The officers stared at her and blinked.

"A good Samaritan," she amended, not wishing to get into a vocabulary lesson.

"So you'll go with him?" the skinny one asked. For such an important job, these men seemed a little dim.

"Yes," Honey said. "I will. If it's not an imposition," she added, turning toward the painter.

"Not at all."

"Here you go, ma'am." Burly Cop handed her a form with a telephone number on it.

"Sorry for your loss," Skinny Cop said.

For a second, Honey thought he was referring to Dominic. Was it still the same day as the funeral? Sweet Jesus. It was just too much.

* * *

Time was up to something; Honey could feel it hopping and skipping, looking for a place to land. The light was confusing, too, flashing on the wings of startled pigeons. As the cops drove off, the painter pulled a set of keys from his pocket. "My car's just around the corner."

Honey nodded distractedly, noticing a shiny rectangle on the ground. Her cell phone? She crouched to pick it up, a delicate scratch on the glass like an eyelash.

"Is that yours?"

"I believe so." She clicked a button, and when she saw the home-screen image of herself with Lara and Suzanne, the ocean behind them, she felt slashed by the sinister illogic of chronology—that such dear friends existed only in the depressing bounty of the past.

Walking out of the alley, she sensed someone lurking behind her. But when she turned to look, there was only her shadow—long and narrow, stretching at each step like gum stuck to her shoes. She stayed close to the man, wondering if he might take her arm again.

He didn't. Well, why should he? They were not walking beside a lake at Bryn Mawr, for heaven's sake. Far from it. The street, in fact, was filthy, littered with more detritus than Joey Ramone's grave. As they turned the corner, Honey remembered why she'd gone down the wretched alley in the first place.

"Michael," she said out loud.

"What's that?" The painter stopped and looked at her.

"Nothing, I just . . . I thought I saw my nephew somewhere around here. Earlier, I mean—when I was driving. It was the strangest thing. He looked like he'd just got out of the hospital. He seemed to be wearing one of those . . ." She gestured fluffily, unable to find the word.

"Is your nephew ill?" the painter asked.

"I don't believe so. It's my *grand*nephew—he's just a boy."

Honey didn't see him anywhere now. Though she did notice the loitering gal again, as well as a few people whispering into the windows of stopped cars, the engines still running. Hurried transactions, the flash of grubby cash.

"They're obviously selling something," Honey said.

"They're selling *lots* of things," the man replied. "Take your pick."

"I had no idea. In my day, people had to go to New York City for things like this. Or Newark, God help you."

"I assume we're talking about the same thing?" the man mumbled quietly.

"Drugs and hookers, yes?" Honey replied—not quietly at all.

The painter's cheeks turned red.

"My boy, I've been around the block. I'm just surprised to see it on the street, not ten minutes from my home. I would have thought this sort of thing was done online these days."

Another woman, in a spandex dress the color of mangos, strolled by.

"Apparently not," the painter said.

"Spandex." Honey sighed. "It is never wrapped around those who deserve it. Rather like Speedos at the beach."

Another loiterer—this time a teenager—emerged from a doorway, sporting hot pants and a black eye.

"I'm surprised the cops didn't throw these gals in the cruiser."

"Probably not their department," the man said. "Well, here's my car."

"*This?*" It was as if the universe were making fun of her. The car was a ragtop Thunderbird, circa 1964. Pale blue, with a white roof.

Perhaps such cars were in again. Though why, Honey couldn't imagine. She'd never liked the design. The front had an unfriendly look, rather sharkish.

"Why on earth do you park here?" she asked. "I can't imagine it's safe."

"I know I shouldn't. But it's free, and it's close to where I work."

When the painter opened the passenger-side door, Honey got in. If nothing else, it was better than driving in the back of a police car. She'd done that once or thrice before.

Of course, the police car might have been more comfortable. The Thunderbird's seats were as hard as cement. Honey longed for a cushion. Thankfully the man drove slowly on the rutted street, minimizing the assault on her pelvis.

When they were on Robby Road she relaxed a bit, and by the time they turned left onto Lefters Boulevard the world seemed to tilt back into place. Honey felt almost confident she'd survive this dreadful day.

The man tapped his fingers against the steering wheel—blithely or nervously, it was impossible to tell. Honey noticed the neatly trimmed nails, the fine, thin hands scrubbed pink. His tanned face was clean-shaven. And though his hair was short, there was a stylish forelock whipped by product into an insouciant wave. Clearly he was gay. Honey smiled at him. "I very much appreciate your kindness."

"Sure. I'm Nathan, if I didn't say."

"Ilaria," Honey said. "But everyone calls me Honey."

"Nice to meet you."

Such formalities seemed silly, considering the circumstances under which they'd met. Honey might have said more, but she was aware of some tension in the air. Surely the young man regretted his decision to offer a ride. She should have taken a cab.

"I should have taken a cab," she said.

"It's fine—really."

They left it at that, and Honey only spoke up when she needed to offer directions.

"This light takes forever," the man said when they were sitting at the intersection of Poole and Moonachie.

"Yes, I often think I should take a nap here. When I was a child, not only was there no light here—there was nothing at all. Swampland."

"You can still smell it," the man said.

"Marsh gas," replied Honey—though, really, she could smell only her geranium.

"So you grew up around here?"

The question was merely an attempt to be polite, Honey knew that, but the silence was no doubt an enemy to both of them, intolerable in the darkening afternoon.

"I've only recently moved back," she said. "And am I sorry? Well, I just might be." She held up the dangling ribbon of her sleeve as evidence. "I'm sure Versace heard it rip."

"Isn't he dead?"

"Yes, but he was always very sensitive. You know, I met him once, at La Scala. Did you know he designed for the theater?"

"I didn't."

"Yes, well—it was a long time ago." Honey held her reminiscing tongue, since the boy's tone did not suggest interest in the subject. "You must ignore the old bore sitting beside you."

"It's fine."

That phrase again. *It's fine.* Meant to be polite, but there was always a barb to it. It was only a slightly more civilized version of the ubiquitous and horrid *No problem.*

Honey rubbed her hand across the dash, the black surface artificially pebbled, perhaps in an attempt to imitate some kind of lizard skin. So many ridiculous design ideas they'd had in the sixties. The car's knobs and dials looked like something straight out of Buck Rogers. Honey glanced upward; a tear in the rag roof was flapping in the breeze. Hadn't someone she'd once known driven a convertible? Who the hell was it?

Honey closed her eyes and tried to ease the constipation of her mind. *Think of nothing,* Osho recommended. *In nothing exists everything.* She felt her head nod sleepily. In hypnagogic flashes she saw a dirt road flanked by trees. She saw the shovel, the plastic tarp. Her head jerked back up. Yes, her uncle Vinch—he'd had a car like this in the fifties. Not a Thunderbird, but a Chrysler Imperial, the color as unabashedly blue as the car she was in now. Sometimes in the mornings he'd show up with the top down and drive her and Enzo to school. Her brother would sit up front while she took the back, a satchel bag on her lap, inside of which was her meticulously executed homework and a pencil case decorated with moons and stars.

Suddenly Honey felt like sobbing.

"Turn right," she said to the young man.

As the Thunderbird veered, spears of sunlight crashed through the windshield. Honey lowered the visor. The flap over the mirror was missing, and in the glass she saw the smeared mascara, the crooked wig—the latter a complete disaster. A swath of her natural white was showing. She reached up to adjust the elastic.

"Why didn't you tell me?" she said to the young man, as if he'd betrayed her.

"Tell you what?"

"And the police said nothing either! You know, a gentleman should always tell a lady if something is off in her appearance. That is, if it's something she can fix."

In the mirror she was only making things worse. Wisps of white were poking out like feathers. Oh, to hell with it. She pulled off the wig and set it on her lap, after which she rearranged her own sparse locks into a quick tight bun. The man, she noticed, was smiling.

"What's so funny?"

"Nothing. I just think it's great that you're so vain."

"At my age, you mean?" She gave him a look of practiced coolness.

"No, I mean—your car was just stolen, and you're worried about your hair."

Of course she was worried! Who wouldn't be? We all came into this world without hair or teeth, without words, and somehow we pulled it off fabulously—but try to take those things away at the end and it wasn't pretty. Well, there was nothing she could do about it now. She sat in the Thunderbird with what looked like a dead squirrel on her lap.

Exposed. The word floated through her head. And why on earth had she introduced herself as Ilaria? She never told anyone her given name. Maybe she *was* going dotty.

"I wasn't making fun of you," the man said after a while. "And, anyway, I think you look great like that. I like white hair."

Yes, now she was certain. Only a gay man would have the balls to flirt with an octogenarian. He probably had a hard-on for her dress, if anything.

"So you're a house painter?" she asked, changing the subject.

"What? No. Well, sometimes. But I'm more of a *painter* painter. Or trying to be. That place was my new studio."

Honey nodded. She'd known a lot of artists, over the years. She'd slept with some living ones, and in museums had silently communed with those long dead. She'd even collected the work of some of the great but overlooked eccentrics. She might tell the young man about the Redon in her bedroom, or the Morandi in the kitchen.

But she kept her mouth shut. The paintings were too valuable to speak of loosely. And the truth was, she really didn't know this Good Samaritan.

"So what's your thing?" she asked. "Figurative? Abstract?"

"I don't like those terms," he said. "But if you put a gun to my head I'd say figurative."

A gun to his head? Had he already forgotten that someone had just done that to her? And not figuratively.

"Right now I'm focusing on animals," he said. "I just did a series of dog-park fights."

Honey grunted vaguely, doing her best to simulate curiosity. The artwork sounded horrid.

As they were approaching her block, she decided to ask the young man to drop her off at the corner. There was no reason he needed to know her exact address.

"I'm the next left, on Bishop. But you can pull over anywhere. Actually, right here is fine."

"Don't be silly, I'll take you to your door. What's the number?"

He was blushing again, for some reason. Gentle eyes, good straight teeth. An honest face, all in all. There was no reason to be paranoid. "Just a few more down on the right, dear. Number eighteen."

As the car slowed, Honey could already feel the relief that would soon come. A glass of wine, a bath. A little blue pill. Dreamless sleep.

But then she saw the girl—or the girl's bottom, to be precise. She was standing on Honey's property, bent over and patting down some dirt with a shovel. The murdered tree had been fully uprooted, and a new sapling was standing in its place.

The Thunderbird was at the curb now, and Honey stared at the un-welcome gardener. She was wearing yet another pair of those ghastly overalls—this time a regurgitated green, rather like pea soup.

"Is this the right place?" the man asked.

"Unfortunately, yes," replied Honey.

The girl—Jocelyn, was it?—was facing away, engrossed in her task. Honey realized there was still a chance to escape. She could ask the young man to take her to the grocery store, say she needed to pick up some milk. Or she might offer to buy him a drink at Mabel's.

"I really don't want to deal with her," she confided.

"Is that your daughter?"

"God, no. And do I look like I could have a daughter that age? She's my neighbor. Listen," Honey said, deciding to propose the drink.

But it was too late.

The girl turned and, seeing the car, waved ecstatically. Honey ignored her, and after a long sigh reached out to shake the painter's hand. "Thank you so much for the lift."

His grasp was pleasingly firm, though his technique was a bit too fervent; Honey's whole forearm flopped up and down like a fish in a bucket. The enthusiasm of the young—it often seemed psychotic. She gathered up her wig and turned toward the door.

"Wait one second, would you?" The young man pulled out his wallet and retrieved a business card. "Not mine," he said, "but just let me . . ."

As he leaned toward the glove box, Honey could feel the heat of him. She waited, trapped by his torso, while he found a pen and scrawled something on the back of the business card. "My number. Just in case you need a ride, or whatever."

He held out the scrap of paper, his confident hands trembling now, as Honey's had been trembling earlier. His dark-lashed eyes betrayed some sadness. "It would just be nice to talk again."

What mysteries people were, thought Honey. What could this dog-painting boy possibly want from her?

Well, loneliness was rampant these days, wasn't it? Especially with the younger set. The gays were no exception. She'd read somewhere that there were cocktail parties that took place by computer, with everyone in separate rooms. Apparently a lot of people had sex like that, too. She accepted the proffered card, simply to be polite.

"Thank you, dear."

As she opened the door, she braced herself. The girl was standing there, waiting in her unsightly greens like the boogeyman.

"Joss!" Honey said brightly. When dealing with monsters, kindness was always the most reliable weapon.

"Cute guy," the girl gushed as the convertible rolled away. "Is that your boyfriend?"

"He's a homosexual, darling."

"Not really a homo car. Plus, he didn't have a gay face. Not that they all do. And, anyway, from the looks of it, you obviously had a wild time." The girl caught her breath, though she seemed to have no intention to stop blabbing.

Honey acted quickly. She grasped her neighbor's hands and spoke gravely, using *The Voice*. "Joss. Listen to me. I'm going into my house now, and I may not come out for a while, and I must ask you to please not disturb me. I'm grateful for the wonderful surprise of a new tree—*incredibly* thoughtful of you. But I just need some time to myself."

"Sure, sure. I've had dates like that, too. Takes a while to recover."

"Yes, it does," Honey said, walking away.

"If you need anything, just text!" the girl called out. "You don't even have to write a message. Just send me an emo so I know you're alive."

What on earth was she talking about? Why would Honey send her a large, flightless bird?

But maybe the girl hadn't said *emu*. Honey limped into the house, wondering if on top of everything else she was going deaf. As she made her way down the hall, she tossed her wig into an amphora she'd purchased a lifetime ago in Bruges.

Or was it Leuven? Maybe it wasn't in Belgium, at all. Maybe she'd bought the thing in Belarus. Her goddamned head was spinning.

Well, at least she knew where she was now.

She was in fucking New Jersey.

The Garden State. Liberty and Prosperity, the motto. The goldfinch, its bird. The common blue violet, its flower. During the Jurassic period, New Jersey bordered North Africa. In fact, Honey had dated an African once, from Trenton. See, she assured herself as she flopped onto the couch, her mind was perfectly in order.

Now where, *where*, were those pills?

8   The Closet

She slept well, too well perhaps. Periods of deep slumber that were no doubt the testing ground for death, followed by the more superficial wanderings of a hungry ghost. Her dreams were circular, a ride on a toy train. Again and again she passed the same little houses and shacks, the same little people standing mutely on painted lawns—so much like people she'd once known. Florence Fini was there, pointing at Honey, the woman's stubby finger erect with judgment, on her face a scowl. Or was it a grimace? It was always a challenge, reading the expressions of the departed.

Here, in this world, it was raining, making the walls of the bedroom look like crinoline. Honey, coming to, thought the patterns beautiful. She stared for a while, lying on her side—but then vanity got her up. Pillows were murder on the face; too long in bed and you ended up with the crisscrossed skin of an elephant.

*   *   *

Though the ringer was off, Honey's cell bleeped and blurped, signaling new messages. The police, surely; the Lexus. She decided to deal with it after breakfast.

Two poached eggs on melba toast, a wiggle of bacon. She was surprisingly ravenous. She even ate the last three biscotti from a Christmas tin God knows who had given her. And then, to be safe, she mixed a glass of Metamucil, which went down, as it always did, like a smoothie made from sawdust. She sipped it slowly, standing near the kitchen window, from where she could see Jocelyn's driveway. Parked beside the girl's station wagon was an unfamiliar vehicle, a pickup with a camper shell. The license plate wasn't yellow, so not New Jersey. The plate was white, with a colored orb in the middle—an orange or a peach. Perhaps the girl had relatives from the South. Trashy, from the look of the truck.

Honey winced at the Metamucil, though really she was wincing at herself. Is this what she'd become—a nosy old woman snooping from a window? She took in the new sapling the girl had planted, another flowering cherry. The former tree, fatally snapped, lay on its side by the curb, looking like a sad haiku.

Cherry blossoms die
When fat girls drive big cars.
Nature—watch your ass!

Honey drained the last of the sawdust and blinked at some tattered clouds drifting away. The rain had passed and the sky was a devastating blue, glazed by della Robbia. God was somewhere in all of this, if you knew where to look. Honey didn't.

Just as she was about to turn from the window, she saw a man come out of the girl's house. A tall fellow, extremely thin. Around his neck there were vine-like tattoos. A baseball cap pulled low cast shadows in his eyes. Honey thought of the boys who'd attacked her.

The girl was outside now, too, talking excitedly at the man's back as he made his way toward the pickup. He turned toward her but said nothing. When it came to conversation, it seemed that no one, not even this tattooed giant, stood a chance against the girl, who—Jesus wept!—was wearing yet another pair of overalls.

The man, perhaps in an attempt to stop Jocelyn from speaking, leaned down to kiss her—and then, for nearly thirty seconds, they made out grotesquely, like gluttons. It seemed to have a palliative effect on the girl. She was quiet now, staring up at the man with a huge smile on her face. She was still grinning as he got into the truck and pulled out of the driveway. But as soon as the pickup turned the corner, her face went blank, almost as if someone had turned a switch. She began to scratch at her arms ferociously, like a neurotic cat.

Honey recalled the Band-Aids she'd seen on Joss's body just the other night. There was definitely something off about the girl. Honey felt a flicker of concern but quickly extinguished it. The last thing she needed was something else to worry about.

She brewed a cup of chamomile and went to sit in her bedroom closet, something she did occasionally. The nice thing about the closet was that it was absolutely quiet. And since it was enormous, she'd been able to fit a lounge chair in there, along with a footstool, a reading lamp, a small table. It was very cozy, and the smell was always calming: the peat of leather shoes, the fresh milk of clean cotton, the deep green swell of cedar, not to mention the phantoms of old perfume trapped in wool or silk.

From the footstool, Honey retrieved a book she'd recently purchased, a feministic potboiler about women in prison. She settled herself in the chair, but after reading for less than a minute, she stopped, stared, breathed. The breathing took some effort.

At the funeral parlor she'd made light of her position, assuming that at her age she'd be a pro when it came to grief (so much experience!). But now the thought of Nicky collapsed her. He was, she knew, the last romance of her life. Selfishly, she was mourning that as well.

While it was true that Honey had always done just fine on her own, it would be dishonest to suggest that she didn't adore being in love. Over the years she'd had so many wonderful affairs. Her sadness about Nicky was like a flare, lighting up all her other romances, both major and minor.

The boy in the tweed suit who'd taken her into the hills above campus. Another boy, a biology major, who made his own wine out of rhubarb. And during a summer at home, there'd been Pio Fini, briefly. Many boys, briefly. Then, in her thirties, the curly-headed cherub at the Self-Realization Center, who chanted during intercourse. In New York, the skinny stockbroker naked in black socks; the Polish swimmer with the girlish bottom. California had brought treasures, too. The cat-eyed actor in Laurel Canyon, twelve years her junior. Most of her lovers, of course, had been older—though no one more than Mr. Hal, who'd had thirty-four years on her, and with whom she'd stayed the longest, well over a decade.

"But who was your *great* love?" Lara sometimes asked, as if life were a novel. The question always annoyed Honey. Why must she decide? They were *all* great loves, in one way or another. Apparently some gals looked down on such a view—either that, or they felt sorry for Honey.

For many women, one man for life was the prize. The proof that you were worth a lifetime.

Honey stared at her hands—the bluish veins, the large brown freckles. In a few months she'd be eighty-three. She recalled Nicky's proposal at Dante's. Would she have wanted that? The pain of his passing was still raw. Though their relationship, admittedly, hadn't been the epitome of passion, Dominic was a true friend, and that was the real prize. Meeting him outside Florence Fini's funeral mass had seemed so lucky. Honey hadn't expected to find much sweetness in New Jersey. She'd come back here after the death of her friends, wanting to die, and then she'd met Nicky and wanted to live.

But now? What was the point? Maybe it was time to call it a day, cash in her chips. The desert-white handgun was somewhere about. Honey closed her eyes and sipped her tea, drifting back, looking for a memory she could inhabit without tears. Surely not everything in the past was filled with grief.

Mr. Hal, for instance. Such a ridiculous man.

Still, if love were flying school—and wasn't it?—then Mr. Hal was the one who'd given Honey her wings.

9 Mr. Hal

Fresh from Bryn Mawr, Honey was living in Manhattan, in a tiny mousetrap-laden apartment on East Seventh Street. Within a week of arriving she'd snagged a job—an assistant at Carrigan's, one of the smaller but well-established auction houses. Her boss, a woman named Sally Bosworth-Previns, felt Honey had promise. During the interview she'd been particularly impressed by Honey's double major (history of art and classical studies), claiming that such a foundation could get a girl through any room, no matter how scratchy the tweed on the gauntlet of men. "Besides, you'll look good around the paintings," she added, with an up-down that made Honey blush. "And there'll be none of this Ms. Bosworth-Previns nonsense. You'll call me BP, as all my girls do." BP's specialty was the nineteenth century, particularly the Pre-Raphaelites. "Dreadful paintings, for the most part," she sniffed, "but a few collectors are going whole hog for them again." When she asked whether Honey was married or had a beau, Honey said, "No and no, and not looking. I feel like I've just been born."

Friendships formed quickly at Carrigan's. Luanne, another assistant—in Jewelry and Timepieces—was a riot, and Honey occasionally went out with her after work. Luanne was around the same age, a bit more zaftig, brunette to Honey's blonde. Salt and Pepper, the men in the office dubbed the girls, who could often be found in a corridor, sharing a cigarette. One fellow, in Rare Stamps, called them Slick and Slack. They never discussed the monikers, but Honey always assumed that she was the slick end of the operation; at night she treated her hair with olive oil and a hot towel, and in the morning, after she washed it, the shining locks gave the impression that someone was following her around with a spotlight. Luanne, aka Slack, had a wilder mane, and her ample bosom seemed perpetually in danger of flying the coop. Honey, though not exactly flat-chested, occasionally augmented things with padding.

The night she'd met Mr. Hal, as a matter of fact, she'd been wearing a padded brassiere.

It was Friday, and the hour happy. Luanne suggested the Chop House, a stone's throw from Carrigan's. Sitting at the bar, sipping martinis, the girls played at elegance. Honey sparkled in glass pearls and a floral dress with a mandarin collar, while Luanne bombed the room in a tight hobble skirt and a silk blouse missing the top two buttons—no doubt intentionally. When after her second cocktail Luanne wobbled off to the bathroom, Honey noticed the older man at the far end of the bar gazing at her. He looked to be in his fifties, positively ancient. And then he was walking over, smiling so crookedly that it was a toss-up as to whether he was drunk, deranged, or the victim of a stroke.

"Forgive me for intruding," he said when he was standing in front of her, "but you are like no else in this room. Do you know that?"

Well, yes, as a matter of fact she did. While sipping her martini, Honey had taken stock of herself in the mirror: the perfectly fitted dress and the spotlit hair, which she'd recently marcelled—a vintage look this late in the fifties, but it suited her. She didn't care for the new bouffants or those awful poodle cuts.

"So what's your name, honey?"

A lot of women hated it when men called them that, but Honey took no offense. How could she? Still, she wondered if she should string this man along with a game of Who's on First. But before she could say a thing, he extended a huge and shockingly hairy hand.

"I'm Mr. Hal, by the way. Well, Hal—but everyone calls me Mister."

"And why is that?" she asked, shaking the interloper's paw.

"Because I'm everyone's boss. Not yours, of course—never yours. But, yeah, I've got a few hundred men under me."

"Really?" Honey cast her eyes downward, in the direction of the man's pants. "No women under there?"

"*Ha ha*," he barked. "Not at the moment."

"Because I might need another job some day," she said. "I've not yet found my groove." Was she actually flirting with this relic? The martini's doing, surely—he was not her type at all.

"So what line are you in, honey?"

"Paintings," she told him, longing for a cigarette; she often found it hard to strike the right pose without one. "I work at Carrigan's—it's an auction house."

"Well, that's just swell, just swell. I'm in insurance," he said, sitting down in Luanne's spot. Briefly, Honey caught a glimpse of the man's profile—the huge nose, the nonexistent chin. *So ugly*. Why on earth was she smiling at him? Plus, that rumpled suit, depressingly beige, with something that looked like dried ketchup on the trousers. At Bryn Mawr, Honey had dated only the cream of the crop. Most of them graduate students, since men weren't permitted in undergrad.

"I'm with a friend," Honey said, "so don't get too comfortable."

"Your friend looks very comfortable where she is."

When Honey turned, she saw Luanne standing against the wall, letting a tall man carry on a conversation with her cleavage. Luanne's catch was older, as well—though only around ten years or so, and he looked dashing in a well-fitting Roman-style suit.

"Let me get us another round," said Mr. Hal. "*Yoo-hoo*," he called out, waving at the bartender like the Queen Mother. The man was ridiculous, a complete cartoon. Honey had no idea why she was mesmerized. Maybe because, despite his age, he seemed like a boy in a costume—one who'd put fake hair in his ears and applied rubber jowls. Even that great hook of a nose seemed a ruse—as if his outward appearance had nothing to do with his spirit.

"I wish these stools swiveled—don't you?" he said, wiggling his hefty bottom.

Honey had no idea what to say, and then she felt a tap on her shoulder.

"I'm taking off, bud." It was Luanne, with Roman Suit lingering at her back. "You gonna be okay with this one?" she whispered into Honey's ear.

Honey rolled her eyes. "I will, if you give me a cigarette."

Luanne handed one over and sashayed away to claim her imitation mink at the coat check. Honey lit her Lucky Strike, while Mr. Hal tapped his fingers against the polished wood of the bar. Neither spoke.

"I don't think I can drink any more," she finally said, looking down at the fresh cocktail he'd ordered for her. "And I really should get home."

"What's at home?"

"Mice," replied Honey, wondering why she was being honest. In such a position, she often said "my husband."

"I see," said Mr. Hal. "Well, have you ever been to the Plaza? We could go there instead. That is, if the mice can live without you for one night?"

"I don't do one-nights."

"Well then, we'll just have to stay at the Plaza forever. How does that sound?"

After stubbing out her cigarette, she informed the man that her name was Honey, not Eloise.

But the reference went right over his head.

*　*　*

Thinking of him as ancient, she was shocked by how good he was in bed. The boys at Bryn Mawr had clearly been doing things wrong. At the Plaza, Honey experienced what could only be called *complete immersion*. Mr. Hal made her incapable of thinking straight, and therefore unable to control the situation, which was always her objective when having sex. Ever since Richie Verona, Honey had learned to keep a part of herself on guard.

But Mr. Hal undid her.

"Why are you going down there?" she asked at one point, as he disappeared under the covers. She had no experience in this department, though she quickly got the gist of it (lie back, do nothing). Afterward, she nearly cried. She felt such gratitude that she was confused when Mr. Hal appeared again from down under and said, "I don't deserve you."

Lying naked in the huge bed, she stretched her arms and marveled at the sheets, so soft and thick they seemed like kindness. And the room was exquisite—nearly twice the size of her apartment, with marvelous inlaid furniture and large windows overlooking Central Park. Under the beautiful antique writing table there were no mice, only lion's feet, and in the bathroom the fixtures appeared to be made of gold.

Honey had grown up around nice things—but nothing like this. Plus, she'd learned at Bryn Mawr that her parents' things might actually be vulgar: the Veronese imitations in their rococo frames, the crystal swans, the black-and-white leather couch, the tasseled lampshades. Just because her family had money didn't mean they had taste. Honey was living in a different world now—especially tonight, at the Plaza—and she wondered if this was where she belonged.

Of course, there was still a lot to learn. For instance, she didn't really understand the problem with the Pre-Raphaelites. BP condemned them as overwrought and sentimental, but Honey rather liked the bright canvases of fat-lipped girls with their ropes of metallic hair. And the verisimilitude was often striking. "Realism is overrated," BP explained. "And can't you just smell the misogyny?"

Honey couldn't.

But she wanted to understand, wanted to better herself. Maybe she could even train herself to talk differently. At college, she'd done a fair job of taming her accent, but why not take it further? Talk more like BP, who grew up in New York but sounded like Alec Guinness, calling everyone *darling*.

"What are you thinking about?" Mr. Hal said, interrupting her reverie. He was lying beside her, buck naked, the hair on his body wall-to-wall, absolutely monstrous.

"I'm starving," she told him. "I've eaten nothing today but an apple and three cigarettes."

He picked up the phone and ordered room service. "Four blintzes, please."

Blintzes? Wasn't it time for champagne and caviar? Not that she really wanted those things, but it seemed like what Jane Russell might order in bed. "Blintzes are boring," she said.

"Not at the Plaza," Mr. Hal informed her.

And he was right. They were marvelous, served on the prettiest little plates, with a sauce made from mint and cognac. On the serving tray, a sprig of tiny crimson orchids curved from a celadon vase.

I don't want this man, Honey thought—but I want this life. As she ate the blintzes in the barge-sized bed, she pictured another man beside her, someone more like Roman Suit.

But then Mr. Hal took her in his Neanderthal arms. Despite his sticky fingers (he'd eaten with his hands!), she allowed him to caress her face, and she almost never let a man do that. At college, whenever a boy dragged his fingers across her cheek, Honey often had the impression he was trying to sign his name there. But with Mr. Hal it was different. There was something gentle about him, and he touched her in a way that seemed to suggest wonder more than ownership.

Honey experienced a sensation akin to melting, and realized that for years now she'd been holding herself rigid; some part of her had frozen. The truth was, she'd never really felt safe around men. It was strange, then, to find herself burrowing deeper into the ugly man's fur. Embracing him in a way that was not her style.

"Tell me something about you," he whispered.

"Tell me something about *you*," she replied.

"Okay, fine," he said, kissing her head, "we'll keep our secrets."

Good, Honey thought. This was exactly how she liked to play it. Cool, with an air of mystery.

But then she was crying. She didn't even know she was doing it until Mr. Hal said, "What is it, sweetheart?" He took her face in his hands and looked at it. "Did I do something wrong?"

"No. I'm fine."

"Well, you don't look fine. You look like someone just ran over your pussycat."

"That would be you," Honey said—and as the blush bloomed in her cheeks Mr. Hal started to laugh. He ran his hand gently down her belly and asked her if she'd like him to do it again.

* * *

After he fell asleep and was snoring like a kazoo, Honey slipped from the bed and stood by one of the windows overlooking the park. Here and there, moon-like lamps illuminated the curving pathways. In the distance, beyond the trees, tall apartment buildings twinkled, a crossword puzzle of windows, some bright, some dark—the checkered unknowability of other people's lives.

It was Friday night, not yet nine o'clock. Honey had the whole weekend in front of her. She wondered if she should steal away now, before the man woke up; waiting till morning would make things complicated. She was still naked, though, and not quite ready to be anything else.

What was she, that night? Twenty-two, twenty-three? Standing in her glory by a window, proud and unashamed and so very confused. Because somewhere to the west was the Hudson, and across that filthy river was New Jersey.

It had been almost a month since she'd spoken with her mother, and even longer with her father and brother. Maybe she should call them, tell them where she was, that she was doing fine—implying *fine without their money.*

Or she could call simply because she missed them, which she did, despite everything. Family was awful that way, as if there were magnets implanted at birth. No child could ever really escape.

Maybe she'd ask her mother to meet her for lunch next weekend, at Dante's. She wouldn't invite her father—not that he'd come, even if she did. They'd said some unfortunate things to each other the last time she was home. A Sunday dinner that seemed like a dream now. He'd called her a *puttana.* She'd called him disgusting, a murderer. It was the first time she'd allowed herself to use that word. Her mother had left the room, her brother too, and then she was alone with the Great Pietro. He didn't speak, only nodded and drank his wine, while she sat there drinking hers, pretending to be brave, waiting for him to slap her, or worse. But he refused to even look at her, and finally she gave in, said she was sorry. *Forgive me, Babbo*—scarlet-faced and pleading, proving she was a coward after all. When, finally, she began to cry, he took his cue. He turned and touched her cheek. Signed his name.

"Bella faccia, bocca brutta," he said. *Pretty face, ugly mouth.*

Honey didn't argue. Because maybe he was right. To have called him a murderer was beyond the pale. Some stories were too terrible to remember, let alone talk about. There was a fairy tale her mother used to tell her, about a girl whose lips were sewn shut with black thread.

But one couldn't sew up the mind—and from the safety of the Plaza Hotel, Honey imagined what a relief it would be to tell someone, just once, about her father. Tell them how he'd forced her to get into a car with Richie Verona, even after he knew what the boy had done. And then she'd tell them how, when she was eleven, she'd seen her father strangle someone.

But who would believe her? They'd say she was crazy. They might even lock her up, claiming that to have witnessed such a thing and not come forward made her an accessory to the crime.

Honey turned away from the window, from the dizzying view of the park, and stared at the snoring giant in the bed. She was cold and afraid, and there was nothing to do but crawl in beside him, press her body against his. Otherwise she'd go crazy, or do something foolish. The room was on the eighteenth floor, and if you looked straight down you could see the blank canvas of white pavement. She'd never really do it, of course. Still, the thought of jumping somehow calmed her. She thought about things like that a lot.

*   *   *

When Honey woke a few hours later, Mr. Hal wasn't in the bed. It was still dark, and when she clicked on the lamp she saw that it was only a little past midnight. There was a note on the bedside table—chicken scratch on the back of a business card.

> *If you are not a figment of my imagination, please call me next week at the office. The room is paid for through Monday. Enjoy yourself.*

Honey wasn't sure whether to feel mortified or thrilled, and since she was too tired to decide she simply turned off the lamp and went back to sleep.

In the morning, after a long bath, she went downstairs and had breakfast in the Oak Room—cinnamon toast with whipped butter and two sides of bacon. It cost a fortune, and she paid in cash, even though the waiter said she could sign it to her room.

Honey wondered how many girls this Mr. Hal had brought to the Plaza. Well, it didn't matter; she had no intention of seeing him again. Checking out early, she walked back to her apartment, where she spent the entire weekend with the mice, one of whom kept staring at her from under a chair, as if concerned about how much she was crying.

A t first she thought the vibration was coming from her chest— her heart perhaps. The old ticker felt strangely out of kilter. But the disturbance, in fact, was the doorbell.

"Coming," she muttered, getting up, a tea stain on her robe and her left foot completely numb. How long had she been sitting in the goddamned closet, daydreaming?

In the real world, the light was indecisive. It was hard to tell if it was day or night. Shuffling toward the living room, her knee throbbing, she made no effort to rush. It was probably the creature from next door. Either that or those Jehovah's Witness ladies with their twinsets and their tracts. The most she could hope for was a handsome pair of Mormon boys to condemn her spirit to prison.

What did it matter? Whoever was there would be no more than an extra, since all the leads in Honey's life were dead.

When she opened the door, she nearly gasped. Standing before her was her brother. He was completely intact, though—no shattered jaw, no bullet hole in his forehead.

And then the clouds parted. The man before her, in the blue velour running suit, was not Enzo; it was Enzo's son.

"Corrado? What are you doing here?"

Her nephew towered above her, alarmingly tall. In his hands was a bunch of pink lilies, though all Honey could smell was the man's cologne, the same vile stuff he'd worn to Dominic's wake.

Corrado was saying something, but Honey couldn't concentrate. She was distracted by the car in the driveway, which looked exactly like her Lexus.

"I don't understand. Is that mine?"

"That's what I was saying. We found it."

"What do you mean, you *found* it?"

"Why don't we talk inside?"

"We can talk here, Corrado."

"Please, Aunt Honey. I won't stay long."

She wondered if he might push his way in—she knew the type. But he only stood there waiting, clenching and unclenching his fists.

Honey looked at the man's dark green eyes freckled with hazel, the thick and enviable eyelashes. He looked too much like her brother. Poor Enzo, dead at forty. Corrado had been a teenager.

Honey stepped back and allowed her nephew into the foyer. His smile, like his fists, opened and closed. Clearly he was uncomfortable, even nervous. Honey prolonged the man's discomfort by not speaking.

"So, yeah," he finally said. "About the car—it's kind of funny, actually."

Honey rather doubted that. "I love a funny story," she said coolly.

Corrado glanced toward the living room, toward the sanctuary of the couch, but Honey didn't budge. Let the man stand on the threshold like a salesman. After a disingenuous laugh, he said: "So, some friends of Peter's—"

"Who?"

"Peter? My son?"

Yes, of course. The older of her two grandnephews. Michael, the younger one, was the drug addict who'd barged in a few days before. Peter was the married one she'd seen at the wake. Infuriating, having to keep all these bit players straight.

"Not really *friends* of Peter's," Corrado continued—"just some people who work with him. They were involved with your situation and—"

"Please don't beat around the bush," Honey interrupted, closing the door. "I was born in the same family as you. So what are you trying to tell me—that your son's friends stole my car?"

"Can we at least sit down?"

"We're fine where we are. Just spit it out."

"Okay, well, I'm trusting you here."

Honey couldn't help toying with him. "Trusting me—really? Do you think that's wise? We barely know each other."

Corrado took no flak. "You're my father's sister," he shot back smoothly. "Or have you forgotten that?"

"I forget nothing, dear." She looked her nephew directly in the eye, and could barely believe it when she said: "Of course you can trust me. I don't betray other people's secrets."

Corrado nodded. "So, as I said, Peter knows these guys. They work for him, actually. But then Peter noticed the name on the registration and he came right to me."

"I see."

"And so, yeah, total mix-up. But we fixed the window and had the car cleaned—and there's a full tank of gas in there."

Was she supposed to thank him? Honey recalled the two men in the alley—how they'd pulled her from the vehicle, knocked her to the ground.

"Your son's *friends* were a bit rough."

"As I said, they're not really friends, just associates. And don't worry, we'll deal with those guys."

"Don't do anything rash," Honey said. The young men who'd assaulted her were no more than boys.

Then again: Why should she care? Hadn't they ripped her dress, called her a stupid old cunt?

Feeling slightly dizzy, Honey leaned against the wall, and before she knew it she and Corrado were sitting in the living room. Someone had placed the lilies in a ceramic water pitcher. Unnerving, the way time was jumping around lately, a game of hopscotch over patches of nothingness. Sometimes being old was rather like being stoned.

"Are you all right?" her nephew asked.

"I'm fine," she said, getting her bearings. "And what am I supposed to tell the police? I've already filed a report, you know. I've even given a description of the men."

"Here's what you need to do," Corrado said calmly.

She didn't like his tone. But she waited, wanting the man to reveal himself.

"You call the cops and say a friend of yours saw the car parked at the side of the road. Keys in the ignition."

"And why would they believe that?"

"Tell them there was some money missing from the glove compartment."

"There was no money in the—"

"Yeah, but just tell them that. That way they'll chalk it up to amateurs—you know, kids looking for drug money or something."

"Someone like Michael, I suppose."

Corrado's face darkened at the mention of his other son. Honey, feeling leverage, went further.

"I believe I saw him, very close to where the car was stolen. He was standing at the side of the street wearing some sort of flimsy getup, almost like a dress."

"A dress?"

"Or a hospital gown, I don't know. What's going on with him, anyway? Is he sick?"

"I don't know what the fuck he is. He's got problems, okay? And I didn't come over to talk about Michael. For Christ's sake, Aunt Honey, I'm doing you a favor here!"

The force of his voice silenced her. And though she didn't doubt her own power, she knew it would be imprudent to show it. Men like Corrado were unpredictable when confronted.

"Of course, dear. I'm very glad to have my car back."

Her nephew's face relaxed. Obviously, stolen cars were a less touchy subject than wayward sons.

"So what do you do with the vehicles?" she asked. "My father—well, your father too—they used to ship them to Eastern Europe. Is that still the arrangement?"

"That's not something you need to know," Corrado replied—not unkindly, but as if he were talking to a child.

Honey felt like laughing. *I know everything*, she would've liked to say. *I know more than you, dear. I know where the bodies are buried.*

Instead, she adjusted the lilies in the pitcher; they were leaning too much to the left. With her head bent over the blooms she could finally smell their sweetness, and perhaps she lingered there too long.

"I'm sorry about your friend," Corrado said. "I'm sure you miss him."

"Yes. But you mustn't worry. I've gotten quite good at missing people."

When she stood, rather abruptly, Corrado followed suit, understanding he was being dismissed.

"Well, I should probably get going."

"Yes," said Honey.

But then, when neither made a move toward the door, Honey sensed that it was still there—that irrepressible magnet of family, fidelity. Even as her mind resisted it, something in her body took comfort—her blood perhaps, with a mind of its own, acting against her better judgment. Because her nephew was ready to go, and here she was turning to him, saying: "Unless you'd like a cup of coffee?"

He looked surprised, something in his face almost innocent. She recalled him as a baby, or perhaps she was seeing her brother.

"Sure," Corrado said, with a crooked smile borrowed from a dead man. "A coffee would be nice."

* * *

Silence, as they sipped their espresso. A slight tremor, on Honey's part, she hoped went unnoticed.

"Coffee's good," Corrado said.

"Sant'Eustachio," replied Honey. "I order it special."

"I don't know that kind."

"From Rome?"

He shook his head. "Never been."

She judged him—*so provincial*—then judged herself for judging.

"But I guess you travel a lot, huh?" he said.

"I used to."

"I remember my father calling you a gypsy."

"Yes, well, that wasn't always a fashionable word. Gypsies were often hated."

Corrado squinted, as if against a blur. "My father didn't hate you."

He said it with such assurance that Honey refrained from correcting him. They were sitting at the dining room table—too formal, too far from each other. Corrado placed the little cup on the saucer, fit it to its groove like a puzzle piece.

"I think my father was just confused why you never came home."

"Did he say that?"

"No, but I often had the impression he was waiting for you. They were all waiting for you—Grandma and Grandpa, too."

Honey only nodded, letting the silence speak for her.

Of course, silence was often dangerous. The empty chairs in the dining room grew significant. And then, as if merely to think of the dead was to summon them, something began to stir outside the house. In the mid-afternoon darkness, there was a rustling agitation.

Corrado blinked and fidgeted. Honey could tell that he wanted to ask her things. But she could tell, too, that behind his curiosity there was anger. She'd been in New Jersey nearly eight months before informing her family she was here. She hadn't been ready to face them. She, too, was still hobbled by anger. The feeling besieged the room—or possibly it was the wind, knocking against the French doors. Beyond the glass, leaves and dust were swirling about; something was blowing in. Honey wondered if the new blooms on the rhododendrons would be ripped from their stems. These spring storms were often spiteful. She could see the cypresses bending, as if whipped by a violent master.

"My father," she began, thinking to tell her nephew something, maybe just a little. But as she looked up to meet his eyes, the glass doors blew open and a burst of warm wet air struck their faces. A vaudeville of leaves danced into the house, defiant of boundaries. The chandelier was singing. Honey stared helplessly into the chaos, but Corrado jumped up and shut the doors, slamming the bolts into the floor with his foot.

"Those doors shouldn't do that," he said. "I have a man I can send over to look at them."

"I have my own man," Honey replied.

"I'm just saying, if you ever need anything . . ."

Why, she wondered, was her nephew really here? She recalled that when she'd gone to her brother's funeral, Corrado wouldn't even speak to her. No doubt he'd spent a lifetime hearing stories of his aunt's betrayals.

So why this sudden kindness? If that's even what it was. He stood there, sweating a bit, his breath audible from the slight exertion he'd made leaping up to close the doors. Probably a chain-smoker, like his father.

"Oh, I almost forgot," he said, digging in his pocket. Honey flinched—but her nephew pulled out only a set of car keys.

When she took them, it felt strangely like a pact. But what was she agreeing to?

"How will you get home?" she asked. "I don't think I'm up to driving you."

"I'll call for a car," he said. "But, listen, we really would like you to come over sometime, for supper maybe. Not a big thing, just the family."

Honey made a noncommittal sound, then rose to lead her nephew to the door.

But apparently he wasn't ready to release her. He lingered in the foyer, smiling. "You know, I remember the gifts you used to send me when I was little—like those funny slippers with the mirrors on them."

"From Morocco, yes. I'm surprised your parents let you keep them."

"Why wouldn't they?"

"How's your mother doing, by the way? She's in Florida, right?"

"She was living there for a while, yeah—but, no, she passed away a few years ago."

"I'm sorry, Corrado. I didn't know."

"Yeah, it sucks. So I guess you're, like, the last one now."

"The last one?"

"I mean, that generation or whatever. The silent ones, right? You guys knew how to keep secrets."

What was he getting at?

"Listen, Aunt Honey, I can't speak for the rest of them, but I'm glad you came back. I feel like there's a lot we need to talk about."

He was still smiling, though it seemed a put-on. There was something about him she didn't trust.

"You better call your car," she said. "Before the rain comes."

"Something's coming," he said. "That's for sure." He bent down to kiss her cheek.

Honey accepted the affection—but when her nephew pulled out his phone, she told him he'd get better reception outside.

* * *

In the bedroom, she checked the nightstand drawer—but it wasn't there. She checked the other nightstand. Again, nothing. Where had she put the stupid thing?

She looked in the large locked trunk that held her photographs; she looked in the blue velvet Crown Royal sack where she used to hide her diamonds; in the Ferragamo box that housed a copy of her will.

Goddammit.

She went back to the closet, remembering that in the eighties she'd kept it in the pocket of a fringed leather jacket. After going through the pockets of nearly *every* jacket, she stuck her hands into the soft canvas sleeves where she stored her shoes. Finally, she found it on one of the high shelves stacked with winter sweaters. The pistol was tucked between a white angora turtleneck and a pale-blue lambswool crew. She could tell from the weight of it that it wasn't loaded.

Which was probably for the best. Surely she was overreacting. Then again, maybe not. Possibly Corrado, beloved grandson of the Great Pietro, wished to finish the old man's business, to hold Honey accountable for her sins. In the kitchen, she opened a drawer beside the sink. It would be a comfort to know where the gun was, a reminder that she had some power, or at least the means to protect herself.

Failing that, she'd simply get on with her original plan.

As she pushed the thing to the back of the drawer, she noticed the clipping—the newspaper article about her and Florence Fini winning a sewing competition. And then, beside that, was the business card the young man had given her—the painter who'd driven her home from that godforsaken alley.

He'd said to call him anytime. And the truth was, she didn't feel like being alone right now. What did it matter that he was forty, possibly fifty, years her junior? Age had never been a factor with Mr. Hal. Besides, the young man was a homosexual; to suggest a friendly drink could not be misconstrued. Still—how awful to be this lonely, to have to call a stranger. Honey had never been in such a position before, and it stuck a sharp pin through her vanity.

She poured a glass of wine and took a long sip before dialing. She wouldn't invite him here, of course. She'd propose a drink at Mabel's, or perhaps a visit to the young man's studio. She'd mention her years at Carrigan's, and at Fitzroy's in Los Angeles. They could chat about art, about paintings, about the goddamn Pre-Raphaelites. When she finally called, though, there was no answer, and Honey was too proud to leave a message.

The air in the kitchen felt thick. The scent of Corrado's cologne lingered. Honey drifted to the window and opened it. The rain hadn't started yet, though every molecule of the atmosphere seemed pregnant with moisture. The light was strange—furtive and rushing about, as if looking for a place to hide.

Honey thought to go back to bed, but found herself standing outside, on the lawn. She looked down at her stained robe and for a moment felt like an actor who'd forgotten her lines. She glanced around at the set—the flowering cherry, the pickup parked next door.

As if in a dream, she crossed the property line and scrutinized the truck, seeing clearly the peach on the license plate and the lived-in mess behind the window of the camper shell.

From the girl's house came the sound of music, and as Honey moved closer she could hear shouting. Then there was a scream, followed by a thud. Honey knew these sounds from her childhood. She pounded on the door.

Almost immediately, though, she realized that what she was hearing was intercourse. *Jiminy Cricket!* She limped away as quickly as possible— which wasn't quickly at all. Back in the safety of her kitchen, she poured more wine, took her trusty Valium.

And then the phone began to ring.

Hello?"

"Yeah, hi, this is Nathan Flores. I just got a call from this number."

It was the painter.

Honey was mortified. At her age, she often forgot that there was no longer any privacy when it came to telephones. One could always be tracked, always be traced.

"Yes," she said. "I'm sorry I didn't leave a message."

"Is this Ilaria?"

Oh, God—now she was even more embarrassed. Is that how she'd introduced herself? Clearly she'd suffered a fit of nostalgia while driving in the young man's Thunderbird.

"Yes, it's me," she said. "Your charity case."

He laughed. "Don't be silly."

But what was silly was having called him in the first place—to have imagined inviting him out for a drink.

Well, she'd end this quickly, put them both out of their misery.

"I just wanted to thank you again for your kindness last week."

"Yesterday, you mean?"

"Was it?" Honey felt a tilt. "Goodness, you'd think I'd banged my head and not my knee," she joked, making light of her confusion.

"How *is* your leg, by the way?"

"Oh, fine," she replied, glancing down at her bruised and grotesquely swollen kneecap. Through the opening in her robe her leg looked like a snake digesting a grapefruit.

On the phone, she could hear music. Perhaps the boy was driving, or at a party. "Well, I'll let you go. It sounds like you're busy."

"Not really. I was just staring at a blank canvas."

"A noble endeavor, I'm sure. The muse rewards the patient."

"So they say. My sneaking suspicion, though, is that she's fooling around with the painter next door."

"Well, darling, it's her job to be promiscuous."

Jesus Christ, was she flirting? It was an old habit she found difficult to break. Barking up the wrong tree was one thing, but here she was barking up a fruit tree; Nathan, after all, was a swish.

And even if that weren't the case, Honey had no carnal interest in the young man—or any man, for that matter. She was done with that part of her life. Dominic had been a lovely farewell; all she wanted now was solitude and celibacy. Perhaps she'd resume her meditation practice, revisit the teachings of Yogananda. Leave this world like a nun. Shaved head, saffron robe . . .

She was drifting again. "Excuse me, dear—what did you say?"

"Just that I'm glad you called. I was going to tell you yesterday about the show, but I was too shy."

"You're having a show?"

"Not a solo exhibition, just a group thing. But I have a piece in it, and—I don't know—I thought maybe you'd like to come to the opening."

In L.A., Honey had attended hundreds, if not thousands, of openings. But since returning to New Jersey she hadn't been to a single gallery; she hadn't even gone into the city to visit the Modern or the Met. And it'd been more than a decade since she'd purchased a painting or a drawing, let alone a print. Which begged the question: Did she still care about art? Still believe it had the power to change a person's life? That it was, at its best, salvation?

Unfortunately, she did.

"So when is this shindig?"

"Not for a couple of weeks. First Saturday of next month. If you want, I could pick you up—since you're without wheels."

"Actually, my car's been found."

"Oh, that's great."

"Well, there was some money missing from the glove compartment," Honey confided, testing Corrado's lie.

"Probably junkies."

"Yes." The subject chafed. She thought of her grandnephew loitering half naked at the side of a road. "So your opening is next month?"

"Yeah, Saturday the third. Five to seven. Like I said, I only have one piece, so it's not a big deal."

Honey knew how insecure artists could be—and how important it was to be kind. "It is a big deal. And I'm very curious to see your work. Why don't you give me the address?"

"Do you have a pen?"

Honey reached for one across the table, clicked it open, and said, "Shoot."

* * *

After she hung up, a tiny bliss, like a champagne bubble, rose inside her chest. What on earth was causing it? Not the boy or the invitation, surely. An art opening in the suburbs—potato chips and onion dip— did not inspire her. Still, there was something.

Maybe just the idea that she wasn't finished. That there might yet be a bit more story left to her, a small parcel of the unexpected. Perhaps the tiny bubble in her chest was hope.

But then, in the bathroom mirror, she saw something horrible: an eighty-two-year-old woman who looked—well, eighty-two. In the woman's eyes no hope at all. Only sadness. Honey blamed Corrado, for making her think of her brother. She blamed Dominic, for leaving. Blamed her father, for everything.

Honey's sadness was so potent that it seemed to have outwitted her plastic surgeries. Her cheeks sagged and her eyes drooped, her skin was pallid and her hair was beyond forgiveness. Had she really answered the door, looking like this? She'd actually done it twice now—once with the neighbor girl and then again, with Corrado. It wasn't like her at all, to allow herself to be seen in such a state. No wig, no makeup. Barefoot like a beggar girl, her toe paint cracking.

Under the harsh light, Honey scrutinized the wreckage of her face. Every little capillary was visible, every little and not so little wrinkle. She sighed; her skin was definitely too thin to survive another lift. For several minutes, she confronted the mirror. Though distasteful, it was important to check in with reality now and then—even to become conversant with it.

"You're slipping," she said to herself.

Maybe she'd take a bath, wash her hair, put on something nice. She might even sit in the yard, under the awning, look out at the burgeoning garden. It was spring, for heaven's sake—and how many of these did she have left?

Honey didn't hazard a guess.

* * *

She did not sit in the garden. It was pouring now, and the wind had turned furious, knocking against the windows in startling bursts.

After a modest dinner of twelve almonds and two squares of bitter chocolate, she put on her cat-burglar pajamas and read for a while in bed, more of the interminable novel about women in prison. The main character was a lesbian named Up Yours who was fond of Jell-O and Jack Russell terriers. Up Yours had murdered a priest. The novelist was clearly concerned with spiritual issues, but her insights were about as valuable as something found in a Cracker Jack box. Honey managed only a few pages before closing her eyes against the absurdity.

Liars, she thought. We are all liars.

* * *

Later, as she dozed, he came to her in a dream. A lover from her youth. When he touched her, in this conjuring, Honey had a different body, a different face. Her heart was made from entirely different materials. How such alchemy had happened—this change between then and now—she couldn't fathom. She woke up strangely bereft, though not unhappy.

Her heart, yet again, was changing. It was harder, darker, a bit like granite. At first this frightened her, but then she thought of Bellini, of Leonardo. She thought of their cliffs, their stones. Rocks shaped like shrouded figures or calcified wings. One painting, she recalled, had a black cave that throbbed with a nearly invisible undercoat of crimson. And she remembered what she'd learned from looking at this master-piece:

That stones were not dead. Stones, in fact, were the mother of this world.

12 Bruises

A few days later—three? four? who could count?—the sun was out, flying toward Earth at alarming speed, not to mention at a jaunty new angle. The natural world was thrown into confusion. Insects darted and plunged, a madhouse of buzzes and clicks. The flowers, too, seemed to be screaming. Even the shy hellebores had opened, revealing their hairy privates.

Honey decided to enter the chaos—test her knee by walking to the corner market. With luck, she'd find some kumquats.

In homage to the weather, she put on her yellow Gucci day dress with the ribbon trim. On her feet, dark brown velvet flats with cushion inserts. As for her wig, she chose the lighter brown one with subtle highlights of red. The color was no cheap trick. The wig had cost an arm and a leg—and, like all of Honey's wigs, it was made from human hair. Sometimes she worried about where this hair had been harvested. Years ago, she'd read an article about roving gangs in China who went around stealing women's ponytails.

But, like so many things, it was best not to think *too* much about the ethics of it. Once you went there, you ended up paralyzed. Slave labor, animal testing, my goodness. You could hardly eat a banana or put on some lipstick. Next thing you knew, your Hermès wallet, in orange crocodile, would have to be sacrificed too.

* * *

No kumquats, sadly. And too early for cherries. Spring was tricky when it came to fruit. Honey grabbed a few Italian plums, no doubt from China, before scanning the vegetables. The artichokes looked excellent, though possibly too heavy to carry. Honey had to consider her knee; though it was much less swollen, the stroll to the market had brought discomfort. Luckily, she had the cane. Grimacing, she limped toward

the checkout. And then her grimace turned into a scowl when she saw
Teresa Lioni entering the store.

Immediately, Honey escaped down the beverage aisle. She'd circle
around to the cashiers closer to the exit—anything to avoid talking to
the woman. Teresa Lioni was good friends with Angela Carini. Both
had been at Dominic's wake—where Angela had whispered *bitch*, while
Teresa had muttered something about Honey's plastic surgery.

Carini and Lioni—the two *i*'s at the ends of their names had always
been snake eyes. Years ago, the women had worked as a team to expose
Honey's affair with Pio Fini, Florence's husband. It was Teresa who'd
spotted the lovers exiting the hotel, and Angela who'd told Florence.
Soon everyone in Ferryfield knew about it—even Honey's parents.
"Peccatrice," her mother called her. *Sinner.* And her father, who was no
stranger to infidelity, said he was ashamed of her.

So much fuss over nothing. It wasn't even an affair; Honey had slept
with Pio only once. But Angela and Teresa went around, talking as if the
plan had been to steal the woman's husband. They'd clearly taken some
pleasure in destroying Honey's friendship with Florence—the only girl
Honey had truly admired.

Flo was more than just a dressmaker; she was an artist. After they'd
won that sewing competition, Honey suggested they open a shop together.
Her father, back then, would have gladly fronted the money. Florence,
though, was terrified of the Great Pietro, and nothing had ever come of
the dream. But if it had—who knows? Honey might have stayed in Ferryfield, married Dominic Sparra at eighteen, instead of dating him at eighty.

No—it never would have worked. In the end she would've gone crazy
in this town, living among the philistines. She'd always been so much
better than them. As she tottered down the aisle, Honey's arrogance
flashed, a welcome respite from her sadness. She held up her head and
limped on. The checkout lane was mercifully in view.

But then—*Oh, shit*—there was Teresa Lioni reaching for a package
of toilet paper. Eye contact was unavoidable, and when it came it was no
simple matter. For what seemed an eternity, the women stared at each
other from opposite ends of a long tunnel. All other shoppers blurred
into landscape, a vague suggestion of trees and hills.

Finally, the old acquaintances approached each other, hands raised in greeting. Clearly they were no better than robots, under the control of some old-world politesse.

"Honey."

"Teresa."

The woman's smile was tentative, though her snake eyes were assured, steely. The lights in the market were far too bright, and Honey was self-conscious about her face. She could feel a tremor in her cheeks.

"Have you hurt yourself?" asked Teresa, gesturing toward the cane.

"It's nothing," Honey replied. "To be honest, I just like the sound of it." And here she tapped it firmly near Teresa's feet, like a burst of gunfire.

Startled, Teresa dropped her TP. As she picked it up, her hackles came up with it.

"So are you headed to a party?" she said to Honey.

"What do you mean?"

"The dress. I mean, you can't be wearing that just to shop."

Oh, these Catholic girls played innocent so well. Honey was much less good at it.

"Civilization would fall, dear, if we all wore sweatpants in public."

Teresa was wearing something quite like sweatpants—though they were dolled up with ghastly appliqués of sparkly silver daisies. Which drew attention to what was best ignored: Teresa's over-ample thighs.

"These aren't sweatpants."

"No, they're lovely," Honey said. "Did you make them yourself?"

"My daughter made them."

Honey nodded—she had nothing to say against this daughter. Teresa seemed to have nothing left to say, either. The two of them stood there silently, their smiles gone, replaced by the natural frown of age. It was then that Honey realized that their childhood grudges were irrelevant, because she and Teresa now shared a common enemy. *Time.*

"I use that same tissue," Honey said stupidly, pointing to the product in Teresa's hand.

Teresa looked down at the grinning bear on the label. "Yes. It's the best."

Under the stark fluorescence, faced with such mundanity—two old rivals talking about toilet tissue—Honey felt the last of her animosity evaporating. "How is Angela doing, by the way? She didn't look well at Dominic's wake."

Teresa's face tightened in defense, but when she saw that Honey's question was genuine, her eyes filled with tears.

"What is it, dear?"

"They had to take her back to the hospital. She's in intensive care."

"Oh, I'm sorry. May I ask what's wrong with her?"

Teresa wiped her face. "I'm sure you're the last person she'd want to know."

"Oh, Tessie—must we, really? It was a million years ago, all that. We were *children*."

At this terrible word, Teresa began to cry in earnest. "Angela's dying," she finally managed to say. "She's at St. Joseph's, and they don't expect her to . . ." Here, the woman made a choking sound, accompanied by a hopeless shake of her head.

As she sniffled on, Honey wondered if dying wasn't somehow worse for these diehard Catholics. The idea of a Christian heaven required a lot of imagination, a thing in short supply by the time one reached eighty. Imagination, like hope, was the province of the young.

She patted Teresa's arm. "I know how close the two of you were."

"Like sisters," Teresa squawked.

When Honey took the woman's hand, it seemed to calm her.

But then, not two seconds later, Teresa pulled away rather abruptly. "I'm sorry for making a scene."

"You hardly made a scene, dear. And what's the point of life if we can't express ourselves?"

But Teresa had already closed herself off. "Well, I really need to get going. Take care of yourself, Honey."

"You too, Tessie."

The woman emitted an odd little laugh. "You were the only person who ever called me *Tessie*."

"Yes, I always liked the sound of it."

"Well, to be honest, I never cared for it. Some of us actually like our *real* names."

As Teresa waddled off without another word, Honey stood frozen with her bag of plums. The temptation to throw one at the woman's head was not easily overcome.

* * *

Walking home, Honey felt a downward pull in her chest, as if someone had hung sopping-wet towels there. The weight wasn't just Nicky. She missed Lara and Suzanne, her friends from Los Angeles. Both gone— and so very young, compared to Honey. One felled by disease, the other by suicide. Horrible, horrible. And yet it was hard not to see some dark intelligence in having left the game early.

It was late afternoon now. The sun was gone, hiding inside a villa of clouds. Somehow, the spring flowers looked prettier in the shade, more poignant. A gaggle of lilacs were nodding in unison, the subject of their agreement a mystery. Scattershot birds tattered the edge of Honey's vision; some were singing. Life was everywhere, glorious, though at the moment its exuberance was more of a slap than a tonic to the old woman limping with her bag of fruit.

Children played on porches, while in little silver leaps a squirrel moved shrewdly across a lawn. And just up ahead, the neighbor girl sat stolidly on her stoop.

Honey had no desire for a conversation, and perhaps Jocelyn sensed this, because she said nothing as Honey approached. She offered only a wan little wave, which Honey dutifully returned.

The pickup truck wasn't in the driveway, so surely the girl was waiting for the man to come back. It was the first time Honey had seen her neighbor in something other than overalls. She was actually wearing a dress, albeit a frumpy one—and on her cheeks there was rouge, though far too much. No doubt she'd tarted herself up for the new boyfriend.

As Honey doddered by, Jocelyn lowered her head, as if she too wished to avoid a conversation. Honey wondered if she'd said something to offend the girl. Against her better judgment, she turned and spoke.

"Are you all right, Joss?"

"What? Yeah, I'm fine." The girl smiled, though it seemed forced.

"I see you've done up your face."

"Just a little, yeah—but it's fine, it doesn't even hurt."

Hurt? Honey squinted, quickly realizing her error. It wasn't blush on the girl's cheeks, but bruises.

"Oh my goodness, what happened?"

"Nothing. It's so stupid."

Honey came closer, and now saw the extent of the injury. Both cheeks swollen, and around the left eye a purple shiner.

"Have you been *mugged*?"

"What? No. I just tripped."

Honey was reminded of her mother, who'd often said the same thing (*Sono caduto*)—a lie everyone accepted but Honey and her brother, who'd regularly witnessed their father's rages.

"I don't see how you could get that banged up from tripping," she said to the girl.

Jocelyn shrugged and pulled out a pack of Marlboros. "I'm a total klutz." She lit up grandly with a purple Zippo and took a deep, ravenous drag.

Honey resisted the urge to mention the ruckus she'd heard the other day, while standing outside Jocelyn's house. She didn't want to expose herself as a snoop. But maybe her suspicions had been correct.

"Oh, sorry," the girl said, holding out the cigarettes. "Did you want one?"

"Darling, it is a vile habit. I smoked for thirty years. It'll kill you, as I'm sure you know, but not before it gives you a thousand wrinkles."

"So do you want one or not?"

"Yes, I'd love one, smart-ass."

It was her second this week. Dominic would be furious. But how smoothly it went into the mouth, the filter almost like silk. As Joss flicked the Zippo and Honey pulled with her breath, she felt once more that small flutter of hope. There was something exhilaratingly primitive about sharing a cigarette with someone.

But then she looked again at the girl's face, and all hope collapsed.

"Are you sure you're all right?"

Jocelyn nodded and exhaled. "Nothing's broken."

Honey pictured the man in the pickup truck—the vine-like tattoos encircling his neck. She couldn't restrain herself. "He better not be hurting you."

"Who?"

"Your boyfriend."

"*What?*" The girl's cheeks flushed redder. "This has nothing to do with him. And he's not my boyfriend."

"Well, his truck's been here for several days, and I saw you kissing him."

"Nosy, are we?"

"When necessary, yes."

The girl stubbed out her cigarette. "Okay, I mean, we're sexually involved, and he needed a place to stay—but I wouldn't call him my *boyfriend*. I met him on Blinder."

"Where's that?" Honey imagined some Greek island she hadn't heard of.

"It's not a place, it's an app."

"A what?"

"A hookup site. But without pictures. Basically Grindr for ugly people."

Honey was completely at sea. All she could think to say was: "You're not ugly."

Joss rolled her eyes.

"And I certainly don't think you should be allowing strangers into your house."

"Why not? All people are strangers at first. And I'm not gonna just give up and be *alone* all the time."

The girl said this with enough force that Honey felt compelled to take a step back. Lonely people were often desperate—and desperate people were dangerous.

But then Jocelyn dropped her defensive pose and, in that bizarre shape-shifting way of hers, began to smile maniacally.

"Plus, Lee is a terrific guy. I mean, okay, sure, he's a little rough, but he's been through *a lot*—and I feel like we're really good for each other. You know how when you're with someone and it just feels right?"

Honey made a vague sound, knowing there was little she could do to disabuse this girl of her foolish notions. Every pair of lovers lived in their own country, with their own laws. Honey had never been able to help her mother, so why think she could help this girl? Despite the idea of women standing together being back in fashion, Honey couldn't rise to it. All she could feel were the bruises on the girl's face communicating with the bruises on her own knee. It seemed a hopeless conversation. She took a final puff of her cigarette, then tossed it to the pavement and crushed it with her velvet slipper.

"You shouldn't give up either," Jocelyn said.

"Excuse me?"

"I mean, with dating and everything. How old are you, anyway?"

Honey was too tired to lie. "I'm eighty-two."

"Wow, really? You don't look it."

"I've had help."

"Well, you should put yourself out there. I mean, there are sites for people like you."

"Yes, I believe they call them gravesites."

"Very funny. *Websites*. And there's a couple of apps specifically for older people. Octoroons or whatever. I could send you some links."

"No thank you, dear. I'm quite off the horse. And I think you mean *octogenarians*."

Suddenly the girl's phone dinged, and she flinched as if something had bitten her. She glanced down to read the text, then twiddled her fat thumbs in reply.

Honey sighed and said she had to go.

"One sec, one sec," Jocelyn muttered, still typing. When she finished, she jumped up and ran into the house. "I'll be right back!" she shouted.

For crying out loud, thought Honey, wondering if the girl had a bladder problem. But not ten seconds later Jocelyn was back with a small, filthy knapsack.

"Would you mind keeping this at your place for a couple of days?"

"What is it?"

"I don't know. But Lee said to get it out of the house."

When Honey hesitated, the girl begged. "Please, please, just take it.

Lee's parole officer might show up today." She thrust the knapsack forward.

"I don't want it."

"Can I at least hide it in your yard?"

"Absolutely not."

But Jocelyn was already sprinting across the lawn.

13 Taster's Choice

She sipped her espresso and stared at the small Morandi she'd hung in the kitchen. Hung carelessly, too close to the stove. It was an exquisite painting, though people who didn't know better often thought it boring. "A bunch of cheap vases," her father once sniffed. "The guy could have at least put in some flowers."

Honey had inherited the canvas from Mr. Hal. She'd been the one who'd convinced him to buy it—a steal, she'd said, at fifteen thousand. That was in 1967, only a few years after Morandi's death. The piece was surely worth at least a million now.

What did it matter, though? She had no one to leave it to but dogs. Car thieves, drug addicts, garbage men.

What Honey liked best about the Morandi was its simplicity—those pale, sweet-colored jars lined up like toys, like a child's sadness. Despite the pastel loveliness, the light in the painting was bleak. It was not the light of the sun, but the light of the mind trying to understand mortality. Honey knew this light—and not just in her dotage. As a child she'd lined up colored things on her windowsill, bits of broken glass she found in the gutter. Rubbish that she wished to redeem. The shards of glass took the light splendidly, clever as any diamond. Even back then, Honey had been interested in transformation.

Was such a thing still possible? Honey longed for change, and yet everything—not just in the world but in her heart—felt tight, trapped, ossified. She asked the Morandi for help, but the canvas only blurred. She was crying again.

Even worse, her mind kept returning to the girl next door—that bruised and banged-up face. Why did such awful things keep happening? Wasn't it time to write a new story?

Don't look at *me*, thought Honey. I'm far too old.

* * *

Eventually she drifted into the yard and knocked about the azaleas, parting their frilly curtains to peer inside. She still hadn't figured out where the girl had hidden the knapsack—which was filled with God knows what. Coke? Cash? Kiddie porn? The tattooed man with the pickup truck was considerably older than Jocelyn, and he had the flattened face of a pervert. Such men often had faces like that; perhaps a lifetime of hiding things made their features implode. Honey had arrived at this opinion through experience; like all pretty girls, she'd attracted a fair amount of perverts in her day.

After the azaleas, she messed about in the overgrown hydrangea—and when she had no luck there, she looked up to see if the pack had been flung into the branches of a tree. But there was nothing. As she headed back to the house, though, she spotted a suspicious lump behind the gingham apron hanging by the outdoor grill.

She lifted the fabric gingerly, and there it was, the filthy green knapsack. She unhooked it from the peg and, glancing around to make sure no one was looking, carried it into the house.

*   *   *

Inside the knapsack was a plastic Taster's Choice container—but instead of instant coffee it was filled with what looked like bath salts. Exactly, in fact, like the scented crystals she often put in the tub. Honey opened the container and sniffed, but there was no fragrance. Surely it was some kind of drug, or perhaps some chemical used to manufacture them. Corrado would know, she thought, or one of his sons.

But the idea of calling them just made her feel depressed, not to mention weak. Besides, she could deal with the situation on her own—simply walk next door and deposit the knapsack on the girl's stoop, or, better yet, throw it at the man's head the next time she saw him. She was done with criminals and their dirty deeds. An angry heat stormed her body, pushing her down the hall to the little powder room off the kitchen—where, without further deliberation, she emptied the Taster's Choice jar into the toilet.

"Bye-bye," she said, and flushed.

A triumph—albeit a brief one. Because almost immediately she felt sick, regretting her rashness. As the water swirled, sucking down the crystals, she thought what the hell have I done? Her worry was less about herself than about Jocelyn. Had she put the girl in danger?

Once again, the annoying thought: *Call Corrado.* She hated that her mind went there.

Honey had always been self-sufficient, and in order to remain so she refused to start relying on her family. She could certainly manage this Lee character herself. The best thing might be to feign innocence, tell the pair next door that someone must have stolen the knapsack. *I know nothing about it*, she'd say. She was—don't forget—an excellent liar.

* * *

Back in the kitchen, she resisted the urge to take another Valium or open a bottle of wine; she'd been doing too much of both lately. She'd always liked her booze—and as far as pills were concerned, the Valium was a newish thing. She'd started taking them not long after Florence Fini's funeral, after the woman's grandson had gone missing. The boy was lovely, and the crime had upset Honey terribly. This world was no place for a child, especially this particular stretch of New Jersey. Prior to the Valium, Honey had only ever taken diet pills—which she'd never really needed, though they did provide a nice burst of energy.

What she required now was calm. Peace. At the table, she attempted a few pranayamic breaths, but the espresso still raged in her blood, making her jumpy.

Or perhaps it was the Morandi, staring at her from the wall, trying to communicate something. Such an intelligent work of art; it was practically an oracle.

"Tell me," she whispered to the canvas.

Its answer jangled her.

Memento mori. Remember you must die.

Not two seconds later Honey picked up the phone—though she didn't call Corrado. She called St. Joseph's Hospital and asked the nurse on duty if she could speak with Angela Carini.

"Ms. Carini is in a coma."

"Oh, my goodness. Well, can you tell me when your visiting hours are?"

"Are you family?"

"Yes," Honey lied.

"Then anytime between nine and six. But you should know that Ms. Carini probably won't be here much longer."

"Where is she going?" asked Honey—but then she answered the question herself.

"Yes, of course. I understand."

14   Whose Hat Is That?

When she woke and turned on her phone, there were two messages from the police and *seventeen* from Jocelyn. Honey decided to deal with the lesser of two evils first. She prepared herself by rehearsing the lines Corrado had fed her—repeating them until she felt her delivery was flawless. Then she called the station and explained that a friend had spotted the stolen car in the neighborhood, keys in the ignition. "Unfortunately, there was some money missing from the glove compartment."

"Huh," the officer replied. "Where was the car found, exactly?"

"Just a block from my house, can you believe it? I was relieved, of course—though, to be honest, I'm still a bit traumatized."

When the officer suggested that a team come to the house to dust for fingerprints, Honey didn't falter.

"I'm such an idiot—I hadn't even thought of that. I've already had the thing washed."

"I see. Can you hold on a second, ma'am?"

After a brief silence, Honey could hear a clicking sound. At first she thought the man was typing, but then she worried that the line was tapped.

A moment later, the clicking stopped and the man was back, asking Honey to confirm the spelling of her last name.

Then he reminded her about coming to the station to look at mug shots. "We can't catch these guys without your help, Ms. Fasinga."

"I'll do what I can," she said, trembling as she hung up the phone.

* * *

To calm herself she took a bath, after which she scanned through Joss's texts. The first two messages—I just wanted to let you know I'm fine and I watered your tree this morning☺—were followed by Where are you? and Why are you ignoring me?

After this, the girl sent several links to dating sites (Highly recommended!)—and, finally, the texts arrived at the subject of the knapsack.

I thought I'd come over and pick up you-know-what.
OK If I come over now?
I'm coming over.
I'm in your yard but can't find it.
Where is it, did you move it?
I'm knocking on your door. Are you deaf???
I'm still here.
I'm going home now. Please call me.
I'm leaving for work now—call me.
Call me!

* * *

The knapsack was still on the kitchen table. Honey retrieved it and stuffed it into the trash, along with the empty Taster's Choice container. Peeking out the window, she saw that Jocelyn's station wagon was gone but Lee's pickup stood guard, parked at an eccentric angle. Honey shut the curtains, feeling like a prisoner in her own home. She checked if the gun was still in the drawer, and then wondered if it was too early for a drink.

It was.

She retreated to the safety of her closet, tried to read but couldn't focus. If only Nicky were here, he could hold her arthritic hand, rub her worn-out feet.

But she was alone. Alone, yet surrounded. There was too much going on, and far too many characters. Honey couldn't keep them straight. When she thought again of the tall fellow next door, with his sleazy jar of bath salts, she confused him for a moment with her grandnephew Michael. She pictured him in that filthy alley, wandering around half dressed.

Was he sick? In trouble? When he'd come over, demanding money, she should have asked more questions. She should have tried to help. Now she wondered if she'd been unkind.

I'll start again, she thought. Let me start again.

* * *

She didn't have a number for her grandnephew, and after some debate decided to call Corrado's landline, on the off chance the boy would be at home. If Corrado answered, she could just hang up.

But it was the wife who answered. *Rita? Rina?*

"Hello, dear, it's Honey, Corrado's aunt."

"Oh, hi. Oh my God, how are you?"

"I'm fine. I was wondering if I could talk to—"

"Corrado's not here," the woman interrupted. "But if you want, I can give you his cell."

"No, I was actually calling about Michael. If he's home, I'd like to speak with him."

"Why do you want to talk to Michael?"

"We had an unfortunate interaction—I think I mentioned it at the wake—and it's been bothering me. I just wanted to apologize."

"You don't have to do that. I'm sure it was his fault. He probably wanted money, right?"

"Yes." Honey felt it best to be truthful.

"You didn't give him any, did you?"

"No," she lied. "May I speak with him, please?"

"He's not here."

"Well, would you let him know I called?"

"He, uh, he isn't staying with us at the moment. In fact, I haven't seen him in weeks. It's just a real mess right now." The woman sounded distraught.

"Well, I certainly don't want to complicate things," Honey said. "I'll let you go."

"No, wait, don't hang up. I just—I'm glad you called. I mean, Corrado's been so angry about the whole situation, and then Peter practically *attacked* Michael, so I can't blame him for not wanting to stay here."

"Attacked him?"

"Well, he didn't really hurt him. I mean, Michael didn't need stitches or anything. Busted his lip, though."

"My God."

"I know—awful, right? Hitting his own brother. I still got blood-stains on the carpet."

Honey had no idea what to say.

"I probably shouldn't be telling you any of this," the woman continued. "I just—I don't know—I think it would be great if you could talk to Corrado. I mean, you've probably got more experience with these sorts of things."

Experience? Honey wasn't following. She explained to the woman that she had no children of her own.

"Yeah, I know. I just mean, you've traveled a lot and so you're probably more open-minded or whatever—and I know Corrado respects you. He mentioned you might be coming for dinner?"

"Maybe, once I'm feeling a little better. But as for Michael, I'm still a bit hazy about what's going on. Is it something to do with drugs?"

"Well, that's part of it. And then he's doing all this counseling, or like *evaluations*. And Corrado refuses to pay for any of it, you know, he's just sick of it. Anyway, we probably shouldn't discuss this on the telephone."

"I agree. And it's really none of my business."

"No—it is your business. And I would really love it if you came for dinner and we could all just talk, you know. Just have a civilized conversation for once. Corrado says you spent a lot of time in Europe?"

"Years ago."

"And he said you were in Egypt, too, and then Africa. You've probably seen all sorts of things."

"A bit," Honey offered modestly, still not sure where the woman was going with this.

"Listen, I'll tell Corrado you called, but when you talk to him, maybe don't mention that I said anything about the boys."

"Of course not, dear."

"Thank you. It's just a sensitive subject—and I don't want him to think we're talking behind his back. I'm sure he'll confide in you eventually."

I certainly hope not, thought Honey.

"So you'll let us know about dinner?"

"I will."

"Because you're always welcome here. I mean, my God, you grew up in this house, right? You probably got a lot of memories."

"I do, yes."

"Well, I'd love to hear your stories sometime."

"Unfortunately, my memory's not what it was."

"Sure, yeah, my mother's getting like that too. Do you mind, though, if I ask you one thing?"

"What's that?"

"It's just—this probably sounds weird—but I can't seem to grow anything in the yard. Everything just, like, *withers*. Maybe it's the soil, I don't know—but I just wondered if maybe your mother had trouble growing things, too?"

Honey felt the kitchen tilt. "As a matter of fact, she did."

"Oh, good. Well, not *good*, but at least I know it's not just me."

"No, it's not. It used to drive my mother crazy, actually, not being able to grow a good tomato—though I recall she had a bit more luck after she put a statue of the Virgin in the garden."

"Really? Huh. I'll have to try that. I get a kick out of those old superstitions."

"Yes," Honey said. "We were very quaint."

* * *

Cursed was more like it.

Was such a thing possible? Of course it was. Honey believed in magic, in curses. Her superstitious nature had been instilled in childhood. Though her parents were less medieval in their Christianity than some of the poorer families, they'd maintained a pious respect for mysterious realms beyond the human. Her mother, especially, had kept a lookout for omens, and she had a plethora of rules in regard to managing one's luck, or at least averting disaster. The statue of the Virgin had been an attempt to purify the backyard. Though Honey's family didn't seem to worry very much about sin, they did worry about retribution. Fortune could turn easily; one had to be vigilant.

"Whose hat is that?" How many times had Honey heard her mother ask this question, when Honey had accidentally left one on a bed? "What are you trying to do, Ilaria—kill us?"

Worse than a hat on a bed was the *malocchio*, the curse that might come from the envious eyes of others. There were many such eyes around the Fazzingas. To ward off the curse, a *cornicello*, a little red horn symbolizing strength and immortality, was placed in all the family cars. Driving around in a fancy car was dangerous, since envy could easily turn into bullets—which, in fact, is what happened many years later to her brother. Enzo, as an adult, had not kept a *corno* hanging from his rearview mirror.

Her father, on the other hand, was never without one. The horn he hung in his Cadillac looked like a twisted chili pepper—a cheap gewgaw, constructed of plastic. But he also had a smaller one made of coral that he wore around his neck and that went with him to the grave.

As children, Honey and Enzo had learned early how to negotiate with Fortune. If they spilled olive oil at dinner, they'd be required to dab a bit of it behind each ear. Enzo balked, but Honey just pretended it was perfume. Sometimes she spilled the oil on purpose.

Luck was a kind of game. If a shopkeeper was sweeping the sidewalk, Honey's mother would whisk her across the street, lest the broom touch Honey's feet and decree—God forbid—that she remain single for the rest of her life.

Her most powerful memory, though, was the day of the black moth. As a child, Honey had loved moths and butterflies, and knew from her mother that these delicate creatures were the souls of paradise come to visit.

But apparently Honey hadn't been given the full rulebook. One evening, at twilight, she opened the back door and a moth flew into the house—black with yellow spots, the pattern absolutely gorgeous, like a dress she might ask Florence to make. It landed on the edge of a chair, and Honey backed away so as not to disturb it. "Come see!" she called out to her mother. But when her mother saw the creature she gasped.

And then she slapped Honey across the face.

Honey hadn't understood that to let a moth in at night, especially a black one, meant death, misfortune. She and her mother spent nearly fifteen minutes attempting to chase the insect out the door, since killing it, apparently, would only make things worse.

When the moth escaped into the darkness of the living room, Honey's mother shook her head and said, "Why, Ilaria? Why do you always do this? *Sfortuna!*" she cried, pointing at Honey as if that were her name.

Honey knew this had something to do with the fact that she'd been born a girl. But she refused to take all of the blame. Because, even as she let her mother scold her, she knew that the real bad luck came from the dead man in the yard.

As she made her way down the soulless corridor, surrounded by exhausted-looking nurses in ghastly flowered smocks, Honey composed a prayer. *Dear God, please don't let me croak in a place like this.* She sent her net wide—to Vishnu and Shiva, Hashem and Allah. And, since this was a Christian hospital, she even batted a small birdie in the direction of Jesus.

When a nurse began to stare, Honey wondered if she'd been babbling her prayers out loud. But then she realized the woman was gawking at the dress. Honey was wearing one of Florence's—a green silk wraparound with a small black bow at the waist. There was something mermaidish about the design—the color pulled from the deep, and the bow marvelously ruffled, crinkum-crankum as seaweed. The fit was slightly tight, and Honey proceeded slowly in two-inch heels.

She tried but failed to ignore the open doors, inside of which metal beds with blinding white sheets sat victim to bleeping technologies. And the patients, of course, lying there like seedless husks, while loved ones peered down bleakly, as if penniless before a wishing well. The floors gleamed viscously and everywhere the smell of disinfectant and excrement, the sour burn of fluorescent light bulbs. *Intensive care.* Could there be a more dreadful pair of words? They made Honey think of a cheap hand cream she'd used back in the seventies.

When finally she stood outside Angela Carini's room, she was afraid to enter. It seemed a trick now—as if the door before her were the door to her own death. *Surprise!* Angela would yell, like a party planned in secret.

But when Honey entered there was only silence, only another woman's doom. Angela, small as a child, was wrapped in a blanket. One arm dangled free, and in her frozen claw someone had inserted a strand of plastic rosary beads. She resembled a papoose, or a mummy. Her eyes were closed but her mouth was open. Tubes traveled to arms and nose—

tubes that would be disconnected soon. Angela was about to be moved to hospice—a deceptive word, Honey had always felt. It sounded like a Swiss auberge run by nuns, though one in which instead of black bread and Emmentaler there'd be morphine and the last bitter licks of time.

Poor Carini. Her face appeared grained like wood, and just as hard, as if she were straining toward some decision. As if death were a choice and not a decree.

Maybe it was.

Honey sat beside the bed and wondered if it would be all right to touch the woman's hand.

No, not yet.

"Can you hear me, Angie?"

Whether she could or not was up for debate. These states the body entered prior to passing remained a mystery. A coma, a comma, a pause before eternity. A moment to collect one's thoughts, pack one's bag—or unpack them, probably. Throw everything out, except the essential core of one's being: the thing that lived in you always, that you could feel but never touch. For lack of a better word—the soul.

Honey stared at the shriveled thing before her.

"Darling," she finally said, "you look terrible." If they were going to have a meaningful encounter, they might as well start with honesty. Besides, Honey was here to look the past dead in the eye.

She wouldn't stay long. Surely some of the woman's real friends would show up soon—the gang that had been with her at Nicky's wake, including Teresa Lioni, who Honey had run into at the supermarket.

"I'm surprised none of them fixed your hair." The woman's silver frizz was a mess, flung upward on the pillow in tufty peaks, like a jester's crown.

Well, what did it matter? There was no man for Angela to pretty herself up for. Like Honey, the woman had never married, and had no children. Perhaps she, too, had been cursed by a broom touching her foot. And now here was the final curse, mortality. The rosary beads would not protect her, though she gripped them as if there were battles yet to fight.

"You were always strong," Honey said. "I'll give you that. You had convictions. Unlike me, though, you didn't have the money to back them up."

"But you were never timid."

Honey recalled a Halloween party—ages ago, in the late forties or early fifties, when she and Carini had been teenagers. Angela had come as a devil, with papier-mâché horns and a tail made of wire wrapped in velvet. Quite clever, actually.

"But I was the real devil, wasn't I? That's what you always thought."

"You knew who we were, my family, and you judged us. Of course you did. I don't blame you. My father strutting around like a king, when your people had nothing. Most of the poorer girls kept their heads down around us, but not you."

Angela had been the only one who wasn't afraid to sneer at Honey, or call her out for her misdeeds. Honey respected that. Not back then, of course—but now.

A firecracker, they used to call a girl like Carini. A lot of power in a little package.

Honey had always been amazed by the smallness of Angela's body. A smallness that was never frail. Even now, as this body neared non-existence, Honey could see in the compact little frame the gnarled muscles of a wild dog. The woman could have been a boxer, or a lawyer.

In actuality, she'd become a secretary for a company that made zippers. It seemed a terrible fate—but perhaps Angela hadn't minded. She'd had friends, she'd made a life.

"Still, you were always so mean," Honey said. "And I know you were jealous."

"But the unkindness, dear, the unkindness was uncalled for."

Honey wondered if the woman had seen a priest before slipping into unconsciousness. And if so, what had she confessed? Had she mentioned how she'd blabbed to Florence about Honey's affair with Pio? Broken the poor girl's heart. Treachery was a sin. In Dante, it was the ninth circle, quite low, the traitors buried in ice.

Honey was a traitor, too.

"And what did we get out of it, Angie? What did anyone get, for that matter? Florence never forgave me, you know."

Honey wished the woman could open her eyes, just to see the dress. Angela had never been able to afford a custom-made frock, even though Florence had charged so little. As a girl, Angela had worn utilitarian skirts made by her mother, and occasionally for her birthday she'd be given some cheap outfit from Ohrbach's or Bamberger's. *From the doll department?* Honey used to wonder. The girl was that tiny. Even at fifteen, sixteen, the boys still thought of Angela as a child, ignored her, or were outright cruel, calling her a dwarf—sometimes Sneezy, sometimes Grumpy. At the same time, those boys fell silent around Honey. They nodded politely, in awe—partially, she knew, in respect for her father, but also for her beauty. By fifteen, Honey was five foot nine—and, in two-inch heels, formidable.

But there was one boy who didn't seem to be afraid of her, or shy. He was older—bold and flirtatious. This was long before Pio Fini, when Honey was still an innocent. The boy would find her after school and give her chocolate bars.

"And I know it drove you crazy, Angie, because you had a terrible crush on him. Everyone knew you loved him. Florence said you told her you hoped to marry the boy one day."

"But he chose me, didn't he?"

"When he asked me on a date, I heard you were sick with rage. *Why does that Fazzinga girl get everything?*"

"And he *was* something, with that dark hair and that tanned skin—not to mention those wonderful hands. All of us swooned over those mitts. Even when he had dirt under his fingernails it somehow seemed sexy."

"Of course, dirt under the fingernails was something you knew from the men in your house, laborers—but those hands were a novelty to me. And he was so very beautiful."

Honey paused. She hadn't meant to speak of Richie Verona, but it was too late now to stop.

"Do you know he attacked me, Angie?"

"That boy you loved but who chose me. He *raped* me."

For a moment Honey wondered who was speaking. She'd never in her life said this word out loud. It was a relief, a reckoning long overdue; she felt giddy. But she was also short of breath.

"It was quite terrible, Angie."

"So you might say I saved you, dear. Because I think he would have done it to anyone—and I felt certain he'd done it before."

Rape. Was the word even sufficient to the boy's brutality?

"Do you know, he didn't even get undressed, he just pulled out his thing as if he were taking a leak—and then afterward he told me to keep my trap shut. Of course, *he* wasn't very discreet, telling all his friends that he'd had me."

The words still stung. *Had* me—as if she were a meal or a cigarette. Not long after the assault she'd walked past Richie and his friends on the street. Richie merely nodded, but his friends had snickered. Honey had run home crying.

"Of course, I said nothing to my father about the boy—but somehow he found out. My mother probably told him, even though I begged her not to. And I was terrified, Angie. I was sure my father would kill me."

"But the funny thing is—he didn't seem angry at all. He actually invited Richie to our house and offered him a job and then, as if it were another bit of business, he said, 'So you're going to marry my daughter, yes?' "

"Richie didn't answer right away. He looked completely petrified. But then he said, 'Yes, Mr. F—of course.' "

"I was sitting there at the table with them—my mother was there too. I remember they'd served Richie coffee."

" 'Come back, tomorrow,' my father said to him. 'I'll introduce you to some people, set you up.' "

"When Richie left the house, I started shaking. I got down on my knees, right in front of my father—and I begged him, 'Please, Babbo, please, I don't want to marry him.' "

"I was beyond frantic, but my father was absolutely calm, saying, 'Shhh, shhh, I know what's best for you, Ilaria.' "

"And the next day, when Richie came back, my father said he had some business down the shore, he wanted Richie and me to come with him, and that afterward we'd go to the beach, have a picnic. He told us my mother had made some sandwiches; that they were in the trunk. 'Yes,' my mother said, 'and your bathing suit is there too.' "

"It was like I was dreaming. It had been only a week since the attack, and my mother had been giving me some kind of pills, I suppose tranquilizers, and I was feeling woozy, utterly confused. And then there I was, driving with my father and Richie to the beach. It made no sense."

"But I think maybe some part of me grasped what was going on. I knew my father, knew his cruelties. And I thought, yes, he's selling me off to this boy. He's selling me off because I've been stained. But for the life of me I couldn't understand why he'd be selling me to the boy who'd hurt me, the one who'd actually *stained* me."

"I can remember sitting in the back seat. Richie was up front with my father—and he was nervous, I could tell. When my father brought up marriage again, Richie turned to look at me and attempted a smile—and I just felt sick. I thought, are we supposed to pretend we love each other?"

"And the more my father talked to Richie and joked with him, the more Richie relaxed. At one point, I even saw my father pat Richie on the back. It was as if he were *rewarding* Richie for his brutality. As if what he'd done to me was acceptable or, I don't know, a way of putting me in my place. I was like you, Angie—strong-willed. *Orgoglio*, my mother called me. Arrogant."

"And I realized that Richie and my father thought this too, and in their agreement they were like brothers. I could hear them whispering up front, and it made me sick, Angie, because I understood how powerless I was."

"I remember thinking, I could just jump out of the car, I could just jump out and kill myself."

"But I could barely move. Maybe it was the pills my mother had given me. Every so often I caught my father's eyes in the mirror and he'd wink at me. It took everything in me not to cry."

"I'm not sure how long we drove for, but it seemed a long time, and then I remember passing the strangest thing—this huge dinosaur made of concrete, an enormous white Brontosaurus. It was in front of a bait and tackle shop."

"Not long after that, my father said he was hungry. 'What about you?' he asked Richie. Richie said he was. And so my father suggested eating the sandwiches early, before going to meet his friends."

"We got off the highway, we were on Route 9, I think. My father said he knew a nice spot he'd been to with my mother. And I was so afraid, Angie, because then we were on a dirt road with lots of trees and I kept having the strangest thought. I kept thinking my father was taking me into the woods so that Richie could attack me again. I felt sure my father was bringing me out here to punish me."

"'I'm not hungry,' I said from the back seat—but my voice was so small I don't think anyone heard it."

"Finally my father pulled over at a trailhead and I saw that there was another car parked there—a blue convertible. And I was confused, because it looked just like my uncle Vinch's car."

"That's when something spun around in my head and I knew—I knew *exactly* what was going on."

"We all stepped out of the car and my father got the blanket out of the back seat and he said, 'Ilaria, why don't you get the sandwiches? Richie and I will find a spot.' He handed me the car keys and put his arm around the boy's shoulders. When they started to walk away, I saw Richie hesitate, as if he were beginning to understand too. He turned to look at me."

"It made sense now why my father had brought me along—because if *I* was there, Richie would think it was safe, you know, that *he* was safe."

"I knew the kinds of games my father liked to play. And I understood that I was expected to play along. It wasn't the first time I'd had to lie for my father."

"So when Richie looked at me—do you know what I did? I smiled. I smiled, Angie, and I said, 'Go, I'll be there soon. It's so hot, I want to put on my bathing suit.'"

"I saw Richie's face relax, and then I watched him walk away with my father. I took the keys and opened the trunk, but of course there were no sandwiches, no bathing suit. I started shaking, I felt dizzy, and when I couldn't hear the men's footsteps anymore I just sat down in the dirt."

"Waited for the inevitable. A gunshot or a scream."

"But it never came. There was nothing. And I was so relieved because I realized that my father and uncle were just going to rough Richie up a little—and that would be all right. I mean, he deserved it, didn't he?"

"I don't know how long I was sitting there, but then I saw them come back out of the woods—my father and Uncle Vinch. When I saw that my uncle had a shovel, I started screaming."

"I wanted to get up and run but I couldn't move, and then my uncle was there and he grabbed me. '*Calmati ragazza,*' he said. '*É finito.*'"

"And then my father told me to get in the car."

"I sat up front with him and I wouldn't look at his hands, because I was afraid they'd be dirty now, like Richie's."

"We didn't talk the whole way home, and at one point my father put on the radio. I can remember hearing Frankie Laine."

"Mostly I kept hearing my uncle's words. *É finito.*"

"But it wasn't finished."

"I didn't know that then, of course. I didn't know that I was pregnant yet."

"Angie? Can you hear me?"

Honey squeezed the woman's hand, then caressed it. What did it matter that, as children, they'd despised each other? They were the last of a certain kind, of a certain world.

And maybe that was good.

"I think there was something cold in both of us."

Honey was crying now, a silent undoing like the melting of ice. There was no redemption, though; no hope. From the corner of the room, death unfurled his fingers, waiting for the women to join him.

"Where are we going?" Honey asked her old friend. "Where are we going?"

Part Two

Honey can recall another life. Just two years ago, in Los Angeles, she was sitting with her friend Suzanne at a slightly wobbly table at the back of their favorite restaurant. A small glittering room with antique mirrors, where exquisite things were served on tiny flowered plates, mismatched sets of Dresden china. This particular day, Honey and Suzanne had ordered at least ten dishes, and the spread before them resembled a tea party set out for dolls. Only women seemed to dine here, middle-aged film and television executives, and Honey often wondered if there wasn't something Freudian going on— all these successful strivers, with their guillotine haircuts and Maoist uniforms, eating precious delectables off princess plates. Honey once mentioned her Freudian assessment to Suzanne, suggesting that perhaps these powerful gals wished to return to the nursery—and Suzanne, in her delightful way, had said, "Fuck Freud." And she was absolutely right—because, really, what did it matter? These were women who'd made it, they could do as they pleased—and besides, the food at the restaurant was excellent, and the wine list eccentric and utterly charming. Who ever heard of a Macabeu, tasting of salted butter and figs? This time they'd ordered a Côtes du Roussillon, which was the earth and all its minerals transformed to silk.

"I've always loved the taste of dirt," Honey said.

Suzanne replied with a smile, though it was merely dutiful; the grief showed through. Honey felt it, too.

It'd been only a few months since their mutual friend Lara died, terribly, of breast cancer that had metastasized to her brain. In the hospital, near the end, Lara could not find her words and had begun to hum her communications. Often Honey and Suzanne had no idea what the woman was getting at, but still they would hum back to her. It had calmed Lara. And what were friends for, if not to sing along as you lay dying?

For many years, it had been the three of them at this restaurant. Honey knew both women from her job at Fitzroy's, another auction house, where she'd been employed for over twenty-five years, before retiring at seventy-two. Fitzroy's had not wanted to let her go. Clients adored her—among them Lara and Suzanne, who'd relied on Honey for information about things that might interest them.

Lara had collected nineteenth-century landscapes: modest pastorals of slender trees and dusty lanes; grassy fields with far-off flecks of sheep. She was particularly fond of Corot, his late, more brushy work, much of it rushed-looking, as if he'd known the end was coming—the leaves a blur and the tree trunks nearly transparent. Perhaps these landscapes represented a longing for the simple life Lara hadn't chosen. Up until her illness struck, she'd been CEO of an insatiable entertainment conglomerate. It was a merciless job, and paintings, as Honey knew, could be a tonic—a resting place, a moment of beauty held longer than was possible in real life.

Suzanne, on the other hand, had no interest in paintings. Her tastes were more eclectic, and surprisingly fussy, considering her no-nonsense personality. Suzanne collected antique vanity cases, with intricate metalwork or elaborate encrustations of gemstones. She also went wild for Art Nouveau hatpins, Lalique or Cartier if she could get them. These acquisitions puzzled Honey, since Suzanne wore little makeup and never hats. The fabulous items were reduced to specimens, which Suzanne displayed in a chilly glass case lit as if for surgery—the hatpins in a neat row like tiny ceremonial weapons.

Since Lara's passing, Suzanne had not been the same. Her Fuck-Freud bravado was gone, replaced by a pensive melancholy. By her own admission, she was depressed. At the restaurant, that day, she seemed particularly lost. She put down her doll cup of espresso and sighed.

"I don't know, Honey—I really don't."

"What don't you know?"

"I'm just so tired."

The woman was only in her fifties—far too young to be tired.

"Hard day at work?"

Suzanne rolled her eyes. "Ryan Reynolds' ass—I mean, what's the point?"

"I can see a bit of a point, dear—and I think millions of women would agree with me."

"Not if you had to look at it all day."

Suzanne, an unearthly beauty, was a former body double who'd become one of the most sought-after cinematic sexographers, basically a choreographer for sex scenes. It was apparently quite difficult to make these scenes work—not only to make them look real but to do so without exposing the giblets.

"I mean, what am I doing with my life?"

"You've already done it, darling. Do I need to remind you how successful you are?"

Suzanne had recently been called upon to help with a Diane Keaton film, in which there were several intimate scenes with Nick Nolte. *A nightmare*, Suzanne had said—but one for which she'd been paid a ridiculous sum of money.

Honey was ready to make a joke about geriatric porn, but Suzanne was suddenly crying.

"Sweetheart—what is it?"

Suzanne shook her head for a worrisome thirty seconds before responding. "This isn't just about Lara. But ever since she died, I just feel like I don't want to fight it anymore."

"Fight what?"

"I pretend. I pretend I'm this person that I'm not. And I fight so hard to make people think I'm brilliant."

"You are brilliant."

"I don't feel that way. I feel empty. And lonely. Which is a stupid thing to say."

"Why is it stupid?"

"Well—let's see—I've dated, like, fifteen men in the past two years."

Honey took her friend's hand. "I hate to tell you this, but men are rarely the cure to loneliness."

"It's not even that. And I know I have you, and I'm grateful. I am.

It's just this *thing* inside me, this . . ." Suzanne clutched at her chest, as if the problem lay there.

Honey felt the riot in her own heart.

"Everything just feels fake," Suzanne said. "It all feels so fake."

She turned and looked out the window of the restaurant. In the courtyard, a jacaranda tree was in bloom, throwing off a purple glow that infiltrated the room and tinged the white tablecloths.

That tree had seemed a brilliant example of the real, of redemption, renewal, and Honey was about to offer some such blandishment to soothe Suzanne.

But Suzanne spoke first—breathlessly, no longer in tears, a flash of what seemed like ecstasy in her eyes.

"Have you ever thought of killing yourself?"

"No. Never," Honey had replied. "And I want you to promise me to banish that thought from your mind."

Later, after Suzanne was dead, Honey often wondered why she hadn't been honest with her friend. *Yes, of course*, she should have said. *I've thought about suicide on and off since I was fifteen. It has been a constant companion.*

*   *   *

Freedom? Oblivion? Strands of light? Honey wasn't certain what she believed anymore about the afterlife. Yet here she was, far from Los Angeles but close to her fate, parked before a quaint-looking building with ornamental shutters and a hand-painted sign. *The Gun Shoppe.* Only in New Jersey would they make such a place look like a candy store.

Honey pulled down the visor mirror and reapplied her lipstick, wondering if they'd want to see a permit. Probably not; she was only buying bullets.

When she entered the shop, an electronic bell chirped like a sickly bird, and an old man—that is, a man of around her age—looked up from behind a glass counter infested with fingerprints.

"Can I help you, doll?"

This sexist greeting did not offend Honey; it actually made her feel more at ease. There was no malice in the man's endearment—and besides, she'd always known how to deal with men like this, old-timers who would never be reborn. If you played their game, they were easy to manipulate.

She approached him with a smile. "Yes, I'm looking for—now what did my son say?" She pretend-rummaged in her orange croc handbag. "Goodness, I seem to have lost the paper." She lifted her eyes winsomely. "Do you have something called nine-millimeter ammunition?"

"What kind of gun?"

"A Glock, I think."

"Your son's?"

"Yes. He wrote down the brand he wanted, as well, but as I said, I lose things."

"Tell me about it. I've lost three wives."

Honey dove in. "Have you? Well, I'm a widow too—though only once." Dominic had been, in many ways, like a husband. And while it was true that her heart still grieved, this heart was well concealed by her attire. In a late nineties Helmut Lang, Honey was a supernova in electric pink.

"So, as for the bullets . . . ," she continued.

"Well, if you want my advice . . ."

"I do, indeed."

"Then I suggest the Winchester PDX Defenders—a little more expensive but definitely worth it. You could also go with the Fiocchi Extrema."

The man pulled down two boxes.

"Oh, I like this one," Honey said, pointing to the Italian ammo in its tasteful blue-and-white package.

"Fiocchi is a good company. The wops know their bullets."

Honey smiled—again, taking no offense.

Besides, *wop* wasn't really so terrible. From *guappo*—in Neapolitan dialect *wah-po*. A flashy, handsome man. Honey had grown up hearing her father use the word affectionately with some of his henchmen.

"Twenty-five or a hundred?" the proprietor asked. "We carry two sizes."

"Oh, I'm sure twenty-five bullets will be sufficient."

"And I'll give you a discount."

"What for?"

"Just because I feel like it," the man replied with a youthful grimace. As he rang Honey up and took her cash, he gave her a lingering appraisal. "I have to tell you, it's nice to see a lady doing herself up before leaving the house. You don't even see that on Sundays anymore."

"At our age, it's important. I see you've made an effort, too." The man was wearing an ancient-looking corduroy blazer, reeking of mothballs.

"I try," he said. "Mind if I ask your name, hon?"

"Not at all. It's Gina."

"Nice to meet you, Gina. I'm Fred."

They shook hands, after which Fred bagged her ammo in a plastic sack adorned with the store's logo: two guns snout to snout, as if kissing.

Fred seemed to have a similar idea. "Listen, I hope you won't think me too forward, but"—he leaned over the counter conspiratorially—"I got a whole bar in the back, if you want to partake of something."

"Oh, I don't drink," Honey said.

"How could a woman in a dress like that not drink?"

"It's my blood sugar. Wreaks havoc."

Fred, unfazed, said he could make her a cup of tea as well. "I got one of those stingers. I can heat up your water in thirty seconds."

"Aren't you delightful?" Honey said. "But my water is just fine."

As Fred laughed, she could smell his high-proof breath. His gaze was steady, though, and his rangy body remained in its hopeful position, leaning slightly toward her across the counter.

"Keep that receipt, now—you hear? It's got my number on it."

To see longing in an old man was lovely—and though Honey had no interest in the gnarled, gin-soaked thing before her, she patted his hand before leaving, to let him know he was worth something.

* * *

On the ride home, with the bullets in her handbag, Honey had the unnerving feeling she was keeping a secret from herself. Not the bullets, or what she would do with them, but some greater mystery about the construction of the self—how she'd become the woman that she was. It was a humiliating predicament, not to know oneself at eighty-two. Honey sighed, causing the Lexus to swerve. Another car blared its horn.

Honey waved at the driver, begging forgiveness as she drew herself back into the appropriate lane. Waving and smiling—a performance, really. Because what was she if not a woman who was always acting, a woman too aware of every gesture, too aware of the sound of her own voice? Perhaps time had stiffened things to grotesquery—stiffened a personality that was already too rigidly constructed. So many years of manners, decorum, personal style, even her particular brand of thorny love—these things were diversions, veneers, that had no doubt alienated her from deeper truths, truths she'd once been so keen to penetrate. Now she toyed with truth, was flirtatious with it, even when it came to matters of life and death.

She'd spent a lifetime blaming others—Angela Carini, her father, her brother. And while these people were by no means innocent, neither was Honey. She was the one who'd broken Florence Fini's heart. Worse than that, she'd played a role in Richie Verona's death. And there were other things, too, should she only dare to look. Look at herself, as she really was. Scratch the precious surface to expose the cheap metal underneath.

It all seems so fake. Yes, indeed. Suzanne had been exactly right. Honey often felt like she was living in a dollhouse.

But when had it started, this sense of unreality? She'd felt it as a child—even before Richie Verona. Perhaps the first tilt came at eleven, when she'd seen her father strangle a man.

The car swerved again, matching Honey's mind. It was a good thing she had the bullets. She'd resolve things soon.

As she pulled into her driveway, she could see the lovebirds next door, sitting on their stoop. Honey reached for the garage clicker, deciding to park inside to avoid them. She refused even to wave. She was done with waving, done with performing.

Done with life.

She turned off the ignition, and when she pressed the clicker again to close the garage, a feeling of peace came down as well.

But not two seconds later, in the rearview mirror, she saw a flash, someone in a white T-shirt ducking under the descending door.

17 The Opening

Honey stepped from the car—a foolish move, no doubt, but she was keen to take control.

"Who's there?" she demanded.

"I didn't mean to scare you," the stranger said, flicking on the light. "I just wanted to chat for a second."

Honey's heart was jabberwocking, but she kept her voice steady.

"Is this how you usually start conversations, by sneaking into old women's garages?"

"Come on, you're not that old."

In this instance, flirtation—Honey's favorite currency—would get the man nowhere.

"Who the hell are you?" she said, knowing exactly who he was.

"I'm Jocelyn's friend," he replied. "I don't think we've met."

"This is beyond ridiculous. Please get out of here." Fear turned to anger. She marched over to the wall and pressed a button to reopen the sliding door. It rose slowly, groaning like a constipated bear. But, mercifully, the sun streamed through.

The man, unfortunately, stayed where he was. "I just wanted to apologize. You know, for that misunderstanding with Joss."

"I don't know what you're talking about."

"Well, it seems she thought I had something I wasn't supposed to—but she was confused. Good kid, but not quite all there, if you know what I mean."

The man was backlit, standing in the open doorway, the sun much brighter than the tiny electric bulb. Honey couldn't quite make out his face.

"If I could just get the backpack," he said. "That is, if you know where it is."

Honey did know; it was in the trash bin right beside her, along with the emptied-out Taster's Choice container.

"I have no idea where your backpack is," she said. "Joss hid it in my yard, so you'll have to ask her."

"Yeah, I already did—and we both looked and it's not there."

As he moved closer, Honey flinched. "I'm quite a good screamer."

The man held up his arms, as if to prove his innocence. "You've got me all wrong. I just wanted to talk."

As Honey's eyes adjusted, she could see that he was smiling. Surprisingly, he had excellent teeth.

"I'm Lee," he said, extending one of his hands.

Did he expect her to shake it? She rebuffed his aggressive cordialness and asked him once again to please leave. "Now."

His green eyes flashed, staring at her as if it were a contest—who would look away first. Men's gazes were always so revealing; they never failed to tell you one of two things—either that you meant something, or that you meant nothing at all. Despite this one's smile, Honey could read his assessment of her: that she was weak, expendable. He held his astonishing virility over her like a weapon. She could almost smell the arrogance. What this man was up to with Jocelyn, Honey couldn't imagine. A taste of metal filled her mouth, and her tongue grew sharp.

"So what was in the backpack? Your schoolbooks?"

The man laughed, the tattoos on his neck flaring. He was older than Joss, and undeniably handsome. Nothing was more irritating than when bad people had good faces.

"Well, if you happen to find the pack," he said, "please let me know."

Honey nodded coolly.

"Again, I'm sorry to bother you. I really didn't mean to scare you."

He seemed genuinely apologetic, and Honey wondered if she'd misjudged him. But then, instead of backing away, he moved toward her again.

"You don't think someone could have stolen it, do you?"

"How would I know?" Honey eyed a shovel hanging on the wall.

"Because I noticed a guy at your place this morning. He looked pretty whacked out."

"No one has been at my house today, I assure you."

"Yeah, he came by while you were out. Young guy, long hair, driving a BMW?"

Clearly, he was referring to her grandnephew.

Honey was trapped against the wall. She was about to reach for the shovel when her phone began to chirp. Immediately the man froze, and Honey took full advantage of his hesitation. "Out," she said, as if to a dog. "Out!"

Miraculously, he obeyed, and as he stepped outside Honey pressed the button to shut the garage. The phone was still ringing, and when she looked at the screen she saw the name Nathan Flores. It took her several seconds to realize it was the painter.

Oh God. She had no desire to talk to him; she'd forgotten to go to his exhibition. But, as she could still glimpse the intruder's feet standing in the driveway, fear got the better of her.

"Hello?" she said, fleeing into the house.

"Are you okay?" the painter asked. "You sound out of breath."

She sat on the couch, certain she was going to pass out. When the boy asked again if she was all right, Honey found she had no access to deceit, to subterfuge.

"I just can't take it anymore," she said.

"Take what?"

"I'm *so* tired." Suzanne's words in her mouth. "And I'm sorry I missed your opening, dear. It's been a rather trying week."

"You didn't miss it. It's this weekend. I just thought I'd call to remind you." His voice was so gentle, so different from that of the man in the garage.

"It was kind of you to call," she said, placing the bullets on the coffee table—"but unfortunately I won't be able to make it to the gallery this weekend."

"Well, the show is up for almost a month, so maybe at some point you can stop by."

In another life, Honey thought, yes, I might.

"I'll try," she said. "No promises."

"You sound different," the boy said.

"Do I?"

"Not that I know you that well—but, yeah."

She had absolutely nothing to say to him, yet she also had no desire to hang up. The silence between them was a kind of oxygen.

"Do you know I own a Redon?" she finally said. "Also a Morandi."

When the boy didn't respond right away, Honey realized that he probably had no idea who these artists were. But then he said, "I wrote my thesis on Redon."

Silence again.

And then: "Ilaria?"

"Yes?"

"Please come to my opening."

18 Brooding

She'd bought the gun years ago, after her brother was killed. An awful time for the Fazzingas. Greed, revenge, rivalry—the family losing ground to other tribes, other thugs. There'd been an attempt on her father's life, as well. Throughout all of this, Honey was still living in New York, though she rarely saw her parents. Her mother, for the occasional lunch at Dante's—though even that had come to an end, her mother claiming it was now too dangerous. Honey hadn't asked for specifics about the nature of this danger. *From whom? To whom?* Their final lunch had occurred several months after Enzo's murder, Honey feeling sick for the entire meal—not from the food but from holding back her tears. It had been a surprisingly sober afternoon, despite the bottle of wine. Her mother had left the restaurant without kissing her, paying the bill with a brusque formality that had felt like a severance agreement.

Honey knew that her parents didn't trust her. The word on the street was that a *cugine* from one of the New York families had killed her brother, but there were others who claimed it was Richie Verona's father. More than a decade after the boy's disappearance, his parents had somehow learned the truth.

And though Honey had never betrayed her family's secrets, never spoken of her father's crimes, it was clear he believed her capable of such a thing. Because if she was not with them, then she was against them. He'd said as much, over the years. He'd said much worse. *Puttana*—whore. And once, when drunk, *pompinara* (Honey refuses to translate). This was when she was still dating the "old Jew," as her mother called him—and, what was worse, the old Jew was married. She recalls telling her father that she loved Mr. Hal, after which her father had slapped her so hard she'd lost her breath. Such astonishing meanness, but it was the cruelty of a broken heart, of a man who'd lost his only son.

For a while, she'd tried to have some sympathy for the Great Pietro.

But when she bought the gun, it was not only for fear of the rivalrous thugs; she was afraid of her father, too. There were times she was sure she'd seen him lurking outside her apartment in the city.

She was in her early thirties then, and the depressions that had plagued her youth were replaced by a reeling anxiety that often spiraled into panic. After her brother's death, it was completely unmanageable. She'd seen Dr. Kleinerman, sometimes three or four times a week. She couldn't eat, she couldn't sleep. At every corner of her mind there was Enzo, though she never knew which version she might encounter. Would she find the boy who for years had protected her, taught her where to hide when their father was in a rage? Or would she find the man with a shovel in his hand, or a gun, the Great Pietro's servant? Together, her father and brother had done terrible things. When Enzo was murdered, Honey, despite her depthless grief, knew that her family deserved to be punished. There was so much she wanted to confess, so much she wanted to share with Dr. Kleinerman.

But when she thinks of those sessions now, she can only recall her dishonesty, how she manufactured a story similar to her own but not quite the genuine article. Full disclosure simply wasn't possible.

Kleinerman had given her medication, and the two of them had talked and talked in circles—the talking supposedly the cure, but for Honey the best part about the words were how they provided a distraction from the shadowy terror of her feelings. When Dr. Kleinerman ventured too close to the heart of the matter—her father or Richie Verona—Honey would bring up a dream, as a way of changing the subject.

And besides, Dr. Kleinerman loved her dreams, many of which she invented specifically for him. This wasn't straight-out deceit. In fabricating her nighttime myths, there was a creative impulse at work. In those sessions with Dr. K, she was not only trying to cure herself but to reinvent her life. And making up a story about one's life that was survivable, surely *that* was the cure.

Honey had long understood that she was different from the people who'd made her; but, somehow, with Enzo gone, she felt bound to them more than ever, her brother's death a dark moon dragging her blood home. This feeling frightened her. What, in the weakness of grief, might she be pulled back into? Sometimes she thought of begging for her father's forgiveness—a confusing thought, since she'd done nothing wrong. Shouldn't her father beg for *her* forgiveness? Honey's upbringing was a hall of mirrors that played tricks with her mind. Sometimes it seemed that she owed her father a child. He'd never learned about the one she'd had at sixteen. Richie Verona's son.

On the fainting couch, Honey often talked about why it was necessary she abandon her family completely. Of course, she didn't speak of the violence, but focused instead on the pettiness, the greed, her parents' racism or vulgarity. She didn't speak of her father's weapons but of his toxic old-world ways, the machismo, the misogyny. She framed everything as a noble battle against hypocrisy. Sometimes Dr. Kleinerman would practically roll his eyes, suggesting she stick to the facts, rather than dress things up with poetry. Still, Honey couldn't stop herself. From the top of her high horse, she condemned her family, hoping to move closer to her goal—which was to remake her very soul.

She can recall lying on the fraying recamier and espousing such romantic notions, the imperatives of art and beauty, borrowing many ideas from BP, the woman she worked for at the auction house. These ideas had become, for Honey, essential truths.

But now, as she sat at the kitchen table and cleaned the old gun, she wondered if she'd spent her entire life deluded. What did any of the beautiful things mean if she'd ended up here, sticking a brush inside the barrel of a Glock and moving it in and out pornographically?

*　*　*

For nearly an hour she wandered about the house and said goodbye to her treasures. In the bedroom, before the Redon, she studied the feathered creature in the painting, rendered wildly in gold and vermilion and slushy streaks of lapis—a riot of excess, compared to the modest Morandi in the kitchen.

All paintings exist in the present, and Honey is there now too—no past, no future. Deathless, almost—the bomb ceasing to tick as she gazes at the masterwork.

Redon's creature is splendid, with wings and taloned feet and curving ram-like horns. But the legs are those of a man, and the sex, too, hanging in the shadows between the stalwart thighs. He stands, slightly stooped, on an ochre cliff, and his eyes are fierce, flecked with highlights of unearthly green. Another creature flies in the sky far above him, a tawny thing, little more than a blur—though one can make out the breasts. This other creature, despite its anonymity, is clearly a woman.

Beasts in love. Honey has always seen it like this. An impossible love, since the female seems to be flying straight into the sun, a kind of self-immolation. Look closely and you can see the small tongues of flame already rising from the woman's head. *The Angel's Dilemma*, Redon has titled the piece.

Somehow it's not unbearably sad. There's a sweet horror to the painting, as well a touch of whimsy. Flowers sprout everywhere, even in the sky—childlike revelations, crudely painted, less like real flowers than like a pattern on some rustic quilt. The *emblems* of flowers, flashing with hidden meaning, as if the mind of God were bleeding through.

Honey returns to the creature on the cliff and stares at him for so long he eventually catches her gaze.

"Yes," she says, meaning, *Yes, I will miss you.*

* * *

With fingers nimble as a girl's, Honey loaded the gun. She did it gently, since this gun was a virgin. It seemed almost a spiritual triumph that the weapon had spent its entire life denying what its creators had intended for it. In many ways, the same was true for Honey, and she felt a flush of sorority with the little thing.

From the Ferragamo box, she took a copy of her will and left it on the bedside table. A flicker of embarrassment to be another lonely spinster leaving her money to charities. The list was long, and though Honey couldn't remember all the beneficiaries, she feared she'd made some less than sensible choices. The Institute of Noetic Sciences, for instance, whose mission was the advancement of human consciousness. Had she left them too much? Maybe she should have put more toward the Women's Legal Fund or breast cancer. At this point, any residual funds were earmarked for LACMA.

A small amount, a pittance really, was going to Corrado. Perhaps the meager gift was crueler than leaving him nothing; it had always been a dilemma. But the truth was, she didn't really know her nephew. Or perhaps the issue was she *did* know him, and her bequest was a kind of judgment. It was impossible to look at the man without seeing the phantoms of her father, her brother.

Anyway, Corrado didn't need her money; he had plenty. And what would he do with a Morandi or a Redon, not to mention the porcelain vases, the jewelry? His wife didn't wear such things. He'd only sell it all and buy a Ferrari, a yacht, a beach house in Lavallette. Besides, Honey's money was not from her father, not from the family. Some of it she'd earned herself; most of it was what remained of her inheritance from Hal. It wasn't Fazzinga money.

Despite these rationalizations, Honey's Italian heart was not without shame. *Family, fidelity, duty*—the old echo, the old pact. It pinched, it pushed, a bully.

Well, at least she'd made a gesture toward the Fazzingas. Though the fifty grand was less than one percent of her net worth—this included the paintings—it certainly wasn't nothing.

Honey had arranged her will in Los Angeles, before returning to New Jersey and reuniting with her nephew. But what was this reunion, really? His son's goons had stolen her car, after which Corrado had stooped to return it, as if he were doing her a favor. This wasn't kindness, it was a show of power. The man had the same strut as her father, the same insidious charm, his love indistinguishable from threat. The way he spoke to her, touched her arm, as if she could be coaxed into submission, his friendly manner doing little to hide what his eyes loudly proclaimed: that Honey didn't know her place. Even at her age, it seemed, she was not allowed authority.

No different from her father, stroking her cheek, writing his name there—or her mother telling her stories about girls who got their mouths sewn shut with black thread.

A skittering fury moved through Honey's gut, and its force surprised her. She'd thought the old pest exterminated—eradicated by all those years of therapy, chanting, meditation. But here, at last, it was as if the secret stuffing were coming out, all the black and dirty bits even the best of spiritual ambitions had failed to cleanse.

Honey glared at the small white gun. It suddenly seemed ridiculous, pathetic. The same could be said of her, sitting there in a satin robe with ostrich fluff at the cuffs. The late-afternoon light coming through the slatted blinds threw bars across her swollen feet, wedged in plumed slippers that matched her robe.

Is this really how she wanted to go, like a mad perspiring bird? Anger—not only against herself but against others—jangled her resolve. The right moment, it seemed, had passed. Honey put the gun in a drawer to wait.

Besides, it wasn't quite dark enough—and, to be honest, she was feeling slightly peckish.

* * *

In the kitchen now, with her hand in a box of crackers, she understood that there was still a lot to think about. A lot to *work out*, as people said—though Honey hated this expression. Life was not algebra, not algorithm; it was more like composing a symphony, and the coda was important: a final flourish that didn't merely sum things up, as in math, but that brought the soul to the surface, illuminating how everything was connected—how the prelude and the sonata, the adagio and the allegro, were a single story. Even if it was a tale of blood and war, the coda brought resolution, or at least symmetry. Honey had devoted her whole life to the subtle art of aesthetics, and it would be a sin not to reach for harmony at the end.

Simply put: to die with anger or remorse wasn't stylish. Not to mention that such feelings would make for a rocky transition into the afterlife, rather like a boat disembarking in a storm. Besides, it didn't have to be today, the deed; she just wanted to be gone before her birthday in July. She dug up another handful of crackers, poured some wine. Slow sips, deep breaths. But she couldn't find the calm. Her thoughts went everywhere, bursting from her hot core like fireworks. The fear again that her mind was slipping. She could hear Dr. Kleinerman's impatient voice.

What do you really want?

* * *

Searching for her Valium in one of the kitchen drawers, she discovered the bunched-up tea towel. Inside of it were the pieces of the porcelain vase her grandnephew had broken. Honey studied the shards. On one of the larger fragments she could see a complete vignette: a snake curling around a forked branch laden with fruit. She found another piece that fit this one, and the branch grew longer. Such a depressing puzzle.

In her mind she pictured her grandnephew, the vandal, with his long hair and dark eyes ringed as if with kohl. She'd assumed he was unwell, but now it seemed more than that. What had his mother said on the telephone? That his brother had attacked him? And she'd confirmed Honey's suspicion that the boy was on drugs.

Honey wondered why she hadn't had more sympathy. The fact was, she'd been under the influence of one drug or another for nearly her entire adult life. Prescribed by doctors, for the most part, but in her twenties and thirties there'd been cocaine, weed, psychedelics.

Part of her reached out toward Michael, to apologize. When he'd come to the house, she'd been flippant and hadn't really listened. She'd been more concerned about getting ready for her date with Dominic. The selfishness of a contented soul. And then he'd broken the vase and she'd thought, *Good riddance*, not caring if she saw him ever again.

But now she wanted to talk to the boy. Because the more she thought about him, the more what persisted was not his rudeness nor his filthy boots but rather his scent, an acrid undertow of smoke and curdled milk. It was the scent of fear. Honey knew it well.

It seemed she'd missed an opportunity. Maybe she could have helped the boy in some way. Maybe she still could. A good deed before her final exit. And apparently he was looking for her, too. Hadn't that ghastly man in the garage said he'd seen Michael come to the house, just yesterday?

Honey was about to phone the boy's parents when she saw the moon appear in the kitchen window, a grimacing orb far too close. Honey squinted and reached for her glasses.

Jesus Christ! It was Jocelyn, her big round face filling the glass.

"Go away," shouted Honey.

But the girl only clasped her hands in mock prayer, begging.

"I'm phoning the police." Honey picked up her cell and showed it to Jocelyn. "I'm dialing."

But Jocelyn called her bluff. "Don't be so dramatic. Just open the window for two seconds."

Honey's fury returned. To be accosted by such lowly people was intolerable. The other one breaking into her garage, and now this one knocking on a window. Plus, the girl was standing in a flowerbed, no doubt crushing the gerberas.

Honey marched from the kitchen, stormed through the living room, and turned on the porch light. When she walked outside, she was fuming. "I could have you arrested for trespassing."

Jocelyn stared at her, dumbstruck. "Why are you being so mean?"

"Are you joking? Please get off my property."

When the girl didn't move, Honey screamed, "You are standing in my gerberas!"

"I didn't hurt them." Jocelyn lumbered away from the flowers. "Look, they're fine." She bent down to straighten some dented blooms. In her squatting position, she was more fully illuminated by the porch light. Her bruises, though nearly healed, were still visible. Honey leaned against the bannister, suddenly short of breath.

The girl was speaking again, but her words arrived in blips of gibberish. A peculiar spinning descended upon Honey. She clutched the railing tighter. Her legs felt made of straw, and she had no choice but to sink down onto the porch steps.

"Oh my God," Joss squealed. "Are you okay?"

"I just need . . ." A word hung in the air, but Honey couldn't grasp it.

"Oh wow, you are totally the wrong color." Joss dashed into the house and several lifetimes later returned with a glass of water.

Honey took it and drank, dribbling much of it down her chin.

"Here, let me hold it for you," the girl said.

Honey sipped, grunting, mortified. She wanted to push the girl away, but the water tasted like heaven. A sensation of light filled her chest, though it made no sense how she could see inside her body.

And then it happened again, that feeling of not knowing where she was. Or even *who* she was, everything around her in deadly inversion like a photographic negative. Darkness bloomed, brightness was deviled to black. Honey closed her eyes, and when she opened them again Joss was sitting beside her on the steps, saying something about dehydration. In the sky there were tiny rips, which slowly confessed to being stars.

Eventually, as Honey's heartbeat slowed, she realized that she wasn't dying; she'd merely had one of her panic attacks. Well, *merely* didn't do it justice—these attacks felt rather like a knife to the chest while simultaneously being buried alive. She hadn't had one in years, and this comeback had been a doozy.

The girl's hand was on Honey's leg, which was confusing, because Honey could recall only that she was angry with this person. This girl who would not stop talking and whose words moved in and out of sense. Now she was babbling about a man, maybe Honey's grandnephew. No, someone else.

"Lee just feels terrible about the whole thing."

"Who's Lee?"

"My boyfriend? Are you sure you're okay?"

"I'm fine," Honey said.

"Anyway, he's really sorry for bothering you."

"*Bothering* me?" Honey harrumphed, suddenly recalling the man they were talking about. "Bothering is what a fly does, dear. Your friend did a great deal more than bother me." She was so relieved to have her mind back that she spoke without thinking. "I flushed it down the toilet, you know?"

"What's that?"

"What was in the knapsack."

"You what?"

Honey made a swishing sound while pressing an imaginary lever.

"Are you insane?" The girl stood. "That wasn't even Lee's stuff. He was just holding onto it for a friend. Oh my God, I can't believe you did that."

"So are you on drugs too?"

"What? *No*—and neither is Lee. He was just doing a favor for someone."

"Are you really that gullible?" An urge to throttle the foolish girl. "That man is clearly using you. Freeloading and—"

"You don't know him!" Jocelyn huffed and walked away—but then she turned, her face as red as Texas. "Not everyone lives a perfect life like you, okay? Other people have to struggle, and Lee's been through *a lot*. And, yeah, he's done some things wrong, but he's *paid* for that."

All Honey could think was: He's got this idiot wrapped around his finger. For a moment it almost seemed sad—but that was before Jocelyn said: "So I'd appreciate it if you weren't such a bitch about it!"

Honey was more than ready to return the insult—but then the girl began to cry, a rather elaborate display, the tears condensing into sputtering accusation. "I thought we were friends!"

Honey had whiplash. "I believe you just called me a bitch."

"Well, you are! But I really *liked* you."

As Jocelyn snuffled on, Honey turned away, glimpsing the sapling the girl had planted. The few pink blooms the tree had produced were gone, replaced by a sparse scattering of fruit. The branches looked withered, despite it being the height of spring. Honey doubted the poor thing would survive.

"I miss my old tree," she said quietly.

To which Jocelyn replied, "I'm doing the best I can." She spoke with her back to Honey, her voice frigid with contempt. "I bet it was *so* easy for you."

"What's that?"

"When you were young. Finding a boyfriend, meeting people. You were obviously gorgeous. You probably could have had any guy you wanted."

Yes, that was certainly true—but how to express it modestly? "I had some luck," Honey admitted.

"Well, it hasn't been like that for me. Some of us actually have to make compromises." The girl pawed at her face, blubbering again.

"Enough with the waterworks," Honey said—"and wipe your nose. Goodness gracious!" She reached into the pocket of her robe. "Here's a tissue."

Jocelyn took it and honked. Her hair was unbraided, foaming like a cataract, and Honey noted the failed attempt at fashion, another frumpy dress—puffy sleeves, a fusty pattern of flowers, vaguely Mennonite. Clearly this girl was not cut out for love. It wasn't her attire, though, or her abysmal posture that exposed her—but rather the impossible-to-miss signage of need plastered across her entire being. Such neediness scared men away. Either that or it attracted schemers.

Honey knew she shouldn't judge the girl—or the man, for that matter. Possibly she was overreacting to this Lee person, doing what she often did with men who had a particular kind of swagger: molding them into the image of her father.

On the stoop, Honey felt her strength returning. Still, she couldn't bring herself to get up. The girl had stopped crying, and a buzzing sound, maybe from a streetlight, had stopped as well. The silence was so complete it was almost menacing. Even the balm of the breeze had been withdrawn. Jocelyn, too, seemed to sense the change. When she sat on the steps again, head down and slouching, Honey had no choice but to take her hand.

When a short while later the pickup rolled into the driveway next door, the women were still touching. Together they watched the man get out of the truck, watched as he waved to them, bowing slightly, as if in apology. Jocelyn waved back, and the man nodded politely before heading into the house.

The women turned toward their tree and said nothing. They were part of the night now, and the night was brooding.

Honey was on the floor, flat on her back, attempting to lift her legs. She groaned, then cursed, tensed and pushed. Anyone watching might have thought she'd fallen—slipped or succumbed to illness—when in fact she was simply trying to exercise. Jesus H. Christ! When had doing leg lifts started to feel like childbirth? It was outright torture. Still, it was essential she keep going.

Yesterday, on the stoop with Jocelyn, Honey realized how weak she'd become—both physically and mentally. During her time with Dominic she'd rarely meditated and almost never exercised. Being in love had made her lazy, as love always did—the great softening.

What she needed now was to reclaim her strength; there was no longer a man to lean on. And though there was always the cane, Honey had no intention of marrying the rubber-tipped monstrosity. The ideal relationship with it would be on again/off again, using it only when absolutely necessary.

Gugghh. Up her legs went, before dropping like sacks of cement. She'd try for twenty and then do some scissors, after which, if inspired, she might flip for a plank, maybe even some push-ups. *Yes, push-ups, ye of little faith.*

Ever since her thirties, Honey had been rigorous in regard to fitness. Though she was skinny by nature, nature was fickle. She'd taken no chances, and over the years had tried a bit of everything: vibrating belts, jazzercise, Jane Fonda, Iyengar. In Los Angeles, spinning—even a little Zumba with Lara. Once, during a minor bout of chunkiness, a doctor had prescribed the most marvelous pills. They remedied the problem in several weeks, though Honey took them for years. They always improved her mood. This morning she'd found an old bottle in the medicine cabinet—expired, but, what the hell, she'd swallowed one.

Fifteen, sixteen, seventeen—only three more to go. When her fait was accompli, she rested and stared at the ceiling, whose whiteness seemed aswirl with tiny black dots; it was as if she could see the very atoms of the air. The swarming dots danced in do-si-dos, fishtailed into paisleys—the sensation rather like an acid trip, though in reality it was probably due to overexertion. Or possibly a side effect from the diet pill. Honey waited for the disturbance to pass before moving on to some crunches.

How, she wondered, have I gotten here? From suicide to sit-ups. From the existential black veil to pale pink leotards. But hasn't she always been like this—capricious, quixotic, vain to the core? And though she senses the gun in the drawer chiding her (*What about me?*), she understands that what she's doing here on the floor doesn't contradict it. As a great sage once said: One must be strong to live, stronger to die.

Old age was not for scaredy-cats. Not for weaklings. Especially if one wanted to break free of its chains, as Honey did. Besides, the end of creation should be as wondrous as the beginning—and Honey wished to go out with a bang, not a whimper.

Her blood was moving now, and with it came clarity. Sweat, refreshing as dew, beaded her forehead. Chopin tumbled from the stereo, though in her mind it was a chandelier hung from a tree, tinkling in the breeze. Every crystalline note inspired her. She pushed and pulled and felt her core growing stronger.

What luck to have found those pills! It was only ten in the morning, but she'd already been quite productive. She'd cleaned the kitchen, the bathrooms. Honey had never been the type for maids, though she could easily afford a battalion of them. Besides, cleaning was a kind of meditation; it bred humility. After working up sufficient sparkle, she'd called Corrado, saying she would accept his invitation for dinner, but on one condition: she wanted Michael to be there.

"I don't know if that'll be possible," Corrado had said.

"Why is that?"

"We don't really know where he is."

Honey had scoffed, said that a man in Corrado's position could certainly locate his own son. "Besides, it just seems that if we're going to get together, the whole *family* should be there." She'd used that word strategically.

Corrado said he'd try, and they'd made tentative plans for the following weekend.

Honey decided that, from now on, she'd make an effort to remain neutral in regard to her nephew—to simply observe him and not judge. What better way to leave the world than to get a good last look at it, make an effort to see it without the blinders of history?

Of course, that was easier said than done when it came to her family. Especially when she was about to visit her father's house, with its menagerie of ghosts. There were other bodies to confront, in addition to Richie's, and one of them lay in her childhood garden.

To go back there was frightening, but the challenge inspired her. Maybe she could rid herself of anger, of fear, in the exact place those things had been bred. *Forgiveness*—it was, by all accounts, a noble venture, though for Honey the idea had been a lifelong irritant, a grain of sand from which she'd never managed to make a pearl. As a final task, though, it seemed appealing.

* * *

The day moved forward, from pale pink leotards to a Samantha Sung flared-skirt dress—blue delphiniums pressed on a sea of red, like flower roadkill. Honey made a second pot of coffee and, despite her efforts to stay in the present, often drifted south, into the past. Possibly it was Chopin's fault; he was still chiming on the CD player, which she'd set to loop. The notes, that tinkling chandelier, were memories.

Sipping coffee, caressing the delphiniums on her lap, Honey was with child again. During her confinement, she'd often worn flower-print frocks, loose-fitting things that Florence had designed to help hide the baby. In addition to her mother, Flo was the only other person who'd known about the pregnancy. Honey had carried light but still required camouflage.

Seeing her in those smocky dresses, her father and brother had teased her. What was she hiding under there? *Il bastone ha le tette?* Does the stick have tits? No part of her, it seemed, was off limits; the men referred to her belly, her bottom, pointing and laughing. Honey swallowed it because their mockery meant success: they'd suspected nothing but a teenage girl trying to hide her chubbiness. Her mother played along, chiding Honey for eating too much cream.

In secret, though, her mother would give her whatever food she wanted, claiming that to deny a craving might harm the baby, cause a hole in a vital organ, or possibly some deformity. Honey took advantage of this superstition and requested a steady flow of Peppermint Patties.

In later months, her mother forbid her from opening windows—not only because a cold breeze might result in illness, but because the action itself, by which Honey would have to extend her arms above her head, would cause the umbilical cord to become wrapped around the baby's neck.

Honey was pretty sure this wasn't true. Still, when she was alone in her room, she often threw her arms over her head, and always with a fair amount of force. She had no affection for this baby. When she asked her mother what they were going to do when the child came out, her mother shushed her. *Non ti preoccupare.* All she admitted to Honey was that when she got too big they'd go away for a bit.

Honey hadn't pressed for more. She kept her head down, a prisoner, living under the protection of Florence's dresses and her mother's witchery. Both of them also prayed for her, for what they openly called her sin. As for Honey's fury, there was no place for it in her father's house; so she'd hidden it in her belly, beside the baby.

Chopin knew all of this. A nocturne was playing now, and Honey tried to heed the warning. *Memory is a trap.* She understood that if she went too far—to the little house in Toms River where the baby was born—then the challenge would no longer be to forgive her family but to forgive herself.

She, too, had done terrible things.

* * *

Often, it was Jocelyn who brought Honey back to the present. It was almost a comfort to run into her. Ever since their moment on the porch, holding hands after Honey's panic attack, something had changed for them—or at least for Honey. She felt a fondness for the stupid girl, as well as a responsibility.

Most of their conversations happened on the lawn, or by the mailboxes—never inside one of their houses. Strangely, during their encounters, they often ended up behind a tree, whispering like spies. This happened more often when the pickup was parked in the driveway.

"Does he not want you talking to me?" Honey finally asked one day, fed up with the Mata Hari routine.

"What? *No*," Jocelyn replied, with that big smile of hers that Honey could see right through. "He's not even mad anymore."

"Mad?"

"You know, about losing his stuff."

"Did you tell him what I did?"

"That you flushed it? God no. I just convinced him that someone probably stole the bag. And I paid him back for what he lost."

"I don't see how that's *your* responsibility."

"Well, I hid the stupid thing in your yard, so. And better he blame me than you, right?"

"Why is that?"

"Because I can handle him. Plus, it wasn't a lot of money. The stuff was just, like, bath salts."

"Do I look like an idiot? I know it was drugs."

"Yeah, that's what I'm saying. Bath salts are what they're called. It's just cheap shit. Anyway, the point is he was able to pay back his friend, so everything's good."

"Why are we whispering then?"

"We're not *whispering*," Joss whispered.

Honey raised a penciled eyebrow.

"Okay, whatever. Lee just gets a little jealous."

"Jealous of *me*?"

"Of everyone. Which I guess is a compliment, right?"

Honey disagreed—jealousy was always toxic—but she played along and nodded. *Detachment*, she reminded herself. All she needed to do was observe and listen. Be compassionate, as necessary.

When Jocelyn glanced in the direction of her house—a fairly common tic during their conversations—Honey asked what she was looking at. "Are you worried about something?"

"No, I was just thinking that maybe one night when Lee is busy you and me should hang out again. Have another bottle of wine."

Honey said she'd enjoy that.

"Maybe next week?" the girl suggested. "I can make more brownies."

Honey, recalling the dusty cowpats the girl had brought the last time, said, "My mouth is already watering."

*　*　*

On a Thursday morning, while Honey was half asleep and retrieving her newspaper, Joss plodded over for a quick hello. This was now a regular thing, since it seemed that Joss left for work around the same time Honey woke up. This particular morning, the girl was wearing another pair of her famous overalls—an obscene lemon yellow—and on her hair was a plastic headband from which two furry ears protruded. Honey had always imagined the girl working on a farm—it was easy to picture her planting potatoes or churning butter—but now she wondered if the girl was perhaps some kind of professional clown.

"What the hell do you do?" asked Honey. "For work, I mean."

"Oh, I'm a dental hygienist," Joss said.

If Honey had had a thousand guesses, dental hygienist would have been somewhere around nine hundred and ninety-nine. "Really?"

"Yeah, and I'm *super* good at it. You should let me do you sometime."

"*Do* me?" Honey laughed. "I appreciate the offer, dear, but I already have an excellent hygienist. Though she doesn't often wear cat ears."

"Aren't these great? Yeah, the kids love them. I do a lot of children." Joss glanced at her watch, which, Honey noted, also had cat ears. "Listen, I need to run or I'll be late." She leaned in and pecked Honey on the cheek.

This intimacy came as no surprise to either of them. Lately, it seemed that almost every conversation, no matter how brief or mundane, ended with a touch—nothing elaborate, often just a quick grasping of hands or a fleeting hug. But it was in these brief landings upon each other's flesh that Honey felt the real conversation took place. No words of affection were ever uttered; it was more a language of breath, or light. Honey consistently felt a flash, something so warm and alive that she made sure to keep the touches brief, for fear she might not let go of the girl.

* * *

The following day, Honey woke up feeling surprisingly clearheaded. She decided to go through some papers, including her letters. No one would care about them after she was gone. Her plan was to read a few, skim the rest, and then burn the things. That there were twelve boxes of correspondence only proved she was a creature from another era.

The first box she opened was tied with a ribbon that must have once been red but was now closer to brown. And then, in her hand, was a letter from Mr. Hal—*11 October, 1973*—sent from his office on West Thirty-Sixth Street to Honey's apartment on East Seventh. Hal often jotted notes to her at lunchtime—many of them sent, extravagantly, by messenger. Less love letters than silly scribbles, since at that point their love was beyond question. Hal was still married, of course—and on the nights he couldn't get away to be with Honey, his notes were always longer.

Dear Skinny-malink, this one began.

Honey stopped there; it was all she could bear. Hal had used this same endearment when he proposed to her. It was six months after his wife had died, and they'd gone to their favorite restaurant in the village. A summer night; they'd sat outside, under fairy lights. The mood was somber, but somehow sublime—Honey's love for Hal distilled by his recent loss into something almost too pure, too potent. The feeling was strangely like terror.

Honey put the letter back in the box. Maybe she'd try to read it later, after a couple of drinks.

Anyway, there were plenty of other things that needed doing. She strolled into the living room, planning to call her lawyer in Beverly Hills. She had decided, rather impulsively and with no regard to fairness, to leave an extra bit of money to her grandnephew Michael. But as she picked up the phone, she was distracted by what she saw out the window. Raccoons, it seemed, had gotten into her garbage. The bin was overturned and the bags ripped open, the contents smeared everywhere.

Honey put on her bathrobe and a pair of rubber gloves and went outside to clean up the mess. It was a complete disaster. The little beast—

or beasts—had gotten into every single bag. As she kneeled on the pavement, she could feel the ache in her knee.

Into a clean sack she deposited fruit pits and cucumber skins, a steak bone buzzing with flies. And since she didn't recycle—why support Corrado's business?—she also gathered up several empty wine bottles. After a moment, she sensed someone watching her. Looking up, she saw that horrible man on Jocelyn's porch, smoking a cigarette. He lifted his chin and smiled. Honey felt a tremor as the man tossed down his cigarette and crushed it with his boot. Something about this scenario—her compromised position versus his superior one—felt familiar, eternal, and terribly depressing. When the man leaned forward to pick up something from the ground, Honey couldn't tell what it was. Then he began to walk toward her.

"Are you looking for this?" he said. He held out the empty Taster's Choice container.

Honey felt no obligation to explain, or apologize. She simply extended her hand and took the plastic tub. When she tried to stand, her legs refused to cooperate.

"Something wrong, Ms. Fasinga? You seem to be having a problem down there."

Honey blinked at the sun. Somewhere a fly darted and buzzed.

The man veered closer. "If you mess with my shit again," he said—not finishing the sentence, leaving his threat vague, perhaps to make it appear larger than it actually was.

"If I mess with your shit—what?" Honey said, placing the Taster's Choice container on the ground. Some devil in her wished to say more, but the man's eyes frightened her; they seemed on fire.

"If you mess with my shit again, you *will* be sorry. And I want you to stay away from Jocelyn. Do you hear me?"

"She's a good girl, you know."

"I know what she is," the man said—smiling again. Abruptly, he turned away.

Honey watched his slow steady stride, watched him step onto the girl's porch and enter the house. When he was gone, there was only the scent of garbage. Honey picked up half an eggshell and crushed it in her fist.

T he man next door was weak—if not physically, then in spirit. Honey intuited this from the well-rehearsed swagger, the nervous twitch of his lips, not to mention the fact that he'd chosen, as his nemesis, a hundred-and-ten-pound octogenarian. Honey knew the type—not necessarily dangerous but despicable nonetheless, the kind of man who got pleasure in making women feel afraid.

Still, it might be a sign of Honey's own derangement that she didn't phone the police. But what could she tell them? Because she had, in fact, destroyed the man's property. His antagonism was not unjustified. Honey often felt the same way, when it came to her possessions. Though she was unquestionably generous, and more than happy to give someone the blouse off her back—if you tried to take it from her, well, you'd be in for a fight.

As for the police, Honey really didn't want to deal with them again. She still hadn't gone to the station to look at mug shots, to help find the car thieves. That was a whole other can of squirms, because of Corrado.

Besides, Honey preferred, whenever possible, to take care of things herself. And, in regard to Lee, it seemed that the best choice was to ignore him. No doubt he'd be moving on soon. Honey recalled the license plate—Georgia, wasn't it?—although she'd detected no accent. Anyway, the point was, he wouldn't be around for long. Everything about him said *drifter*. In his face something pitiable and lost, even sad. But what of it? Honey's compassion could only go so far.

* * *

It was Saturday afternoon, defiantly gloomy, the sun no more than rumor behind the clouds. Honey hadn't left the house in days. She was morose and petulant, waiting for the weather to turn. The only thought that gave her comfort was one that also embarrassed her—which was that she wanted to go to that young man's opening. Embarrassing because she didn't care a jot about Nathan's art; her desire to go was purely a factor of loneliness.

But the idea of putting on a nice dress, fixing her hair—it filled her with longing. Even if it was only for amateur hour at a strip-mall gallery in the suburbs. Not the swan song she might have hoped for—though why be snobby? Perhaps the painter had some skill. And even if he didn't, at least he was gay. That in itself would be a tonic, an antidote even, against the toxicity of Lee.

The only problem was how to stay awake for the silly thing. Honey had been up since four in the morning, and the opening didn't start till seven. Plus, it would be bad form to show up before eight.

No, it was quite impossible. The sunless day was already encouraging slumber. Honey picked up the breakfast things and limped toward the sink (pure dramatics; her leg was absolutely fine).

Then, while scouring egg muck from a fork, she remembered the expired bottle of diet pills. There were only two or three left, but that would be more than enough to get her out the door. Suddenly she felt inspired. The effect of thinking about the pills was nearly as good as taking them. To hell with the clouds! And if the rain came, all the better. In fact, let it be a storm. Electric lights on wet pavement, the carcasses of dead umbrellas—how Honey had adored nights like that when she was young in New York City. Nighttime had always been her element.

In fact, she'd been born at night, at 3:00 a.m., during a summer storm. A blackout, to boot—the story being she'd slipped from her mother's legs by candlelight, and when her father asked, "Figlio o figlia?" the midwife needed to stick her hand between Honey's legs to check. "Sorry, sir," the woman said. "There's nothing there."

*　*　*

Honey was suddenly aflutter, her mind racing. Though there was pleasure in this, she knew to be wary of her spurious enthusiasms. Dr. Kleinerman, too, had been skeptical of these ups and downs of Honey's, seeing them not as legitimate biorhythms but as an illness that required treatment. And while Honey understood that her symptoms were damning, she'd always felt her fickle temperament to be part and parcel of her soul.

To impede such energies seemed spiritually unwise. Honey had stopped taking mood stabilizers years ago, right around the time she'd moved to California. Her "illness," she'd always suspected, had a lot to do with geography.

In her closet, she spent an inordinate amount of time considering which dress to wear to the young man's opening. In the end it came down to two: either a Chanel ice-princess suit or a modest blue Florence. You would think there'd be no choice here—but the Florence was made of charmeuse silk, and it was the kind of blue one finds only in the nacre of certain seashells. The white Chanel would look better with her auburn wig, but, then again, maybe she'd go without a wig tonight. A radical idea, though possibly evolutionary.

Honey had been wearing wigs for nearly two years now, ever since her return to New Jersey. She told herself it was because her hair had become too thin, too fine. And though it was true that her endowment was not quite what it had been in her heyday, it really wasn't so terrible. The wigs, to be honest, were a ridiculous attempt at disguise. When Honey came back to Ferryfield, she didn't want people to recognize her. Which of course they did, even in fake hair. Still, she'd continued to wear the things. Somehow they offered a feeling of protection.

In Los Angeles she'd never considered a wig. In fact, Suzanne had often complimented Honey's hair, its enviable softness, its uniform whiteness. Virgin snow, she'd called the shade, claiming that many women paid a fortune trying to mimic Honey's natural hue. Hadn't the young painter said something, too, in praise of the color?

Honey played with it in the mirror. Straight down it looked too witchy, so she maneuvered it up and around into a tight chignon. *No*— she looked like the Ghost of Christmas Past. She loosened the knot a bit, pulled a few strands into tiny spikes, until the effect was both dignified and wild. Ikebana punk.

After doing her makeup, she dabbed geranium oil on her wrists and neck. On her ears she placed moonstone studs, dreamy little things, delicate as drops of water.

* * *

She decided to call an Uber, in case she had a drink—though maybe that wouldn't be wise, what with the diet pills. She'd taken only one so far, but the spares were in her purse. When the car was two minutes off, she waited in the hallway, telling herself she didn't wish to catch a chill. The truth was, she was hiding from Lee, whose pickup she could see from the window. As the Uber arrived, she dashed out, got in, and immediately locked the door.

"Everything is all right?" the driver asked, his accent lovely but indeterminate.

"Perfect," Honey said. She asked where he was from.

"Fez," he replied.

"Oh, Morocco. I love Morocco."

In the rearview mirror the man beamed, baring impressively white teeth. "You," he said, "are very smart woman."

"Just being honest, my friend. I ate very well in your country. What I wouldn't do for a good zaalouk."

"Oh, man." The driver shook his head. "You are saying all the right things." He put on some music—a peaceful Malhun—and Honey nodded appreciatively. A wonder to her why only strangers could be loved in this way—which was to say, completely.

This particular stranger, whose name was Dalil, drove slowly, carefully, lightly humming. Rainbows flickered across the warped tinting on the windows. Beyond them, the world sparkled deceptively, like a vision in a sorcerer's mirror. Honey realized she hadn't been out at night in a while. Everything seemed unreal. The flash of other cars, of traffic lights and neon signs—it was as if she were at the bottom of a bassinet, looking up at a spinning mobile of moons and stars.

As the car approached the area in West Mill where the gallery was, Honey grew confused. What had once been a poor neighborhood, with crumbling apartment houses and working-class shops, was utterly transformed. Honey felt quite sure that they'd come to the wrong place.

"Is this Jackson Street? In West Mill?"

"Yes, we are almost to where you want."

"So many people," Honey commented.

"Saturday night," Dalil said. "Always like this."

Couples and small groups were strolling about, laughing and buoyant, not to mention underdressed—many in shorts, some in flip-flops. It was only May, for heaven's sake. Honey had thrown a cashmere cardigan over the blue dress.

Even more surprising than people's attire was the renewal of the neighborhood. There were cafés and bars, boutiques and pastry shops. It was rather disorienting, and Honey wasn't sure she wanted to get out of the car. But, finally, encouraged by Dalil's smile, she did.

On the street she peered about, dazed by all the activity. Everyone was speaking louder than necessary. She watched two young men meet on a corner, greeting each other with the word *bra*. Honey was baffled. Luckily the gallery seemed to be right in front of her.

Peering in the window, she saw that the room was packed. She felt oddly nervous and wondered if it was the diet pill. Maybe a drink wasn't the worst idea. Across the street was a bar, but the interior was too brightly lit, a fishbowl of modular furniture in the color palette of a candy shop. Honey didn't care for these sorts of places, the kind where when you ordered a martini the bartender asked, "What flavor?"

For a while she just stood there on the sidewalk, watching the revelers glide by. Most of them seemed to be in their twenties or thirties, though there were a few middle-aged couples. Certainly no one of Honey's age.

From a nearby street cart she purchased a small bottle of water and took a second pill. "Vitamin," she said to the vendor. A few sips were all she allowed herself, since surely there'd be lines for the restrooms. At her age, one had to be careful. After a restorative sigh, she tossed the bottle into the trash and floated toward the gallery.

* * *

Inside, there were so many men with beards and mustaches that for a moment Honey felt like she'd just entered a West Village gay bar circa 1978. Of course, many of the men here had women at their sides. Honey struggled to understand the latest obsession young heterosexual men had with facial hair. And they were so ridiculously fussy about it. Some of them looked like baby Hercule Poirots. It was quite amusing, actually, and Honey suppressed a giggle.

She didn't see Nathan anywhere, and as she looked around, a freak-ishly tall woman approached. She had a sweaty face and was dressed from neck to toe in imitation leather.

"The sculptures in the middle are mine," the woman said.

"Are they?" Honey had no choice but to move toward the monstros-ities: milk-white mannequin parts—all female—on which the artist had glued a fair amount of beads, or possibly gumballs. Yes, gumballs, because the next piece Honey perused was a torso on which there were wads of grayish muck, clearly bits of chewed-up gum.

"Accumulation art," the woman said sullenly.

"Indeed," replied Honey. On another pedestal was a leg. The little red balls glued to it gave the impression of boils or some type of skin disease.

"Fascinating," Honey muttered, quite cornered.

The woman perked up. "Thanks, yeah"—she joined Honey beside the infected leg—"this is my personal favorite. I call it *Razor Burn*."

When Honey tilted her head quizzically, the sculptress smiled like the Buddha. "My artist statement is on the wall."

"I'll check it out," Honey said, moving away.

Nearby she spotted a serviceable little still life, dull but not embar-rassing; she rather hoped it was Nathan's. The gallery was stuffy, and as Honey took off the cardigan, her arm got caught in the sleeve. Just then she heard someone say, "Ilaria!" When she turned, Nathan was moving toward her.

"Here, let me help you," he said.

Her elbow, stuck awkwardly in the sweater, was flapping like a chicken wing, and it took Nathan several seconds to jimmy her appendage free.

"Well, as you can see," she said, "I've always known how to make an entrance."

Nathan smiled. "I'm glad you came."

Honey couldn't help herself: a smile rose to her lips, as well. Some-thing about the boy made her happy.

Though, really, he wasn't a boy at all. She could see that quite clearly now, under the bright unflattering lights. He was wearing glasses—he hadn't been, the day they met—and around his eyes and lips were deli-cately incised lines, merely starter wrinkles but wrinkles nonetheless. In the alley she'd assumed him to be in his late twenties, but he was more likely in his thirties.

Dutifully, he complimented her dress. Honey returned the favor without effort. Nathan was wearing an impeccable blue suit, and his hair was perfection.

"We rather match," she said, putting her sleeve close to his.

"So you're doing okay?" he asked. "How's your leg?"

"Fine," she chirped. "Good as new."

"And you got the car back, you said?"

"I did, yes."

When Nathan spoke again, there was a sudden rush of voices in the space and Honey couldn't hear him. She gestured toward her ear, and he leaned toward it: "I just said I'm glad!" And then, as he pulled away: "Is that geranium?"

"You have a good nose," she told him. "Most people can't place it."

"Well, my mother was big on essential oils."

Oh dear, thought Honey. *His mother.* And that *was* of his—the tense implying that either the woman was dead or that he was estranged from her. Honey wondered if she'd been invited here tonight as a kind of maternal substitute.

No doubt she'd be taken around to meet the painter's compatriots, introduced to the boyfriend. Surely Nathan had one. Honey had rarely seen a sweeter face—olive-skinned, dark eyes, throw-pillow lips. He looked a bit like a boy she'd dated at Bryn Mawr.

For a moment neither knew what to say. Glancing around at all the dreadful art, Honey's mind felt like a seesaw. She now considered the possibility that she'd been invited here less as a mother and more as a potential red dot. The day they'd met, perhaps the boy had sniffed out money and pegged her as an easy customer.

"Shall I meet your friends?" she said.

"Actually, I'm here by myself. Well, I know some of the other artists, but not that well."

"Yes, I bet you're all very competitive with one another. But as for me, I'm *dying* to see your paintings."

"As I said, there's only one."

She could see that the boy was nervous, intimidated perhaps by the fact that she'd mentioned owning a Morandi and a Redon.

"So which one is yours?"

"May I?" He took her arm, and as he guided her through the fray Honey caught a glimpse of something large and frightening at the back of the room. Surely not that!

But then Nathan led her toward it.

21 The Witness

Honey isn't sure what's happening. She seems to be looking through a window: a rush of color crashing across the sky, though whether sunset or storm it's impossible to tell. The clouds are red-bellied as flaming dirigibles, tilting at impossible angles.

Moving closer, she can see more of the canvas. In the foreground there's a caustic green lawn—and rising from it are two animals painted with the grandeur of mythical beasts, though they're merely dogs. Pets, no less; you can see the collars and the tags, rendered roughly with quick streaks of black and silver. The two beasts stand on their hind legs and are fighting, fighting viciously. The larger dog, a golden German shepherd, has its teeth sunk into the neck of the smaller one, a dark ruffian who's snarling in pain and fury.

The fur on both animals is more like plumage, fluttering in the wind, or perhaps rising on thermals of emotion. Gleaming black eyes strain heavenward, as in paintings of martyrdom. The smaller dog digs the claws of one paw into the German shepherd's chest; there's blood, just as there's blood at the smaller one's punctured neck. The animals' muscles are taut, rendered in precise exaggeration. It's almost impossible to look away from the battle, but if you do, you are rewarded.

In the shadows of the background, there are humans—chatting, smoking, slack leashes hanging from their fists. None of them look at the dogs. These humans are no more than phantoms, clever congregations of dots and flecks. One woman seems to be laughing at another woman's joke. The only face turned toward the dogs is that of a child, painted in primitive simplicity, to mark only what's necessary. The eyes wide-awake, the mouth open with the wonder that precedes terror. The child sees everything, and though he wants to scream the painting holds him back, in the just-before.

Are you crying?"

"No," Honey said. "Am I?"

The painter pulled a handkerchief from his pocket. "Here. It's clean."

She took the cloth and dabbed. "This is your fault, entirely." Offering a smile, to lessen the blow.

The boy smiled back—more of a grimace, actually. "It's an awful painting, I know."

"I wasn't expecting this," said Honey.

"Expecting what?"

"You're very talented."

"I don't know about that."

"Well, you are."

"Even if I were, why is that surprising?"

"Look around!" She gestured at the other artwork. "The company you keep!"

"*Shhh*," said Nathan, laughing.

They both felt the clarifying effect of honesty. Honey handed back the boy's handkerchief.

"You sure you're all right?" he asked.

"Please, let's not talk about me. I feel foolish enough. Let's talk about this"—she pointed at the canvas. "What's it called?"

"It doesn't have a name. I just marked it *Untitled*."

"That's lazy. It needs a title."

"What do you suggest?"

"Haven't the faintest." Honey regarded the animals again, the dream figures behind them. She was still overwhelmed, and not ready to speak about the horror the painting made her feel. But she could certainly discuss the formal qualities, the historical references. "What I love is the collision of styles," she said. "Like Seurat waking from his park to a nightmare. Waking to Bosch, for heaven's sake."

"I was thinking Goya, too."

"Yes. And do you know the dog paintings of Jacobz?"

"No."

"Well, you need to look at them. Much more romantic than this, but he's worth considering, if only for the brushwork. I can lend you a catalog if you'd like."

Nathan said he would, yes.

Honey took a breath, wishing to go a little deeper, to move from style to story. "And as for that little dog, you captured his pain perfectly. The twist of his neck is terrifying. Still, I don't think it's necessarily curtains for him."

"Neither do I," said Nathan.

"Somehow it seems a fair fight, despite the size difference. And there's no David and Goliath here. They're both brutes. It's simply their natures."

"Absolutely."

"But the child . . ."

"Yeah," Nathan said, softly. "That's . . ."

When he paused, Honey took the lead. "That's really the heart of the painting, isn't it?"

"Yes."

"Maybe that would be a good title," she suggested.

"What's that?"

"*The Child*, or, I don't know—*The Witness*?"

They both nodded, and silence reigned for a moment before Honey said, "It's really marvelous, Nathan."

"Thank you."

"I love how the mouth is open—the child's, I mean—and the way you can see his teeth—the same white as the fangs. They sort of communicate with each other. The child's teeth even seem a little sharp, the way you've rendered them. He's terrified, on the one hand, but he's also learning something, isn't he? It's an education. Which might be another good title."

The boy stared at her, mute, and Honey suddenly felt self-conscious.

"I'm babbling. Why don't *you* tell me something, dear?" She gestured toward the canvas. "What brought this on?"

"You make it sound like a fever."

"Well, I imagine it must be—no?"

"I guess, yeah." He peered at his own painting and looked baffled. "I'm not very good at talking about my work."

Honey noticed that his hands were trembling slightly, and she patted his arm. "It's not a test."

"I don't know," he said. "The dogs, maybe. This probably sounds weird, but I sometimes see dogs like that in my dreams."

"Well, that's to be trusted then. So how long does it take to do something like this?"

"This one was almost three months."

"Do you usually paint so large?"

"Recently, yeah. Because of my new studio, which is pretty big. The place you saw when we . . ."

"Yes. The white room I thought was heaven."

He smiled again. "You should come visit sometime. See the rest of the series."

"I'd like that," Honey replied, knowing she'd never do it. For her, the season of calendars, commitments, was over.

She studied the painting more closely, particularly the little dog, particularly the neck, where a drop of blood glistened as if it harbored some irrefutable idea. It was hard not to think of her father.

"What's the matter?" the boy said. "You look sad."

"You must ignore my face—it's a great liar. You can't trust the faces of old people. Gravity, you know."

"I like your face. And anyway, I know my paintings sometimes upset people. I often feel ashamed."

"For what?"

"For doing such heavy work. Depressing or whatever."

"I don't think it's depressing at all, because it feels true, and that always wakes one up. Besides, why be ashamed for sharing what's in your heart? You certainly don't want to stifle that."

"Yeah, but sometimes it seems that's exactly what an artist has to do to become successful. Soften things, you know. Even lie."

"Now *there's* a depressing thought."

They smiled again, and Honey felt something very similar to what she'd felt the last time she'd spoken with Nathan. Which was her ease with him. This gentle boy who painted violent things. She felt quite unable to lie to him.

"I think maybe I *have* been a little sad lately."

"I don't think it's just you," he said. "I've been feeling the same way. I think there's something in the air."

They fell silent again, gazing at the dogs.

Eventually Nathan murmured, "*The Witness.* I like that. Do you mind if I steal your title?"

"Not at all," said Honey, adding that she'd expect only a ten percent cut.

"That seems more than fair."

As they continued to banter, people around them probably thought, How nice to see a boy so chummy with his mother. Some: a boy with his grandmother.

But in their own minds, they talked as peers, as equals. As lovers of art. Honey found herself telling stories she rarely shared with anyone. The night she'd spent with Lucien Freud in a freezing loft (he'd promised to paint her but never did). She talked about the auction house she'd worked for in her twenties—about BP and the Pre-Raphaelites. She even brought up the recent shattering of the priceless vase, though she didn't mention her grandnephew.

Nathan asked about the Redon, and Honey described it for him. She talked about the Morandi, as well. She told the boy that what she loved most about painting was the way it could make peace between what seemed to be irreconcilable ideas. In the Morandi, it was a truce between beauty and sadness; in Redon, beauty and madness. "And in your piece," she said, "between beauty and violence. Which is the trickiest feat of all."

Honey had missed talking like this—intimately, about aesthetics. But when Nathan asked, "So what about you? What have you been up to since I last saw you?" Honey paused. What could she say? *Oh, I've been sitting in my closet, dear. I've been shopping for ammunition.*

"Just some gardening," she replied, before turning the conversation back to art. When she looked again at the painting, she realized that not only did she love it, she coveted it. A collector's greed was something she hadn't felt in a while. It was an invigorating sensation—though, in this instance, ridiculous. She could never fit the canvas in her house; the thing was nearly eight feet high and at least ten wide. And to buy anything at all, when she was still debating where her current possessions should go, was simply impractical.

Still, it was infuriating to see so many red dots on other paintings in the gallery—God-awful hack-jobs—while there was no apparent interest in Nathan's triumph.

"What are you asking for the piece?"

"Oh, I'm not sure. I think six thousand."

"Is that including the gallery's percentage?"

"Yes."

Honey scoffed. "That's a terrible price."

"Too much?'

"Too cheap!"

"Well, that's what the gallery suggested."

"They're idiots," declared Honey. "You shouldn't even be showing here. You should be in New York, in London. Los Angeles, certainly. I still have colleagues in all these places." She explained that, for her, working at auction houses had never been merely a job—it had been a passion. "People often say they live for art—but for me it would be more accurate to say, I lived *because* of it. Sometimes I even think I might have died without it."

Oh, for Christ's sake, she thought, *shut up.* The boy was strangely quiet, and Honey suspected she was overdoing it. Showing off. Holding court, as she used to do at parties. She blamed the pills. Her heart was absolutely galloping. Spotting some chairs against the wall, she asked if they might sit down.

"Sure. Why don't I get us some water?" Nathan said. "It's pretty warm in here, huh?"

Honey took a seat as the painter ran off. The gallery was less crowded, but those that remained seemed more animated than before. Great gusts of laughter blew through the room, and nearly everyone had a little plastic cup of wine in their hand. Where, Honey wondered, was this mysterious elixir hidden? She'd seen no trays going around, no waiters, no bar. She reached up to check that her wig was straight, only to remember she'd gone commando.

She sat for a while—a long while, it seemed—and finally she understood that Nathan wasn't coming back. Clearly she'd frightened him away with all her blather.

What the hell was she even doing here?

Honey's melancholy sharpened, bright as a knife. The room hardened around her, and she found herself staring at her lap, at the miraculous sheen of the blue fabric. Everything blurred, became water.

Years ago, she'd worn this dress on a ship with Mr. Hal. It was not long after her brother had died. Hal said she needed to get away, and that she shouldn't be alone. Though Honey couldn't remember where they'd gone, she could still remember the ship. In the center of it a huge spiral staircase. How strange that had seemed, a velvet nautilus in the middle of the sea. She'd climbed it every night, on her way to dinner, attempting to rise above her grief. And every morning Hal had given her flowers—a mystery where he'd gotten them, thousands of miles from shore. Hal had been so kind, though Honey felt she didn't deserve it. Sometimes she argued with him, for no reason, acting like a child, hoping he'd disown her, the way her parents had. But Hal never took the bait. He remained steady, affectionate, loyal—and, even worse, perceptive. "You won't get over this," he said about her brother—"but, for what it's worth, I'm here. I'm here for you, baby."

Slowly Honey's mind drifted back to the gallery. She saw Nathan chatting with a muscle-bound man with short hair and serious eyebrows. Then they embraced, and the man whispered something in Nathan's ear. Honey could see the painter blushing as the weightlifter strolled away.

Go with him, you fool, thought Honey—who, being a fool herself, imagined all whispers to be whispers of love.

It was clearly time to go. Honey reached for her purse, and when she stood Nathan was there, apologizing—in his hand, two cups of wine. He handed her one.

"Oh, thank you, dear—but I really should get home."

"Come on—one drink won't hurt you."

They toasted wanly, a wordless clunk of plastic.

The wine was dreck. Honey refrained from comment, though Nathan said, "*Ucch.* This stuff is terrible." And then: "Should we get a drink somewhere else?"

"Please, you don't need to feel responsible for me anymore. You did your good deed."

"What do you mean?"

"Just that you're too sweet. The old woman is fine—and apparently you have an admirer over there."

"Who?"

"That man with the muscles."

"*Steven?* No. That was just one of the other artists. He flirts with everyone. Besides, I'd rather talk to you."

"Why?" asked Honey, genuinely baffled.

"I just, I don't know. I like you." The boy blushed again, and Honey felt her own face reddening. The situation began to feel uncomfortable.

"How old are you, dear?"

"Thirty-five."

"All right—and I'm eighty-two."

"You can't be."

"I am. I'll be eighty-three in two months."

"Well, you don't look it. I assumed you were in your sixties."

"Even so!"

"Why are you upset?"

"I'm not. I'm just confused."

"About what? I thought we were having a good time."

"Yes, we were. But I'm sorry, I really do need to go."

"Wait." The boy touched her arm, peering at her in a way that made Honey wonder if she'd pegged him incorrectly.

"Why did you invite me here?" she asked.

"Because I wanted to spend more time with you."

"That's very sweet, but—"

"And also," he said, though quietly now, "I'm attracted to you."

"That's absurd!" cried Honey. She pulled away. "What are you playing at?"

"I'm not playing at anything. I just . . ."

He flushed again, and what she saw in his eyes horrified her. She saw innocence, desire.

Honey, on the other hand, felt something like shame. She looked down at the little gold watch on her wrist. It was after midnight—which made no sense. Had she been talking to the boy this long? Time, somehow, had disappeared.

But the spell was broken now. Honey was old again—her wigless head a pumpkin, her blue dress dissolving to dust. As she tottered away, the room began to spin. The door appeared to be in several places at once, and Honey moved toward the most likely reality. The boy came behind her, too close. "Nathan," she said. "Don't."

She looked helplessly at the swaying crowd, their fabulous hair. There seemed to be music coming from the ceiling, the sound raining down like liquid metal. A twisting pain pierced her chest.

"Ilaria," he said. "Are you all right?"

Suddenly she was in a forest of mannequin parts, quite unable to breathe. The room tilted past recovery, and as she started to fall there was no one to catch her but the boy she was trying to flee.

23 Abnormal Tendencies

The tests came back completely normal. No evidence of a heart attack, a stroke, dementia of any sort. Dr. Blewis—ridiculous name!—said it wasn't uncommon for someone her age to have moments of confusion or dizziness. Honey waited for him to use the phrase "senior moment," because if he did, she was going to strike him.

"I completely passed out," she said. "They had to take me away in an ambulance."

"Have you been under a lot of stress lately?"

"A bit, I suppose."

"Related to . . . ?"

Honey didn't want to get into all of it: family nonsense, problems with the neighbors, sexual advances from minors. "Just the normal stress of living," she said.

"And medications, let's see"—Blewis looked at her chart. "You're on something for your blood pressure, and I see we prescribed some Valium a while back."

"Yes, but I hadn't taken any that day."

"Just the blood pressure meds?"

"Well, to be honest . . ."

When she mentioned the diet pills, he asked, "What kind?" and when she told him, he threw up his hands. "Ms. Fasinga, those pills were taken off the market years ago. They're *much* too strong. How many did you take?"

"Just one," she lied.

"Well, I want you to throw the rest of them out. *I* certainly didn't prescribe them."

"No, they were from my previous physician. I got them when I lived in Los Angeles."

"Well, you're not in Los Angeles anymore."

"I realize that, dear. What's your point?"

He didn't have one.

"I never had a problem with diet pills in the past," she said, shrugging.

"Why would you even need them? You're very trim."

Honey refrained from saying she thought of them more like vitamins. But she did ask if he'd be kind enough to renew her Valium prescription.

"I'd prefer not to," said Blewis.

"Very funny, Bartleby."

Unfortunately, the reference only baffled the man. "You do know my first name is Leonard, right?"

"Yes, of course. But as for the Valium, I find them quite helpful."

"Just one more refill," Blewis grumbled—"until you get over your stress. But use them sensibly. Why mess with your luck? You're in excellent health."

In Honey's opinion, this wasn't the greatest news. She pressed for something more depressing. "I still don't understand what's going on. It isn't just the passing out. I grant you I was agitated, but I find my mind wandering more than ever. Sometimes I forget where I am. Or even *who* I am."

Blewis didn't look fazed. "As I said, that's normal at your age. The mind tends to drift."

"Well, my mind drifts abnormally. Ruthlessly, in fact."

Honey wondered why she even cared, this close to the end. Didn't she want to be free of this pageant of tomfoolery called life? So why not just let herself drift right off the cliff? The only issue was, she didn't want to forget to shoot herself. *Ha*, it was almost funny.

Honey sighed. "Sometimes I feel I understand less and less as I grow older. My life seems to be this vast landscape broken to bits, completely indecipherable."

"Yes," Blewis muttered, in a tone suggesting that he was growing weary of this conversation. "Aging can be difficult. And really, it sounds more like a psychological issue."

"Of course it's psychological," said Honey. "I'm gathering you're not very holistic in your approach to medicine."

"My job is your body. The pump and the pipes, as we like to say."

Goodness, he sounded like a plumber. Honey missed Dr. Kalani in Los Angeles, whose office smelled like sage and who was much less Calvinist in regard to medication.

"Maybe you'd benefit from speaking to a counselor," Blewis said.

"Excuse me?"

"We have a woman we work with from the senior center. A few of our older patients have found her quite helpful."

Honey said she wasn't interested.

"Let me ask you something, Ms. Fasinga. Do you have a *community*?"

Oh God, Honey despised that term, the banner family types liked to wave in the faces of wanderers.

"I have some friends, yes," she said, hearing the embarrassing crack of defensiveness in her voice. Because who *did* she have? The screwball girl next door, and a young man she thought was a homosexual, but who was actually a—well, she didn't know *what* he was. A pervert?

"And you have family you're in touch with?"

"I do. We're not exceptionally close, but I'm planning to have dinner with my nephew and his children this weekend."

"That's good. And who is this Dominic Sparra we have listed as your emergency contact?"

"Oh, just a friend—but you might want to cross him off. Might be a bit difficult to get in touch."

"Has he moved?"

"In a way, yes. He's dead."

"Oh, I'm sorry."

"Thank you."

"So who should we put down as a replacement? Someone from your family, perhaps?"

"No, just leave it blank."

"We really should have someone on file."

"Please, just leave it—I'll be fine."

"Ms. Fasinga—"

"What do you want me to say? The truth is, I don't really have anyone to replace it with—at least not anyone I'm completely comfortable with."

"Okay. Well, let's just put your nephew down for now."

"No," Honey said. "Just put, oh God, just put my neighbor there. Jocelyn."

The doctor scribbled. "And her last name?"

"I have no idea."

"This is one of your friends?"

"Yes. Here's her number." Honey retrieved it from her phone.

The doctor was looking at her oddly, and she said, "What? Do you know all the last names of all of *your* friends?"

"I do, actually." And then: "Are you angry about something, Ms. Fasinga?"

Somehow the question calmed her. "Oh, Dr. Blewis." She smiled. "I am. I'm absolutely furious."

* * *

Later that day, and the following, there were several incoming calls from Nathan, as well as a few from Jocelyn. Honey didn't answer, nor did she respond to the texts, also from both of them. But when the name Teresa Lioni appeared on her landline, Honey intuited the reason and immediately picked up.

"She's gone, isn't she?"

"Yes," said Teresa. "I didn't think anyone else would call you, and I didn't want you to read it in the paper."

Teresa sounded businesslike. No doubt she was phoning everyone in her book, sharing the loss widely so as to claim it as her own. "The viewing is this weekend," she said. "And the funeral's on Tuesday, at St. Margaret's."

"Donations or flowers?"

"Angela wanted flowers."

"Good for her. And how are you doing, Teresa?"

"I just can't believe it, you know."

Honey said, yes, she knew what it was like to lose one's best friend. "No repair there."

"But at least I know I'll see her again," the woman declared—in reference to the afterlife party Honey knew she wasn't invited to.

"It's funny," she said to Teresa—"I was thinking recently about a Halloween bash from when we were teenagers. Angela came as a devil of some sort, and she'd made the most marvelous tail from a piece of wire covered with velvet. It was quite sproingy, and all the boys kept touching it. I was very jealous."

Teresa said she remembered the costume. "And didn't you come to the same party dressed as Rosie the Riveter? Jumpsuit, red polka-dot kerchief around your head."

"Exactly. And I recall Angela asking me who was I supposed to be, Aunt Jemima?"

Both women laughed, then self-corrected.

"God, we were awful," said Honey.

"Some of us," said Teresa. "And I'm surprised to hear you remember those days. We all assumed that after you left, you didn't ever give us a thought."

"I didn't, actually," Honey said. "But I never forgot you, either."

For a moment they lingered on the line, not quite enemies, not quite friends, but certainly the last of their kind—and in this regard they were of a feather.

"Light a candle for Angie," said Teresa.

And Honey said, "Of course."

* * *

Ever since her return to New Jersey, it seemed that everyone was croaking—Florence, Dominic, now Angela—while Honey herself was apparently invincible. *Why mess with your luck? You're in excellent health.* The doctor's diagnosis felt more like a curse.

Honey drifted into the bedroom. When she took out the gun, it acted sullen; it wouldn't even speak to her. She put it back in the drawer and ate some chocolate—four squares, bitter, no chaser.

From room to room she wandered, a game of hide-and-seek with ghosts. Florence had died first, just a month or so after Honey moved back to Ferryfield. She'd had every intention of visiting her old friend, but she kept putting it off, and then it was too late. When she'd finally seen Florence, it had been at the woman's wake. Honey had apologized to the lifeless body in the casket, apologized for sleeping with her husband. She'd thanked the corpse, too—for the dresses, for the dream that had never come to be, the clothing shop they'd planned to open.

She'd met Flo's grandson at the wake—an eight-year-old cutie-pie she'd immediately fallen in love with. No doubt she'd frightened the child, going on and on about his grandmother. Not long after their encounter, the boy was abducted. It had seemed like a dream—the child's pale face on posters around town. Though Honey barely knew him, she'd prayed every day.

During the nearly nine months that the boy was gone, Honey often thought of her own child. He'd been abducted too, in a way. Taken from her by forces she barely understood. Such terrible memories. The blood-stained blanket, the hole somewhere in the woods, a hole she'd filled in herself. No marker, no gravestone. The same fate as his father.

Well, at least the Fini boy had been found. *Edgar*, that was his name. She really should visit him, tell him more about his grandmother's dresses.

* * *

The cell phone was squawking again. Goodness gracious, the noises it made! It sounded like a sick chicken—cheeps and chirps—and of course Honey could never remember which meant a text and which an email. She ignored the thing and sipped daintily, pinkie out. She was halfway through a bottle, absolutely shit-faced, when the cell began to ring. Glancing at the screen, she saw the name of her new emergency contact. Honey didn't answer, and a few seconds later a text arrived from Joss.

> If you don't call back soon, I'm going to break down your door. Just kidding. I miss you!

At the end of the message there was a minuscule image of what appeared to be an ice-cream cone, or possibly a slice of pizza. What was it with all the hieroglyphics lately?

Now that the phone was in her hand, Honey saw the ridiculous number of missed calls and texts—mostly from Jocelyn, but a few from Nathan, as well as from Corrado. She was drunk enough to listen to the voice mails.

When she heard Nathan's gentle voice, he sounded to her like a sixteen-year-old. Maybe it was this softness that had made her think he was gay. In his message he said he was sorry if he'd offended her. *But I just think you're fantastic. There aren't a lot of people I feel comfortable talking with. Especially about art.*

And then Honey found herself wincing as he repeated the dreadful words: *I'm not going to lie about being attracted to you, but we can skip all that and just—*

Honey stopped listening at this point, feeling again the anger she'd felt at the gallery. Normally she wasn't so judgmental in regard to a person's sexual fancies; in fact, she prided herself on being open-minded. But, in this case, the only apt word seemed to be the one that kept ringing in her head. *Pervert.*

Strangely, she'd never thought this in L.A. whenever a younger man had flirted with her. But those other men had *gigolo* written all over them, and Nathan seemed the furthest thing from that. What was even more curious was the fact that, in the past, Honey had always been able to gracefully dismiss passes from men she had no interest in. But with Nathan she was completely flummoxed. And his attraction to her hurt; it was *physically* painful.

To distract herself, she began to plumb the depths of Jocelyn's texts—a continuous stream of them, stretching back for weeks, even months. Had she known the girl this long? It was a vast catacomb of messages, stacked one upon the other like small gray bones. Honey took another slug of wine, and put on her readers.

* * *

For the most part, the texts were bland but affectionate pleasantries.

Let's have our brownies soon.
Everything A-OK over here! You???

As Honey swiped further, she discovered the links the girl had sent to various dating sites.

Just some examples, in case you want to try your luck.

Attempting to delete one of the texts, Honey accidentally clicked on a link and fell into a rabbit hole—a site called Craver. On the screen appeared a grid of faces, and above them the phrase *What do you really want?* The query was sexual in nature—and the users of the site could respond in one of three categories: Mild, Medium, and Freaky.

Honey, being Honey, clicked on Freaky, and began to read the most astonishing things. She sensed her face growing hot, reading about a man who was looking for a woman to—No, Honey's mind refused to preserve it. Disgusting, she thought. Not to mention sad—the way certain individuals found it necessary to look for love in the trash.

Still, she was curious—and as she continued to explore the site, she found herself more and more intrigued. The world, it seemed, had grown wild while she wasn't looking. Or perhaps it had just grown more honest, now that people could hide inside these caverns of technology.

When Honey perused the Mild section, it didn't seem mild at all. She was expecting to find things like *Young woman looking for a travel companion*, but found instead: *Young woman looking for full-time slave. Young woman looking for*—No, again Honey's mind shut down.

Attempting to click her way out of this hellhole, she found herself directed, as if by magic, to a gay site. Here, she wandered through ill-lit hallways hung with shadowy photos, gasping when she saw a close-up of a man's rear end. Good Lord! Was that the best he could do for a headshot? The photo was so detailed it looked like an image from laparoscopic surgery. Quite horrible.

As she made her way through the other profiles, fearful she might be mooned again, she came across several terms she didn't understand. One man described himself as a "power bottom"—which sounded, to Honey, rather like a pair of sequined slacks she'd worn in the seventies. There were twinks and unicorns, pans and fairies. She giggled at the designation "verbal top"; it made the dominator sound like a toddler who'd just learned to speak.

Oral submissives, pillow biters—an endless parade of monikers. And the descriptions of what they wanted, it was all so dreadfully specific. Everyone seemed to know exactly, but *exactly*, what they required in the bedroom. Bodies reduced to shopping lists of proclivities and preferences, everything so rigid it seemed that the point of another person was merely to assume a certain position, press a particular button.

Occasionally, someone exhibited a refreshing flexibility: *Mainly bottom but can be versatile.* (Once again, Honey imagined this sartorially: a miniskirt that might also work as a halter top.) For the most part, though, everyone had their roles down pat. Even those describing themselves as "gender fluid" were looking, it seemed, for a very definite type, a concrete channel through which to pour their fluidity. There seemed to be little room for self-discovery or imagination. Which was what sex was all about, was it not?

Another text from Joss read, This one might be good for you! The site was called StillKickin, and featured older people with bizarrely blurry faces. *Seventy but feel thirty*, one of the users proclaimed. Which no doubt meant *Eighty and deluded*.

After closing the various pages, Honey found herself back at the original website—the grid of headshots. As she swiped through them one last time, she studied the faces: some of them stiffly smiling, as if for school photos; others cool and detached, fugitives on a passport. Honey swiped faster, then paused when she saw a shadowy image of a round-faced girl who looked familiar. The girl listed her name as HotSauce, and she seemed to have some sort of medal on her chest that was catching the light—but as Honey squinted she realized it wasn't a medal but a buckle on a pair of overalls.

Dear God, it was Jocelyn!

Honey clicked to read the profile. It wasn't very long, but it pierced her like a knife.

Twenty-six, full-figured, open to pretty much anything. You tell me!
Long term would be nice. Stronger men preferred.

Honey put down the phone, feeling sick. She was very drunk.

Suddenly it seemed imperative to talk to the girl, straighten out that silly head of hers. A strong man was fine—Honey had liked them that way, too—but brutality, *no*; it was never acceptable.

The more she thought about it, though—about Joss and Lee, the drugs, the bruises—the more she understood that the only choice was to stay out of it. Every woman was free to invent her own apocalypse.

Honey closed her eyes and wept.

Honey was halfway out the door when she realized she'd forgotten something. She went back to the bedroom and found the vial of geranium oil. Moistening two fingers, she deftly punctuated herself: commas on the wrists, periods behind the ears. Only a little was necessary. The oil's purpose was not to allure. No, today she was using it as a witch might—for protection. Honey hadn't been to her father's house in nearly fifty years.

As she pulled out of the garage, it was just after one o'clock. Corrado had told her to come at two, but she wanted to stop at the cemetery first, say hello to Dominic. It was Sunday, and she drove slowly down peacefully deserted streets. Spotting a market, she decided to buy some flowers. When she stepped from the car, though, a homeless woman blocked her path and began to coo like a pigeon. "I just love that dress of yours. Where can I get one?"

"You can't," said Honey.

"And why is that?" the woman asked, in an offended tone. "You think I can't afford it? Because I'll have you know I don't really look like this"—she gestured at her weather-eaten face. "I'm in disguise."

"Aren't we all, dear?" said Honey. "But I only meant that you can't get a dress like this because it's one of a kind, and the designer is *dead*."

The woman seemed to think this was a riot; she slapped her filthy thigh and cackled phlegmatically. "Good for her!" And then, not missing a beat: "Got any cash?"

Honey handed the perceptive loon five dollars and returned to the car, forgoing the flowers.

* * *

Distractedly, she made her way into the poorer part of Ferryfield. Maybe, instead of going to the cemetery, she might stop by Florence Fini's old house, show the little boy another example of his grandmother's handiwork. The dress Honey was wearing, a simple but elegant shift, was a Florence.

She parked across the street but didn't immediately get out of the car. Though she'd met Flo's family at the wake and had visited them occasionally after that, she wondered how they'd feel about an unannounced visit on a Sunday—a precious day for the working class.

Honey stared at the small white house: 21 Cressida Drive. The address had once seemed magical, lucky—though it'd turned out to be quite the opposite. The Fini family had been cursed with more than its fair share of tragedy. When Florence's son died on that bridge . . .

No, the story was too long, too terrible. And, more important, it was not Honey's to tell. Someone else would have to write that book. Suffice it to say: other people suffered, too.

Honey waited, spying from behind a tinted window. Eventually the family came outside and sat on the porch. The first thing Honey noticed was how happy they seemed. Edgar, the albino boy, was smiling, as was his mother, Lucy, who was drinking a beer. When the boy took his mother's hand, Honey understood how easily love comes, and how easily it is ripped apart.

It seemed she might speak with Edgar about what it had been like when he was abducted. To Honey it was almost as if the boy had been to the underworld and back. What had he seen there? Strands of light, or only darkness? Had he felt the presence of his grandmother?

Honey was ready to get out of the car and make her way to the porch.

But then she thought, What am I doing? I have no right to be here. The boy and his mother were laughing now. Why disrupt their Sunday idyll to reminisce about the dead? Besides, these lovely people were not her family.

Honey pressed the gas and sailed away, unnoticed.

* * *

Soon she was at her father's house, now the domain of Corrado and his wife. Honey still couldn't remember the woman's name—Rita? Rina?

Sitting in the car, Honey gazed out the window at the handsome prison where she'd spent her early life. The bones of the estate were pretty much the same, a sprawling three-story villa with a facade of beige blocks chiseled to look like stones. On the second level there were two good-sized balconies, and at the very top several arched windows with borders of stained glass.

Honey noted the addition of burglar bars on the ground floor—ornate wrought-iron curlicues. A pity, really; from the inside, the bars would spoil the view. The property was huge, with a park-like yard. Some of the old trees had grown so large they delivered an electric shock to Honey's sense of time.

The driveway was new, significantly widened, with black tiles that sparkled as if embedded with diamonds. The path curved dramatically and was flanked by elaborate landscaping, featuring topiary hedges and enormous concrete urns—a Las Vegas version of Versailles. Honey drove up and parked behind a Hummer. Five minutes later she was still sitting there, debating whether to turn and drive away.

But then she sighed, scolding her fear. It was just a house, for heaven's sake. She checked her face in the mirror, adjusted her hair. After pinching her cheeks for color, she picked up the pricey bottle of Barolo and opened the Lexus door.

25 All Good Men Have Hairy Chests

As she crossed the diamond driveway, the click of her heels was accompanied by the dull thud of the cane. Though Honey's leg was feeling just dandy, she'd brought the cane for more esoteric reasons. The scratched-up wreck of cherrywood, with its horrible rubber tip, had belonged to her mother. Honey had taken it from the hospital room at the very end, knowing she would inherit nothing else. Her brother Enzo was already dead, by then; her father too. Everything from her mother's sizable estate had been left to Enzo's son—who was now opening the front door, saying, "Aunt Honey!" Kissing her on both cheeks, asking if she needed help.

"I'm fine, dear. Here, this is for you." She handed Corrado the bottle of Barolo.

"Wow—this looks great."

He stared at the label a bit too long, and Honey navigated the awkward silence with a theatrical sniff. "Smells wonderful in here," she said.

"Yeah, Rina's making manicotti."

Rina. Honey drilled the name into her head, so as not to forget.

"Can I take your, uh, thing?" Corrado asked. "Your scarf or . . ."

"No, the wrap is part of my ensemble."

"Oh."

"Plus, it'll keep me warm. I get cold easily."

When her nephew offered to turn down the AC, Honey said she was all right, at the moment. Not quite true. The house was only slightly warmer than a meat locker.

"If you want," Corrado said, "we can eat in the backyard."

"No," Honey replied, too quickly. "Inside is fine."

"Good. Because, to be honest, Rina's made a big fuss with the table. Come on, she's in the kitchen."

Corrado led her down the hallway—a wide passage that, after all these years, remained jarringly familiar, exerting an intimacy that felt almost inappropriate. The colors of the walls were different, the furnishings, but the architecture hadn't changed, nor the way the light came through the windows—and it was these more subtle forces that surrounded Honey, owned her.

As they moved toward the kitchen, Rina appeared in the hall and embraced Honey with damp arms, her apron smelling faintly of garlic. Honey wasn't offended; in fact she found the scent endearing. When was the last time she'd had a home-cooked meal? At her own house, she'd done little more than nibble lately. Here, it smelled like heaven—though perhaps too much so, because it made her think of Dante's. Of Dominic. She willfully brightened, squeezing Rina's hand.

"I hear you're making manicotti. My favorite."

"And I'm using your mother's recipe."

"Yes," Honey said, "I thought I detected nutmeg."

"I've also got meatballs and braciole, broccoli rabe—and Corrado made cheesecake."

"You cook?" she said to him.

He shrugged. "I try."

The three of them stood there stranded, smiling.

"Where are your sons?" asked Honey.

"Peter's in the living room," Corrado said. "Why don't we—"

"Yeah, you guys relax," Rina said. "I'll join you in a bit."

Corrado gave the bottle of Barolo to his wife and then placed his hand on Honey's arm, escorting her toward the living room, as if she might not know the way.

Peter, the older grandnephew, was lounging on the couch, watching a television the size of a billboard, his white-socked feet resting on a coffee table. When he saw Honey, he raised his head and offered a silent wave.

"Get up," barked Corrado. "Say hello to your aunt."

The boy rose—handsome, unshaven, more robust than his drug-addled brother.

"Nice to see you again," Peter said, shaking Honey's hand.

"Likewise. Is your wife joining us?" Honey recalled meeting her at Dominic's wake.

"Yeah, she's around somewhere. In the bathroom, I think."

"Can I get you a drink?" Corrado asked

"Yeah, I'll take another beer," Peter said.

"Not you, you idiot. I was talking to your aunt."

Honey smiled. "I wouldn't mind a beer."

"You don't want some of the wine you brought?"

"No, save that for dinner. I'll just have whatever Peter's drinking."

Corrado nodded and headed back toward the kitchen.

As Honey stood beside her grandnephew, she could see the effort he was making not to look at the television. There was a baseball game going; no doubt he had a bet on it.

"I don't mind if you watch, dear."

"Thanks." He returned to the couch. "You can—" He pointed at a large padded chair that looked like a throne. Honey rested the cane beside it and sat.

"Is your brother here?"

"No."

"But he is coming?"

"She invited him."

"She?"

"My mother."

Tension in the boy's voice. Honey recalled Rina saying on the telephone that the brothers had gotten into a fight. She thought it best to change the subject.

"Would you remind me of your wife's name? I seem to have forgotten."

"Addison. We call her Addie. She's not Italian"—this last bit delivered sotto voce.

"Well," Honey said, "we'll forgive her."

Peter smiled tightly, as if unsure if she was joking.

"I dated a Jew once," Honey continued, "and it didn't sit well with my parents."

The boy looked confused, not to mention alarmed. "Addie's not Jewish."

"No, I wasn't implying . . ." Again, she changed the subject. "So how much do you have on the game?"

"A lot," he said, turning back to the television. "And it looks like I'm getting screwed."

*   *   *

A little while later, they were all seated at the dinner table—well, all of them except Michael, who was late. Honey was eager to see the boy again. Perhaps, at some point, they'd have a chance to speak privately. If he wanted to discuss his problems, she'd attempt to be more sympathetic, maybe even tell him about her own struggles—not only with drugs but with the family. She was glad to see that they'd set a place for him right beside her.

But what an elaborate fuss they'd made! The napkins were done up like opera fans, and there was a huge centerpiece of silk flowers—eternal peonies in a funereal-looking urn. The tablecloth, disturbingly, was black.

Corrado opened the wine, saying, "We might as well get started on the antipasto."

Rina suggested waiting a few more minutes, but when Corrado shot her a look, she said, "Fine, I'll bring it out."

Peter's wife jumped up. "Let me help." She followed Rina, leaving Honey alone with the men.

"This is great stuff," Corrado said, sipping the Barolo.

"I'm glad you like it. The Piedmont reds are my favorite. This one always reminds me of clay mixed with roses."

Corrado nodded vaguely, while his son gulped the stuff like it was grape juice. Honey realized she should have thought like a Fazzinga and brought several bottles.

When the women returned, they were loaded down with platters—a ridiculously excessive antipasto. Cheese and olives. Roasted peppers swimming in a lake of oil and garlic. There was prosciutto and mortadella, a big tray of stuffed artichokes.

"Goodness," said Honey. "What a feast."

"Well," Rina said, "we wanted it to be special." She took her seat, saying quietly to Corrado, "I left him a message." And then loudly to every-one else: "Eat, eat."

They all dug in. Even Honey spooned up more than was her custom, wanting to be a good guest. The peppers were done just the way she liked them, perfectly charred, the thin slivers of garlic completely raw. It was the kind of thing you could eat only in the company of friends, of peo-ple you trusted. Honey took the raw garlic to be a gesture of goodwill; at least it would have meant such a thing, in her parents' day.

Still, there was a distinct feeling of unease at the table: the weight of history, of time, of all the things left unspoken for so long they were now impossible to put into words.

But this unease was handily covered by murmurs of appreciation for the food—grunts and yums standing in for real conversation. Rina smiled nervously at Honey, and though Honey didn't fully understand the woman's agitation, she returned the fraught smile with a reassuring one of her own. Polite questions ensued: asking after Honey's health, her leg, a brief mention of the stolen car, after which Honey said to her grandnephew Peter, "I hear it's you I have to thank for its return."

She hadn't meant to shame him, but he seemed to take it that way. He grimaced and looked down, miserably shoving a pink flap of pro-sciutto into his mouth.

Addie, the young wife, turned to Honey and said, "Peter told me you haven't been to the house in a while, but that you grew up here."

"Yes," Honey said. She wanted to say more, something clever or sweet, pick one good apple of reminiscence from the wizened tree—but nothing came to mind. She looked down at the platters: her moth-er's *maiolica*. On the border of one was a pattern of vines and lemons; on another, tiny split pomegranates with scrolls that unraveled into birds. "Those platters," she said, "are from the Deruta factory, one of the oldest producers of *maiolica* in Italy. And, in my opinion, one of the best."

No one responded to this, so Honey continued to babble. "I actually visited the factory once and saw the artists at work. When they apply the glazes, they're so unerring and quick it's more like they're *thinking* the colors rather than *painting* them."

Silence again. Honey sipped her Barolo.

"Yeah," Addie finally said, "the colors are really pretty."

"Really bright," added Rina.

"Well, you know," Honey said, quite unable to shut up—"to get that luster, the pieces are fired several times, a technique that started in Arabia, probably Baghdad, then brought to Italy by the Moors. Though perhaps that's a derogatory term, these days, I don't know. The Moorish Spaniards, maybe that's the more ethnically sensitive way to put it."

Peter looked at her oddly, and then turned to his father as if to say: *Why have you let this lunatic into our house?*

Why, indeed, thought Honey. Why *was* she here? Not only did she have no idea what these people wanted from her; she had no idea what she wanted for herself. She felt confused, embarrassed, and more than a little tipsy. The overblown art lesson was clearly an attempt to obfuscate what was really in her heart, something not unlike terror. In the very next room, Honey had watched a man die.

"Forgive me," she said. "It seems that I'm full of useless information."

"No," Rina said, "it's fascinating. I didn't know the history of the plates. Did you, Corrado?"

"I didn't," he replied. "But I know my grandmother loved them." These words were directed at Honey, though she couldn't detect if they contained a barb. When saying "my grandmother," he was of course referring to Honey's mother—perhaps feeling it fair to claim ownership of the woman, since everyone knew that Honey had abandoned her.

"We really do treasure them," said Rina, and it took Honey a moment to realize they were still discussing the *maiolica*.

Corrado repeated the sentiment, adding that the past was something one shouldn't forget.

Honey, chastened, pushed aside a piece of garlic on her plate. Perhaps she was not among people she could trust.

But then the tension, or Honey's imagining of it, dissipated. Conversation softened again into unchallenging mundanities—recipes, the weather. The wine was a panacea.

Corrado's mood lightened, and he mentioned how, when he was young, "My aunt here"—he gestured toward Honey—"used to send me all these funny little gifts." Again, he brought up the little gold slippers she'd sent him, with beads and tiny mirrors sewn into the fabric.

"Sounds like something Michael would like," Peter said with a sneer.

"Leave your brother out of this," said Rina—and then, to Honey: "He'll be here soon."

Corrado ignored this mention of his other son. "Where were those slippers from again?" he asked.

"Morocco," Honey told him. "I went there with a friend." And then, turning to Peter: "I think I mentioned the Jewish fellow to you earlier."

Peter nodded warily, and Honey wondered if she were goading him on purpose. He really was a sullen creature. When Honey was young, such behavior would never have been tolerated at the dinner table. The boy was practically brooding, as well as eating like a *gavone*. Even worse, he was wearing some kind of jogging suit, completely inappropriate attire for dinner, not to mention a sign of disrespect. And though Honey thought of him as a boy, he wasn't a boy at all—he was a grown man, a *married* man, in his mid-twenties at least.

Honey attempted once more to draw him into a civilized exchange. "I see you liked the Barolo." He was finishing the dregs of it.

His response, alas, was wordless, a grunting smirk.

"I definitely enjoyed it," Corrado said, getting up to fetch more booze. He returned almost instantly, as if any delay would be fatal—in his hands two fresh bottles, a cabernet and a pinot grigio. "Probably not as good as yours," he said to Honey.

"I'm sure they'll be excellent." Honey pointed to the pinot. "Santa Margherita is always reliable."

"That's my favorite," said Rina.

Corrado poured some for his wife, and then for Honey. Switching from red to white seemed prudent, and Honey willed it to serve as metaphor: a shift from bloodshed to surrender. She had nothing to prove.

Corrado lifted his glass. "*Cent' anni*," he toasted. When Addie didn't drink, Rina asked if she was all right.

"My tummy's a little off," she said.

Honey advised the girl to try a bit of the raw garlic. "Very good for the stomach."

Conversation veered back to food—Corrado telling a story about his grandmother once putting a clove of garlic in his ear when he was ill. "I was five or six, and I started crying. I thought she was gonna cook me."

Honey laughed. "She used to do the same to me and Enzo."

But then she swallowed her amusement, thinking about her brother. When Enzo died, Corrado was still a teenager. After the loss of his father, he'd grown very close to his grandparents, whereas Honey had drifted away.

As she considered these things, it changed the shape of reality, or rather brought it into focus. Corrado's face was so like her brother's— and this offered a wild, impossible relief. For so long the only image of her brother she could recall was his face after he was killed—the shocking hole in the forehead, the shattered jaw. For some reason, Honey's father had insisted she go with him to the morgue to see the body. She understood later that he blamed her, believed she'd been unfaithful to the family, disclosed their secrets—and that somehow this had led to Enzo's death.

Did Corrado believe this too? Who knew what the Great Pietro might have told him. It occurred to Honey that the last time she'd actually been in this house was after Enzo's funeral. She hadn't stayed long. Her father had not been kind.

Perhaps she should have fought harder to keep Corrado in her life. Perhaps she might have been a good influence on him. Instead, she'd abandoned him to her father, who'd surely taught the young man well, about pride and power, fidelity and vengeance.

"Something wrong, Aunt Honey?" It was Corrado.

"No, dear. I just—to be honest, it's a little strange to be back here." Again, she wanted to say more, but there were so many things she couldn't speak of, especially with Peter's wife present.

Corrado looked as if he, too, had more to say, though he proceeded lightly. "You're always welcome here."

"I'd forgotten," Honey said, "what a pretty house it is."

Once more they fell into pleasantries. Maybe it was good Peter's wife was with them; they could all remain safely on the surface.

After a while, Rina and the girl got up, and out came the manicotti, the meats, the broccoli rabe. No one mentioned Michael, nor took his place setting away. Honey was on the verge of saying something, but as Corrado served the pasta and some of the tomato sauce spattered onto the tablecloth, it seemed a sign to avoid the subject.

Honey tasted the manicotti. It was, as she feared, superb—the nutmeg handled perfectly.

Corrado, well oiled by now, was leading the conversation. He was talking more openly about the past, and it didn't seem in any way an attack on Honey. She found herself relaxing.

As Corrado wiped up the red sauce, he mentioned that his grandfather—Honey's father—was extremely superstitious. "If anyone spilled salt, he made them throw a bit of it over their left shoulder. It *had* to be the left."

"Do you know why that is?" asked Honey. And when Corrado shook his head, she explained: "Because the left side is where the Devil enters the body—and so to throw it over that shoulder was to throw it in the Devil's face."

Addison seemed startled and made a quick sign of the cross.

"I didn't mean to scare you," Honey said. "I gather you're Catholic?"

"Of course she's Catholic," Peter said.

Honey, taking the temperature of the room, decided to avoid any further mention of the Devil. Pouring herself more pinot, she mentioned how her father, as a young man, was famous for his jokes. "There was one he told quite often." She asked her tablemates if they'd like to hear it.

"The floor is yours," said Corrado.

Honey sipped her wine, cleared her throat. "Okay—so there was this girl named Theresa, who just got married, and she was a virgin, of course. On her wedding night she stayed at her mother's house, and she was terribly nervous. When she finally went upstairs with her husband, she came back down almost immediately, saying, 'Mamma, Mamma. Silvio took off his shirt and he has a very hairy chest.' 'Don't worry, Theresa,' her mother says. 'All good men have hairy chests.' So she went back up, and her husband took off his pants—and Theresa runs downstairs again. 'Mamma, Mamma. Silvio took off his pants, and he has very hairy legs.' 'Don't worry, Theresa,' her mother says. 'All good men have hairy legs.' So up she went again, and this time her husband takes off his socks and she sees that he's missing three toes. Downstairs now it's, 'Mamma, Mamma. Silvio's got a foot and a half!' '*Really?*' says Mamma. 'Here, you stir the pasta, Theresa, and I go up. This is a job for Mamma!'"

For a moment the only reaction was silence, but then her sullen grand-nephew put down his wineglass and burst out laughing. Everyone else, as if given permission, followed suit. Even Addison—who seemed to be blushing.

A general feeling of ease descended, and Honey felt a pleasing warmth. Even the brutal air conditioning couldn't extinguish the fire. Honey smiled at the patterns on the *maiolica*—the lemons, the pomegranates, the birds.

But when she looked up again, she saw a table full of strangers. Even more disconcerting was that these strangers had the faces of people she'd once known, people she'd loved. She glanced at the empty place setting, hoping Michael would get here soon. Perhaps he was the only one she had any real business with.

Rina was speaking again.

"Excuse me?" said Honey.

"I was just saying, you haven't tried an artichoke."

"Oh, I'm really quite stuffed."

The woman was clearly disappointed, and Honey said, "They do look delicious. Maybe someone would care to split one with me?"

"I'll have the other half," said Addie. "I love splitting things."

"Yes, I can tell," Honey said. "You have the figure of a splitter." The girl was an absolute twig.

"Thanks," she replied, "but just wait a few months." She looked at Peter and whispered, "Should we tell them now?"

"Tell us what?" said Rina. "Oh my God—are you?"

When Addie looked at her husband, he gave a gesture of permission.

"Yeah," Addie said. "I'm pregnant!"

Rina jumped up to kiss the girl, while Corrado reached across the table and shook his son's hand. "Well done, Pietro."

Everyone was talking excitedly now. Rina was crying. Corrado mar-shaled the chaos with another toast: "*Sempre la famiglia.*" Honey found herself unwilling to repeat the words. She felt a confusing mix of despair and jealousy. Addie was beaming, and when Corrado asked if she knew the sex, she said, "Not yet. But we're hoping for a boy."

Nothing ever changes, thought Honey.

Rina was already talking about the christening, what hall they should rent for the party. "You'll be a great-great-aunt," she said to Honey. "You'll have to come."

"Yes," replied Honey, knowing she'd be gone by then.

Corrado asked the young couple where they were going to live. Apparently, they had a place just up the street, but everyone agreed they'd need something larger now. When Rina suggested that maybe Peter and Addie look for a house closer to downtown, Addie said that some of that neighborhood was sketchy.

"A lot of Asians," Peter said.

"That's true," agreed Rina. "How do you like where you're living, Aunt Honey? You have a house not far from the library, right?"

"Just around the corner. Yes, I like my little place—and it has a lovely garden."

Addie asked Honey if she felt that area was safe. "Do you like your neighbors?"

"For the most part, yes. Though there's a man who's just moved in with the girl next door, and I think he's rather a bully."

"Well," Peter said—chatty now, pumped up with his virility—"if he keeps bothering you, just let me know. I'll come over and talk to him."

"Very sweet of you, dear. But I think I can manage things on my own."

"Should I get the dessert?" asked Rina. "Corrado, do we have champagne?" She stood, collecting the dinner plates, and when she took away the clean one that had been meant for Michael, Honey couldn't help but think of that other missing son—her own.

Suddenly feeling unwell—too much wine, perhaps—she excused herself, asking where the powder room was. And then: "What a ridiculous question. I know exactly where it is. I was born here, for heaven's sake!"—repeating these words silently to herself as she left the room.

She has a dinner party to return to, but she's paralyzed in the hallway of her father's house. She's standing at the bottom of the stairs, where at age eleven she witnessed something terrible. Her mother, her brother, had seen it too. A secret the three of them had kept all their lives. Again, this sense that she shouldn't even think of it, as if the memory itself is a crime.

But there's no forgetting that awful night.

She'd woken from a sound inside a dream—a dream in which she'd been stamping out a fire. But then this sound bled through to the waking world; it seemed to be coming from downstairs. Honey got up to investigate.

In the corridor outside her bedroom, the windows were iced with moonlight. She moved toward the sound, and from the top of the stairs she saw two men down below, dancing. They were in an odd position, though—one man's back to the other's chest. The one facing out, facing toward her, was a stranger. Her father was embracing this man, a slim fellow frantically stamping his feet. In Honey's mind, still powdered by sleep, the scene suggested a continuation of her dream. That is, until her mother appeared, turned on a light, and began to scream.

Then Enzo was there, too—the three of them on the landing, watching as the scene condensed into reality, which was her father with his hands around the stranger's neck.

What Honey remembers most clearly is the thing that, above all, she wishes to forget—the way the man had looked at her. She knew exactly what he wanted. He wanted to live. But neither Honey nor her mother or brother did anything to help him.

How could they? They knew the Great Pietro's rages, knew the best thing was to stay away. Honey was screaming now too, but the sound exhausted itself before the man was dead. Finally he fell to the floor with a sound that was as brutal as it was trivial—a stack of newspapers tossed from a truck.

Her father, sweating, wiped his face and told Enzo to come downstairs. He spoke calmly, but when Enzo hesitated her father shouted, *Vieni qui!*

Later, from her bedroom, Honey saw the two of them in the yard, standing at the edge of the property line where the woods began. She saw the shovels and the tarp. She saw her uncle Vinch appear, as the sky turned a lovely shade of pink. Only then did she remember it was a school day, and she had a test in mathematics.

But what was she going to wear? The question disturbed her, and as she sorted though her dresses, she kept forgetting how to breathe.

* * *

"You okay? Aunt Honey?"

When she turned, her nephew was there, standing in the hallway. She could tell he was drunk; his eyes were at sea, his cheeks splotched with crimson.

"Just thinking," she told him.

"What about?"

Honey shrugged and changed the subject. "So, you're going to be a grandfather."

Corrado nodded, unabashedly proud. When he asked if she was ready to have some champagne, Honey only stared at him; she could summon no words.

But then something spoke through her, perhaps the Valium she'd taken in the bathroom.

"Do you know I saw a man die in this house?"

Corrado blinked, as if she were speaking a foreign language.

"Right there, in fact," she continued. "Right where you're standing."

For a brief moment, as her nephew gazed at her, Honey felt the old familiar fear. Fear of the man in the fairy tale, who sewed up the lips of children. Still, she managed to say the long-unspoken word. *Strangled.*

Corrado, strangely, didn't seem surprised at all. He simply glanced around the hallway as if to gauge the extent of their privacy, and then he took Honey's arm and guided her around a corner, closer to the basement door.

"What are you doing?"

"Nothing, I just . . ." He was whispering. "I think I know what you're talking about."

"How could you know?" She found herself whispering, too. "What I'm referring to happened before you were born."

Corrado nearly smiled. "My father told me the story."

"First of all," Honey said, "it's not a *story*—and why on earth would your father tell you? Surely we're not talking about the same thing."

"You're talking about the guy who broke in, right? The *intruder*?"

Honey stumbled on this word; she'd never thought of the man as a criminal. For her, the villain in the drama had always been her father. The stranger, she'd unthinkingly assigned the role of victim, of innocent.

"I'm talking about a man that was *killed*. By my father. By your grandfather."

"So am I," Corrado said, but as if he meant something very different.

Honey took a step back; her shoulders touched the wall. "And you're saying what, exactly—that this man was some kind of burglar?"

"No. I don't think he planned to steal anything."

"Then what was he doing here? You seem to know more about this than I do."

"Only what my father told me."

"And what is that?"

"He said the man came here to . . ." Corrado finished the sentence with his eyes.

Honey knew what her nephew meant, but she wanted him to say it. "Came here to what?"

"To hurt you."

"Hurt who?"

"All of you. You, my father, Grandma."

"That's ridiculous," snapped Honey.

"Why is it ridiculous?" Corrado spoke calmly, without antagonism.

His nonchalance was frightening, and Honey fell silent. What he was saying made sense. The Fazzingas had never lacked for enemies.

"Grandpa was only trying to protect you."

"That's a convenient way of looking at it."

As Honey lurched away, Corrado's face hardened; he was not a person accustomed to being dismissed. "Why are you so angry?" he said. "With all the luck you've had."

"Luck?"

"Yeah. If Grandpa hadn't stopped the man, you'd be dead. My father would have died back then, too. I wouldn't be standing here with you."

Honey could smell the alcohol, the garlic.

"That's always the game, isn't it, Corrado? We try to justify these terrible things."

"I don't see what's so terrible about taking care of one's family."

He was slurring a bit, though his voice had the confidence of a made man. The tone disgruntled Honey, and she spoke without thinking.

"Family is overrated."

For a moment her nephew looked stunned, but then he turned on her, his crimson face growing almost black. "How would you know? You've never had a family. You've never had children."

"What are you saying?"

"I'm saying you have no idea what it's like to love someone like that."

"Like what?"

"So much you'd do anything for them. You stop being selfish."

How dare you, thought Honey. As she moved away, Corrado blocked her path, and in that gesture she saw everything.

She willed herself to breathe, to look into her nephew's eyes. Because she was not entirely without sympathy. Corrado, no different from her, had been *made* by violence, schooled in it. And in Corrado's case, one always had to remember how his father had died. An execution.

The two of them were quiet now, staring at each other, ashamed—or at least that's what Honey felt. They'd said far too much. Somewhere a clock was ticking, chiding them.

At last Honey found her voice. "What's the first rule?" she said. "Do you remember?"

"First rule of what?"

"Of family. Of *our* family."

Corrado looked down and nodded, as if he understood.

Say nothing.

In the hallway, with her nephew, it was no different from standing with her brother.

So when Corrado held out his hand, she took it.

In the dining room, it was clearly the Venetian hour. In addition to cheesecake, there was a lemon tart and a large platter of cookies and pastries—pignoli, sfogliatelle, cannoli. A Carmen Miranda of fruit towered above little bowls of nuts, and two sweating champagne bottles waited to be popped. Everyone was laughing, though they stopped when they saw Honey and Corrado.

Peter was obviously drunk—even more, it seemed, than his father. "Aunt Honey!" he shouted, in a way that seemed to imply a joke. The wife nudged him, as if to say *Cut it out*.

Honey took her seat beside the empty chair. Rina was pouring espresso.

"None for me," Addie said. "I don't think caffeine's good for the baby."

Honey realized she hadn't yet offered congratulations. Maybe, as the eldest, she should make a toast, give her blessing—finish this dinner playing the role required of her. As Corrado undid the foil wrappers on the champagne, he winked at Honey, but when he released one of the corks she turned away. There was something vaguely pornographic about how he held the black napkin over the bottle's neck.

"Just a splash for me," she said, gesturing toward her glass. The antique flutes had belonged to her parents. More like goblets, really—knobby monstrosities with pompous golden lips.

When everyone had their share of bubbly, Honey lifted her glass. The others followed suit, Addie joining in with a cup of water.

"*No*," cried Rina. "Water's bad luck." She poured the girl some cola.

Honey waited, and then began: "I just wanted to say . . ."

Well, what *did* she want to say?

More important: What did *they* want to *hear*? It was all pageantry, anyway—all performance. Though, in truth, some part of her felt genuinely moved to be sitting here again at the family table. A barb of emotion snagged in her throat. Corrado was still looking at her, rather chummily. His bloated face no longer seemed grotesque, but more like a cherub's, the ruddiness almost endearing. She remembered seeing him as a baby, just a few weeks after he was born. There'd been a minor truce with her father at the time, and Honey had been invited to the christening. And though she'd been happy for her brother, she'd felt jealous, too, that he'd been allowed to keep his child. When Enzo deigned to let her hold Corrado, Honey's legs had gone weak with that peculiar elixir of joy and sadness only mothers are susceptible to.

"I'd just like to say," she continued, "that I feel grateful to have been invited here today."

Did she mean it? Was she stoned? She had no idea. "Grateful to share in this moment of good fortune," she chirped on. "I sincerely hope it continues for all of you." She turned to Addie. "And for your children, as well. *Tanti auguri!*"

Corrado and Rina repeated the words, and everyone drank. It was a good bottle of Veuve, a reserve. Honey noted the descriptors on the label—*Extra Brut, Extra Old*—thinking they'd make an excellent epitaph. As she sipped the stuff, the bubbles entered her like metaphor; they seemed, in fact, to enter everyone as such. The mood lightened, lifted, eyes less guarded, more honest. At least this was the case for Honey—who, after speaking with Corrado about the past, felt unburdened. She'd been carrying that stranger's body for such a long time, a punishing weight, like a soldier's rucksack. And having previously laid down Richie Verona's corpse at Angela Carini's bedside, Honey felt ready to move on, move upward—though she wasn't drunk enough to imagine the bubbles would take her to heaven. Though lighter, she was not without guilt, or remorse. But it was as if the quality of the blackness had changed. Still terrible, of course, but somehow, by being confessed, a little less so.

Corrado asked how she liked the champagne, and she complimented it—then told a story of an artist she'd once known in Los Angeles, named Piper Heidsieck. "And the funny thing is, she detested champagne. Only ever drank milk. Quite the eccentric. She painted these fabulous little canvases of dead birds, mostly sparrows. I know it sounds morbid, but they were very beautiful, very poignant."

No one seemed to know what to say in response to this, though they murmured politely. That is, everyone but her grandnephew, who was staring at her in a way that suggested suspicion, if not outright contempt.

Honey sipped her Veuve and returned Peter's gaze openly. She wondered if she'd given too much attention in her toast to the wife, and had failed to sufficiently note the boy's virility. She asked him if there was something the matter.

"Yeah," he said. "I was just curious why you talk like that."

"Like what, dear?"

"Like you weren't born here."

Honey smiled. It was exhausting to her that others sometimes heard her voice as *wrong*, a put-on, when she'd spent her entire life striving to become a truer expression of herself. And now, having achieved this, she was often belittled for it, especially by those from her homeland. It was curious how something as simple as losing one's accent actually *angered* these people.

Personally, she didn't think she'd lost the sound of New Jersey completely; there was still a roughness to her voice, like the base note in a good perfume. Certainly she didn't think of herself as a phony, and to prove this she spoke honestly to Peter.

"I suppose it's true that when I left New Jersey, I did everything I could to reinvent myself. Even my mother said I was arrogant. But I think, really, I was just curious."

"So that's why you talk like the Queen of England?"

"*Peter*," Rina scolded.

"No, it's fine," Honey said. "I appreciate the boy's directness." When she looked at him again, he was chugging his champagne like it was water in the Sahara.

Honey noted that Corrado hadn't stepped in to defend her, and so perhaps he too was waiting for an explanation. Rina was the only person who spoke on Honey's behalf. "Your aunt's traveled all over the world. That changes a person."

"Yeah," Peter replied. "She even changed her name."

Honey looked at the boy, uncertain how he knew this. She played innocent and asked him what he meant.

"When I got your car back," he said, "I saw the registration. Your last name—you spell it different."

Corrado suddenly perked up. "Is that true?"

"Yeah," Peter said—"she spells it with an *s* instead of two *z*'s."

Everyone, even Rina, stared at Honey as if this were nothing less than sacrilege, as if she'd not only removed the two zeds, but murdered them.

Honey decided it was best to stay in the vein of honesty. "Yes, it's true, but it has nothing to do with any of you. When I did it, *you* weren't even born yet," she said to Peter. "And the fact is, as I'm sure you're aware, no one ever seems to know how to pronounce *Fazzinga*."

"They know how to pronounce it around here," replied Peter.

Oh, for God's sake—she was too old to have to explain herself, justify her actions. But she chose not to become defensive. "I was quite young when I did it, and in hindsight I can see it might have been an overreaction. But what you have to understand," she said to her grandnephew, "is that I had certain disagreements with my father."

When the boy sneered, Honey had no choice but to up the stakes. She lifted her chin and turned it checkmate toward Corrado. "Shall I tell him more?"

"No. Water under the bridge," Corrado said. "Peter, just leave it."

The boy grumbled and reached for the second bottle of champagne. He opened it quickly, spilling foam, and after pouring liberally for himself, he put a bit into Addie's empty flute.

"I guess one sip won't hurt me," she said, looking distraught.

Everyone was slightly on edge now, and Honey decided to extend an apology to the boy. "I didn't mean to offend you, dear."

When her grandnephew's face failed to soften, Honey understood she'd made an error. In this world, the world of the Fazzingas, an adult would never apologize to a child; that was a sign of weakness. And so, in extending this kindness to Peter, Honey had made herself vulnerable.

Rina seemed to sense this too, and as if to prevent further trouble she pushed large pieces of cheesecake and lemon tart on everyone. A balm of sugar and black coffee, things no Italian could resist.

Conversation eased again into culinary compliments. The praise was genuine. Corrado's cheesecake was excellent, made with ricotta rather than gummy Philadelphia. "Lemon zest?" asked Honey.

Corrado nodded. "Orange, too."

Her mother's recipe.

This was the problem with going home: no matter how vile, you still wanted to taste it again, if only to understand what you were made of.

For a moment, as Honey ate the soft, delicious cake, she could no longer recall how it had happened, the great rift—if her family had turned against her, or she against them. A dolorous lethargy came over her. Even the champagne bubbles seemed to be slowing down, as if weary of elation. Peter, Honey noted, was still stewing, eating a cannoli like it was a piece of rebar. When he caught her staring at him, he began to chew with his mouth open, a secret message of scorn, just for her. He looked like a dog.

Animals. Isn't that how the younger brother had put it, when he'd come to Honey's house? As she watched Peter devour the pastry, she had a strange cascade of thoughts. Yes, they were brutes, these people—that couldn't be denied. And she, of course, stood above them. Her very *nature* was different. Yet as she looked at the boy, with his mouth full of cream, Honey experienced an odd feeling of envy. Because she knew that it was not the meek who would inherit the earth. Nor the kings. And certainly not the connoisseurs. But rather the pigs. In the end the pigs would rule.

When she glanced at her grandnephew again, he was still sneering at her. She felt a tremor in her limbs and turned away—and as she did she dropped her fork, which fell presciently onto the empty chair beside her. When she reached out to retrieve it, she let her hand rest for a moment on the cushion. Rina seemed to be the only other person who recognized the significance of this, and Honey smiled at her. "Maybe he'll still show up."

"No, he won't," said Peter. "He knows better."

"*Sta' zitto*," hissed Corrado.

Honey looked from one to the other. "May I ask what the problem is, exactly?"

When neither responded, she said, "I believe I mentioned that Michael came by my house a while back? And if I may speak honestly . . ."

Everyone looked aghast at the prospect.

"When I was young," Honey continued, "and even not so young, I also dabbled in drugs. And when I saw Michael, it was pretty obvious what was going on. I'm not completely unaware. I do know that this crack, as they call it, is quite a problem with a lot of young people."

Peter put down his cannoli and let out a horrific, barking laugh.

"*Crack?*" he said. "Is that what you think? That the psycho's on crack?"

"Enough!" Corrado banged his hand against the table.

"Why shouldn't she know?" said Peter. "If you say she's part of the family."

"I'm warning you," said Corrado.

But the boy kept going. "My brother's not on crack, Aunt Honey. The problem is, he fucking *wants* a crack."

Corrado stood now. "Shut your mouth. Do you hear me, Pietro?"

Honey had no idea what they were talking about.

Addie began to gulp her champagne, and Rina had her eyes closed, as if praying.

Peter got up to face his father, and when Addie tried to tug him back into his chair, he pushed her away.

But for once, the girl showed a little spine. "Don't be such an asshole, Peter. It's not a big deal."

He scoffed at her, spittle flying from his mouth.

"It's not," she insisted. "I knew a gay guy in college, and he was really nice. I mean he had that kind of voice and everything, but he was basically a normal guy."

"So Michael's *gay*?" Honey said, nearly laughing with relief. "Is that what this is all about?" She wanted to laugh, too, at her faulty judgment. It seemed that the people she thought were gay were straight—and the people she thought were drug addicts were homos.

"He's not gay, he's not gay," Corrado muttered, as if reciting a mantra.

"No," Peter said, with a grimace. "It's fucking worse than that. He actually thinks he's a woman."

At this point, Corrado reached his hands across the table and grabbed his son's neck. Rina shrieked and tried to separate them. "Stop it! Both of you! *Stop it!*"

The men backed away and fell into their chairs. Corrado's eyes were wet with tears. Peter, as if to prove his victory, inhaled another pastry. "Fucking sick," he said.

These words seemed to induce a hex: Addie clutched her belly, excused herself, and rushed from the room.

Honey felt queasy, too.

"Michael's just *confused*," Rina said to the men, before turning pleadingly toward Honey. "I mean, maybe it's not so bad, right? I don't know. On TV I saw this program, and they said—"

Corrado glared at his wife—a deadly look—and she fell silent.

"What did I tell you, goddammit? Don't even mention his name. In fact . . ."—and here Corrado got up, dragged the empty chair away, and jammed it ferociously against the wall.

Moments before, when he'd throttled Peter, Honey had assumed Corrado was punishing the boy for insulting the younger brother. But, no, it wasn't that at all. Clearly, Corrado was ashamed. Or worse: possessed by a hatred so great he couldn't bear to hear it named. He returned to the table, glowering, breathing through his nose like a bull.

To see such rage was awful, though it didn't shock Honey; it was too familiar to shock. She dared to pursue the matter.

"I'm sorry, but I'm still confused. Are you saying that Michael"—she paused, wishing to be delicate, choose the exact right word. "Are you saying that Michael's a *transsexual*?"

"Oh my God," Peter said, covering his face, convulsing, though it was hard to tell if he was laughing or choking.

Corrado seemed to have completely stopped breathing.

Honey took a moment to consider her grandnephew's recent visit. She recalled the oversize shirt that was nearly a dress, the shoulder-length hair, the eyes so dark it was as if he were wearing makeup.

I'm trying to change, he'd said.

No one was speaking, so Honey filled the void. "When I talked to him, he was very upset. His behavior was extremely erratic."

"The pills do that, I think," Rina said.

"So he *is* on drugs?"

"Not exactly." Rina's face was quivering and pale. "He's taking hormones," she whispered.

"Oh my God." Peter moaned again, as if his anger were a kind of torture. His hands were still on his face.

Corrado, too, was hiding, looking down at the tablecloth like he wanted to burn it with his mind.

"I think the pills mess with his head," Rina said. "I feel like I don't even know him any more. I was hoping you could help, Aunt Honey."

"How can *she* help?" said Corrado.

"We don't *need* help," said Peter.

Honey wasn't sure how to proceed. As open-minded as she was, she'd never given much thought to this particular version of beingness. She was out of her league, and decided the best thing would be to discuss practicalities. "Well, if he's taking hormones, I imagine he's under the care of a doctor. So that's a good thing, yes?"

"No," Corrado said. "I took him off our insurance. I'm not letting him use it for *that*."

"So he can grow tits," Peter added.

"*Shut up*," barked Corrado.

"He gets the pills off the street," Rina said. "That's what he told me."

Honey thought of the filthy alley where she'd seen the boy. "This is awful," she said. "This is just awful." Recalling Michael's car, filled to the brim with boxes, she felt a rising fury. "I gather you've kicked him out?"

No answer.

"Yes, I suspected that. I think I told you that when he came to my house he asked for money. And I noticed he was driving Corrado's old Beemer."

"He stole that," Peter muttered.

"He didn't *steal* it," Rina said. "I gave it to him."

"Well, he seems to be living in it now," said Honey. "Did you really invite him here today?" she asked.

"We did," croaked Rina, bursting into tears.

"Enough with the waterworks," Corrado said.

Rina wiped her face and turned to Peter. "Maybe you should check on Addie."

"She's fine," Peter said. "She's probably just throwing up."

"More coffee, anyone?" Though visibly trembling, Rina made a play at normalcy. "I can make more espresso."

But there were no takers; everyone stared at the demitasse pot as if it were an unfathomable mystery. Not a word was uttered; there was no sound but the hum of the air conditioning.

Honey took a breath. "I'd like to ask just one question, if I may?"

Her family looked at her, and she pulled the pashmina tighter around her shoulders before speaking.

"Do you love him?" she asked.

Corrado, as if deeming the question an ambush, said, "What are you—the expert now? You're gonna tell us what to do?"

"I have no wisdom," Honey said. "But you *have* to help the boy."

"And why is that?"

"What was it you told me? When you have children, you stop being selfish."

Honey braced for an attack, but somehow her comment failed to trip Corrado's anger. Instead, his eyes welled with tears. "It's humiliating," he muttered, drying his face with one of the black napkins. For a moment he seemed in danger of collapsing. But then he recovered.

"You lose people," he said. "That's just the way it is."

* * *

Later, Honey stood with Rina in the backyard. The light was fading, though taking its time, lingering in the spaces between the trees. For several minutes neither woman spoke. At one point Rina reached out to take Honey's hand.

There seemed to be nothing more to say about Michael. Rina pointed to the garden, mentioning again her struggles with growing tomatoes.

Honey refrained from any mention of curses. Most likely, the man wasn't even there anymore. Her father and uncle—maybe her brother too—had probably moved the body one night while she and her mother were sleeping.

"You have to find him," Honey finally said. "What if he's living in his car? Do you even know if he has an apartment?"

"I don't know *anything*," Rina said, which Honey found infuriating.

"How can you not know?"

When Rina started to cry again, Honey wanted to scold her. Collaborators did not get to cry.

"Send him to me," she said. "He can stay at my house."

The woman barely nodded. "I know you think I should let him come home, but I can't go against Corrado."

Honey held her tongue. Her judgment. Because, in many ways, she still hadn't gone against her father. A lifetime of silence had made her a collaborator, too.

"Send the boy to me," she repeated.

And then, as if on cue, the garden lights came on. A miracle, it seemed—though the miracle was only melancholy.

28 Ovid

On the way home, she took her time, let the car drive her like a needle on a Ouija board. She passed through the ramshackle part of town where the warehouses were, where she'd seen Michael in that flimsy dress. It was dark now, after eight o'clock, and some of the streetlights weren't working, quite a few of them shattered. As before, cars came and went, stopping briefly, the transactions hurried. Honey watched a buxom woman climb into a truck, her frizzy hair flapping from a window as the vehicle pulled away. Nearby a man seemed to be selling something from his trunk. It was almost impossible to make out anyone's face, and Honey knew she was being ridiculous. Even if her grandnephew were here—which was unlikely—she'd never be able to spot him in this hellish gloom. She drove onward, passing what appeared to be a clothesline strung with tarps, or maybe a makeshift lean-to. When her wheels crunched over some broken glass, she chided herself for not having a Saint Christopher in the car. Accelerating slowly, she steered around a small mountain of garbage bags, and then found herself turning into the alley where the painter's studio was.

She hadn't meant to do this.

Or had she?

Again, it was the Ouija.

Honey wasn't thinking straight. She was frightened—and not just of this place. Frightened of life, of death. Most of all, frightened of herself. There was something inside her she didn't recognize, a small skittering beast clawing at her heart. The dinner at Corrado's had shaken her up more than she'd realized. She stopped the car. *Where are you, Michael?*

When she thought of the boy's family—*her* family—she was torn. Perhaps she should have talked with them more, tried to help them understand. Then again, it wasn't her job to help these people evolve. Let the Fazzingas keep their *z*'s, stay asleep in their petrified minds. They were never going to be—what was the word now—*woke*?

When Honey glanced at the metal door of Nathan's studio, she could see the tiny crack of light along the bottom edge. He was probably in there, working. Painting his dogs, his brutal epiphanies. For all the confusion of that night at the gallery—the confusion of Nathan's desire—Honey rather wished she could talk to him now. Despite his faux pas, the young man was smart, and obviously open-minded. Honey needed a friend, not to mention a cigarette. Besides, it would be a balm to talk about art, to climb out of the mud, into the realm of the conceptual.

But the little beast inside her seemed riled by this thought. It clawed at her cowardice, her wish to escape the facts at hand. She knew the beast was right; there was no escape. Plus, to be honest, she wasn't sure a man—even a man of Nathan's sensitivities—could understand. The truth was, Honey had never felt more like a woman.

Gazing at the liquid edge of light limning the metal door, she imagined another life. A life in which she was a man, a man who made things, an artist. She'd always wanted to become someone else. In many ways it wasn't difficult for her to inhabit her grandnephew's predicament.

Tiny shadows moved at the far end of the alley—rats, perhaps, or the twitching feet of derelicts. Honey reached for her purse and set it on her lap. Inside the leather Birkin was the little Glock. It seemed funny, for a second—*Glock-in-Birkin*, like some village in the Black Forest. And then the needle swerved again—from funny back to frightening. She opened the bag and thrust her hand inside, to check if the gun was really there. Such audacity, such foolishness, to have brought it to Corrado's house. What the hell was she thinking? The fact was, she barely remembered taking it—and it was this lapse that troubled her most of all.

When she pulled the gun from her bag and opened the chamber, she saw that it was loaded.

*　*　*

In the garage, at home, she sat for a while in the hushed timelessness of a vehicle going nowhere. To Honey, the inside of a parked car had always seemed a sacred place, a kind of church—and if one was alone, a confessional.

Earlier, when she'd witnessed Corrado's rage—and Peter's, as well—it had seemed so familiar, and Honey had attributed this to her father. But, sitting in the quiet car, she understood that the real reason it was familiar was because the rage was her own. Her own mind, her own flesh. It was everywhere, in every thought. How had she managed to hide this from herself—and for so long?

Apparently, she *was* an artist—a maker of fictions. Unfortunately, she'd believed her own bullshit. Believed that she'd rid herself of anger, *worked it out*. Kleinerman had used those words, and Honey had imagined herself healed, when all she'd done was push down the worst of herself, fenced it in with a decorative border. So much energy spent on spiritual endeavors, meditation, the mining of the soul—and all for naught.

Maybe the only true thing was rage; maybe *that* was the Holy Grail. Certainly men understood this, and they often used it to their advantage; sometimes they even achieved greatness by means of it. They weren't afraid of their anger; they weren't *taught* to fear it, like women.

Honey recalled all those self-help seminars she'd attended in Los Angeles. There was one teacher, female of course, who said that anger was the leading cause of aging. To stay calm, she'd insisted, was to stay beautiful. Honey and an auditorium full of women had eaten up this drivel.

Maybe the goal now, in these final days, should be something quite antipodal. To nurture her anger and make it grow. To become a man—or at least die like one.

Honey got out of the Lexus, crossed the lawn, and knocked on Jocelyn's door.

* * *

"Sorry," Lee said. "She's not home."

"I can see her car." Honey pointed at Exhibit A, Joss's station wagon.

"Yeah, she's taking a walk. Trying to get more exercise."

The man was smiling—honestly, it seemed—and Honey had no choice but to believe him.

"Well, would you ask her to give me a call when she has a moment? I know you don't want us speaking for some reason, but it's really none of your business."

Honey wanted to say more, wanted to shout at the man, say all the things she'd not said to Corrado. But then the man before her was suddenly apologizing.

"I'm really sorry about the other day. I was upset about stuff, and I guess I took it out on you."

Honey, not expecting civility, faltered and fell silent.

Lee continued, cordially. "When Joss gets back, I promise I'll let her know you came by."

Under the bright porch light, Honey had an excellent view of the tattoos on the man's neck. They were not vines, as she'd thought at first, but rather strings of barbed wire.

He noticed her staring. "I did it a long time ago," he said. "I was pretty drunk."

At that moment, Honey felt the force of her own intoxication. Wine, champagne, a dim memory of taking a pill. The man was backing away, ready to close the door.

"Do you have a cigarette, by any chance?" she asked him.

"I don't smoke."

Honey didn't find this credible; in fact she could smell the smoke on his clothing. He was still smiling. Behind him, the sound of television—plush voices and something like the peal of bells, a jangling soporific. Honey leaned on her cane. "Well, I'll let you go."

But as the man began to close the door, she told him to wait. Because maybe it wasn't a television. It sounded now like a clatter of dishes, running water.

"What is that?"

"What?"

"That noise. Are you sure Jocelyn's not in there?"

"I already told you she's not home."

"Well, *someone* is in there."

The man grinned tightly. "Now you're being annoying. I'll tell her you stopped by. What more do you want?"

I want to show you what's in my bag, thought Honey, picturing the gun. She didn't trust Mr. Barbed Wire one bit. In a white T-shirt that displayed his muscles, he brought to mind Richie Verona.

"Do you need something else?" he asked.

Part of her wanted to push him aside, barge into the house—but by now she'd lost her nerve. She shook her head and walked away.

* * *

In the kitchen she drank more wine and thought about Michael. She had his cell phone number in her purse. Rina had scrawled it on the back of a ShopRite receipt. Tomorrow, when she was sober, she'd give the boy a ring, maybe take him to lunch. Perhaps she'd give him her cherished copy of Ovid's *Metamorphoses*, one of the few books she still had from her time at Bryn Mawr.

"Everything changes. Nothing is lost."

In her drunken mind, she knew exactly what to tell him.

All the things she'd never told her son.

A month or so before the baby is due, Honey's mother comes up with a plan. They'll drive to Toms River, to visit a relative. It's summer, and they leave Ferryfield under the guise of a vacation. "Solo per le ragazze," her mother says to the men. *Just for the girls.*

They pack lightly, sharing a single suitcase, hard and glossy as a chestnut. When they arrive in Toms River, Honey sees no river, only seeping puddles and scratchy patches of wild blackberry. The relative is an old woman Honey hasn't met before, supposedly a great-aunt or a distant cousin, though Honey suspects it's a lie. The woman speaks little English, and her house is horrible, rotting in the damp air, with floors that reek of eucalyptus and bleach. In the bedroom where Honey sleeps, there are so many plaster saints and flickering votives that she's afraid her mother has taken her here to die.

The old woman's cold hands are often on Honey's belly, massaging things into the taut skin, fragrant oils and tarry homemade lotions. There are mumbled prayers, or what Honey takes to be prayers. She's told to stay in bed, even during the day—a kind of torture, since she doesn't feel sick.

One morning she sneaks outside and wanders among the berries. Eats her fill, until her arms are scratched and her mouth black. On the way back to the house she sees a crushed snake that looks like a melted candy cane. That night she wakes to gut-wrenching pain. "I ate too many berries," she tells her mother.

But it isn't the berries.

The old woman leans inside Honey's nightgown, and then straight inside Honey. The pain gets worse—constant waves of it, unbreaking. Her mother sits silently in the corner of the room while Honey cries out to angels she no longer believes in. The world splits in two, and it seems that only one half can survive.

Time becomes water, becomes blood. Something from the nuns comes back to her, something one of them said in Sunday school—that in Hell the clocks ran on a sinner's blood. Drop by drop, eternally.

Who knew there could be so much of it, though? When finally the old woman pulls the baby out, its face is streaked with war paint. Honey doesn't hear a breath, a cry. There's only silence. Somehow it's over, and Honey falls asleep, or dies—or maybe someone else, someone like her, dies. Either way, it doesn't matter.

*   *   *

When she wakes, the bed is dry, and the old woman places the shriveled creature on Honey's chest. The war paint has been washed away. Honey wonders how a lifeless thing can be so warm.

But then the little mouth attaches itself, a barnacle. Honey stares at the boy—the black hair, the nub and fig between the legs. She keeps her hands at her side, offering no comfort beyond what her body gives without consent. When she looks away, she sees the white blanket stained with blood. Everything hurts, even the light. She wills herself back to blackness, and sometime later—hours? days?—she hears a car approaching. Immediately she thinks, *Richie Verona*.

Then she remembers that he's dead.

She gets up and goes to the window, where she sees a Cadillac, though not her father's. His is black; this one's a metallic green. Her mother is standing there with the baby, who's wrapped in a clean blanket. She thinks that the two of them are going to get into the car, but then a woman, a stranger, steps from the back. The woman is ugly, with dents in her face, her thin hair the color of mercury.

Honey watches as her mother hands the woman the baby, and then watches as the car vanishes into the forest. She feels relieved, even grateful.

But years later, after Enzo's death, after she's no longer part of the family, she'll worry that they've played a trick on her. That maybe, after the baby was taken away, her parents somehow reclaimed it.

She knows these thoughts aren't real. It's only sickness, only panic. Dr. Kleinerman gives her pills. But still, she goes on imagining it—

that the baby has been hidden inside her father's house. Even now, it might be there, waiting to be used. A soldier.

There'd been no paperwork, no names—no buyer or seller. Her mother kept no records.

Before they left Toms River, Honey took the bloodstained blanket and buried it in the woods, pretending it was a body. She'd shed no tears. It was finished. She was free.

Or so she'd told herself.

Part Three

The morning arrived strangely faded, as if in the night there'd been an existential theft. Every surface in Honey's house was stripped of its vitality. The yellow Scalamandré throw pillows looked tawdry, while the raspberries in the fridge seemed to need a transfusion. Even the paintings appeared bereft, bleached of their former glory.

Honey was fading, too. What had happened to her life in color? She recalled a red dress from her youth, a full-length gobsmacker made of crepe georgette, a gift from Mr. Hal. How she'd adored that gown—a blazing crimson, the color so deep and true it had suggested the lambent interior of a flower. Honey hadn't seen a red like that since at least 1962.

Perhaps her eyes were going. Or worse, her mind. Her pounding headache suggested a hangover, as well. She poured more coffee and with a sharp poke woke up her computer.

* * *

"Transgender," she typed in the search window, shocked to find over two hundred million entries. Honey scanned the first page and clicked on "Let us answer your questions about transgendered people." Good, because she had a lot.

After reading an overlong and slightly confusing treatise on gender, she moved on to more of the nuts and bolts. It seemed that *transgender* shouldn't necessarily be equated with *transsexual*. Some individuals didn't wish to change their sex—and among these, there were a plethora of categories: *crossdresser, genderqueer, gender nonconforming*. There was the bonus pack of *multigendered*, as well as a more mysterious classification, *third gender*. In regard to her grandnephew's place in all of this, Honey had no idea.

She recalled how troubled Michael had seemed the day he came to visit. The website explained that people who existed outside societal norms often faced a number of challenges. Sometimes they suffered from debilitating anxiety or depression. Honey's hands were shaking as she read the phrase "injustice at every turn," because apparently there were countless hate crimes against people like Michael. It wasn't a surprise to learn that transgendered youth were often evicted by their parents; many were homeless. Honey was beside herself with fury—and when she turned away from the computer, the faded room flooded with color.

* * *

Dialing Michael's cell phone, Honey felt nervous. The boy mightn't have a fond memory of their last interaction. Then again, she *had* given him a check—which, according to her statement, had been cashed. "I have plenty more," she'd tell him.

The phone rang and rang. Honey lifted her chin, preparing to leave a message—but there was no voice mail. After fifteen seconds or so, the line emitted a series of quick sharp beeps and disconnected.

Undaunted, she composed a text. This is Aunt Honey. Please call me back. I'd like to see you.

She considered adding *I miss you*, but decided this would seem suspect to Michael, to whom she'd never given much attention. Had she even once sent him a birthday card or a present? The question was disingenuous; Honey knew quite well that, over the years, she'd sent the boy nothing. When Corrado was young, she'd at least made an effort, sending him the occasional toy or trinket. That had stopped, of course, after her brother died. At that point, Honey was persona non grata.

As she sat on the couch, mulling over the situation, she didn't go easy on herself. She even went so far as to question whether this wish to help Michael might be some perverse attempt to validate her own black-sheep story. Even kindness, if one looked closely, might harbor vanity. Still, it was better than doing nothing. Besides, Honey had been the recipient of so much kindness throughout her life; she had a debt.

She thought of Mr. Hal, how good he'd been to her after her brother was killed, when she'd suffered not only grief but a paralyzing fear of her father. Hal had watched over her—comforted her trembling body, eased her fragile mind. He'd taken her on all those cruises, where the wide and hopeful terror of the sea had put the smallness of Honey's story in its place.

And how had she repaid Hal's kindness? After his wife had died, and he asked Honey to marry him, she refused, thinking, I don't owe him that. She'd always been rabidly independent, and by the time Hal proposed, it was far too late to change.

To her credit, though, she hadn't abandoned the man. In fact, she'd been beside Hal when he died. Well, most of her had been there—because, of course, she'd always held back a part of herself. She'd wanted to protect Hal from the worst of who she was. But she wondered now if, by keeping secrets, she'd been a failure in regard to love. When Hal left her the lion's share of his money, she was both shocked and inconsolate. It had been a fortune—much more than she'd deserved.

So, yes, she had a debt—and when the doorbell finally rang, Honey knew exactly how to proceed. She promised herself not to use *The Voice* with Michael. She wouldn't be imperious, nor pretend she had all the answers. She would speak to the boy honestly. More important, she would listen—and, together, they'd work things out.

* * *

"Hi. Lee said you wanted to see me."

It was Jocelyn at the door; it was *always* Jocelyn. Still, Honey acted without thinking and leaped at the girl, encircling her with a robust and uncharacteristic hug.

"Okay, wow," Joss said. "You really missed me, huh?"

Aware that she'd overdone it, Honey stepped back and adopted a brusquer attitude. "Don't just stand there gawking at me. Come in, if you're coming in."

"I can only stay a minute," Joss said, though as soon as Honey had closed the door, the girl made her way into the living room and plopped herself down on the sofa.

"Would you like some coffee, dear?"

Joss pointed to the empty bottle on the table. "Do you have more wine?"

"Does the pope shit in the woods?" replied Honey.

"Probably," said Joss.

Though Honey was loath to admit it, it was a relief to have the girl's company. As for the wine, it seemed a bit early in the day, but then, in the kitchen, Honey saw the clock. It was after four. Apparently she'd been sitting on the couch, waiting on Michael's call, for more than three hours.

Jocelyn was shouting from the other room. "Lee said you were acting really strange last night."

"What does that mean?" scoffed Honey, returning with two glasses and a bottle of Viognier.

"He said that you accused him of lying."

"I thought I heard someone in the house, that's all."

"Well, now he thinks you're off your rocker."

"Darling, I'm not the one with barbed wire around my neck. I simply came over to check on you. I hadn't seen you in several days, and I was worried."

"About what?"

The girl played innocent so well—so well, in fact, that Honey wondered if perhaps there was nothing to be concerned about. Still, she scrutinized the clown makeup on Joss's face, to see if it might be hiding another bruise.

"Why are you staring at me?"

"I'm not." Honey turned away to pour the wine. She made some small talk, not her greatest skill. "So what have you been up to, dear?"

"Just working. And I'm trying to get more exercise."

"Yes, Lee mentioned that."

"Yeah, it was his idea. Not that he thinks I'm, like, gross or anything, but he just thought it would be good for me. And I've already lost two pounds."

"Wonderful," mumbled Honey, glancing at her phone.

"You okay?" asked Joss.

"What? I'm fine."

"Really? Because, to be honest, I sort of agree with Lee. You have been acting a little weird lately."

"Look who's talking. You're not exactly the poster child for *normal*. I seem to recall you wearing a pair of cat ears to work."

"Yeah, well, Lee also said you were really drunk."

Honey, sipping wine, wasn't in a position to defend herself. She felt it best to change the subject.

"Let me ask you something—since you seem fairly knowledgeable about the current sexual landscape."

Joss nodded, as if this were an accurate appraisal.

"I just wondered," Honey continued, "if perhaps you knew any trans-gendered individuals. It seems I have a family member who might be in this camp, and I just—well, I really don't know what to do."

"Why do you have to do anything? Just be supportive."

"That's the thing. I don't even know where he is. And his family doesn't, either—and some of them are being quite nasty about it. So I just thought, if you knew anyone in a similar situation . . ."

"Sorry, I don't. And even if I did, it's not like they all live on the same block."

"I realize that. I'm just concerned about him."

"Maybe you should call the police. I mean, if he's missing."

"I think that's premature. But I was thinking of going to Mabel's. Ask if anyone's seen him there."

Joss frowned. "Mabel's is a pretty uptight gay bar. You might do better at the Shelter in West Mill—it's a little more alternative."

Honey picked up a pad and wrote down the name.

Joss poured more wine. "Is this what you came over last night to talk about?"

"No. I just wanted to see you." Honey looked at the girl's large doughy face, wondering why her affection for Joss sometimes felt like pain. "I was thinking maybe we could get together this weekend. You know, just the two of us."

"Maybe, yeah."

"How about Saturday? I could roast a chicken."

"Well, I have to check with Lee first, see what he has planned."

"Of course," Honey said brightly, masking her disappointment. She managed to hold this laissez-faire pose quite well, but when Joss stood and said she had to run, Honey blurted, "Wait!"

"What's wrong?"

"I just . . ."

Honey realized she had nothing to say. Yet the idea of the girl leaving felt unbearable. She spoke rashly, bringing up something she'd promised herself never to mention.

"I saw your ad."

"My what?"

"Remember, you sent me all that information about those dating sites? Well, I looked at some, and I saw your picture on one of them."

"Oh." Joss smiled, as if this revelation were no cause for embarrassment. "So, what did you think?"

"Frankly, I was perplexed."

"By what?"

"By your honesty, I suppose."

"Isn't that the point?"

"Well, I'm not sure exposing yourself to strangers is the wisest thing."

Jocelyn shrugged. "Romance is always a risk."

Romance? That seemed a stretch. As far as Honey could tell, Lee didn't even *like* the girl—telling the poor thing she needed to exercise. And God knew what else he was making her do.

"I'm just worried about you."

"Why do you keep saying that?"

Jocelyn was obviously annoyed—this was an argument they'd had before—but Honey couldn't help herself.

"I just wish you had a little more self-respect."

The girl turned a peculiar shade of pink—anger tinged with shame. Mostly anger. "I told you, I'm fine. I know you don't like Lee, but this is my life, not yours. So can you do me a favor and stop interfering?"

"I'm not—"

"Yes, you are. And I know you care about me and I appreciate it, but you're not my mother."

"I'm not trying to be your mother, for heaven's sake."

"Good. Because I don't need someone else in my life judging me all the time."

"I'm not judging you."

"No? You just wish I had a little more self-respect."

"I'm just saying, as a woman it's important to—"

"I didn't come over here for advice."

"Fine. But just tell me one thing. Were you really out last night when I stopped by?"

"Oh my God, you're relentless."

"Well, I heard *someone* in the house. In the kitchen, maybe."

"And what if I *was* there? What if Lee just wanted me to himself? Is that so terrible? And how is it even your business?"

It's my business because I love you. But Honey didn't say this, since surely it wasn't true. It was no doubt some kind of sordid transference.

"You're absolutely right, dear. It's not my business."

The girl still looked angry. "Thanks for the wine," she said. Barely two seconds later, she was out the door.

"Let me know about Saturday!" Honey chirped from the porch.

But Jocelyn didn't answer.

Blackouts were nothing like sleeping, they were an algebra of delirium. Honey's dreams existed as senseless equations. A man divided by a woman, multiplied by violence. Subtract time. Add fear.

After Jocelyn's departure, Honey had polished off the rest of the Viognier. On the sofa she tossed fitfully, rolling toward consciousness only when she heard the birds. Birds that had somehow gotten inside her phone. She answered shakily, trying not to slur.

"Michael? Is that you?"

"No, it's—it's Nathan."

"Who?"

"Nathan Flores. The painter."

"Why are you calling me in the middle of the night?"

"It's not—it's not even eight o'clock."

Honey blinked, confused, as the man continued to chatter. He seemed to be apologizing.

"I've just been upset—you know, that I upset *you*."

"No, no. Please, just forget it. I'm sure I overreacted. I was recently informed that I'm a judgmental bitch."

When Nathan laughed, Honey asked if she'd said something funny. "Listen—why don't you go back to bed, young man? I'm very drunk. We can talk tomorrow."

"You want to talk? I thought you were mad."

"Oh, I am. I'm furious. Call me around eleven—all right? We'll sort it out then."

Honey dropped the phone and instantly fell asleep.

* * *

In the morning, she had no memory of the night before and couldn't understand why she kept thinking about the painter. Perhaps it had something to do with that bar Jocelyn had mentioned in West Mill, which was also where Nathan's gallery was. She looked at the slip of paper where she'd jotted down the name. *The Shelter.* If she didn't hear back from her grandnephew in the next few days, perhaps she'd visit the place, see if anyone there knew him. Of course, she'd have to get a photograph from Rina—though surely Rina wouldn't have any photos of her son in mascara and a dress. Well, people would just have to use their imagination.

Honey wasn't going to do anything quite yet. She had a piercing neuralgia in her skull; it was rather like being accosted by tiny demons with electric pitchforks. When she went to the kitchen and discovered she was out of coffee, she wondered if her sins had really been *that* bad, to deserve such punishment. Over black tea and a piece of toast, she opened her calendar and saw that it was the day of Angela Carini's funeral.

"No, I can't. *I won't.*" She said these words out loud, indulging her petulance—because, frankly, she'd had enough. This dying thing was becoming a bore. The only death Honey was interested in was her own. And if it weren't for her grandnephew's predicament, she'd join Angela in a heartbeat, if only to escape the pitchforks. Then again, there might be even larger pitchforks in the world to come.

In penance, she cleared away the empty wine bottles (there were two in the kitchen, two on the coffee table, and one in the bedroom). She brought them to the garage and even deigned to put them in the recycling bin.

* * *

When Honey finally called Rina and asked if she'd heard from the boy, Rina said yes, that he'd come to the house.

"Thank goodness. How is he?"

"I didn't really get to talk to him."

"What do you mean?"

"He was . . ." Rina paused. "Can you hold on one second? Let me just go upstairs." She was whispering, as if worried about being overheard.

Honey was impatient. "I don't understand why you didn't speak to him."

"He had an argument with Corrado. In the driveway. He didn't come in the house."

"Did you tell him he could stay with me?"

"Like I said, I didn't have a chance."

"Why didn't you just go outside?"

"Corrado asked me not to."

"And so what happened?"

"They yelled at each other, and Michael took off."

"Where did he go?"

"No idea."

"What did Corrado say?"

"He didn't. The two of them really had it out. Afterward Corrado was a wreck. He still won't talk to me about it."

Honey mentioned that she'd tried to call the boy, but that something seemed to be wrong with his phone. "I wasn't able to leave a message."

"Yeah, Corrado took him off the plan, so that number won't work anymore."

"Are you joking? So now you can't even get in touch with him?"

Rina was suddenly defensive. "You don't know what he's put us through, Aunt Honey. Coming to the house like that—just throwing it in his father's face."

"What did he do?"

"I mean, he didn't even make an effort, you know, to even *pretend* to be normal. You should have seen what he was wearing, and it was the middle of the day. I'm sure the neighbors saw him."

"So what? You can't let the opinions of others—"

"Maybe you can't. But Corrado has a business to run."

"This isn't about Corrado. This is about Michael. And I thought you were on his side."

"I am. But he's got to make an effort too. It can't just be all about what *he* wants."

"Why not?"

"Because it hurts people. You should have seen how upset Corrado was. He had agita all day."

Honey sighed. "Well, I'd still like to talk to the boy."

"Maybe it's better if you don't."

"Why is that?"

Rina paused. "I don't know. It just might be better if he went away."

"What do you mean, *went away*?"

"Move away. Corrado said Michael mentioned something about leaving town."

"No. You can't just let him leave."

"Why do you suddenly care?" asked Rina. "After all this time."

Honey reminded the woman that she'd solicited Honey's opinion. "You invited me to dinner to discuss the matter."

"I know. You're right. And I thought you could help, but we've talked about it and we both feel it might be better if you don't get involved."

"By *we*, I'm assuming you mean you and Corrado?"

"It's not that we don't want to see you anymore, Aunt Honey. We do. But we're not looking for advice about our children."

"Of course," said Honey, attempting to keep her cool. "Well, can you at least send me a photograph of Michael?"

"Why?"

"Indulge an old woman. I'd just like a picture of my grandnephew. A recent one, if you have it."

"I don't want to argue, Aunt Honey. But you should have seen him when he came to the house. I didn't even recognize him at first."

Rina seemed to be crying now. Honey felt no sympathy.

"So you'll send a photo?"

"I'll text you one."

"Thank you."

"I better go," Rina said. And then: "I'll let you know about the baby shower."

After hanging up, Honey felt short of breath. When her phone emitted a plaintive *ting*, she jumped. Tapping on Rina's text, she saw Michael's face—and, as suspected, no mascara, no long hair. The photo looked like it had been taken several years before, possibly during high school—the face so young. In the image the boy was smiling, his dimples dutifully displayed. Honey didn't know this Michael. In fact, she didn't know *any* Michael. Her relationship to him was purely a conceit. So why on earth did her heart feel broken?

* * *

She was still breathless when the phone rang again. Assuming it was Rina, Honey picked up immediately.

But it was the painter, saying bizarrely that he was sorry to be late.

"Late?"

"Yeah, you said to call at eleven. But there was a water leak at the studio, so I had to deal with that."

Honey had no idea what the hell he was talking about. "When did we speak?"

"Last night? You said to call back today. I guess you were a little . . . You said you'd been drinking."

"Oh, yes," Honey replied, since to pretend otherwise would only make her appear more foolish than was already the case. She spun a quick white web. "I had a party here yesterday, with some friends. We all got pretty loaded. You must have called in the middle of that."

"Okay," the painter said, as if not quite buying it.

"And remind me, please, why I wanted you to call me?"

"I'm not sure. You said that you thought maybe you'd overreacted."

"To what?"

"That night at the gallery, maybe? You know, when I . . ."

"Yes. Well, I probably did. To tell you the truth, I'm not myself these days."

When he asked what was wrong, she said, "*Everything* is wrong."

"I know I offended you."

"No. You didn't really. Well, you did—but it's not important. You were just being yourself, and I had no right to judge. Still, I hope you'll respect my decision."

"Which is?"

"Which is that my dancing shoes are locked away."

"I wasn't proposing dancing. I just thought that since we had such a great conversation at the gallery, we could at least get together and talk about art. And you said you'd like to come to the studio and see more of my work. Plus, I'd love to see the Redon you mentioned."

Honey felt cornered.

"What is it you like about me?" she asked. She wasn't fishing for compliments; she was genuinely perplexed.

Nathan answered simply, with no taint of flattery. "I like your honesty, your intelligence. I love the way you talk. Your style."

"Are you sure you're not gay?" asked Honey.

Nathan laughed. "I'm sure."

"Listen, dear—I don't think I'll be able to come to the studio. I just have a lot on my plate. To be honest, it's been a difficult few weeks."

Nathan asked if there was anything he could do to help.

"Why are you being so nice?"

"Do I have to repeat myself?" the painter said. "I like you."

Inwardly, Honey sighed; outwardly, she blushed. And then she said: "Maybe there is something you can do to help."

"What's that?"

"Have you ever heard of a bar called the Shelter?"

U nable to settle her mind, she picked up the novel she'd abandoned months before, the one about women in prison. The
pages, though, seemed to be made of lead; turning them
wasn't easy. But, since Honey was a finisher by nature, she sat in the reading nook of her closet, giving *The Scent of Something*—asinine title!—
a second chance.

Up Yours, the main character, was still incarcerated. Well, it was a
life sentence, so of course she was. The woman had murdered a priest.
Years earlier, this priest had touched her inappropriately, and it was fairly
obvious that more horrendous crimes against a young Up Yours were yet
to be revealed, if Honey could just keep reading. A prison, mind you,
wasn't the most dynamic setting. It would be like writing a novel about a
woman sitting in a closet. And since only so much could happen within
the confines of a cell (Up Yours was currently in solitary), there were
frequent narrative breakouts, in which the woman reflected on her previous existence as a free agent.

Life, it seemed, had conspired against the protagonist; she was poor,
obese, abused—and though this was sad, the book's discussion of female struggle tended to value philosophy over emotion. It was evident
that the author had a bone to pick, politically, which made it difficult
for Honey to invest in Up Yours's reality. Every once in a while the in-
mate would say or think something so disingenuous that Honey would
find herself flipping back to look at the picture of the authoress on the
flap. *Shut up*, she wanted to tell her, *and let the damn character get a word
in edgewise*. But as it stood, Up Yours remained a puppet, and Honey had
no choice but to set the pantomime aside.

Drowsing in the armchair, she had a peculiar wish that she could re-
write the book, that she could save Up Yours from the clutches of the
author, who seemed to have such a narrow view of her main character.

In Honey's opinion, a narrow point of view was as disastrous in fiction as it was in life.

Even the character's name was problematic. Funny, yes, in a bawdy sort of way, but entirely too obvious. Up Yours was a nickname, of course, and one that the character had bestowed upon herself, transmuting how the world had shoved things inside her—spiritually, emotionally, anatomically—into an outward expression of hostility. A simplification, as Honey understood it, in regard to a woman's rage. That a tragic history could only lead to further tragedy—it was absurd, pigheaded even. Violence spawned violence spawned violence, while on the other side of the concrete wall a rose was a rose was a rose. Why must these two equations be kept apart? Why not violence to violence to roses? Honey was mumbling as she nodded off. Why not a little alchemy, a little magic? A little self-determination?

Honey had only recently considered her own rage. And though she no longer wished to deny it, she also allowed herself the belief that she'd transmuted it into something better—even if only a militant insistence on elegance. Just before she fell asleep, though, she thought of the gun. It was curious, that she'd chosen it as her exit strategy. Why this little horror and not the more subtle undoing of pills? A gun for someone so vain—it was an odd choice, no? The blast would deform her face.

But maybe that was precisely what she wanted. To blast through the veneer and see what was underneath. Maybe it had to end in violence. Maybe the roses were merely illusion.

* * *

When she woke from her nap, it was still morning. There were hours yet to kill. The painter wasn't picking her up until six. Honey felt nervous, though not about Nathan. This wasn't a date, she'd made that clear; he was simply accompanying her to the Shelter. Moral support, you could say. When she'd mentioned what was going on with her grandnephew, Nathan didn't show the slightest bit of prejudice. In fact, he'd applauded the boy's bravery.

Honey's nervousness had more to do with her own lack of clarity about her grandnephew. She had a strong intuition that she'd find Michael, and she wondered what, exactly, she'd say to him when she did.

In many ways, they were strangers. When Michael was a child, she'd spent time with him only once. Sadly, it had been at her mother's funeral. At the repast afterward, the boy—four or five—had sidled up to her, implicating himself in her dark cloak. "You smell good," he'd said, hugging her. She'd picked him up, a skinny scrap, light as a bird. Almost immediately, though, she'd sent him on his way. She was in Jersey solely for the funeral, and since she was staying only a few days, it didn't seem wise to get attached to the child.

Still, she'd never forgotten his embrace, the warm wet confusion of it. A little thing her heart had made too much of. No one else in the family had shown her any affection that day.

*　*　*

In the kitchen she prepared a light lunch—a hodgepodge of greens, a little cheese, a few almonds. As she whisked the dressing, she could feel the strength in her arm. For over a month now, Honey had been exercising regularly. *One must be strong to live, stronger to die*—in many ways it had become her mantra. Her eighty-third birthday was just six weeks away, and there was so much yet to accomplish. To-do lists scribbled across her despair. It was strange how the will to live and the desire to die were not mutually exclusive. Honey nibbled her salad, standing up, looking out the kitchen window—a terrible habit, but she often ate like that now.

Beyond the glass, the flowering cherry continued to languish, and the lawn had yellow patches like a sickly jigsaw puzzle. Over the past few weeks Honey had neglected the watering. Often, from the window, she saw Jocelyn and Lee coming and going. Such frenetic existences. When the pair weren't kissing, they were arguing. A general feeling of tawdriness prevailed; the property itself had grown trashier—a broken bicycle on the stoop, oil stains on the driveway. Lee was often working on his truck, with an exasperated look on his face, while Jocelyn smoked madly by the front door, scratching at her arms. Everything over there seemed frazzled. Throw in some dogs and cats, and you'd have a George Booth cartoon in *The New Yorker*.

And lately there'd been other people—strangers to Honey—who regularly paid visits next door. Perhaps Lee was selling more of his Taster's Choice. Honey occasionally thought of phoning the police, but she never did. She'd been brought up to believe that the worst crime of all was to be a snitch.

The man's pickup was currently parked in the drive. Honey put on her readers, which also worked for distance, and jotted down the license plate number. Surely one could look up such a thing; gather information about the owner. A snoop wasn't the same as a snitch. Honey simply wanted to appease her curiosity.

But after doing a little research on her laptop, she was quickly disappointed. It seemed that the only way to obtain a driver's personal information from his plate number was to submit a formal request to DMV, and provide compelling reasons for requiring this information. Well, to hell with that.

And really, why did she care? Even if she discovered something horrible, what could she do? Jocelyn had made it clear that she wanted Honey to butt out of her affairs. Apparently she'd insulted the girl when she told her that she lacked self-respect. Honey's mother would have approved of a girl like Jocelyn, who had the good sense to compromise—unlike Honey, who was arrogant. *Orgoglio.*

The fact of it was, Honey hadn't ever wanted to live with a man. Not even Hal. She was her own woman, irrefutably independent. It was a stance she'd rehearsed her whole life. Maybe in some small way she was jealous of Jocelyn, who was willing to give up a part of herself for the sake of love.

Then again, Honey refused to accept that the girl was *in love* with that man. Clearly, she was acting out of loneliness. And while Honey wanted something better for Jocelyn, in regard to romance, what she wanted even more was that the girl be stronger, less gullible. Less of a pushover.

* * *

An hour later, when both the pickup and the station wagon were gone, Honey put on an old utility jacket Dominic had left behind. In one of the larger pockets she stuffed a pencil and a pad. When she went outside, she walked down the block, well past Jocelyn's house, just to make sure that none of the other neighbors were out and about. When the coast seemed clear, she turned back toward home, pausing before Jocelyn's mailbox to take a quick peek inside.

There were three letters, bills it seemed, all of them addressed to Jocelyn. But then at the bottom of the stack was a small envelope with a yellow forwarding sticker on it. The name on the sticker was Lee Czernik, and though Honey couldn't make out the full address beneath the sticker, she could at least make out *Swainsboro, Georgia*. How apt, she thought, jotting down the details.

Back at home she used her credit card to pay for a membership on an online site that allowed you to check a person's background, including any criminal records. The whole process was surprisingly easy. There was only one Lee Czernik in Swainsboro, Georgia—age thirty-three, which seemed about right. Formerly of Monroe, formerly of Cordel, formerly of Eastman—all of these in Georgia; and before that his places of residence included cities in Florida, Michigan, and New Hampshire.

As she scrolled down to the criminal records section, she was disappointed that it was not as damning as she'd hoped. There was no record of assault, sexual or otherwise. He'd been arrested once for extortion and once for possession of a controlled substance, this last offense fairly recently, and most likely what he was currently on parole for. It seemed he'd served no prison terms. There was a DUI charge, as well, though Honey couldn't hold that against him, since she'd had one of those herself, in Los Angeles.

With a sigh she closed the laptop, having uncovered nothing but the obvious: drugs and threats, both of which she already had direct experience of in regard to Mr. Czernik. She stood and headed for her bedroom, wanting a bath. Wanting cleanliness.

* * *

After she was dressed and ready for Nathan, she still had nearly an hour before he was due to pick her up. Looking out the window, she saw that only the station wagon was in Jocelyn's driveway. Honey texted the girl, asking if she'd wouldn't mind coming over for a quick chat.

I'm busy, the girl texted back.

Honey typed, Please. The word on the screen turned pink, and when she pressed another key, the word became an image of praying hands. Honey sent this.

Almost instantly the phone dinged.

Five minutes, the girl replied. I'll meet you in the backyard.

Honey went outside and waited by the grill. When the girl showed up, wearing one of her famous pair of overalls, Honey couldn't help but smile. Jocelyn, though, was stony-faced. "What?" she said, with a bravado that was almost convincing.

Honey wanted to say, *I'm sorry*. But the sentiment seemed cheap— and besides, she wasn't completely sorry for having given the girl a talking-to.

"Are you well?" asked Honey.

Jocelyn grumbled affirmatively. "You?"

"Yes," lied Honey, and then padded the lie further. "You look nice."

But the girl didn't thaw.

Honey applied more warmth. "I just wanted to say that I'm here for you, should you need anything."

"I don't need anything," the girl said.

"But if you ever do," reiterated Honey. "I trust we're still friends?"

Jocelyn shrugged, vaguely, attempting to hold her stance, but then her eyes filled with water. Honey took this as an opportunity, and touched the girl's hand.

The affection was not returned. Jocelyn pulled back her arm and said she had to go. Her eyes were smudged with a disturbing blackness—not bruises, but fatigue. At least, they didn't look like bruises.

As the girl walked away, Honey felt that her words had been insufficient. *If you ever need anything*—it was an empty phrase. People often said it blithely, knowing they'd never be held to their promise. But, in this instance, Honey actually meant what she'd said.

She hoped Jocelyn knew this.

33 Teena

At six on the dot, the painter arrived in his ridiculous Thunderbird. Honey stepped from the house wearing charcoal slacks and a lampblack turtleneck, a buttery confection of three-ply Mongolian cashmere. Nathan had on a white sports shirt, short-sleeved, his arms thin but strong, and tanned as if it were already midsummer. Honey, despite the fading light, wore sunglasses, movie-star monstrosities that covered her worst flaws and made her look at least ten years younger.

"I imagine this is a little strange for both of us," she said.

Nathan shrugged. "I'm just glad you asked for help."

"I really didn't want to go by myself, so I'm grateful."

"What time are you supposed to meet your nephew?"

"Grandnephew."

"Right."

"To be honest, I haven't talked to him in weeks. Months, really. So there's no plan, exactly. In fact, I'm not even sure he'll be there."

"Oh."

"I just had a feeling. And I've always run my life like this—on intuition."

Nathan said it was the same for him, as a painter. "Of course, it doesn't always turn out like you expect."

"No, it doesn't. I had a spiritual mentor who used to say, 'Surprise me, Holy Void.' He said if we had to choose a single prayer, it should be that."

As Nathan shifted into gear, he smiled. "I like a good surprise."

Then he asked how he should refer to Honey's grandnephew.

"What do you mean?"

"*He? She? They?* All of them?"

"All of them?"

Nathan said he had a friend who accepted any pronoun.

Honey sighed and said, "For now, let's just call him Michael."

* * *

There was very little traffic, and within fifteen minutes they were parked in front of the Shelter. The sign reminded Honey of the one outside Dante's—the name in red neon, sizzling with cosmic significance. Ever since Dominic's death, Honey had refused to dine at her old haunt; she even refused to drive past it, afraid the doors might fly open and she'd be sucked inside—a date not with Nicky but with Virgil.

"You okay?" Nathan asked.

Honey nodded. They were standing on the street now, a few feet from the entrance—a great slab of wood painted bright orange, as if in warning. Nathan easily pulled it open, and in they went. For a moment there was nothing but blackness. Then Honey remembered her sunglasses. She removed them, and the room slowly came into focus. A rustic tavern hijacked by fairy lights and pots of plastic shrubbery. The floor was sticky, and there was a migrainous pulse of music. The place was dead, except for two men on barstools and a tiny woman seated at a high table near the bathrooms. The smell was just shy of despair. Bleach and beer and drugstore perfume. As they approached the bar, the bald man tending it said something Honey couldn't make out over the music, though surely it was the obvious query.

"A martini," she shouted.

"What kind?" asked the bartender.

"The *gin* kind," replied Honey. "Dry, with olives. What about you, dear?" she asked Nathan.

"The same," he said, or seemed to say—who could tell with this ruckus? Dance music, apparently, though no one was dancing. Honey asked the bartender if he'd be a darling and turn down the music. When he did, the relief was profound, like surviving an avalanche.

"Goodness, I don't know how you deal with that sound, night after night."

"I go into a zone," the bartender said.

Honey watched closely as the man made up her order. Over the years, she'd come to rate bartenders by the way they splashed the liquor into a glass, and this man had a very good splash. When he applied the vermouth, it was with a swiveling tilt of his wrist. And the olives were deposited gently, like babies into bathwater.

Nathan asked if they should take a seat.

"I suppose we should, yes."

There was a mirror behind the bar, and Honey's impulse was to check her hair, but the place was too dark to see much of anything.

"It's like a cave in here. Has there been a power outage?"

"Our patrons prefer it on the shadowy side," the bartender said with a wink as he set down the drinks.

When Honey lifted her glass, Nathan lifted his and held it aloft. "I hope you find what you're looking for." After a modest clink, they sipped with their heads bowed, as if praying. The gin lacked nuance. But the second sip was better, and the third better yet—the law of inferior liquor.

Now that it was quiet, Honey realized that the two men at the end of the bar were chatting in Spanish. And now that her eyes had adjusted, she saw that they were not, in fact, men at all. Despite the crew cuts and the work shirts, their hips were robustly feminine. There was also, on one of their collars, a plastic pin of interlocked Venuses. Honey had always liked the symbol. She'd actually considered becoming a lesbian during her early days at Bryn Mawr, but the idea had been reaction more than truth.

As she watched the garrulous couple, she sensed that they were not lovers but friends. They looked like a pair of plumbers shooting the shit after work. Their jeans were preposterously baggy, no doubt in an attempt to disguise their figures. Honey didn't judge the women, since it was clear that their attire wasn't the result of laziness. This was more like art. The pair seemed perfect in their mannish duds. The inversion suited them, possibly because their outward form matched their sense of self—which was what all fashion aspired toward.

Sipping her drink, a little less shyly now, Honey felt confident she'd come to the right place. Still, she was out of her element. She glanced at the woman seated at the high table near the back of the room. Her delicate doll-like body was adorned with what seemed to be liquid silver, a dress that collected and reflected the limited supply of light in the room. The woman moved slowly, patiently nursing a glass of ruby wine. When she noticed Honey staring, she lifted a hand in greeting. Honey waved back.

"Do you know her?" asked Nathan.

"No, I was just being friendly." She touched her cashmere for comfort and then glanced toward the entrance.

Nathan caught her impatience. "It's early," he said. "I'm sure more people will show up eventually."

Honey nodded and sipped, willing herself toward equanimity. Michael would come or he wouldn't. Whatever fate decreed, there was nothing she could do to change it. It was pointless to worry. Besides, she was being inattentive to Nathan, who was on his best behavior. She asked him what he was working on. "Any new paintings?"

"Always," he said. "Sometimes I have three or four going at a time."

"More dogs?"

"I'm afraid so. I'm kind of obsessed with them right now."

"Me too," said Honey, thinking of Corrado, not to mention the man next door.

"I didn't know you had a dog."

"I don't." When Nathan looked confused, she said, "Half the things I say are nonsense. Sometimes it's best to ignore me."

Nathan smiled and said he'd rather not. "I like listening to you."

Honey feigned immunity to the compliment and changed the subject back to the young man's paintings.

"Have you been working as an artist a long time?"

"Well, like I said, I do other work as well, to keep me going—but, yeah, I've been drawing or painting since I was a kid."

"And you mentioned writing a thesis on Redon. So I gather you went to art school?"

"In Rhode Island." He said this quietly, and then repeated it—"Rhode Island, yup"—this second time mainly to himself.

Honey suspected there was more to Rhode Island than art school; something about Nathan's face and tone suggested he'd lost something there, or left something behind. There was a sadness in his eyes—she'd seen it before. She didn't press him on the subject. Instead she returned to Redon.

"What was your take on him? In your thesis."

"Well, it started with a quote of his. Something like, 'I've made an art according to myself.' And so I was thinking about that, but also how he has all these mythological references in his work. You know, stories from the Greeks, from Christianity."

"From Eastern religions, too," said Honey.

"Yes. Definitely. But my point was, he didn't treat any of these ideas academically, say like the Pre-Raphaelites. It was much more personal for Redon, much more connected to his own life."

"To be honest," Honey admitted, "I really don't know that much about him, outside his work."

"Well, he had epilepsy as a child and was sent to live with an uncle in the country, which is where he started to draw. Ten years old when he first picked up a piece of charcoal. And then for the next forty years he worked only in black and white."

Honey exclaimed that she loved Redon's *noirs*. "That large winged head of the boy floating in the sky over the little boat—so wonderful."

"But I think it also speaks to the torments of an unhappy childhood," argued Nathan. "It's almost like he had some kind of psychic resistance to color."

"Still," countered Honey, "he did make his way to color eventually. Think of the paintings he made when he was older. And then all those glorious flowers he did at the end of his life."

"But they have a sadness, too."

"I'm not sure I agree," said Honey. "They're melancholy, and that's not the same thing. Melancholy is the song of life. Besides, I've lived with a

Redon for a long time, and I don't think he's so easily interpreted—that's the beauty of him. You have to surrender to the dream he presents. And in my experience, he seems to want you to dream *with* him. Ultimately, the viewer gets to choose her own story."

She was rambling again, and Nathan was staring at her like a dumbstruck squirrel on a country road. Just as she was about to apologize for monopolizing the conversation, the door flew open and a crowd of people blew inside, dressed in such exuberant colors that it was as if they'd appeared to bolster Honey's argument. There was even a fellow whose hair was dyed to mimic peacock feathers. Another arrival had a harlot skirt stretched over an enormous bottom, a sartorial sin one could almost forgive due to the skirt's color, a stunning Turkish blue. Plus, she—*he? they?*—had the legs to pull it off. Something about the crowd reminded Honey of former days. Two of the gals had hair that cascaded to their shoulders in luxuriant swoops, like Breck girls from the fifties.

Honey suddenly felt self-conscious in her black turtleneck and proletarian slacks. Rarely, anymore, did one see people having fun with fashion, and Honey sensed she'd missed an opportunity. She should have worn a Florence, or the Sies Marjan with the purple cape. As it stood, she and Nathan probably looked like tourists.

As another wave of revelers entered the bar, Honey could briefly see outside, see that the sun had set. Perhaps the customers here were vampires. Or, to be more generous, night-blooming flowers. Unfortunately, Michael wasn't among them.

"I have a picture of my grandnephew," she said to Nathan. "Maybe I should show it to the bartender?"

"You should."

Honey pulled the phone from her bag and found the photograph— the one Rina had texted. Nathan put on his glasses, and she showed it to him first, before signaling the bald man behind the bar.

"Another?" he asked.

"Not yet, dear. But would you mind if I asked you some questions?"

"That depends. Are you a cop?"

"Aren't you adorable? No, I'm just looking for a family member. If you'd be a doll and look at this photograph . . ." She held up the phone.

The man leaned in and squinted.

"You have to imagine him with longer hair," said Honey. "And somewhat older. And a little thinner."

"Sorry. Doesn't look familiar."

"Are you sure?"

"He's cute, so I'd remember."

"He's less cute now," Honey explained, "a little more rough around the edges."

"Story of my life," the bartender said. He glanced again at the picture but offered nothing more.

The place was getting crowded, and Honey let the man get back to work.

"Why don't I ask our neighbors?" Nathan gestured toward the plumbers at the end of the bar.

Honey handed over her phone, and then watched as Nathan approached the pair and spoke to them in Spanish. He spoke it beautifully; perhaps it was his native tongue. Nathan *Flores*, wasn't it? He was clearly charming the plumbers; they were smiling. And then he showed them the phone.

"Mis amigos, ¿conocen a este apuesto joven?"

They shook their heads but remained curious, asking some questions of their own.

When Nathan pointed toward Honey, the women lifted their beers in her direction. Then one of them spoke to Nathan. "Saludos a la dama. Ella es muy convincente."

After the painter returned, Honey said, "I gather they don't know him, but what was that last comment? My Spanish is a little rusty."

"It was nothing." Nathan was suppressing a smile.

"What? Tell me."

"She said you were very convincing."

"*Ha*. Well, I try." Honey raised her empty glass toward her admirers.

"You want another?" asked Nathan.

"No, thank you. I'm really not much of a drinker."

As soon as she said this, though, she realized that when the young man phoned the other night, she'd been absolutely plastered. Luckily he didn't call her on it.

"Do you mind if I get one?" was all he said. "Though maybe I shouldn't, since I'm driving."

"Please don't be sensible on my account."

"You sure?"

"Yes—have one. And, what the hell, I'll have a second too. Drown my disappointment."

"Don't give up. We can stay as long as you want."

"The truth is, I'm not sure I'll last much longer."

"I'll keep you awake," Nathan said.

As he leaned in to order the drinks, another customer approaching the bar banged into Honey's shoulder. When Honey turned, she saw a Turkish-blue moon.

"Excuse me, dear, but would you mind not putting your tush in my face?"

The woman shifted her stance. "Sorry." She seemed genuinely apologetic. "This bar is way too small, and I'm just desperate for my Choo-Choo."

"Is that a cocktail?" asked Honey.

"You've never had a Choo-Choo?"

"I haven't, no."

As the woman began to extoll the charms of vodka and chocolate milk, another woman approached the bar to inquire what was up with the music.

"Oh, that's my fault," said Honey. "I asked that it be turned down."

"Why?" Turkish Blue asked with a clown-school pout. "I always feel naked without music."

"Your outfit appears to be doing most of the work," said Honey.

"Isn't it great? Twelve bucks at Goodwill."

Turkish blue turned fully toward Honey at this point. A bulge at the front of her skirt was proudly on display.

"What a bargain," said Honey, excusing herself and returning to Nathan.

"Do you wanna leave?" he whispered. "I'm sensing you're not comfortable here."

"I'm fine, darling. I've been to the rodeo before."

The truth was, she couldn't wait to get out of the place. Not because of the culture of blur, of otherness—she was comfortable with all that. It was just the press of bodies, and also the fact that she'd started to doubt her intuition. What the hell was she doing, playing Ms. Marple, not to mention getting tipsy with the painter?

Still, she picked up her second round and sipped. The bad gin tasted like heaven. Christ, what she wouldn't do for a cigarette! Despite her attempt to play it cool, a sigh escaped her vigilance.

"What's wrong?" asked Nathan.

She wished she could tell him, say *I'm sad, I'm tired*. But if she went anywhere near the truth, she might start crying.

"I was just thinking about what you were saying earlier, in regard to our friend Redon." She asked the young man what he thought of *The Cyclops*, one of Redon's most famous pieces. She said that in her opinion no artist had ever painted a sweeter monster.

"Don't change the subject," Nathan said. "I can see that's a habit of yours. I have plenty to say about *The Cyclops*, but that's not why we're here."

"Why are we here?" asked Honey, hoping the boy wasn't about to make a romantic overture.

"We're here for your grandnephew, right? So let's show the photo to some other people, see if anyone knows him."

"You guys looking for someone?"

It was Turkish Blue, still lingering, sipping her dreadful sludge-colored cocktail.

"Yes," said Nathan, picking up Honey's phone and refreshing the image.

Honey both liked and didn't like how the young man was taking control. In some ways it was a relief, but Honey also knew that a man sometimes did this as a kind of mating dance—the puffed-up dramatics of a frigatebird.

"My friend is looking for a relative," Nathan said. "We'd appreciate your help."

Friend? We? Honey felt this language to be a bit presumptuous.

But then Turkish Blue examined the photo and said, "He looks *sort of* familiar. But isn't he a little young to be coming to a bar?"

"He's a bit older now," Honey chimed in.

"What's his name?"

"Michael."

"I can't say for sure. Why don't you ask Teena?"

"Teena?"

"The owner. That's her in the back." Turkish Blue pointed to the tiny woman in the silver dress.

"Do you want me to go talk to her?" asked Nathan.

"No. I'll do it." Honey took back the phone.

"You sure you don't want my help?"

"I'm not an invalid, dear." Her tone was sharp, perhaps unfairly, but she didn't apologize. She lowered herself from the stool—no easy task making it look elegant with an arthritic hip.

"I'll be back," she announced, setting off, martini glass in hand.

The bar was humming now. In addition to the more colorful customers, there were several businessmen in suits, as well as a group of bearded men who looked as if they worked for the forest service, two of them in khaki shorts and ragg wool socks. The common denominator of this crowd was not to be fathomed.

As Honey made her way to the back of the room, she felt herself limping, and now that she was in motion she was doubly aware of the gin; the room lurched oceanically. In a bid for decorum, she moved slowly, a bride stalking the altar.

When the tiny woman saw Honey approaching, she gestured toward the empty seat at the small round table.

"Thank you," said Honey, "but I'm fine standing." She wasn't keen on climbing onto the dauntingly vertiginous chair.

"Please," the woman said, "I'd like it if you joined me."

Honey obliged, and once she was situated on the mountaintop she saw things differently. First of all, the woman was not as young as she'd seemed. From across the room, she'd appeared to be in her thirties. But she was clearly closer to fifty. And her silver dress was slightly worn, less transcendent in close-up. There were patches of sequins missing, a disco ball with mange.

Still, what couldn't be denied was that this woman was lovely, almost alarmingly so—the symmetry of her face too perfect, the lips too full. Honey suspected surgery.

"I noticed you before," the woman said.

She had an accent—a mix of elements Honey couldn't quite place. Asian? Eastern European—Czech, perhaps? Either could account for the almond-sliver eyes—that is, if the eyes hadn't been pulled.

"Yes, I noticed you too," said Honey.

"And you've come here looking for someone?"

"How did you know?"

"I saw you showing the phone. So who have you lost? You're clearly heartbroken."

Honey made a sound, almost a scoff. Mainly because the accusation was true.

"My grandnephew is missing—well, not missing—but, anyway, I thought this was the sort of bar he might frequent."

"Why is that?" The woman's question was slightly spiked, and Honey was careful to say the right thing, to avoid offense.

"Apparently my grandnephew is struggling with his identity."

"*He* is struggling with this—or *you* are struggling?"

Honey found herself perplexed, as if in the presence of the Sphinx.

"And you have a picture?" the woman said.

"I do, yes—and forgive me, I haven't properly introduced myself. I'm Honey."

"Teena. Two *e*'s, no *i*."

The woman extended her hand and Honey shook it, noting the expertly manicured nails lacquered into orange flames, the same color as the door.

"I really do admire your establishment," Honey said.

"And I, your cashmere. It is Mongolian?"

"Yes."

Teena smiled and asked to see the photograph.

Honey put the phone on the table. "Just tap the screen."

Teena did—and as she looked at the image, her face betrayed nothing.
"Do you know him?"

The woman didn't answer, and Honey asked again.

"I know him well," Teena said quietly. "But if you are family, then I
don't wish to speak to you."

"Why is that?"

"Don't play games. I think what you've done is disgusting."

"Excuse me?" protested Honey. "I think you misunderstand who I
am. I'm not involved with the rest of the family."

"You're Michael's aunt?"

"Great-aunt, yes."

Teena still seemed suspicious. "He never mentioned you."

"Well, we're not exactly close, to be honest. I've been out of the picture
for a while. But I very much want to help him. I know what it's like to be
in his position, so . . ."

"How do you *know*? Cis people always think they know everything."

Honey wasn't quite following. "I'm his grandfather's sister, that's
true—but I'm not sure of the relevance of that. I just want to be supportive, since I know Michael's having a hard time. Surely it's a very confusing moment."

"Confusing for you, maybe. *I* am not confused. And neither is Mica."

"Listen, perhaps I don't have the right language, but really I'm a very
open-minded person. At least I think I am."

When Honey queried about the correct pronoun to use, Teena said,
"This is not the issue at the moment. Besides, Mica is—"

"I changed my own name once," Honey blurted. "Not that I mean to
equivocate, but . . ."

As she continued to babble, the woman stared coolly.

"And I really *do* want to help," repeated Honey.

Teena slid the phone back across the table. "A little late for that now,
isn't it?"

"What do you mean?"

"You honestly know nothing of the family, what they've done?"

"Well, I know about the brother," Honey confessed. "I heard there
was a fight that ended with Michael getting punched."

Teena waved her hand dismissively. "That was nothing. Nothing compared to the father."

"I know about that, too," admitted Honey, "about the argument. I spoke to the boy's mother and she was very upset."

Teena laughed, a frightening sound.

"The mother is no better. Watching her husband do that to her son."

"Yes, I gather it was quite the nasty argument."

"Why do you keep using that word—*argument*? It was no argument. His father—"

At this point the music in the bar began to pound again. Honey couldn't hear what Teena was saying. But then the woman raised her hand in a sharp gesture, and the music returned to its former volume. Teena took a sip of wine before repeating herself.

"The father attacked him."

"No, the brother is the one who did that."

"Who is telling this story—you or me? Did Mica come to *you* after the 'argument'? No. He came to me."

"Is he all right?"

Teena's breath was audible as she reached for an oval purse that resembled a Fabergé egg. She clicked it open and pulled out a phone.

"You have shown me a picture. Now I show you a picture."

She swiped her flame-tipped fingers across the screen, then handed the phone to Honey.

"I don't have my glasses, but . . ."

Honey squinted and saw her grandnephew as she knew him, with longer hair. There was makeup too, smeared and rather ridiculous. Honey gasped. Not makeup, but blood.

"Scroll," Teena said calmly. "There's more."

Honey did as she was told, and saw a detailed shot of the boy's face, the left eyelid cut open, and then another in which his gaping mouth exposed a missing tooth.

"I took them, thinking maybe I show the police. But Mica says no. He doesn't want me to get in trouble."

"Where is he?" asked Honey.

"I let him stay in the back. I had to call a doctor. A friend of mine. You are aware the family took him off the insurance?"

Honey's hands were trembling. "Yes." She asked if she could speak to her grandnephew.

"He's already gone."

"Do you know where?"

Teena's gaze was unflinching, a psychic X-ray.

"You can trust me," said Honey.

"I trust no one. Especially *family*." The way Teena used the word, it was as if she knew something about Corrado, about his associations.

"As I said, I'm not part of the *family*. In fact, I'd like nothing more than for Michael to separate himself from them entirely."

"Not always so easy," said Teena. "I know people like this. Where I come from . . ." She paused, and almost seemed to stop breathing. "After my surgery, things were very difficult."

It took Honey a moment to understand what the woman was talking about. But then she grasped it. Beneath Teena's sublime femininity was the ghost of another life. Though, somehow, this only made the perfection of her face more poignant.

"My father was the same," Teena said, looking down at her hands. "He used the same words. Threatened to kill me if I ever came back."

"Is that what Corrado said?"

Teena looked up, as if annoyed. "I don't think you know this man very well."

"I know him," said Honey. "Please tell me where Michael is."

"Why do you want to help? You say you are not close to him—so why?"

Honey wasn't sure what to tell the woman; the history was too complicated. "I suppose I'm sick and tired of the same things happening over and over. I'm just *sick* of it."

Teena briefly shut her eyes. "I have friends," she murmured sadly. "Mica's going to them."

"In New Jersey?"

"Are you not listening to me? I told him not to come back here. I gave him some money."

"Well, I'd still like to speak to him."

Teena shrugged. "Not possible."

"Please."

"He'll be fine—don't worry. Mica is actually a very happy person. In his heart he's happy with who he is. You say he's having a hard time, but that's only because of you."

"Me?"

"Well, maybe not you—but your people."

As Honey looked at the woman, she could feel the tight cord stretched between them, which was the effort they were both making not to cry. "I don't understand," she muttered.

"What don't you understand?"

"Life. *Men.*"

"How is that possible? You are an old woman."

Honey felt her body stiffen. But it was merely reflex, the prick of vanity. The pain passed quickly and was replaced by gratitude, that someone had the balls to say it so directly.

"Yes, I am," said Honey. "I'm eighty-two."

Teena softened slightly and raised her eyebrows. "But you have a young lover, no?"

"Excuse me?"

Teena gestured toward the bar, where the painter was peering at them, his eyes full of concern.

"No," said Honey, "he's just a . . ."

Suddenly she felt it even more—her age, her utter confusion. She turned away from Nathan without acknowledging him, and asked Teena to take down her number. "I'd be grateful if you called me, if you hear from Michael."

"He may not want me to call you."

"That's fair. But if he does . . ."

Teena nodded and produced a pen and paper from her purse. "For your number. I don't want it on my phone," she explained.

Honey began to write, but after setting down the first three numerals she found herself unable to continue. Her hands were still shaking.

"It's all right," Teena said. "Here's my card. In a week or so, you call me. Mica is driving, so it'll take him some time to get there."

"California?" asked Honey.

When Teena didn't answer, Honey looked down at the business card. *The Shelter. Teena Novak*. It seemed a talisman, the white satin embossed with orange letters. Impulsively Honey grasped the woman's hand. There was something important she needed to say—but suddenly she couldn't remember.

"It's okay," Teena said. "I believe you."

A warm wind blew into her face, whatever kindness it carried not meant for humans. Still, there were humans everywhere, carousing on the sidewalk, many of them laughing. Someone shouted, "Ilaria!"—a name no one called her except her father. When a hand touched her shoulder, she turned, ready for a fight.

But it was only Mr. Hal—the relief so profound that she embraced him. He seemed surprised, stepping back to adjust his glasses.

No, not Hal. Hal was old, and the man before her was young. But she knew this one too—didn't she? He had a very pretty name, something to do with flowers.

* * *

In the car she told him everything. Well, not everything; just everything about Michael. The painter made no attempt to comfort her, which in itself was a kind of comfort. That he didn't offer assurances or anything with feathers made her feel she was with someone she could trust. At one point, when referring to the boy's parents, he used the same word as Teena. *Disgusting.* Honey thanked him.

"For what?"

"For being outraged."

"How could anyone not be?"

"You'd be surprised," she said.

When they were parked at the curb, neither made a move to get out of the Thunderbird. They only stared through the windshield, at dark lawns glazed by lamplight. Honey turned to see the little tree Jocelyn had planted. As if to taunt, the sapling had finally begun to thrive, the last late blooms emerging in silver pink and the first leaves coming in, the impossible green of innocence. Trees were thieves, weren't they? They stole precious things—air, water, sunlight—yet they weren't criminals.

In nature there was no morality. All the rape and pillage served the common good.

From somewhere came the sound of music. For a moment Honey thought Nathan had turned on the radio, but then she realized the noise was coming from Jocelyn's house. No discernible melody, only the heartbeat of the bass, a pounding like the music at the Shelter.

Jocelyn and Lee were no doubt rolling about, flesh to flesh, howling like animals. Or maybe he was hurting her. Honey put her hand to her mouth, but it was too late. A sob erupted violently, like sickness. And then it happened again. Honey was unable to control herself. And since she didn't like being out of control, she did something she hadn't done since she was a child. She pinched herself to stop the tears, dug her nails into the soft flesh on the side of her hand. After several deep breaths she managed to speak. "This isn't me," she explained. "I'm not myself."

The young man said nothing, though he looked at her without flinch or fear. He seemed to have no wish to escape the dreadful position she'd put him in.

Honey, too, wanted to be brave. And since she couldn't bear the idea of being alone, she asked the young man—not caring if it sounded like a pickup line—if he'd like to come inside and see her Redon.

* * *

In the kitchen they drank large glasses of water, gulping shamelessly. Perhaps they drank to avoid speaking. Even after putting the glasses in the sink, they remained silent, the length of this silence impossible for Honey to gauge, due to her tipsiness. Finally, she asked Nathan if he'd like something to eat, and was relieved when he said no. She would have felt like his mother making him a snack.

She turned on another set of lights and gestured toward the painting. "Did I tell you I had a Morandi too?"

Nathan nodded and approached the piece. His blank expression Honey read as awe—but then he grimaced.

"I've never really gotten Morandi. I mean, I think it's beautiful—the colors and the composition, but, I don't know, it doesn't drive me crazy, the way I want a painting to. Maybe it's just too calm."

"And what's wrong with that?" said Honey. "There has never been *enough* calm, and there never will be. Not on this planet."

Nathan stepped closer to the canvas. "Those pale blues and yellows are pretty great. Like something you'd want to spread on toast."

"Exactly," said Honey. She stood beside the young man and told him a bit about the history of the piece, how and when she'd acquired it.

What she really wanted to talk about, though, was the light in the painting—her interpretation of it, anyway, which was that the light on the objects was not the sun, but the glare of consciousness, perhaps Morandi reckoning with mortality.

Instead, she spoke about the arrangement of the jars and bottles on the deftly rendered tabletop.

"I've always seen the painting, I suppose, as a sort of metaphysical chess game, in which Morandi has forced chaos into checkmate. When I look at those objects, they seem very brave, very intelligent."

Nathan tilted his head, puppy-like, as if to consider this idea. His eyes were eager, and as he fell into the painting, Honey did too—though for her it wasn't a painting, but an old friend.

All her life, she'd been turning something in her mind, an agitating math whose solution seemed a matter of life and death. Perhaps it was an attempt to factor out violence. There'd been no success until she'd entered the world of art, of paintings. Morandi, in particular, provided a consistent charge of hope. To her this canvas was more than a still life; it was a history painting. Those sweetly colored bottles stood there in a line—familiar, mundane, huddled in a way that might be interpreted as frightened. And yet they were brothers, sisters, working together to resist something in the atmosphere surrounding them, something terrible.

"I think it speaks to what humans are incapable of—selflessness, harmony." She said that, in a way, she saw the bottles and jars as sages. "Think of those Tibetan thangkas, with the rows of bodhisattvas, all those heavenly beings and guardians who refuse to dissolve into the void because they feel compelled to protect us."

When Nathan turned to her, she felt slightly breathless. "I do go on, don't I?"

"No. I love the way you talk about art."

"I have my lines," she said. "All very well rehearsed."

"Great lines, though. You have a unique way of putting things."

"Yes, I've been told that before, and it wasn't always a compliment."

Nathan studied the Morandi again, and then he surprised her by asking if she wanted to talk more about her grandnephew.

"I don't," she said. What the young man didn't understand was that she was, in fact, still talking about her family. *Guardians, protectors*— things the Fazzingas had failed to be. She, too, had failed. What had she ever done for Michael, let alone her own child?

Honey steered her heart back to the painting. "Do you see the curving neck of the green vase, the way it leans toward the bottle next to it— the extraordinary kindness of that?"

Nathan sighed appreciatively, then asked if she believed in God.

Honey rubbed her eyes. "I'm not sure I know how to answer that question anymore. If you'd asked me a year ago, I would have said yes. Hell, if you'd asked me yesterday . . ."

The painter was quiet again, though now it felt strained. Honey glanced at the clock. "It's late," she said. "I'm sure you need to go."

"I thought you were going to show me the Redon."

"You still want to see it?"

"Are you kidding? Of course. Unless you're tired?"

She was. She was dead. But she told the boy: "I'm never too tired to talk about art."

* * *

When they were in the bedroom, though, she said nothing. Nathan said nothing. It was Redon who took the floor. Uncannily, he seemed to be speaking about the two people standing in front of him. *Don't pretend*, he seemed to say.

The accusation was complicated. *Don't pretend you're not alive* went alongside *Don't pretend you're not miserable*. The creature standing on the cliff had never looked more lewd, more beautiful; the woman in the sky had never seemed closer to the sun, her tiny feathers more incandescent.

"The flowers," Nathan said, referring to the eccentric overlay of blossoms stitched across the sky, like psychic weather.

"Brilliant, aren't they?" said Honey.

Nathan took a step back and sat on the bed. He shook his head. "It's incredible. Why have I never seen this before? I mean, like in a book or a catalog?"

Honey explained that the piece had never been exhibited. "I've always been selfish with it."

What she didn't tell him was that there'd been some doubt about the painting's provenance, a rumor that it might be stolen. This had put the auction house Honey worked for in a tricky position. They couldn't risk selling the piece publicly, and it had sat in limbo for nearly a year—at which point Honey, using her inheritance from Hal, had been able to acquire it. Under the table, shall we say?

When Nathan asked the title, she sat beside him. "*Le Dilemme de l'Ange.*"

He nodded. "Yes. Wow. The Angel's Dilemma. It's fantastic." And then he laughed. "But I can't believe you keep it *here.*"

"What do you mean?"

"Most people would put it where everyone could see it. Show it off. The Morandi, too. I mean, who keeps a painting like that in the kitchen, and *that* close to a stove?"

"I've always lived dangerously," said Honey. She tossed this off lightly, but when she looked again at the little beast flying toward the sun, she began to cry.

Nathan hesitated only briefly, before taking her hand.

*   *   *

Frozen. Burning. How is it possible, she wonders, for two bodies not moving, barely touching, to give off this much heat?

Don't pretend you're not alive.

Don't pretend you're not miserable.

In the morning, she was afraid to open her eyes—the presence beside her undeniable. For several minutes she lay there paralyzed, a plank of wood over a bottomless pit. But then she looked and saw that she was still in her clothing. The same went for Nathan. Surely nothing had happened. Still, it was embarrassing to see him lying on his side, as if he'd fallen asleep looking at her. He slumbered on, his breathing slow and easy, unlike Honey's.

She slipped from the bed and soft-stepped into the bathroom, where another surprise awaited her. In the mirror her face was unforgivably bloomy, flooded with color. The whites of her eyes were clear, as if they too had nothing to repent. Her black turtleneck, though, was despicably wrinkled and covered with lint, white specks that made her think of insects. She closed the bathroom door and removed the sweater, after which she donned the terrycloth robe hanging near the tub. The thing was pink and fluffy, with scalloped cuffs. Honey hoped it was sufficiently old-ladyish to frighten the young man, or at least knock some sense into him.

Or perhaps it was she who needed to be knocked.

Since there was no possibility of risking a shower, she only washed her face and brushed her teeth, did a bit of damage control on her hair. She applied no makeup. Her plan was to go back into the bedroom and wake the painter. She'd make up an excuse, some emergency that required her to leave the house immediately. The last thing she wanted was a fuss or some dreadful postmortem. The night was over, and they'd be wise to leave it behind them.

But when she returned to the bedroom, she paused. Dawn was creeping in, a terrible elixir of light whose tiny streams touched not only the painter's brow but the bedside table beside him. The paradox was troubling—the boy sleeping peacefully, while only inches away, in a drawer, lay a loaded gun.

Honey stood there, staring—and as the seconds passed, it was less at the drawer, and more at the boy. The *man*. The clever light had found his wrinkles, especially those around his eyes and mouth. They were not unlovely; the blade of time had not yet cut too deeply. Besides, it was different for men, whose wrinkles were often judged as war paint, while a woman's were judged as scars.

Honey dared to move a little closer, since the painter seemed nowhere near to waking. From his mouth a sound like tiny waves crashing upon a shore. She could see now that his eyes were moving under the lids, a shuttle weaving dreams. She took in the pretty lashes, long and dark. And the lips, like something carved from stone, with a subtle upturn at the corners that was almost feline.

Beauty was often said to be relative, or subjective—but really, it wasn't. There was clearly a hierarchy, and Honey placed Nathan somewhere near the top, a place she'd once lived. His adorable hair was mussed, sticking up on one side like a horn, and as the sun forced more reality into the room she could see a touch of gray just above his left ear. Honey felt grateful for that—less like a monster.

She knew she had to wake the painter and ask him to leave, but she stole another moment. Because when would she have this again? Another soul breathing in her room. A warm body in her bed.

What was terrible to admit was that she was attracted to this man—that even at her age, birds of desire still nested in her belly. Ridiculous, to have this kind of hunger, at eighty-two. Did other women her age feel this way? None of them ever spoke of it. Perhaps they'd learned to hide such feelings. Honey's mother, other female relatives too—all of them at a certain point had ceased to be sexual. By their sixties, the clothes went drab, the body shop was closed. Often they padded on the calories—a way, it seemed, to protect themselves, to keep the men away. At the same time, the men in her family—her father, her uncle Vinch— had stayed slim and dapper, continued, even in their later years, to have steady goomahs, not to mention the occasional prostitute in Atlantic City.

It was a disheartening dilemma, possibly a disgusting one. Honey escaped it by forcing her mind back to Corrado. Back to Michael. Deciding what to do about the two of them was where she needed to put her energies, not in reveries about sexual politics. Though, of course, the two subjects were related.

She touched the painter's shoulder and gently shook it. He seemed unwilling to rise from his dream. She shook him again, harder, and this time he rolled onto his back and opened his eyes.

"Ilaria," he said, blinking, startled—a look of cosmic wonder, as if he'd just been born.

S he was the patron saint of hoboes, of the falsely accused, of midwives and single mothers. Also under her wing were or-phans, the mentally ill, and prostitutes. It was a lot to take on—which was probably why the statue of her looked like an exhausted washerwoman who'd done everyone's laundry but her own. She was dressed in a dingy brocade that seemed to be stitched of rags and wilted flowers.

The last time Honey had been in this church was for Florence Fini's funeral. The priest, a chubby little man with a sweaty face, had delivered an uninspiring eulogy. He spoke of Florence as if she were a cardboard cutout that needed to be propped up by clichés. *Bore her struggles with a stony grace. A devoted wife, a loving mother. Led a quiet, humble life.* No doubt these things were true, but there was so much more to Florence—or at least the Florence Honey had known. Where was the girl who made the most gorgeous dresses; who played the piano as if pos-sessed by the devil? And what wonderful legs she'd had! Perfection in stockings, and when bared on the beach the pale mounds of her calves were like scoops of vanilla ice cream.

Long gone, those days. That girl. In the church Honey was alone.

After Nathan left the house, Honey's nerves had felt frayed, jumpy as live wires. She'd thought the chill of the old stone church might sub-due her. Unfortunately, it had the opposite effect; it disturbed her. The cold, empty church only brought to mind her own chilliness, the way she'd treated Nathan that morning. She hadn't been mean, exactly; she'd repaid the young man's kindness with expressions of gratitude, though she offered these only as a prelude to her main point—which was that their friendship was untenable. She'd said this to him before, but her reasons, now, were entirely different. The first time she'd rejected him, it was because she'd been offended by his behavior; this time, because she was offended by her own. If not her behavior, then her feelings, those ridiculous tremors of desire.

Plus, she really didn't want the painter involved in the tar pit of her family. She'd told him it would be better if she dealt with the situation herself. When he said, "I'm happy to help in any way I can," she'd thanked him, saying he'd already done enough—and when he persisted in his offer, it made her angry. She told him to stop being so damn nice. Honey didn't trust niceness; she never had. And at this point in her life niceness would be of little use. In fact, it stood counter to what she needed to accomplish.

Besides, people as sweet as Nathan needed to learn a lesson. She was simply doing the boy a favor. He would get nowhere as an artist without a little grit.

Despite Honey's sharpness, the painter had never risen to defensiveness. He'd only looked at her with those mournful, long-lashed eyes, and accepted her verdict—though at the door he'd hesitated, asking if he might kiss her goodbye.

"Absolutely not," she said, hiding her confusion by turning it into a weapon. She told the young man that he should go and play with someone his own age.

"Fine," he said, finally getting it, finally showing some grit, though this grit was thrown in Honey's face. "I thought you'd be more open-minded," he muttered as he turned and walked away.

After Honey closed the door, she went back to the bedroom. She walked in circles like a madwoman, counterclockwise, as if she could undo the past. Even if she could take herself back just a few months, to the morning that Michael had come to the house and broken the vase— that would be enough. Before Nicky died, before the car thieves knocked her to the ground, before she met Nathan, before Corrado showed his true and disgusting colors.

Finally, sick of pacing, Honey sat on the bed and took the gun from the drawer, held it in her hand, as if to weigh it. It felt good in her grip, strangely familiar, not so different from the spray nozzle she used to water the azaleas. It was a friend, this gun; it could take her home.

Such sentiments, though, were short-lived. Because the more she looked at the gun, the more it seemed that its intentions might be different from her own. Apparently the gun thought there were other people it could be aimed at, much better targets than Honey.

Frightened, she'd thrust the thing back into the drawer and driven straight to St. Margaret's.

* * *

As she approached a dark alcove near the front of the church, a tiny grotto where the Virgin Mother lived, Honey recalled the promise she'd made to Teresa Lioni—to light a candle for Angela's soul. The dead woman was not undeserving of respect. Honey realized that what she admired most about Angela Carini was her anger—her lifelong decision to hold Honey accountable for her sins. Perhaps it would be wise to light a whole bank of candles for Carini.

Entering the votive garden, Honey saw that there were no longer the elegant burning tapers, but something that looked like a pinball machine: a metal table into which one inserted coins to ignite electric flickers of light. Half of the fraudulent candles were already turned on, and they blinked erratically, as if suffering from brain damage.

Honey took several coins from her purse and inserted enough to light three flickers. One for Angela, one for Florence, and one for Michael. The Virgin Mother, stationed above the ghastly arcade, seemed indifferent. Though she was dressed in a finer gown than the patron saint, she somehow appeared less pious, placidly staring down at her prayerful hands as if considering a manicure. Honey took more coins from her bag and lit another flicker for her grandnephew. The poor thing, driving away to start a new life with a missing tooth.

"What do you think of that?" Honey asked the Virgin, who surely had a lot to say about fathers and sons.

But the Virgin said nothing. She never did.

* * *

Back at home, Honey parked on the street, planning to leave again shortly to pay a visit to Corrado. But first she needed to eat something. Her blood sugar was low; she felt confused and wobbly. As she approached the steps that led to her front door, she noticed that the Talavera pot in which she'd planted a gardenia was broken; a large chunk had fallen off, exposing dirt and roots. "Jesus Christ," she muttered. Could this day get any worse? When she turned and saw that the matching pot, on the other side of the porch, was broken too, she immediately intuited the culprit.

Without any hesitation, she picked up a piece of the broken pottery and walked across the lawn toward the driveway next door. When she was a few feet from Lee's truck, she flung the shard at the side window. Unfortunately, only the Talavera broke, the one shard becoming two. The window, as far as Honey could tell, had suffered no damage.

Once she was back at the house she didn't even pour herself a glass of wine. She lay on the couch, defeated. The roof was creaking. It seemed there was an animal up there. Honey stared at the ceiling. *A cat? A squirrel?* No, larger than that. The creaking grew louder, as if at any moment the sky itself would come crashing down.

37 Preparations

She didn't go to Corrado's. What would be the point? Corrado would only deny the attack—and Rina would no doubt support her husband's lies. Besides, Honey knew if she went to visit the Fazzingas, she'd end up saying more than she should.

As Teena described it, Rina had watched Corrado attack Michael—watched from a window and done nothing. For most women—most humans, for that matter—this would seem implausible. But Honey was a Fazzinga, and her own history with that blood assured her that Teena had spoken the truth. Honey's mother, Honey herself, had witnessed cruelty—not only cruelty, but murder—and done nothing.

Honey had even witnessed brutality against her mother. Hadn't she seen the Great Pietro hold his wife's hand over a flaming stove and threaten to burn it? In the end he didn't do it, but his roughness was such that he'd broken the woman's wrist. Honey had been sitting right there in the kitchen—and despite her terror, she'd made desperate attempts to rationalize. Surely her mother must have done something to deserve this punishment. It made no sense otherwise. Why would a man hurt a woman for no reason? Honey's fear permitted faulty logic. That her father never struck her mother in the face had somehow made his violence seem less awful.

But what about Michael, who *was* struck in the face, and quite brutally? Was it possible that a person like him, to men like the Fazzingas, deserved even less respect than a woman?

Honey planned to get in touch with Teena that weekend, to inquire about the boy. Until then, there was nothing to do but wait. Wait and prepare.

* * *

She removed the paintings from the walls—not only the Redon and the Morandi but the lesser pieces too. The oil sketches by Gregory

Gillespie—phantasmagoric interiors, like funhouse Vermeers. She took down the three Diebenkorn drawings and the small pastel of a sleeping girl—French, eighteenth century, artist unknown. It was only a fraction of what she'd once owned. Much of her collection had been sold before leaving Los Angeles, some of it donated to museums.

Kneeling on the floor, she prepared the crates she'd had custom-made to ship the pieces to New Jersey. She used an electric screwdriver to remove the lids. Honey was proficient with the hand tool, having spent so many years, early in her career, working in the shipping department of Carrigan's. BP, her mentor, had always felt it was important not to get too fancy for the job. "We *sell* art," she'd often remind everyone, "we don't *make* it." That Honey could roll up her sleeves and get her hands dirty was all BP's doing.

As she thought of the woman now, in light of Michael's situation, Honey had a new insight about her. She realized that the woman she'd worked for in the fifties and sixties was more than simply a lesbian. BP had dressed like a man, walked like one, smoked like one. Sometimes she came to the office looking like a sergeant in the cavalry, black boots and polished buttons. And though this had often confused Honey, she saw now that these contradictions were what had made BP so inimitable: the complex wiring of her spirit. No wonder she despised those frilled-up Pre-Raphaelite maidens, like dolls that would never be removed from their boxes.

*   *   *

Later in the afternoon, Honey called her lawyer in Beverly Hills. She'd been with Johnny Lavin for more than forty years now; the man had to be close to ninety. His assistant intercepted the call, claiming Mr. Lavin was unavailable. "How can I help you?" the woman asked. Honey didn't feel comfortable talking to an underling about private things. Besides, she'd dealt with this assistant before and didn't like her.

"I'd prefer to talk directly to Johnny."

"Well, can I at least tell him what you're calling about?"

"Tell him that I need to make some changes to my will."

"Again?" the assistant muttered, doing little to hide her irritation.

"Do I know you?" said Honey. "I don't believe I know you."

The woman, a longtime employee of the law firm, understood a subtle attack. "All right, Ms. Fasinga, I'll have him call you back, but it probably won't be until the end of the week."

"Why don't we say *tomorrow* then," replied Honey, thanking the woman profusely and hanging up.

To be fair, the assistant's irritation was not unjustified. In the last decade, Honey had changed her will several times. After Lara and Suzanne died, she'd had to remove them as beneficiaries. Such a pity not to be able to leave money to the dead, petty cash for paradise. As for her current revision, Honey knew exactly what she wanted to do. First and foremost, the insignificant fifty thousand to Corrado and Rina would become a zero. As for Michael, Honey was still determined to leave him a sizable gift. The idea filled her with something almost like happiness, and this feeling was well worth all the unexamined and possibly foolish reasons behind the decision.

By the following afternoon, she still hadn't heard from her lawyer. But around four o'clock, there was a text from Jocelyn. I saw what you did.

It was like something from a juvenile horror flick. Honey ignored it.

A few minutes later there was another message. I won't tell Lee.

And then, after a longer interval: I miss you.

Finally, nearly an hour later, came a fourth: You were right.

To what was the girl referring? Right about what? About Honey's claim that Jocelyn lacked self-respect? About Lee? The advice not to wear overalls when one had massive breasts?

And as for I saw what you did—was that in reference to the pottery chucked at the pickup, or to the invasion of Jocelyn's mailbox? To be honest, Honey didn't care what Jocelyn was referring to. She had no time to care about the girl, at all. One imaginary child was enough.

* * *

The next morning, Honey decided to ring Teena. It was sooner than planned, but Honey was feeling impatient. "Have you heard from Michael?" she asked.

"I haven't," said Teena. "But I wasn't really expecting to."

"What do you mean? You said you'd tell me when you heard from him."

"I said, *if* I heard from him. Mica's on his own now. He's got a car, he's got the money I gave him. It's probably best if he forgets all about us."

Teena didn't say this coldly, and Honey understood what she meant— that to make one's way in life it was often necessary to burn some bridges. Still, Honey didn't like Teena including her in a list of those who should be forgotten.

"I have some money for Michael, too," she said, trying not to sound competitive.

"That's great," replied Teena. "But maybe you should have given it to him before he left."

"I'm not talking pocket change," explained Honey. "It's quite a bit. Enough that he won't need to feel restricted."

"He'll still feel *restricted*," said Teena. "Whatever he does, it won't be easy."

"I realize that."

"And though money is nice," the woman added, "it isn't everything."

An irritating cliché. Honey had no choice but to parry. "It's better than a punch in the face."

"I agree with you there," said Teena. "But, more than money, what I hope for Mica is love."

"Yes, of course. I hope that as well."

"Because he's a wonderful person. Wonderful musician, too. Have you heard him play?"

"I haven't, no."

In fact, Honey had no idea that Michael was a musician. She had a vague recollection, though, of seeing a guitar in the back of the BMW, the day the boy had come to the house. She also recalled that she'd asked him nothing about it. Another example of her selfishness.

"I actually have a notebook he left behind, with some lyrics in it," Teena said. "If you want, I can send it to you. There are other things in there, as well, that you might find interesting."

"I'd love to see it. I'll text you my address."

"He sings too, you know." Teena was clearly proud of Michael, and as she shared more of her thoughts—about the boy's music, his intelligence, his sense of humor—Honey felt a creeping shame, that she'd reduced her grandnephew to one dimension. Not unlike that horrible novelist writing about women in prison. As if all people were no more than a set of problems waiting to be solved. It was wrong to think of Michael as a victim, as she had the other day. Probably she'd put too much emphasis on the issue of the boy's gender. To even see it as an *issue* might be evidence of Honey's limited mindset. As Teena had said at the bar: Michael's only real problem was his family.

Still, Honey remained confused about the nature of the boy's body— or was it his soul?—and so she felt compelled to ask. "Do you know if he's planning to have surgery?"

Teena sighed, as if exasperated by the questions of a child. "It's not so black and white anymore. Boy and girl, girl and boy. Mica likes where he is—in between. He's not really interested in surgery. And the question itself is rude." Teena paused. "I could tell you more, but you're probably too old to understand."

Though Honey didn't like hearing such a thing, perhaps the woman was right. Surely at a certain point there was no moving forward for the old guard. And it was true that there were a great many things that confused her. She asked if she should still refer to Michael as *he*.

"Yes, he still uses that. He uses all of them. But as for his name, he prefers Mica now."

After an awkward patch of silence, Teena told Honey that she should come back to the bar sometime for a drink. "And bring your pretty friend, too."

"Thank you, but we had a bit of an argument."

"So come by yourself, then. And, really, you shouldn't worry about Mica. They can't hurt her now."

"You're right," said Honey, though in reality she didn't believe that Michael was safe from his family. Yes, they wanted him gone, but at the same time his escape would infuriate them. That was the problem with the Fazzingas. Even as they pushed Michael away—as Honey's parents had pushed her away—they would still blame him for betraying them.

"I'm always right," said Teena. "He'll be fine."

"Where are you from?" asked Honey, changing the subject. "You never mentioned it, and I can't quite place your accent."

"The country I come from," Teena said, "no longer exists." And then she made a small sound, like an explosion.

In the garage, she found two old flowerpots of unadorned terra-cotta. They were large enough for the gardenias, and she used them to replace the broken Talavera. Why should the whole neighborhood know that her life was falling apart?

No news from Teena. Nothing from Michael. At least Johnny Lavin had called. They'd had a pleasant chat, Honey trying her best to sound like her old self. Thankfully, Johnny offered no resistance when she informed him of her decision to add Michael to the will. "At our age," he said, "what's more important than friends and family?"—admitting that he was tempted to deliver Honey's paperwork himself. The two of them could have a weekend together, he said, maybe even drive to Atlantic City. "I wouldn't mind that at all," Honey replied. "I miss you, dear."

This flirtation, of course, didn't lead to any real-world plans for a rendezvous, only to a promise on Johnny's part to send, along with the paperwork, some sea-salt truffles from Teuscher, a superb chocolatier not far from his office. Chocolate that tasted like tears. *Perfect.*

As the days passed, the weather grew warmer, the air more fragrant. Was it June already? Honey had no idea, but she played at cognizance. She got her mail, watered her plants. She paid her bills, brushed her hair—all the while sensing the absurd circles of life, the same hopes, the same hopelessness. A few times, when Honey was at the mailbox, Jocelyn waved from inside her house. Less a wave than a frantic metronome, keeping time with what was probably some drug-fueled internal sound track. Or perhaps it was simply the girl's native mania. Either way, she appeared as no more than a blur behind the glass.

Honey's only response to these greetings was a gesture of her own—a quick tap to her wrist, signaling her white-rabbit status. *I'm late, I'm late.* And with that, she'd rush back into the house. Besides, if the girl wanted something, she should step outside like a grown-up, instead of gesticulating from behind a window, or sending melodramatic texts to Honey's cell phone. The last one had been over the top: I know I probably disgust you. But please don't abandon me.

Though Honey's thoughts were somewhat confused in regard to Jocelyn, she'd decided that the girl had made her own bed. Unlike Michael, who was at the mercy of bullies, and was therefore worthy of her sympathy.

And the truth was, the girl did disgust her, a little. It wasn't Jocelyn's size or her slovenliness, her clownish demeanor—these were part and parcel of who the girl was, and Honey had even come to find these traits endearing. What bothered Honey, and now more than ever, was what the girl had written on that online dating site.

Stronger men preferred.

Well, clearly she'd gotten what she'd asked for. The girl had chosen to dance with the devil. And despite the fact that she now seemed to be questioning this choice, the more telling fact was that she continued to dance with him. Lee's truck was still parked in the driveway. Occasionally, Honey could hear the pair of them arguing.

Unbelievable that this affair was still going on, after Honey's talks with the girl, heart-to-hearts in which she'd attempted to make Jocelyn see the error of her ways. Hadn't they sat together on the steps of Honey's porch, holding hands, crying for heaven's sake? Honey had hoped the girl would take something from those moments, take the gift that was being offered—advice about how the world worked, how a woman needed to protect herself. That Jocelyn wasn't following this advice—well, it pissed Honey off.

* * *

The following morning, an invitation arrived in the mail. The silvery envelope was addressed to *Ms. Honey Fazzinga*—the last name spelled in the old way, no doubt intentionally. The invitation was from Rina. She was hosting a baby shower for Addie, the daughter-in-law. The front of the card had a cartoon of an elephant on it—a cutesy beast, with ribbons tied to its floppy ears. At the tip of its upraised trunk was a tiny brown nut with a sketched-in face.

A LITTLE PEANUT IS ON THE WAY!

Inside, there was a personal note from Rina: *Would love you to come, Aunt Honey. Please mark the date.* Addie, the mother-to-be, had also scrawled something: *So nice meeting you! Hope you can celebrate with all of us.*

Honey was nearly knocked flat by the absurdity of the situation: *Now that our problem child has had his lights punched out, let's throw a party.* Unbelievable, how it was all played with a straight face, with glee even— the foul mechanics of compartmentalization. And to add insult to injury, the baby shower was to be held at Dante's.

Honey closed the card and stared at the drawing of the elephant. Like a child, she wanted to grab a black Bic and scratch out the eyes, or replace them with X's. On the animal's red ribbons there was a thick paste of glitter, and bits of it fell onto the table like bloody sugar.

She read Rina's note again, recalling what the woman had said on the telephone. "You don't know what he's put us through, Aunt Honey. Coming to the house like that, throwing it in his father's face."

Honey picked up a pen and checked the second box: I REGRET I WILL NOT BE ABLE TO ATTEND. She put the card inside the stamped return envelope and carried it to the mailbox.

39 Toothbrush, Comb, Revolver

She once asked her brother if he ever had nightmares. "No," he said. "Do you?" This conversation had happened not long after the man at the bottom of the stairs. When Honey admitted that, yes, she often had bad dreams, Enzo said, "Well, you better just forget them. Don't be stupid." They were standing in her brother's bedroom, and he shut the door to show his seriousness. "This isn't a game, Ilaria. Just pretend it never happened."

When he lit up a cigarette, Honey noticed the tremor in his hands. Something was different about him, his eyes especially; they were always moving. Plus, ever since he'd been asked to help their father that dreadful night, Enzo's body had started to thicken. He was still muscular, but over his muscles there grew an extra layer of padding. Even back then, Honey understood what it was. It was a suit of armor. Her brother had become a soldier. He was given a car, a gun. He started to dress like a *guappo*. Puffing himself up, as a way of protecting himself. But Honey could tell that inside this new skin, her brother was still afraid. He spent hours alone in the basement, lifting weights.

Strangely, their father remained as skinny as ever. He seemed to have no muscles at all. He was like Honey, a stick. But while Honey was a willowy twig, the Great Pietro was an iron rod capable of shattering bones.

Later, when Honey considered going away to school, her brother seemed heartbroken. Eventually, though, he started to mock her, even berate her, angry that she had the audacity to imagine freedom.

Somehow she'd managed to escape, while her brother had accepted his fate. When Enzo was killed, Honey didn't blame the men who'd shot him. She blamed the family. She blamed her father.

By that point, all of life had become a nightmare—and to forget any of it seemed impossible. But after many years, Honey finally got the hang of it. Somewhere, deep in middle age, she'd accrued enough psychic peace that it had kept her safe even at night. For several decades she'd slept sweetly, unaccosted by demons.

But now that peace was shattered. Over the last few nights, she'd dreamed of Michael lying by the side of a road, calling for help. The hateful strangers who'd hurt the boy had already fled.

And then she remembered. They were not strangers at all.

* * *

Time crept, a mixture of dread and apathy. Honey remained sober—no booze, no pills. She ate very little. Days folded into night, into a thick gray batter. She found herself thinking about God, His mean trick of separating us into various forms, so we'd forget that we were all the same—a single piece of fabric stitched into different costumes. It was this persistent delusion that lay at the root of all human strife. If Honey could offer a single prayer, it would be this: God help the child born different—the one not only misunderstood, but despised. To be despised by those who made you—it was agony.

Waiting for a call from Teena, Honey was beside herself. At times she was sure that her grandnephew was dead. Possibly Corrado and Peter had found the boy and done something awful. It wasn't beyond reason. Hadn't Honey's father and brother threatened her when they'd suspected disloyalty? Honey hadn't been a proper daughter, just as Michael wasn't a proper son. His willfulness, his audacity to express himself, to turn away from the gifts he'd been given, his manhood in particular—to the Fazzingas, such things would be both crime and insult. And to insult prideful men—well, Honey knew exactly where that led.

* * *

Sometimes she drifted for hours. Without the art on the walls, there was nothing to stop the eye—or even the body, for that matter. The china-white latex of the living room receded into space, a fog one could enter and get lost in. The house grew shapeless, unfamiliar, unmoored. Honey felt like a character in a Beckett play, a vagabond awaiting wisdom. Or, better yet, like the woman in *Happy Days*, buried to the waist in sand, babbling as she removed things from her handbag—toothbrush, comb, revolver.

Honey was poisoned by ambivalence. Part of her still longed to die. But how did one die in the spring, in that glory and fullness? How did one take action in the lethargy? The heat had come, but Honey was loath to turn on the air-conditioning. Air-conditioning was cruel, unnatural, a sensory preview of Hell. In Honey's opinion, the poets had got things wrong, completely upside down, in regard to the climates of the afterworlds.

In the dining room the French doors were open, a warm breeze blowing in, carrying the scents of bee-stirred blossoms. Ever since Honey had stopped drinking—stopped taking the Valium, as well—everything was cut with a crystal clarity; the plainest views seemed almost hallucinogenic. Her memory was sharper, too. Honey recalled a drunken night, when she'd first met Jocelyn. Over Viognier and brownies, they'd chatted about their lives. What was it she'd said to the girl? *Facts are not what you have to master. Illusion is the only hope.* An idea that seemed ridiculous now. Surely the exact opposite was true. Surely facts were the only hope—a conviction born from the startling clarity of sobriety.

As Honey stared at the garden, her reverie was punctuated by a *ding* on her cell phone. It was extremely annoying that thoughts of Jocelyn often led directly to her manifestation: the text was from her.

Can I come over?

Not a good time, Honey texted back.

When the phone rang a few minutes later, she didn't pick up. But when the voice mail arrived, she listened to it. It wasn't Jocelyn, though, but Teena, saying to please get in touch.

Such a relief, to finally hear from her. Honey sighed and let down her hunched-up shoulders. She almost felt like crying. She collected herself and dialed.

"Hello," she said brightly when Teena picked up. "I'm very glad you called. So what's the news?"

"I was actually calling to see if *you* had any news."

"What do you mean?"

"If you've heard from Mica? I only ask because I talked to my friends, and they say he hasn't arrived yet. He should have been there yesterday, or the day before."

"Maybe he's just enjoying the scenery," said Honey, trying to be positive. She recalled her own slowpoke drive, years ago, when she'd fled to California. What might have been a five-day trip had turned into a fifteen-day meander. Perhaps Michael was doing something similar, taking his time to get his thoughts in order. When she explained this to Teena—talking about the boy as if she knew him better than she did—Teena wasn't convinced. "Maybe," she said. "Or maybe he's going somewhere else."

"Such as?"

"I have no idea."

"Well," Honey reminded her, "you did say that he should begin a new life. Forget all about us."

"Yes," said Teena. "But am I not allowed to worry?"

Though Honey had her own worries, she didn't share them. What seemed a better choice was to offer comfort. "We can't let our fears get the best of us." A comment she compounded with a small white lie. "My intuition tells me that he's fine."

"I don't trust that sort of thing," said Teena. "I think we better pray for him."

"I wouldn't have thought you to be the religious type."

"Why not? I can't have God, too? My bar, in fact, is named after a psalm in the Bible."

Honey smiled, her first smile in weeks. When she told Teena that she was grateful to her, the woman didn't succumb to sentimentality. All she said was, "I sent you Mica's notebook, by the way. You should have it tomorrow." And then, in the same businesslike tone, she asked Honey if she was ready to pray.

"Right now?"

"Why not?"

Honey hadn't imagined the woman was proposing they do it together, on the telephone.

Having no idea what kind of prayer to offer, Honey suggested that Teena take the lead.

"Sure," replied Teena, exhaling audibly. "Let me just finish my cigarette."

When Honey saw the Hummer pull into her driveway, she felt frightened. Then angry. The unsent letter that Mica had written to his parents, the one she'd found in his notebook, still raged in her heart. She had no intention of opening the door, but then an even stronger feeling presented itself. Curiosity.

Corrado stood on the porch, looking at his shoes—tasseled loafers freshly polished. He seemed uncomfortable, almost sheepish. Honey kept her face strategically neutral, though in her heart the verdict was in.

"Yes?" she said.

Corrado began to speak, then stopped. He looked from his shoes to his hands, as if the words he couldn't find were hiding there. "Rina said I should come."

"I see. Is she upset that I'm not coming to her party?"

Corrado ignored this comment and stepped into the house.

"What are you doing?"

"Is he here? Rina said he might be staying with you."

"Who? Michael?"

"Let me talk to him."

Honey was suspicious. She wondered if Corrado were performing this lack of knowledge about his son to create an alibi.

"He isn't here," she said. "Don't play games."

Corrado was breathing heavily. His face was hard to read. He looked irritated, but at the same time he swiped at his nose as if attempting to stifle a more complicated emotion. When he put his hand on the cloisonné amphora sitting on the foyer table, Honey wondered if he'd break it. But he only touched the pattern of clouds and birds, and said, "Well, if he shows up . . ."

"If he shows up—what? Do you think I'd tell you?"

"Why wouldn't you tell me?"

"I know what you did," she said, sounding as melodramatic as Jocelyn.

The words were effective, though. Corrado fell silent. Again, he looked at his feet.

Honey asked him to leave—though just before he was out the door she said, "Wait. I have something for you."

And then she gave him Mica's notebook.

41 Sempre la Famiglia!

Dear Mom and Dad—I'm still going to call you that. I'm not sure why I'm writing this, it'll only make you angry. You think I'm the angry one, but that's not true. I have a friend who tells me I should never speak to you again, never see you. But even after everything that's happened I can't imagine that. That's what's so fucked up. It's weird, because you taught me all these things growing up, about family and loyalty. About what's important in a person's life. But it was just a lie. And I know you told it because you wanted me to love you. And I did. I do. You don't want that, though. The hardest thing to tell you is I'm happy. Or I will be soon. And even if I go away, don't worry, I'm here. I exist. You have to live with that.

Sempre la famiglia!

The following morning, a package arrived from Johnny. Honey pulled the cardboard tab to open it. She didn't remove the documents, though—the changes to her will—but only the chocolates in their pretty yellow box. She untied the rumpled bow and, not bothering to sit, ate two of the fleur-de-sel truffles for breakfast. After that, she carried the official papers to her bedroom and tossed them in the nightstand drawer, right beside the Glock.

* * *

In the afternoon, Corrado called. Honey didn't answer, though she listened to his voice mail, which was short and to the point. *I'm sorry, Aunt Honey. Please forgive me.*

Strangely, these words did nothing to warm her heart. In fact, a chill came over her, radiating from her chest to the very tips of her fingers. Quickly, in reply, she composed a text.

I'm not the one you need to apologize to.

When her nephew phoned again, Honey ignored the call and retreated to her closet. Not twenty minutes later, there was a loud banging on the front door. This Honey also ignored—though admittedly with a hope that Corrado (she assumed it was him) would break into the house and force her into a confrontation.

* * *

She ran a bath and while soaking let her head slip under the water, opened her eyes. It was something she used to do as a girl, to test the shimmering surface of the world. Back then, the experiment had cost her little—but now, with such a low reserve of breath, she came up gasping.

After climbing from the tub, she stood before the full-length mirror as tiny rivulets of water flowed down her torso. It was then the tears came. She sat at the vanity and wept. Wept for many things, a constellation of piercing distances whose primary star was Michael.

Honey longed for someone to talk to. She considered calling Teena, though she didn't want to add to the woman's worries. She thought about the painter, too, who'd been so kind when Mica had first gone missing. But what right did she have to get in touch with Nathan? She'd already enacted a rude dismissal so he'd keep his distance.

When Honey finally picked up her cell phone, it was not to call anyone, but simply to look at the photograph of Michael, the one Rina had sent. In the formal shot, staged before a dark gray curtain, the boy had fashioned a smile out of confusion. There was a stunned transparency to his face. His short blond hair was combed fetchingly to the side, and his long pale neck rose from the open collar of a periwinkle oxford.

Honey swiped the photo away and, in an attempt to distract herself, scanned through other texts, a mess of sloppy prose and hieroglyphs. Most of it was from Jocelyn.

You were right.
I know I probably disgust you.
Can I come over?

Honey couldn't recall when she'd last seen the girl, or how they'd left things. As if in a trance, she began to compose a reply, writing it as if it were a letter.

Dear Jocelyn, please forgive me for not responding to your messages. I'd just like to say . . .

It was no easy task, pecking out words on the minuscule keyboard. Honey tapped the voice-dictation icon and spoke into the microphone.

Perhaps you feel I don't care about you, but this isn't the case at all. That being said, I'm not sure I can be of much help. And certainly I've given you far too much advice already. But if I were to say one more thing, it would be this. Be mindful of your choices. They may seem like little things now, but these things will add up. They will accrue and form a pattern from which you won't be able to escape. Later, you'll call it your prison, when in fact it was you who designed it.

Honey held the phone as if it were a compact. In the glass screen she could see a ghostly reflection of her face.

You do not disgust me, dear. Not at all. But I am afraid for you. Please be careful.

When Honey squinted to review what she'd written, she realized it was ridiculous. She flicked at the screen to delete it, but somehow this flick was misinterpreted. The phone made a *whoosh*.

"No!" Honey reached out her hand, as if trying to catch a moth.

But the damn thing had flown out the window.

43 Sorry for Your Loss

When she finally decided to visit the Fazzingas, she dressed as if for a funeral—a black Jil Sander tunic that was stylishly rugged. Honey felt it offered a slightly military effect. Which was good, because she needed to be strong, or at least appear as such.

Ever since reading Mica's unsent letter to his parents, Honey had been plagued by fits of trembling. During the worst of these, her teeth would chatter and her mind would fling itself in wider and wider circles, each one taking her farther from the self she knew, the self she trusted.

As for Corrado, Honey wasn't sure what she wanted. Did she want to attack him, or did she want an explanation, to understand his violence in a way she'd never understood her father's? In her heart there was no clarity. Everything was filtered through the dirty sieve of the past, sabotaging any hope of deciphering the present.

As she was backing out of her garage, a brightly colored blob appeared in the rearview mirror. Honey stomped on the brakes, and not two seconds later the bright blob knocked on the driver's-side window. It was Jocelyn, in an orange baseball cap and bug-eye sunglasses. Honey experienced a jolt of fear, which quickly melted into embarrassment when she recalled the text she'd sent to the girl.

Jocelyn, her hand raised in greeting, was dressed in her mustard-colored overalls, the same ones she'd been wearing the day she'd driven into Honey's tree. A senseless nostalgia struck, and Honey found herself rolling down the window. Several seconds of breathy silence ensued; neither seemed to know what to say. Finally, Joss, in her signature style, began to gush.

"Wow, it smells so good in your car. What is that?"

"I believe it's me," said Honey.

Jocelyn nodded one too many times, as if to give both parties a chance to figure out what came next.

"I just wanted to thank you for your message." The girl spoke quietly, and laid her fingers on the edge of the open window.

Glancing at the stubby chewed-up digits, Honey had an appalling desire to kiss the girl's hand.

"Where are you off to?" asked Joss.

"There's been a death in my family." It hardly seemed a lie.

"Oh my God—are you okay?"

"Actually, I'm quite the opposite."

"Is there anything I can do?"

Honey said there wasn't. "But thank you."

"Well, I'll let you go." The girl lingered, though.

"Is there something else you needed, dear?"

"It doesn't seem important now, but, yeah, I just wanted to tell you that I broke up with Lee."

When Honey peered in the direction of the pickup parked next door, Jocelyn seemed to notice.

"He's moving out soon. I promise."

"Why are you promising *me*? I would hope you're doing it for yourself."

"I am."

"Good."

"We're just waiting for him to find somewhere to stay. I still care about him, even if that seems fucked up." When Jocelyn turned her head slightly, Honey glimpsed the bruised patch of skin at the edge of the dark sunglasses. The girl drummed her fingers nervously. "I know you think I'm an idiot, or a loser or something . . ."

"First of all, I don't think of you that way. And secondly, you shouldn't care so much about what I think."

"Why not? You're a lot smarter than I am."

"Darling, if you want to know the truth, I'm the idiot. But let's talk about this later, all right?"

Jocelyn nodded. She seemed to be crying. "Sorry for your loss."

* * *

When Honey arrived at the Fazzingas', she found it difficult to breathe. She longed for a Valium. Nearby, the leaves of a maple fluttered wildly, as if they too were gripped by panic.

Rina's blue Mercedes was in the driveway, the Hummer nowhere in sight. This arrangement was somehow calming, since it might be best to speak to Rina alone. But when Honey knocked at the door, no one answered. After she rang the bell, she could hear someone moving about inside. Several minutes later, though, she was still waiting, staring at the security camera above her head. She wondered what it was that kept Rina from responding. Shame? Anger? Pride? The best she could hope for was regret. Honey was tempted to walk around the property and knock on the windows, shout the woman's name. In her purse there was a book of matches; the thought of torching the place hissed across her mind.

But she only straightened her spine, as if the evil in the world might be vanquished by good posture. She knocked again, counted to ten, then turned and walked away. Before getting in her car, she marched into the garden and ripped a frail pink rose from a bush in need of pruning.

S o many mistakes. So many misunderstandings. It was hard, at Honey's age, not to see the knottiness of time as some horrible work of macramé, a mass of connected tangles in which she was trapped, like a fly entombed in silk. Was there no way out? As Honey glanced at her hands on the steering wheel, she noticed the blood—and it took her a moment to remember that she'd scratched herself on the rosebush. The little flower she'd plucked lay on the passenger seat, so wilted it was nearly flat. Not a flower, but a memory.

When she got home, an unfamiliar car was parked out front—a modest beige Toyota. The woman that emerged was blurred by sunshine. A bandage dress of ruched white layers gave her the appearance of a sophisticated mummy.

It was Teena.

"I have good news," she said.

Honey embraced her. "Thank God! Tell me everything."

"May we speak inside?" Teena extricated herself, as if uncomfortable with the hug.

"Yes, of course," said Honey. "I'm so glad you're here." As she fumbled to unlock the front door, she felt slightly dizzy. Good news was the last thing she was expecting. This day was nothing if not a Ferris wheel.

"Would you like a drink?" she asked, when they were in the house.

"I can't stay for long," Teena replied. "But I felt I should talk to you in person."

Honey led the way to the living room, where Teena composed herself stiffly on the armchair. "So, I just wanted to let you know that your grandnephew is fine. He called me yesterday—and you were right, he was only taking his time, trying to figure things out."

"Where is he?"

Teena looked down. "I'd rather not say."

Honey assured the woman that she wouldn't share the information.

"I just want the chance to speak with him. If you could give me his phone number . . . ?"

Teena nodded, but remained silent.

"Are you sure you don't want something to drink?"

"I'm fine—thank you." The woman was clearly ill at ease. "What's important is that Mica is safe. He even has an appointment with a dentist next week."

"I can help him pay for that," said Honey. "And if you'd rather not share his number, maybe you could just ask him to give me a ring. That is, if you plan on speaking to him again?"

"I do, yes. But, the thing is, he doesn't wish to be in touch with the family."

"That make sense," Honey said—"though I'm sure he meant his parents and his brother."

At this point, Teena pulled no punches. "He actually doesn't want to speak to any of you."

"But—"

"I know, I know. I told him that you came to the bar. I told him what I thought, but he was very firm about it."

"Did he mention me by name?"

"He did."

"I see." Honey looked down at the thorn slashes on her hand.

"Mica just feels that you're part of it—of what she wants to get away from. I'm sorry."

"No. There's nothing to be sorry about." Honey arranged a smile. "The boy is absolutely right. The girl, I mean. Or . . ."

"It's okay."

Stealthily, sunlight shadowed the empty, artless room.

"I suppose sometimes you lose people," said Honey, repeating Corrado's words.

"But you and I will keep in touch," replied Teena. "You'll come and see me at the bar, yes?"

Honey, though grateful, could make no such promise. "It might be better if I don't. My heart isn't what it used to be."

Teena seemed to understand. "Well, I should go."

When they were at the door, Honey felt the panic again. But she spoke brightly. "It's as it should be, with Mica. I did the same when I went away."

"Me too," said Teena.

"The baby with the bathwater."

"Yes."

The women paused as, inside of each of them, a lifetime passed, a city burned. Honey's knees felt weak, and when she faltered Teena held her.

Neither said goodbye.

Part Four

45 No Respect

The clouds were losing their edges, slurring toward summer in the rising heat. In the garden late camellias, in stunning bloom, lay scattered on the ground. Such stupid flowers, camellias, always falling while still in their glory, as if their waxen perfection dulled the will to live. Honey leaned against the window. Inside, outside—nothing made sense. Snippets of conversation moved through her mind like venom. *I bet you looked like her when you were younger.* That was Teena, speaking to Honey about Mica. Then, there was Corrado on her voice mail. *What's going on? Call me back. Why are you being so mean?* Every time Honey heard one of his messages, her heart dropped like a stone. While she was happy that Mica was safe, her own demons had her surrounded.

She sat on the edge of the bed and tried to put her thoughts in order, though the task seemed futile. Her thoughts were jagged, alarmingly sharp, and none of them fit together.

She attempted a silent meditation, along with some simple breathing exercises. But the outer world intruded. Next door, the psychotic lovebirds were squabbling again in the driveway. Over the past week it had been a constant annoyance, and Lee's voice had started to grate on Honey.

Today's argument was a goddamned donnybrook. And since it was impossible to ignore, Honey had no choice but to listen. When she was able to make out a word or two, they often came from Lee, and were surprisingly nasty. From Jocelyn, Honey could make out an occasional *Sorry* or *Please*—though whether the girl was finally evicting the man or asking him to stay, it wasn't clear. Either way, it pained Honey that Jocelyn had to resort to begging.

But what could Honey do? She was a woman of ideas, not action. Useless, in fact. She'd never been of any real help to anyone.

* * *

Around eight the next morning, Rina called. Honey thought to share
the good news that Mica was safe, but before she could say much of anything, Rina interrupted her. "I can't believe you gave that to Corrado."

"What did I give him?" asked Honey.

"The *notebook*. Why would you do that?"

"I was only trying to—"

"Why would you want to hurt us? That's what I don't understand."

Honey was flabbergasted. "I wasn't trying to hurt you."

"Where did you even get it?"

"I've been in touch with one of Michael's friends. Someone who's
helping him."

"Helping him? Helping him how?"

Honey didn't want to betray any confidences, so she simply said, "I
just thought you and Corrado would want to know what was in the
boy's heart."

"Why don't you worry about your own heart?" said Rina.

"I do worry," said Honey.

"And I can't believe you're talking to Michael's friends behind our
backs. It's as if you have no respect for us. For this family."

"What I have no respect for is cruelty. What Corrado did—how can
you accept that?"

"Corrado's not the only one," said Rina.

"What does that mean?"

"I'm just saying, if Corrado didn't do it, someone else would have."

"So your son had it coming—is that what you're saying?"

Rina was silent. "He was such a sweet baby," she finally said.

"He still is," said Honey.

"You barely know him," scoffed Rina.

"It's true. I really don't know any of you."

Rina grumbled agreeably. She seemed satisfied, almost conciliatory.
But then she said: "Why did you even come home, Aunt Honey? What
good has it done?"

As a kind of last rites, Honey took a moment to consider her crimes. There were hundreds of them, though perhaps only a few that had indelibly marked her life, her soul. Above all else were the bodies. Three unforgivable silences. Not only the silencing of death, but the black thread stitched across Honey's lips. To have waited a lifetime to speak of these deaths—it was another kind of murder.

She included the baby here, since when she'd buried that blood-stained blanket in the woods, she'd pretended it was the child—that she was putting him in an unmarked grave, like his father. So much cruelty, so early. It had hardened her, and there were times in her life when kindness had seemed impossible.

She thought of Mr. Hal. Her refusal to marry him. She'd convinced herself that she was protecting him, but really she was protecting herself. She'd broken Hal's heart because *she* was broken, and frightened that any further intimacy would expose this fact. The same was true of Florence. The woman had idolized Honey. What choice was there but to smash the golden statue? Besides, keeping her distance from people, from love, was how Honey had made her way in life.

Michael, too, had gotten the short end of the stick.

Thinking back to that morning with her grandnephew, Honey recalled how angry she'd been, assuming the boy was on drugs, only interested in her money. She'd barely been able to look him in the eye, to see him for who he was, or what he'd really wanted.

Because it was clear to her now that Michael had wanted more than money. He wanted to talk, he wanted solace. But when he asked questions about the past, she'd been glib, evasive. And then she'd turned on him, telling him to get out of her house. In fact, she'd shouted these words at him. A detail she'd conveniently edited from her memory.

Why lie anymore?

There's no point now in lying. There's only the brightness of pain, the shadow of longing. Honey opens the nightstand drawer and pulls out the gun.

But where should she put it? Her head? Her heart? When she places the barrel in her mouth, the metal tastes like blood. She takes it out and breathes, waiting for a sign. Her indecision galls her.

Quickly she releases the safety on the weapon, turns it toward her face. Peering into the cyclops eye, she feels a tremor in her bowels.

Maybe she should wait.

She doesn't want to wait. She's tired, furious, finished. She puts the barrel to her head—and *bang*.

Honey blinked, confused. Her hands were shaking, her guts were on a trampoline. Standing brought a sudden vertigo.

Bang. Bang. Bang. Not in her head but at the door, the timing unforgivable. Honey couldn't possibly deal with company.

Nor was she dressed for it. She had on a flowing kaftan, a fruity thing she hadn't worn in years. In the brighter hallway, where the morning light burst in abominably, she noticed the silk was fraying, slightly torn at the hip. She had no memory of putting on this shmata, which looked like a costume for Ophelia's mad scene.

"*Let me in!*"

The voice was so hoarse it sounded demonic. Honey's heart leaped at the sound, and before she could say "Go away," the demon shouted "Please!"

It was Jocelyn.

Though Honey had no intention of responding, she watched in horror as her hand undid the locks. Immediately the girl rushed in, pushing Honey aside to take control; she slammed the door shut and quickly re-did the bolt.

Not a second later, there was another voice. "Open it! Open it!" The doorknob jiggled, straight out of a nightmare.

I won't have this, thought Honey. "I won't have this," she said to Jocelyn. "Take your business outside."

The girl seemed to be in shock, staring dumbly. Only then did Honey see the tears in her eyes and a muddle of red lines around her neck. The bruise on her cheekbone, shiny as a plum.

"Come on!" Lee shouted. "I'm sorry!" His voice was sharp, with the hysterical keen of a chainsaw. Again he apologized, though this time softly, plausibly sincere. "I'll do whatever you say. Okay? Baby, are you listening to me?"

Jocelyn grimaced and moved toward the door.

"Don't you dare," said Honey.

"I thought you *wanted* me to leave."

Lee was nearly crooning now, pleading, offering more endearments.

Joss looked torn, and Honey shook her head in warning, before addressing the man behind the door. "Please get off my property, or I'll phone the police."

"Why don't you mind your own business?" said Lee, barking again.

"Don't talk to her like that!" shouted Jocelyn. "You can talk to me like that, but don't be rude to my friend."

"Your *friend*? She's not your *friend*. I see the way she sneers at you. She's a fucking snob. Baby, just come outside so we can talk."

"I'm calling the police," said Honey. She patted the pockets of the kaftan, checking for her cell—but the stupid kaftan had no pockets.

"Give me your phone," she said to Joss.

"I don't have it with me."

"I'm sorry," Lee hissed. "I don't know what gets into me."

Jocelyn touched the door as if it were her lover's flesh.

Just let her go, thought Honey.

For a moment there was silence. No banging, no yelling—a chance to catch one's breath. It seemed that Lee had given up when suddenly the door juddered, as if kicked.

"Get your ass out here! *Joss!*"

Both women took a step back.

Honey, planning to use the phone in the kitchen, turned away—but at that exact moment there was a horrendous cracking sound. Jocelyn screamed as Lee came stumbling into the foyer.

Honey retreated against the wall while Joss ran toward the living room.

"You fucking bitch," said Lee—and as he made a move to follow the girl, Honey extended one of her hooves and tripped him. He went down hard.

Quickly, Honey grabbed the cloisonné amphora from the foyer table and chucked it at the man's head. It shattered spectacularly, the bright shards spilling festively to the floor. Lee lay motionless, stunned or possibly unconscious. Jocelyn stood by the couch, her mouth slashed open like a jack-o-lantern.

"*What did you do?*"

"I didn't care for his tone," replied Honey.

Jocelyn started to walk in circles. She seemed to be hyperventilating. "Is he dead?"

"Does he look dead?" asked Honey. Lee's back was visibly rising and falling. "Can't you see him breathing?"

For several seconds both women stared at this blunt evidence of life. "Thank God," said Joss.

"Thank God?" shot back Honey. "*Thank God?*"

When the girl asked if they should call a doctor, Honey said they weren't calling anyone. "There's some rope in the garage. Top shelf. I want you to go and get it."

"What do we need rope for?"

"Just go!" ordered Honey. "Before your friend wakes up. You can use the side door, just off the kitchen."

After Jocelyn scurried off, Honey tested Lee with her foot, pushing her toes into his ribs. He made no sound. She jabbed again, harder.

Nothing. Nothing at all.

S he hoped she hadn't hurt him *too* badly—though if he woke
to some pain, well, that would be all right. He was definitely
going to have a bump. *But, oh, the poor amphora.* Honey had
bought it in Belgium, on a trip with Mr. Hal. It wasn't priceless, like the
vase Michael had shattered, but it was no less beautiful.

When the girl returned with the rope, she was trembling. "What are
we doing?" she asked.

Honey said she wasn't sure. "But I don't trust him. Better to have him
contained, and then we can figure out who to call."

"What do you mean? The police?"

Actually, Honey wasn't thinking of the police. Her first thought had
been to phone Corrado. But, no, that wouldn't do. "I don't know *what*
I mean," she said to the girl. It was not as if she were thinking straight.
Just minutes before, she'd been contemplating suicide, and now she was
looking down at a body sprawling dangerously close to her white carpet. Luckily, Lee's head didn't seem to be bleeding. "Let's just restrain
him, shall we? And then we'll figure out what to do."

Jocelyn nodded and handed Honey the rope. The transaction seemed
oddly familiar. Honey had a sense that she and the girl had rehearsed
this day, and were finally being thrust onstage to perform it. The feeling
was less one of déjà vu than of fate, of secret waters rising to the surface.
These waters formed a pool in which Honey could see her face, see it as
it really was. She told Jocelyn to go into the kitchen and get the scissors,
in the bottom drawer to the left of the sink. "The heavy ones. The fabric
shears."

The girl hesitated, a flash of terror in her eyes.

"What?" said Honey. "I'm not going to cut off his doodad. I just need
to snip the rope into smaller pieces."

Several moments later, after they'd tied up Lee's hands and feet and were dragging him away from the foyer, Joss dropped her end and asked, a second time, what the hell they were doing. She said it made no sense to bring him farther into the house. "Won't it be easier for them to take him away if he's by the door?"

The two women stared at each other—and again, for Honey, this sense of seeing her own face reflected in dark water.

Jocelyn, as if she, too, sensed some disturbing undercurrent, forced the subject toward mundanity. "You don't even seem out of breath. Don't you find him heavy?"

"Not really." Honey explained that she'd recently started exercising again. It was uncanny, actually, how invigorated she felt.

"I should exercise more," said Joss. And then: "This is weird, right?"

Honey, thinking it unnecessary to reply to the obvious, simply said, "Let's go, already. Grab his feet."

Jocelyn resumed her part of the bargain, and once they'd managed to get Lee into the bedroom closet, the girl was absolutely winded. She appeared on the verge of a heart attack. "This is your closet?" she managed to say, looking around as if she'd never seen a walk-in with approximately five hundred dresses and no less than three hundred pairs of shoes. Once she'd recovered, she began to scratch her arm ferociously, a peculiar habit Honey found distasteful.

"Stop doing that. Why are you always scratching yourself?"

"It calms me down," Joss said.

"What are you nervous about?"

"Very funny." The girl peered down at Lee. She stared at him a long time, as if trying to decipher something in his handsome and oddly flat face. "I mean, it wasn't like he was going to *kill* me or anything. He just ..."

"He just *what*?"

Honey looked at the girl, at her bruises. It seemed astonishing, suddenly, how young Jocelyn was—twenty-six, wasn't it? But somehow, with her puffed-up face, she appeared even more like a child. Today she was dressed not in overalls or one of her Mennonite-style dresses, but in a pair of too-tight sweatpants and a white tank top insufficiently bleached, the color slightly muddy at the underarms. Clearly she'd had to run from her house before she could second-think her appearance. Honey was about to scold the girl for her lackadaisical attitude in regard to self-preservation when, suddenly, Lee began to moan.

Joss flinched, jumping back as if there were spiders on the floor.

"It's all right," Honey said. "Don't freak out."

Lee's eyes remained closed, his body still limp. Honey bent down and took up his arms. "Help me lift him, and we'll put him in this chair."

Lee mumbled incoherently as they roughly maneuvered him into the splendidly reupholstered Louis Seize. After they'd plopped him down, Honey quickly wrapped the remaining length of rope around Lee's chest and fastened it behind the chair.

* * *

For a while he seemed to be dreaming, a dog's dream of tiny yelps and sighs. At times his eyes fluttered, as if he were slipping in and out of consciousness. Honey was slightly worried she'd done some real damage. Whenever Lee's eyes opened, which they did only briefly, he seemed to have difficulty focusing.

Jocelyn had retreated farther into the closet. She was half obscured by a rack of dresses—a tribe of headless mothers that could do little to protect her. These limp guardians were from another world, a world in which there existed such a thing as civility. As Honey tied a second knot at the back of the chair, Jocelyn was whispering to herself, as if praying.

"What are you saying?" asked Honey.

"Nothing." The girl grimaced, mauling her arms again. She looked deranged.

"Are you on drugs, dear? Tell me the truth."

"Why do you keep asking me that? *I'm not.* I'm just *confused.* I mean, what are we doing in your closet?" Jocelyn gestured at the dresses, and then began to bat at them as if they were cobwebs she'd become entangled in.

When Honey shouted at the girl to pull herself together, Lee moaned, as if the order were directed at him.

"He doesn't sound right," Joss said. "If we're not gonna call the police, maybe we should call an ambulance."

When Honey made no reply, the girl grew petulant. "I don't understand what you want."

"What *I* want?" said Honey. "Did this man not hurt you? Did he not do that to your face?"

"It's complicated," said Joss.

"No, it isn't. Did he hurt you or not? Yes or no?"

"He has problems!"

"Be that as it may," Honey said, "violence is not therapy. And there's no reason you need to subject yourself to such things. You're a good girl."

When Jocelyn disagreed, Honey said: "I'm telling you—*you are*. And you deserve better."

Jocelyn grimaced again, covering her face in the dresses. Possibly she was crying. After a moment, she grabbed a lacy sleeve and brought it to her nose like a handkerchief.

Honey said, "Darling, look at me. We are in this together, all right?"

"But what about when he wakes up? What'll we do then?"

Honey hadn't a clue; she was riding a wave of inspiration she barely understood. She felt giddy, delirious, and slightly nauseous. "I really don't get people like him," she muttered. "So I'd just like to have a little chat with the boy, that's all."

Honey wondered if she were losing it. Well, she'd already lost it, but maybe she was in the final fall toward complete insanity. She watched Lee's hands, twitching as if in code. His eyes fluttered more and more, though he seemed unaware of his surroundings. *A patient etherized upon a table*, thought Honey. *An insect pinned to a board*. She moved closer, to study the specimen. There was something pleasing about seeing the man's head drooping to the side, his arms and chest gullivered into submission. Honey felt the anxious pride of a Lilliputian. She leaned forward, examining the tattoos on Lee's neck, the vines that were actually strands of barbed wire. Honey had never liked tattoos, the idea of flesh as canvas.

At rest, the man's face possessed a ruddy sweetness, the wrinkles around his eyes less pronounced. Though his skin was weathered, it was not from age. He was simply a person who'd lived hard; she could see that now in his features, in the flattened face that had clearly suffered, more than a little, the grindstone of life. For a moment Honey veered close to sympathy for the horrid man in front of her. She reached out to touch his head, to see how badly she'd injured him. When she felt farther toward the back of his scalp, searching for the bump, Lee gasped, as if in pain, and his eyes shot open.

"*Wha—what?*" He jerked away from Honey's hand, frightened.

Honey stepped back, too.

"Where am I?" he said, blinking desperately. He glanced around the room, and when he attempted to speak again, he made no sense, uttering a mash of garbled syllables. Finally, this gibberish congealed into words. "Where's Joss?" he asked, plaintively. He whimpered, as if very near to tears. A moment later, though, when he came to terms with the fact that he was bound to a chair, his tone grew sharper. "What the fuck," he said, struggling against the ropes.

Honey watched, fascinated, as the man wriggled like a worm. He turned his head to the left and right, his vision blocked by the wings of the armchair. "Joss!" he called out. "*Joss!*"

Strangely, the girl didn't seem to be in the closet. Maybe she'd disappeared deeper into the dresses. Or possibly she'd snuck back into the bedroom. Honey worried that she might be phoning the police.

Lee was fully awake now, straining so hard against the ropes that the chair was vibrating. He lifted his bound feet and kicked over the ottoman. Despite this aggression, it was obvious he was still frightened, and this arrangement was soothing to Honey. She felt weirdly relaxed. Even when Lee screamed, "I'll fucking kill you!" she looked him dead in the eye and said that she expected nothing less.

Just then Jocelyn emerged from the depths of the closet, coming through the dry-cleaned dresses in her stained white shirt. Honey noticed for the first time that the girl's feet were bare, and not terribly clean. When Lee saw her, he stopped struggling against the ropes.

"Baby," he said. "Thank God."

The couple locked eyes, and though Joss was silent, Honey could read her confusion. How easily that simple word—*Baby*—seemed to act on her like a drug. Honey hated to admit it, but it was painfully clear that Jocelyn was a fool.

"Come here," Lee crooned. He asked the girl to tell him where they were. He asked if his head was bleeding. And then, when she was close enough, he asked her to untie him.

Honey watched and said nothing. Though she wanted to rush forward and stop Jocelyn's stupidity, she also wanted to witness this stupidity. She wanted to understand once and for all how it happened. How a man succeeded and a woman failed. Because that was clearly what was about to occur. Especially now, after what they'd done to Lee. Men like him were dangerous when humbled.

Jocelyn, noticeably perspiring, didn't immediately undo the ropes. She simply stood, facing Lee, her lips quivering as if she had something she wanted to say. Honey could see the man's impatience, even as he made a show of pretending to give Jocelyn his full attention.

"What?" he said. "Talk to me."

The girl produced only tiny squeaks, rusted attempts at words. It took her nearly thirty seconds before she managed to say, "You hurt me."

"I know," Lee replied, with a wonky smile. "I'm sorry. I just got upset when you asked me to leave."

Jocelyn was scratching herself again—and somehow this seemed to increase Lee's power.

"Because I know that's not what you want," he said, speaking quietly but insistently. "You just let *this one* get inside your head"—a flash of his eyes toward Honey. "You're not thinking straight, baby." And then he moaned, beseechingly, said his skull was killing him. "I should probably get to a doctor. You gotta untie me."

Joss nodded, though she continued to stand there passively.

Lee's pretense at patience began to fray. He asked her what she was waiting for.

Joss shrugged, said nothing. Maybe she was smarter than she looked. Maybe, like Honey, she was waiting for the man to flare again, to expose himself. The silence seemed to be driving him crazy.

"What do you want me to say?" he asked her. "I have some bad habits, sure. But so do you."

"Like what?"

"You want me to say it in front of her?" Lee cocked his head toward Honey. "Because I will."

Joss looked down at her feet, as if she were ashamed.

But then she lifted her head and met Lee's gaze. She told him, yes, he could say whatever he wanted in front of Honey.

"Untie me first."

"Just tell me."

"For fuck's sake," Lee grumbled, gritting his teeth.

"I don't do drugs," said Joss. "I don't *steal*. So what's so bad about me?"

"You like it when I slap you around."

"I don't like it. You go too far. You take advantage of me."

Lee scowled at this assessment. "We made a contract."

"What does that mean?"

"You know what it means. Don't act naive. We made a contract with our minds. With our *bodies*." He held her gaze, his eyes as unyielding as a hypnotist's.

"No," Jocelyn said. "I just wanted to . . . I only wanted to play."

"*Play?* What are you, a child?"

"I just wanted to be what *you* wanted. And I don't even mind it when you get rough, but I never wanted you to punch me in the face!"

"That was a mistake," Lee said. "I'm sorry."

"But you've done it more than once. He's done it more than once," she said again, turning toward Honey.

"Leave her out of it. Just talk to me, baby—okay? Let's put all that shit behind us. You know I love you, right?"

Joss looked back at Lee, as if terrified. "You never told me that."

"I'm telling you now." Lee was writhing again, straining against the ropes, though he kept his eyes steadily on Jocelyn. "I'm stupid. You know that, babe. I never do anything right. I'm a fucking mess."

Joss began to tremble.

"I'm a fucking mess," Lee repeated.

"Me too," said Joss, in a spluttering rush. She didn't say it with anger, though, but as if whatever mess she shared with the man were a kind of salvation.

Lee continued to wriggle his body, attempting to edge closer to Jocelyn. She, too, took a step forward. Honey stood there frozen, paralyzed by the train wreck of life, of love.

"Kiss me," said Lee.

At these words, something seemed to break in Jocelyn. Her legs visibly weakened.

Honey tried to will something into the girl, some part of her own spirit. But it was of no use. Jocelyn leaned forward and pressed her lips against Lee's.

Sickened, Honey closed her eyes. But a second later she opened them as Jocelyn screamed. Her face was still pressed against the man's, even as she struggled to pull away. When she finally managed to do so, her lips were smeared with blood.

Lee was rocking his torso more freely now, and though his hands were tightly bound, the rope around his chest was coming loose. Honey ran behind the chair, grabbled the slack cord and pulled it so hard that Lee gasped. Then she made not one, not two, but *three* knots.

Jocelyn wiped her bleeding mouth and told Honey to call the police.

She walked into the bedroom and found her cell phone. But as soon as she picked it up, she put it down. Because also on the nightstand was her old friend, resting on his side.

The white Glock no longer looked harmless, like the spray nozzle on her garden hose. Having turned this gun against herself, she understood exactly what it was. She picked it up, its weight somehow a comfort, a kind of ballast. It would keep them safe until the authorities arrived. She could still hear the man, ranting inside the closet.

"Everything all right?" she shouted out.

"Did you call them?" said Joss.

"Calling them now," replied Honey.

Why was she hesitating?

Possibly it was the matter of what to say to them. A crazy man broke into my house. My friend is bleeding. It seemed incredible. Had Lee actually *bitten* the girl?

Well, she didn't need to tell them everything. She'd just say, domestic abuse, come quickly. Once again she replaced the props, putting down the gun and picking up the cell.

Still, something felt off.

To be honest, the police didn't seem a satisfying ending to this story. Honey was thinking this, perhaps, because also on the nightstand was a book—the ridiculous novel about women in prison. Honey couldn't help but wonder what Up Yours might do, in this situation.

Of course, Honey didn't actually want to *hurt* the man. She abhorred violence. She just wanted to have her little chat with him. And she wasn't opposed to making him feel a tiny bit of fear. If she could accomplish that, then, yes, she'd happily call the police.

* * *

When Honey returned to the closet, she stood in the doorway, where Lee couldn't see her. His restraints looked secure, and he no longer struggled against them. He seemed calmer, and was once again trying to cajole the girl, offering more of his useless apologies.

Joss didn't appear to be listening. She had her back to him, holding a dress in her hands, which she then began to tear. The sound went through Honey like a bayonet.

"What are on earth are you doing?"

"I can't listen to him anymore."

"Well, how is destroying my property going to help?"

Joss didn't answer. She continued to tear a long trip of fabric, after which she made a bundle of knots in the middle of it.

"Don't you fucking dare," Lee said, as if he knew what she was up to. He began to toss his head from side to side as the girl walked behind him and tried to wrap the fabric around his face. After several failed attempts, during which Lee continued to curse, she managed to get the cloth over his mouth, with the knots, just so, jammed between his teeth.

Honey was shocked by Jocelyn's ability to fabricate a gag, though she refrained from questioning the girl about her expertise.

With the fabric over his mouth, the man became even more garrulous—and though his words were muffled, the gist of them was frightfully apparent. His face was purple with rage.

"*Shut up!*" said Honey. And then, more softly: "I would think you'd want to conserve your energy."

At this point, Joss turned to Honey and asked if she'd called the cops.

"Yes," she lied. "They'll be here soon."

The girl nodded, then dropped to her knees, as if exhausted. She seemed not to have noticed the gun—or if she had, she made no mention of it.

When Honey walked farther into the room, where Lee could finally see her, he fell silent—his eyes going straight to her hand. He blinked; he twitched. She could hear his nostrils hissing, feel him calculating his next move.

Jocelyn, perhaps in reaction to the fact that Lee had gone mute, looked up. This time she saw the gun.

"Wait"—she pointed at it—"is that real?"

"It feels real," said Honey.

"But where did you get it?"

"I honestly don't recall. I bought it a long time ago." She held up the pistol, to show it to Lee—sideways, for safety. "What do you think? I assume it still works. I cleaned it just a few weeks ago."

"Is it loaded?" asked Joss.

Honey opened the chamber to display the bullets—first for the man, and then for Jocelyn. "Fiocchi Extrema," she explained. "Very reliable ammo, I was told by the gentleman I purchased it from."

Jocelyn stood, her mouth agape—though whether she was horrified or intrigued, it was impossible to say. She flinched when Honey snapped the chamber shut.

"How's your lip, dear? Has it stopped bleeding?"

The girl distractedly touched her mouth. "I think so."

"Why don't you go into my bathroom and clean yourself up. There's hydrogen peroxide in the medicine chest."

"No, it's fine."

"It's not fine. There are goddamned *teeth marks*."

When Lee attempted to speak, the women turned toward him and watched the gag bobble along to the ape sounds rising from his throat.

Honey was unmoved. She looked at Joss, who seemed nervous, and told her again to go into the bathroom and wash up.

"I don't think I should leave you alone in here." And then, glancing at Lee: "Do you think he can breathe?"

"He can breathe, don't worry."

The man grunted, as if to disagree—a grunt he directed at Jocelyn.

"It's just, it can be hard to breathe in those things."

"It was *your* idea. But feel free to take it off if you'd rather listen to him berate you."

"I just don't want to get in trouble."

"Darling, you've been in trouble a long time. What we're doing is getting you *out* of it."

When Lee grunted again, Honey ignored him.

"All we're doing is protecting ourselves. And *this*"—here, she held up the gun, allowing the barrel to briefly swing toward Lee's face—"is just a little insurance."

Honey was aware of the tremor in her hands. She still felt queasy, but she also felt exhilaration, the amusement-park pleasure of falling from a great height.

But this was more than simply a roller coaster. Here, in the closet, the stakes were higher. In Honey's mind it seemed important to show the girl how to act when confronted by violence. That is, how a *civilized* person should act—a person who, though she had every right to reciprocate that violence, would refuse to play some biblical endgame. *An eye for an eye.*

Instead, Honey would demonstrate how a person could take control with power, not force. Gain the upper hand, with words, with reason, with intelligence and a bit of cunning. How a person could prevail without resorting to the mentality of an animal. The gun was merely symbolic.

The girl was babbling again, second-guessing the gag. "It's just, some-times he has trouble breathing at night. He has that thing, you know, with his nose."

Honey was undeterred. "Your heart," she said, "is too good. It has made you suffer."

"I just . . ." The girl shook her head, and her eyes welled with tears. "I wish you'd stop saying that."

"Saying what?"

"That I'm *good*."

"Joss—listen to me—"

"No, you don't understand. I *asked* for certain things. I put an ad online."

"Yes, I know. I saw it, I told you that."

The girl covered her face.

"Stop it. There's no need to be ashamed. So what if you have certain proclivities? I don't judge you for that."

"Yes, you do." There was pain in the girl's voice. "You said I had no self-respect. You said I was weak."

"I don't think that anymore. I understand that a person can't always control what she wants, especially what her body wants. But the point is that this man went *beyond* what you wanted. He took advantage of you, to use your own words—did he not?"

Lee was grunting again, but Honey plowed over him. "Do you know what your friend here said to me one day? The day he snuck into my garage? He said you weren't so bright. I believe he said, 'She's not all there.' He's the one who thinks you're a fool. He also threatened my life."

When Joss asked Lee if this were true, his gargled reply—"*Onwah anghhh*"—was accompanied by a flipper flap of his bound feet.

"You accused me several times of ignoring you," Honey continued. "But the only reason I've kept my distance is because I've been afraid. Of *him*."

Honey took a step forward. "So if you're wondering what I'm doing with this"—again she flashed the Glock very near to Lee's face—"it's because it infuriates me when people frighten me. I spent nearly half my life terrified of certain people."

When Jocelyn began to cry again, Honey told her to stop the waterworks—and then, when the girl had difficulty doing so, Honey asked her if she'd like to hold the gun.

Lee began to grunt more volubly.

"Go ahead," said Honey. "Just hold it."

"I don't think that's a good idea."

"Why not?"

"I just think you should keep it. You know how to use it and everything. I mean, not that we're going to use it, but . . ."

Lee continued to squirm, his face so purple it resembled an eggplant. The hissing from his nose was worrisome, even Honey had to admit. Maybe he *was* struggling to breathe. A moment later his eyes began to bulge, and there was a disconcerting sound coming from behind the gag, a wet gurgling not unlike a clogged drain.

Honey stared, appalled, trying to steel herself.

But finally she relented. "Take it off him."

Jocelyn didn't move. "You want me to?"

"Well, we don't want him to suffocate, do we?" Lee's throat was grossly inflated, giving him the appearance of a bullfrog.

The two women watched the terrifying transformation of the man's face—and it was several seconds more before Jocelyn walked around to the back of the armchair and untied the gag.

Lee's intake of breath was profound, a vacuum that changed the weather inside the room. The air felt thinner, hotter. Lee's chest filled, then emptied, each cycle seamless and greedy. Something about the intensity of his breathing disoriented Honey. She could feel the shortness of her own breath. The more she watched Lee's chest expand and collapse, the weaker she felt.

The man didn't scream or curse or condemn his captors. He simply kept his eyes shut and edged his way toward equilibrium. Slowly his breathing grew steady, more confident. His eyes remained closed for so long that Jocelyn eventually said, "Lee?"

The tiniest nick of a smile. "Do you realize?" he said, "how fucked you are?" At last he opened his eyes. "Do you have any idea what you've done, Joss? This is *kidnapping*. Do you want to get yourself arrested?"

The girl didn't answer.

But when Lee cocked his head toward Honey and said, "Obviously your friend here is a criminal," Honey told him to shut up. In fact, she shouted it so loudly that Jocelyn took a step back.

"Just listen to her," said Lee. "She's not a stable person. You said yourself, Joss, that she seemed a little crazy. Well, look at her now. She's got a gun—*a fucking gun*."

When Honey tried to speak, Lee interrupted her. "She can't be trusted. That's why you're gonna untie me, babe—okay? And we're gonna get the hell out of here."

"No," said Honey, though her voice lacked conviction. And there was no disguising the tremor in her hands.

"Just ignore her," the man said. "She's not gonna do anything. She's a liar. Acting like she knows us. She doesn't *know us*, Joss. She doesn't get it."

The more he spoke, the more Honey trembled.

"Maybe you should give me that?" the girl said, reaching for the gun.

Honey retreated, confused—and when she looked again at Lee, it was his gaze that undid her. She knew that gaze. It had belonged to her father. All her life, Honey had only pretended to have any power over it.

And yet she couldn't stop herself from looking into the man's eyes, at the nick of his smile—a cutthroat sneer. How on earth could men like this still exist? Hadn't they been eradicated, or reformed? Honey could feel Lee's anger, feel that in many ways it was stronger than her own. He wore it proudly, a birthright. And he wasn't alone. There were still armies of men who hated women.

Lee's gaze was a revelation. Honey realized she'd been naive to believe in evolution, in *progress*. Men had only learned to wear a mask, to hide their hatred. She looked into Lee's eyes as Jocelyn knelt at his feet, struggling to undo the knots.

"Hurry up," he grumbled, frustrated at the girl's ineptness with the rope.

"You're a piece of shit," Honey said to him.

"Oh, yeah?" he replied, with deadly calm. "And you're nothing but a dried-up cunt."

Even Jocelyn stopped what she was doing to look up at him. No doubt he'd used that word against her, too.

For Honey, it was an old word. The first time she'd heard it was from Richie Verona. Then later, more terribly, from her father. And just recently, hadn't the car thieves used it?

"How dare you."

"What," Lee scoffed, "is it not accurate? I *see* you. The way you act. The way you talk. Walking around like a fucking peacock. Dressing up like you still want to suck a dick."

Honey froze, but only briefly. Because, a second later, her hand flew from her side, slamming the gun against Lee's face.

He gasped loudly. On his cheek there was blood, smeared like war paint. When his vocabulary failed to improve—"*You fucking cunt*"— Honey struck him again, this time with even greater force. The sound was significant, a thuggish punctuation. She watched his head swing grotesquely to the side. He moaned, seemingly unable to bring himself to an upright position. His tongue lolled dumbly inside his mouth. Eventually he looked down and spit. With the bloody saliva came a tooth. It landed beside the girl.

"*I'll kill you*," Lee said. And then, to Jocelyn: "Can't you untie a fucking knot? Are you that stupid?"

"I wasn't untying it, asshole!" Joss replied. "I was making it tighter." After which she turned to Honey and said, "Do it again."

How simple it was. Honey realized how wrong she'd been, all these years. Violence was only hard to imagine. Doing it was easy. Almost natural. Honey's rage was spectacular. Before her, they were all there. Richie Verona, the car thieves. Corrado.

Again, she struck Lee's face. And then several times more, until she could see his fear, until he became a mirror, one in which they could regard each other as equals.

"*Stop*," he whimpered. "*Stop*."

The sound of his voice terrible, familiar. Her own voice, at fifteen.

"Just let me go," Lee said, "and I'll leave you alone. *I promise*." He was crying, pleading.

Neither of the women moved.

"*Please*," Lee said. "I promise."

But Honey didn't trust him. She trusted no one.

"I'll be right back," she said to Joss. "Do *not* untie him."

"Where are you going?"

"Calling the police again."

When she walked into the bedroom, though, she changed her mind. She picked up the phone and called Corrado.

When Honey was growing up, her parents had in the house a small replica of a sculpture by Giambologna. *The Rape of the Sabine Women*. It sat on a pedestal in the entryway—the living figures immobilized, like deer, by the spotlight hanging above them. As a child, Honey, too, was transfixed. It was hard not to stare, particularly at the curly-headed woman, breasts exposed, held aloft in the arms of a naked man.

"But what is he doing?" a six-year-old Honey once asked her mother.

"*Eh*. He's taking her away, that's all," her mother replied.

"Taking her *where*?"

"Like when you're tired, and your father carries you to bed."

When Honey said that the woman didn't look tired, her mother said, "She's tired, believe me."

"And what about the other man? Why is he crying?"

At which point, her mother pinched her arm. "*Basta con le domande!*" Enough with the questions! "You gonna learn soon enough."

* * *

"Why don't you go home?" she said to Jocelyn. The girl was crying again, grasping Honey's arm a bit too tightly. They were sitting in the bedroom, waiting for Corrado to arrive—though the girl still believed it was the police who were coming. There was blood on Honey's hand, blood on Joss's cheek. It seemed like a dream.

The man remained as he was, bound in the closet. They could hear him muttering, cursing. Perhaps ashamed that he'd begged and cried, he renewed his bravado by tossing off threats. "Just you wait," he yelled. "You'll be fucked!" He used the C-word again.

Honey focused on her breathing. It was already ten minutes since she'd called Corrado. She felt nervous, impatient. Her mind was spinning, weaving excuses. She found herself saying things to Jocelyn that her father had said. Her brother, too. "If someone breaks into your home, threatens your family . . ." She paused to collect herself. "What we've done here is not a *crime*."

Honey knew she had to get the girl out of the house. She told her to go back to her place and pack up Lee's belongings. "Get everything. Put it all in his truck. Get the keys, too, and leave them in the ignition. Then I want you to go back inside and wait. You don't need to get involved."

"Won't the police want to talk to me?"

"I think it's better if I do it alone."

"*No.* I'm staying with you."

At which point, Honey told her the truth. "The police aren't coming, dear. I've called a friend. A relative."

"I don't understand. What friend? What are you talking about?"

"Enough with the questions! Please, just do as I say."

When the doorbell rang, Honey pushed the girl. "You really have to go. Trust me." She shepherded Joss into the dining room, and then out the French doors that led to the garden. "*Go!*"

* * *

Corrado was already standing in the foyer, kicking at the shattered amphora.

"What the hell happened?" he asked. "Are you all right?"

Before Honey could respond, Corrado's son Peter appeared, fingering the busted door.

As the two of them stared at her, she saw not only her brother in their faces; she saw herself, as well.

She led them into the house, and after explaining the situation, Corrado asked her bluntly: "What do you want me to do?" He didn't say it unkindly, though he gave her an odd look, as if he wanted her to admit something—perhaps that the two of them were not as different as she liked to pretend. He was probably still angry about how she'd shunned him, or the fact that she'd befriended the enemy. Surely Rina had mentioned that Honey was in touch with Teena.

Standing in her bedroom, he asked, "Why are you helping this girl? Who is she to you?"—as if to say, *She's not family.*

Honey said, "The man's done awful things to her. To me, as well. He threatened my life."

When Corrado tilted his head and asked his terrifying half-question—"So you want me to . . . ?"—Honey spoke plainly. She told her nephew that she didn't want the man to come back and harass them. She said, "Intimidate him, if you must. But please don't do anything drastic."

"Such as?"

He seemed to want her to say it.

But Honey did not say it. She was trained not to say it. To say it would be to admit that murder was a *thing*, that it *existed*, that it could easily be arranged.

Still, she felt it was important to be clear about what she wanted—which is to say, what she did *not* want Corrado to do. But before she could clarify, he whispered, "Trust me. You don't have to worry."

Honey, suddenly breathless, leaned against the wall.

"So where is he?" asked Corrado.

When they were in the closet, Honey felt sick again. Lee had the look of a mangled animal, and he was so agitated by the new arrivals that he wet himself. They all watched the dark stain spreading between his legs.

"Holy shit," said Peter—though this seemed to be less in reference to the urine than to Honey's accomplishment.

Lee squirmed in his constraints, then started to cry. He seemed to intuit the nature of the men who were in the room with him. Honey spoke calmly, reassuringly: "They're just going to drive you away."

"Where?"

When no one answered him, Lee asked again, more plaintively. "*Where?*"

"Shut the fuck up!" barked Peter, who appeared to be enjoying this a tad too much.

Honey led her relatives out of the closet and told Peter to please give her and Corrado a moment of privacy. The boy was agreeable, strangely whistling as he left the bedroom.

Honey wasn't sure what to say to Corrado. For a distressing few seconds, her mind went blank. She knew it was important to be clear about what she was asking her nephew to do. But she found herself bringing up something else.

"Your son," she said.

Corrado glanced toward the hallway, where Peter had gone.

"Not that son," Honey said. "Michael."

"What about him?" Corrado tensed, a coiled thing it was surely unwise to provoke.

And yet Honey couldn't help herself. She needed to know.

"Tell me," she said. "How on earth could you hurt him like that?" She mentioned the photos she'd seen on Teena's phone.

Corrado stared at her, clenched his fists, his body enraged by the question. "Don't worry," he said. "I'll pay for my sins."

Honey was tempted to tell him that he'd pay very slowly, to explain what she'd learned in Sunday school, how the clocks in Hell ran on a sinner's blood. Drop by drop, eternally.

But surely Corrado already knew this. Besides, Honey couldn't bear to speak any more about Michael. She shifted the subject back to the matter at hand.

"So my friend in there," she said, gesturing toward the closet.

Corrado seemed relieved to move on to other people's crimes. When he muttered, "I'll take care of it," Honey felt something constrict in her chest. This discussion about Lee's fate was far too murky.

"Just get him out of New Jersey. That's all you need to do," said Honey. "Take him to Connecticut or something."

Corrado nodded. "You must really care about this neighbor of yours," he said. "The girl, I mean."

"I do," said Honey.

Corrado's breathing was audible, aggrieved.

Honey knew her line. *I care about you too, dear.*

But it seemed she was of two minds—and their only compromise was silence.

Part Five

T hey didn't hurt him, did they?" Jocelyn asked.

"No," said Honey. "Don't be silly."

"But what were they doing in the house for so long?"

"Well, they couldn't take him away in broad daylight. It seemed prudent to wait until dark."

"That sounds ominous."

"Just practical," said Honey. "No reason for the neighbors to know our business."

She was trying her best to appear calm, to speak matter-of-factly about the previous evening, though the previous evening seemed to have nothing to do with facts. It seemed a dream, in which some alternate version of herself had run amok, said *va fangool* to the laws of time and space. Other laws had been broken, too.

"Where did they take him?" asked Joss.

"Do you really care? You wanted him gone, and he's gone."

"Yeah, but what if he comes back?"

"He won't."

"How do you know?"

"Darling, you can either believe what I say or not, but please stop with the questions. I know it was a nightmare, but it's over."

The girl nodded, though she didn't seem convinced. They were sitting in Honey's living room, before a tray of espressos. Joss stirred in enough sugar to kill an elephant. Finally she looked up and said, "So how do you *know* people like that?"

"Like what?"

"I mean, my God, they arrived in a *tank*."

"Don't be dramatic. It wasn't a *tank*. It was a *Hummer*. And I already told you, they're members of my family."

"I thought you weren't on friendly terms with your family."

"I'm not. It was a convenience to call them, that's all. I have no plans to see them again."

"But you trust them?"

"Unfortunately, I do—in certain ways. It's complicated."

"I just wonder if it would have been better to call the police."

"What's done is done," said Honey. "And listen to me, Joss—I need to make something very clear. You cannot speak of this, *ever*, to anyone. Do you understand me?"

"Yes. Of course."

A clock ticked as witness, as the women sipped their espressos.

"Signed in blood," murmured Honey, and Jocelyn repeated the words.

The girl kept her head down, lost in her little cup—but eventually she began to glance around, as if confused. "Wait a second."

"What?"

"I just noticed how empty the room is. Where are all your knick-knacks?"

"My knickknacks?"

"You know, all your stuff. And where are the paintings?"

Honey sighed. "I took them down. I was—I don't know—I was considering going away."

"*Moving?* Where?"

"Don't be nosy. And, anyway, it doesn't matter, because I've decided to stay. For a little longer, at least."

"You *have* to stay," exclaimed Joss.

"And why is that?"

"Because I . . . I can't imagine not having you here." The girl's face flushed with emotion; she looked like she might start weeping again.

"*Don't*," said Honey. "As my mother used to say: You won't get far on a river of tears."

"I can't help it." Joss mashed a napkin against her schnoz. "It's just—it's all so friggin' weird. I mean, I keep thinking about last night—thinking, *was that me?* You know, am I *that person?*"

Honey had been asking herself the very same questions.

After a while, Joss got up. "I better go or I'll be late." She made her way into the foyer, stopping at the broken door jimmy-rigged with masking tape. "This isn't safe. You can't just leave it like this."

"Don't worry. Someone's coming later to repair it."

The girl touched the splintered wood. Lingered.

"What is it, dear?"

"Nothing. I just . . . I mean, how am I supposed to go to work and pretend everything's normal?"

Honey agreed it was a trick. "Plus, it's unfortunate you have to spend the day with your hands in other people's mouths."

The girl grimaced, perhaps thinking of Lee's tooth. She seemed hesitant to leave. "Hey, I was wondering if you might want to come over for dinner tonight. I really don't want to be alone."

"May I take a rain check? I suspect I'll be too tired."

"I can do Italian," persisted Joss. "I make a really great chicken parm. Well, a variation of it. I do it without the cheese."

"That's quite impossible, dear. The whole point of chicken parm is the cheese. Listen—why don't you come over here, instead. I'll make you a real Italian supper."

Jocelyn nodded, then lurched at Honey, enveloping her in a wet and snuffling hug. "I love you."

"Yes, yes," said Honey, pushing the girl away. "There's no need to get maudlin about it. Off you go."

* * *

What she wanted more than anything was a hot bath. But she was afraid that if she took one she'd dissolve. There seemed to be very little holding her together. Maybe the great enterprise of her life, the construction of a glittering self, was merely a shell game, and one that had gone on for so long that she'd lost track of the little ball of chaos hiding underneath.

It had shocked her, of course, when she'd first struck Lee with the gun. But then she'd done it again, hadn't she? And though she wanted to be appalled by this, the truth was, she was not appalled. The feeling from earlier remained—that the brutality was somehow a relief. It was a reckoning with both her power and her weakness.

Prior to her suicide attempt, she'd made an accounting of her crimes. But there were others, far worse. When Honey had told the story to Angela Carini, about what her father and uncle had done to Richie Verona, she'd left something out. She'd mentioned the men coming out of the woods, her uncle with the shovel in his hands. She'd told Angela how she'd started screaming, how terrified she'd been.

But she hadn't told the dying woman about what had happened afterward. How, later that night, when she was finally in bed, safe, clean, in a cream-colored nightgown with embroidered daisies, she'd had a change of heart. In her childhood room, with the little pieces of colored glass on her windowsill and her schoolbooks piled neatly on her desk, she'd stared at the ceiling and felt relieved that Richie was dead. More than relieved, she'd felt *glad* about what her father had done. She even hoped that just before the boy died, he'd felt something similar to what she had felt, when he'd forced her down on his bed and entered her. A feeling of powerlessness, of being trapped, unable to change his fate. No longer master of his life.

That night, a fifteen-year-old Honey had slept surprisingly well, and the next morning when she went downstairs and saw her father in the kitchen, she kissed him on the cheek. She'd done this, partly, because she was afraid of him, and wanted to appease him. But she'd done it because she'd been grateful, too. Never before had her father done something *just for her.* Was it not, in some way, an act of love? Later, of course—especially after her years with Kleinerman—she recognized the error in her thinking, understood that what her father had done was an act of pride, of domination, an animal thing.

But, despite this knowledge, she can't help but go back to the heart of the girl who'd been glad, *glad*, that Richie Verona was killed in those desolate woods, while she waited in the warm sand, beside her uncle's baby-blue convertible.

Maybe she was her father's daughter, after all.

A few nights later, Honey shared another contemplative dinner with Jocelyn. The girl was uncharacteristically quiet, and the clank of the flatware against the plates produced what Honey felt to be an ecclesiastical effect, like bells praising the Eucharist. And praise was called for, surely. Honey had made a spectacular dinner. Pasta al profumo di funghi. Braised broccoli rabe with hot pepper and garlic. A panzanella of radicchio, fennel, and olives. Somehow a vegetarian dinner, which is to say a bloodless one, seemed appropriate.

At one point, while eating the mushroom pasta, Jocelyn's eyes grew glassy. "I've never tasted anything like this," she said. "It makes me want to cry."

Honey assured the girl that the reaction was perfectly reasonable. "Food, my dear, is one of the great romances of life." She admitted that, once, in Marseilles, she'd succumbed to tears over a particularly fragrant bouillabaisse.

"I thought you only ate crackers," Jocelyn mumbled, her mouth full. "Who knew you were such a great cook."

"Well, these are very simple dishes," replied Honey, attempting modesty. "A lot of my recipes I learned from my mother."

But as Honey looked at the table, she realized that not a single thing she'd cooked had come from her mother. Everything was straight off the menu at Dante's. In fact, what Honey had prepared for Jocelyn were the exact three dishes she'd ordered the night that Dominic died. Of course, she'd never had a chance to partake of them that evening, since Nicky had keeled over before the meal was served. She recalled the owner, Tarantelli, blathering at the other patrons: *Don't worry, people, it's not the food. They haven't eaten yet.*

As Jocelyn blissfully chowed, Honey put down her fork, unable to swallow, now that the meal had become a memorial. "Have more," she encouraged the girl, spooning out some greens.

"Thanks. I like how spicy they are."

"Aleppo pepper in the olive oil," Honey explained.

After a while the girl looked up, with a contented sigh and a bit of funghi on her chin. "Do you remember the day we met?"

"Of course," said Honey. "Food on your chin, dear. Why do you ask?"

"It's just"—the girl dabbed away the mushroom—"I was sort of afraid of you."

"Afraid of *me*? I think you've got it backwards. I recall coming home to a station wagon atop my cherry tree, pink blossoms screaming from under the wheels."

Jocelyn laughed. "It wasn't *that* bad."

"Wasn't that bad? It was like Dorothy's house coming down on the poor old witch."

"Exactly," the girl said, smiling. "You were really mean that day."

"I'm never mean."

"Well, maybe not mean—but you definitely intimidated me."

"Don't be silly. I recall being nothing but polite."

"It was just the way you were dressed, the way you talked. You told me your name was Gina Lollobrigida."

"Did I?" Honey laughed now, too. "Well, I have to admit, I wasn't sure I wanted to get chummy with you. At my age, one isn't really looking for friends."

"But we're friends now."

"Obviously."

A chaotic happiness flew through the room, casting confusing shadows. The women sobered and wiped the smiles from their lips, perhaps feeling that their good humor was inappropriate, considering recent events.

Jocelyn noisily chewed some fennel. After a while, she surprised Honey by saying: "I don't know, I just . . . I guess I've never liked myself very much. Even when I was little I didn't like myself." She began to scratch her forearms, in that unfortunate way of hers. "As a kid, I actually hated myself."

Though Honey knew nothing of Joss's family, she could sense the story. "I suspect it was other people who hated you, dear—and you simply got confused."

"Maybe," Joss said. "I never thought about it that way."

"Take it from me—you'll like yourself more, as time goes by. You just have to be careful not to destroy yourself before you get there."

"It's not like I haven't thought about it."

"Have you?"

In lieu of an answer, Jocelyn rolled her eyes and snorted. "Wow, I'm really being a downer tonight."

"You're just being honest. And I applaud that."

"I know I talk too much."

"We all have faults. I *drink* too much."

"I *eat* too much."

"Darling, it's not a competition."

Jocelyn had a crumb on her T-shirt, and Honey removed it.

"Oh, thanks."

When the bottle of Viognier was nearly finished, Jocelyn leaned forward in her chair. "Do you mind if I ask you a personal question?"

Honey murmured receptively.

"I was just wondering what was up with that friend of yours?"

"What friend?"

"The guy with the convertible. Where's he been?"

"I have no idea," Honey said, a bit too sharply. "I haven't talked to him in ages."

"I thought I saw his car in your driveway, a few weeks ago. Like, parked overnight."

Honey sensed her face changing color.

Jocelyn caught it. "What's going on?"

"Nothing's going on."

"Come on, if I'm being honest, why can't you do the same?"

"I am being honest."

"So you didn't sleep with him?"

"Absolutely not. For God's sake!"

"Because I'd totally understand if you did. I mean, he's a really handsome guy."

"He's a *child*."

Honey could feel the acid on her cheeks. It was intolerable. She began to babble.

"He's just a painter I know. He helped me out of a rough spot one day—that's all. And then I was considering buying one of his pieces. But I decided against it. It was much too large."

"Was it?" said Jocelyn, with a suggestive tilt of her head.

"Oh, just shut up," said Honey. "And get your mind out of the gutter."

* * *

The following day, Honey rehung the paintings. Why not enjoy them while she could? Surely there was very little art in the afterlife. As a great lama once said: there are no connoisseurs in heaven.

It was sweetness itself to see them again: *Le Dilemme de l'Ange* in the bedroom, the Morandi in the kitchen—which she hung in the same place, too close to the stove. When she was finished, she opened the junk drawer next to the sink and gently lifted out the tea towel, inside of which were the fragments of the broken vase. Michael's doing. Honey no longer blamed him; she blamed herself.

She unwrapped the pieces and laid them on the counter, moved them around like a puzzle. The breaks were clean, and she was able to fit two pieces together without any interruption to the pattern. As she continued her efforts, other fragments came together in happy matrimony.

Honey wondered if Frantzen and Sons were still in business. For generations, they'd been the best art conservationists in New York City. Even if they didn't work with porcelain, they'd be able to provide a reference. Honey decided to give them a ring tomorrow.

Give them a ring. What a lovely phrase that was. So many people, too many, could never be rung again.

53 Do You Ever Ask Yourself?

Corrado had called several times, but Honey didn't answer. At the sight of his name on her cell, she'd feel a tightening in her gut. She knew that she'd have to speak with him eventually, and she knew that he'd be discreet when discussing what had happened. What concerned her was the thought that her nephew might think the two of them had reached an understanding and could now be friends. For Honey it was quite the opposite. That messy little episode in the closet, and Corrado's willingness to provide the cleanup, seemed a perfect way to end things, to punctuate a long history of violence among the Fazzingas. A history in which Honey was by no means blameless.

When she finally answered one of Corrado's calls, she greeted him cordially. He seemed in a good mood, though possibly in a hurry. He began by saying that he'd taken care of things, not to worry. Then he quickly transitioned to a dinner invitation.

"Your birthday's coming up, isn't it? We thought we'd do something at the house."

Honey replied that it was kind of him to remember, but that she'd never been big on birthdays. "This year, I was thinking I'd spend it alone." She said she might go to the cemetery, to visit Nicky's grave. "So I won't come to dinner—but thank you for asking."

Corrado didn't push. He said he understood. He said that he, too, had been spending more time by himself lately. "But maybe we could at least meet for coffee one morning. Just the two of us."

"I'm sure we'll run into each other at some point," Honey replied, evasively. "And please know that I'm grateful for all you've done . . ."

Corrado scoffed. "I can never tell when you're being sarcastic."

"I'm not. Believe me."

Corrado fell silent, and when he spoke again, it was with an air of belligerent affection. "I'm not gonna leave you alone," he said.

Honey laughed and asked if that was a threat.

"I admire you, Aunt Honey. You've got balls. And no, it's not a threat. It's a promise."

"I appreciate that," she said. "I really do. Please give my best to your family."

And with that, she hung up the phone.

* * *

Corrado didn't call again. Despite his promise, he left her alone. Weeks passed, without any interaction. They didn't run into each other at the bank or the supermarket. Honey never dreamed of him. She could feel her nephew flattening, fading, like a blossom pressed inside a book.

Then, one morning, while waiting outside for Jocelyn, Honey's phone began to chirp. When she pulled it from her handbag, she saw that the call was from a private number. Though she usually ignored such calls, she felt compelled to answer.

The voice on the line was bright and sharp, vaguely familiar.

"Aunt Honey—hi."

"Who is this?"

"It's Rina. Sorry for blocking my number. I just . . . I was worried you wouldn't pick up if you knew it was me."

"Don't be silly."

"Well, we didn't exactly leave each other on the best terms. And I really wanted to apologize."

"You don't need to—"

"Yes, I do. I was rude, the last time we spoke. I guess I was upset about you talking to those people."

Honey wondered if Rina was referring to people like Teena. But before Honey could ask for specifics, Rina shifted gears.

"Listen, I was just calling because the baby shower is this weekend. And I know you said you weren't coming, but we'd really like to have you there."

"That's very kind." Honey was surprised by this unexpected chumminess.

"It won't be a huge gathering," the woman continued. "Maybe twenty people. And no men, so . . ."

It was a tricky moment, but Honey felt she had to speak honestly. "I don't think it's a good idea, Rina. For me to be there."

"Why is that?"

When Honey replied that it simply didn't feel right, that it was probably best for everyone if she stayed away, Rina wasn't satisfied.

"Didn't Corrado just do you a favor?"

"What does that have to do with this?"

"I'm just saying, I don't understand why you can't take two hours out of your day to be with us."

Honey played the age card. "I just seem to be less and less cut out for these kinds of things as I get older. Knowing me, I'll end up saying something that will upset everyone. And I don't want to ruin your party."

"You're not gonna do that," Rina said, reassuringly. Then, rather astoundingly: "And, I mean, why do you have to say anything at all? It's just a day for everyone to enjoy themselves. If people have differences, it's not the place to air them."

"No—of course not."

"Plus, the food'll be fantastic. You know it's at Dante's, right?"

"I do."

"I told everyone to just forget about their diets. Mr. Tarantelli's doing a fritto misto with the appetizers. Then, for dessert, we're having a cake of course, but since Addie likes her sweets, we're having a sort of Venetian hour too. Sfogliatelle, frittelle, cannoli . . ."

As Rina enumerated the pastries, she spoke quickly—a rush of words that seemed to be a way of running from what really mattered.

"It all sounds delicious," said Honey.

"So you'll come?"

Honey paused. "The truth is, Rina, it would be hard for me to come to a party with you and never bring him up."

It was Rina's turn to pause—and when she spoke again, her brightness was stained. "Like I said, this is a happy occasion. And anyway, I really don't want to discuss my son with you. Why can't you respect that?"

"I do respect it—and that's why I'm not going to come."

"Fine. To be honest, I didn't even want you there. I was doing this for Corrado."

"I see."

"He feels it's important that you be included. So I'm respecting his wishes. And I don't understand why you can't do the same. You're all he has left. His parents are gone, his grandparents."

"We share a great deal, I realize that. But I just think we'll all feel more warmly about each other if we keep our distance."

"You're unbelievable."

"I'd still like to send Addie a present, though. Shall I send it to your address?"

"Don't bother, okay?"

"It's no bother."

"I'm sure. Just like all those presents you used to send Corrado when he was a kid, as if that replaced actually being there."

This one hit the mark, and Honey found herself at a loss for words.

Rina filled the gap: "Do you ever ask yourself how you ended up being such a cold person?"

"Please, let's not argue."

"So what am I supposed to tell Corrado?"

"Tell him I love him."

"But that you won't come to a party for his grandchild?"

"That's correct. The thing is, dear . . ." Honey wanted to put a finer point on this, to explain herself further. But then she heard a clicking sound.

"Sorry, I have another call," Rina said, her voice bright again, armored with civility. "If you change your mind, you know where to find us. Saturday. Two o'clock."

*　*　*

When Jocelyn arrived in her station wagon, Honey felt an inordinate relief. She put the phone back in her bag and approached the car.

"Sorry I'm late," Joss said. "I had a guy with a shitload of tartar. I mean, it was like *cement*. What's the matter? You look upset."

"I'm not upset. But I do have a question."

"Shoot," the girl said as she pulled away from the curb.

"Do I seem cold to you?"

"What do you mean?"

"I mean *cold*. Not warm. Chilly. Unloving."

"I don't know—I guess sometimes you can be sort of chilly."

Not the answer Honey was hoping for.

"On the other hand," said Joss, "I wouldn't call you *unloving*. Maybe I'd think that if I didn't know you. But I completely get the whole thing you do."

"The *thing* I do?"

"Your act. Whatever."

Honey harrumphed and put on her sunglasses. The car was sweltering.

Jocelyn apologized for the broken AC, pulling at the damp sleeves of her ghastly orange T-shirt.

Thank God they were going clothes shopping.

* * *

At the mall, though, the task proved difficult. After bemoaning Joss's predilection for colors that seemed best suited to jelly beans or plastic beach pails, Honey proposed a compromise. She'd tolerate a few of the garish hues, on the condition that the items were well cut, and flattering to a figure so outrageously full that it required prudence more than permission.

"Huh," Joss said at one point, cocking her hip before a trifold mirror. "I actually look good in this."

"That's the point, dear."

"Oh my God, look at my butt!"

"Yes, very nice. Unfortunately, those other things you're fond of wearing often have the appearance of diapers. These slacks complement your endowment without insulting it. And the blouse presents your case, as well, but doesn't oversell it."

"Only problem is, I can't afford these. We can probably find knock-offs at Marshall's."

"We're not going to Marshall's."

"What about Big Lots?"

"*Big Lots?* The name alone is offensive. No. I'm buying the ensemble for you. Let's just call it a birthday present."

"My birthday's in December."

"All the better. Because I hate shopping during the holidays."

"You don't have to do this."

"That's true. But I want to. Turn around, let me see the back again," commanded Honey.

"You think it looks all right?"

"More than all right. You're quite the hot tomato."

"Why are you crying then?" said Joss.

"Am I?" Honey looked in the mirror. It was true; she was visibly verklempt.

When the girl pressed for a reason, Honey claimed it was seeing such a transformation.

"Do I look that different?"

"You do. You look like *yourself*."

round ten o'clock on a Sunday night, Honey received a text from Teena. Watch this, was all it said. Below the message was a link, but Honey was hesitant to tap it, since among the jumble of letters that composed the link was the word *falling*. It seemed a dangerous proposition, bringing to mind outcast angels and broken hips. Still, Honey took the risk.

Almost instantly she arrived at a website featuring a young woman strumming a guitar. The woman looked a bit like Honey's mother. After applying a pair of readers, Honey was forced to admit that the woman equally resembled her father. Nothing complicated here. The woman in question was Mica.

He was sitting on a straight-backed chair, in a sparsely furnished room. An open window beside him let in too much light. The video flickered in and out of focus. The sound, on the other hand, was excellent, and Honey turned up the volume to better hear the music. It was a hummable confection, deftly played by Mica's long, pale fingers—the melody so disarmingly sweet that Honey was unprepared when her grandnephew began to sing. The voice was nothing like his speaking voice. What emerged now, from a painted mouth, was a kind of weapon—a quick sharp blade, keening in trenchant melancholy. Completely engrossed by the sound, Honey failed to absorb the words; only slowly did they stake their claim.

Can you see how far it goes?
Can you see into my soul?
If we take a step we'll fall.
Baby, take my hand.
Baby, let's just go.

Honey recalled reading a version of these lyrics in Mica's notebook. They hadn't seemed anything special, just a bit of adolescent pap. But now, reunited with their creator's breath, they came to life.

When I saw you on the corner,
You were crying black mascara.
Then you turned and called my name.
Baby, take my hand.
Baby, let's just fall.

At this point, Mica leaned in deeply to his playing; his torso seemed to fold as his voice soared into a perfectly calibrated falsetto, the sound so unnaturally pure it was almost frightening.

Falling, oooh, oooh, oooh
Falling, oooh, oooh, oooh
Where our tears fly up like swallows,
All things free, yeah, all things rising.
Falling together, babe, we're flying.

Honey listened to the remainder of the song in amazement, slack-jawed before the wizardry of the human voice. The high notes were miraculous, seizing ecstasy from heartache. As the performance was ending and the strumming came to a peaceful repose, Mica looked up and stared directly at the camera. He smiled shyly, revealing a triumphant set of teeth.

The video had nine hundred and ninety-seven views, but over the next ten minutes Honey brought it to a thousand.

*   *   *

First thing the following morning, she called her friend.

"That song," she said. "It's marvelous."

"I told you," said Teena. "She's the real thing."

When Honey mentioned that her mother, too, was an excellent singer,

Teena replied that, in her opinion, Mica's talent was born of itself. "Sui generis," she proclaimed mordantly.

For several minutes the women blabbed and burbled like a pair of competitive godparents. Teena took the upper hand when she admitted that she'd actually *spoken* to Mica. Though Honey had a thousand questions, she held her tongue, knowing it wasn't within her rights to press for information.

"He's a strange one," said Teena.

Honey replied that she didn't find the song strange at all. "I thought it was rather brilliant, the sweetness of the melody against that ferocious voice. He seemed hell-bent on reversing the laws of the universe—what's up, what's down. Don't you think?"

"I think you talk too much," said Teena. "Besides, I wasn't talking about the song. I was talking about something he told me on the phone."

Honey waited as the woman took a cigarette-puffing pause.

"He said he was concerned about his parents." Teena's tone was dismissive. "He wanted to make sure they were 'okay.'"

"I don't understand," muttered Honey.

"Of course not. None of you understand. Mica is a very caring person. His parents don't deserve him. Before he left, you know what I said? I told him he should never see them again, never *talk* to them." Teena grunted in frustration.

"He's not planning on coming back, is he?" asked Honey.

"No. I don't think so." Another long and agonized pull from the cigarette. "But he wanted me to ask you about them."

"About his parents?"

"Yes. So you tell me what you know, and then I tell him."

"I'm sorry," said Honey, "I have no idea how they are. I mean, I know they're still angry. But to be honest, I haven't had much contact with them. And I'm surprised that Mica would be concerned."

Honey's comment was slightly disingenuous. She knew, from her own experience, about the brainwashing of Italian blood. For years she'd worried about her parents, too—especially her mother.

"He suggested that you go and see them," Teena said. "Talk to them."

"Do you think that I should?" asked Honey.

"Personally, I think they should be shot."

"They're victims of their history," Honey countered mildly. "Still, I really don't want to see them."

"It's fine," Teena said, sounding relieved. "Besides, I think Mica's just being sentimental. She'll forget about them eventually. Get on with her life."

Honey knew that Teena's inconsistency in regard to pronouns was not laziness. Rather, it was a kind of strategy, a way to stretch the boundaries of the world. Maybe she was also testing Honey, to see if she could flow, be open, be fluid.

"One day soon," Teena repeated, "Mica will forget all about Mommy and Daddy."

"Yes," murmured Honey. "I'm sure you're right."

* * *

But she wasn't sure, at all. She knew too well that the pull to reclaim the love of one's family could be hard to resist. Despite her attempt to condemn the impulse as brainwashing—or, as Teena had called it, sentimentality—Honey couldn't deny the power of family romance, which was love in its primary colors, its building blocks. The foundation for all love that came after it. What child would not want to take the pieces of the toppled castle and attempt to rebuild it? Especially a child whose castle had been so horrendously demolished.

Honey understood exactly where Michael was coming from. Still, as for his request that she talk to the family, she just couldn't bring herself to do it.

Once again, she prayed for the boy. For the girl. She prayed that they would never come home.

oney rose early, to enjoy a little coolness before the temperature soared. The prediction was for a high of ninety-three. In some ways it seemed a gift: ninety-three on her eighty-third birthday. It almost made her feel young.

Still, a heat wave in New Jersey was never pretty. By ten o'clock, it was already beastly. Honey put on a pale yellow sheath, rather slim-fitting, that made her look like a stick of butter. On her feet, a pair of Franciscan-style sandals in creamy caramel, featuring toes done up in Sunset Peach, a color she'd banned since April. It had been Nicky's favorite.

When she left the house, the sun, behind a humid scrim of heat, looked misshapen, vaguely sinister. Honey drove too fast, to the tempo of a frolicsome Vivaldi, and when she arrived, rolling through the open gates, she headed to the north side of the cemetery, where her parents and brother were entombed.

But wait, she wasn't here to see her family. She pulled over, confused, realizing she hadn't a clue where Nicky's grave was located. She'd only watched the burial from a distance, hiding behind an oak tree—and every tree in this goddamned cemetery looked the same. Honey had no choice but to go to the office and inquire.

She parked before a large, squat building of red brick and blinded windows, surrounded by a curving battalion of cypress. Inside, the tiled floor was very clean, with a dizzying pattern of black and white squares. There was no human in sight, only a long unwelcoming hallway with a series of massive wooden doors, all shut. Finally, spotting an open one, Honey walked in to find a gentleman in a crisp white oxford eating a hoagie. He looked up, still chewing. Honey averted her eyes, giving him a chance to swallow.

"Sorry," he said. "We don't usually have a lot of traffic on a weekday." He wiped a paper napkin across his mouth. "How can I help you?"

"I'm looking for a friend who's buried here. But I don't know where the gravesite is. Might I trouble you to look it up?"

"I'd be glad to. What's the name?"

"Dominic Sparra. S-P-A-R-R-A."

"Age?"

"I'm not exactly sure. I think he was eighty-four when he passed, possible eighty-five. It was just earlier this year."

"My condolences," the man replied dutifully. There was a piece of lettuce stuck in his teeth, though somehow this seemed touching.

"Middle name, Giovanni," offered Honey, "in case you need that."

"I might. Thank you. Our computer system's down, so just give me a sec."

The man stood and turned to a shelf behind him, on which there was a collection of large black volumes, lettered A through Z. He pulled down the one marked S, splayed it across the desk, and tenderly turned the pages, as if not to disturb the inhabitants.

"Got him. Says here he's on North Star Lane. Section three, row eight, grave fourteen."

The man put an X on a flimsy map, then handed Honey the paper.

"Thank you." She stared at the black-and-white maze. It was completely unreadable. Suddenly an impulse struck: "Oh, and I'd also like to get a key to my own family's mausoleum."

"What's the name?"

"Fazzinga. F-A-Z-Z-I-N-G-A."

The man took down another book, thumbing the pages more impatiently. "Let's see . . . I have a Pietro here, with a Sophia and an Enzo."

"That would be them."

"Okay, so it looks like a set of keys was issued to the family. And then of course we keep another set here."

"Well, I'll need yours then," said Honey.

"You're a member of the family?"

"Yes. The deceased are my parents and brother."

The man nodded and approached a large built-in cabinet to his left. Inside there were hundreds of keys hanging from a primitive grid of nails. It looked like something one might find in a medieval hostel. The man took down a ring with two keys—one large and ornate, the other smaller, sleeker. "There are two doors," he explained—"the main one, and then an outer gate."

"Yes." Honey recalled as much. "I've been in there before."

"I just need to see some ID," the man said.

"Of course." She set down her purse on the desk and took out her driver's license. "Terrible picture," she muttered, handing it over.

The man looked at the license a long time. Young people often did this, flabbergasted by the year of birth, which, to them, probably appeared prehistoric. Also, they could never seem to align this number with the woman before them; there were regularly comments like "You couldn't possibly be this old" or "You don't look a day over such and such." Honey smoothed her dress and waited for the compliment.

But the man, it turned out, wasn't looking at the birth date.

"I'm sorry, this is . . . the spelling of the last name isn't the same as that of the deceased."

Honey blinked, momentarily derailed. "Yes. It's a long story. But I can assure you that it's the right mausoleum."

"Okay, but I can't give you keys if you're not family."

"I just said that I *was*."

"Well, the ID says otherwise."

"Oh, for goodness sake. Can't you just take my word for it?"

The man said he couldn't, that even with proper ID he wasn't really supposed to hand out keys. "I'm sorry, I'm new here and I don't want to get in trouble. But, listen, I'd be happy to call the contact number I have on file"—he glanced again at the book—"for, uh, Corrado Fazzinga. And if he says it's fine—"

"No. Never mind." Honey sighed elaborately.

How absurd, to be denied access to the family tomb while being assaulted by the scent of salami. The half-eaten hoagie sat blithely on the desk, Cerberus reduced to lunch meat.

"It's for security purposes, ma'am. And to respect the family's privacy. I'm really sorry."

The man seemed genuinely apologetic, and Honey softened. "It's not your fault. And you're right, of course. One can never be too cautious. I might be a grave robber, for all you know."

"If it were up to me, I'd give you the keys, but"—the man leaned forward and adopted a whisper—"they probably have cameras installed in here."

"Forget about the cameras," replied Honey. "It's the dead you should worry about. They're watching, too."

"I don't doubt it," the man said, handing Honey back her license.

* * *

She sat in the Lexus and let her emotions zing about like bats. Why would she even want to enter that horrible mausoleum? She pictured the pink granite monstrosity, with its bas-relief columns, not to mention those carved scrolls inscribed with pompous epitaphs. Inside, it was like a clubhouse, furnished with bunk beds essentially, enough to accommodate twelve guests. Her parents had once hoped for a pride of grandchildren. Well, maybe Peter and Addie would make up for it. Years from now the clubhouse might be full. Honey, though, would never be a member—neither by choice nor invitation.

As she rolled away from the office, the sun was high, casting everything in bleak perfection. Without shadows, the pieces of the world looked uprooted, unmoored. The cemetery was nearly deserted, and the graves appeared tired, many of them adorned with dusty plastic flowers. When, after twenty minutes, Honey failed to locate Dominic's grave, she crumpled the map and stuffed it in her purse. What a way to spend her birthday.

Before leaving the cemetery, she decided to at least *drive* past the family tomb. To find it, Honey had no need of a map. She made her way slowly down the narrow streets, and soon she was parked on Cherry Blossom Lane, before the Fazzinga mausoleum. The surname was chiseled triumphantly above the doors, in a Romanesque font with tiny blade-like serifs.

This close, she could feel the chill of the bodies. But she willed herself out of the car and approached the tomb. The inner doors had small windows of double-paned glass, and the outer doors were basically gates. Which meant that if she stood on the very top step of the entryway, she'd be able to peer inside. But when she did this, pressing her nose between the metal bars, she could see nothing, only a darkness that refused to unfold.

She stepped back and traced her hand over one of the carved scrolls beside the doors.

BREVIS IPSA VITA EST
SED MALIS FIT LONGIOR

It was Honey who'd suggested this epitaph, after her brother was killed. Her father, at first, had scoffed at what he considered his daughter's arrogance. But when she translated the Latin for him, he fell silent.

Life is short, but made longer by misfortune.

It wasn't arrogance. It was simply the truth. And no one could deny it.

* * *

On the way home, while stopped at a red light, Honey heard what sounded like thunder. When she turned her head, she saw two dogs on the sidewalk, lunging at each other. Their human counterparts—one a small woman, and the other a child—seemed incapable of untangling the animals. The growling was horrendous, and the child, clutching a taut leash, was crying.

Honey watched, fascinated and appalled, with a startling sense of clarity. It was as if something inside her chest had opened its eyes. She immediately understood what she needed to do. When the light turned green, she drove on, breathlessly.

There was very little time.

Part Six

S ince her no-show at the baby shower, Honey hadn't heard a
peep from the Fazzingas. But in early October a large cream-
colored envelope arrived, an invitation to the christening. The
ceremony and after-party were in mid-November, on a day that Honey
had already scheduled an appointment. It was as if the universe had decided for her.

Besides, it was not as if they were begging her to come. On the card
there was no personal note, or even a signature. Also, Honey's name and
address, though seemingly handwritten, were clearly generated by a computer program designed to mimic penmanship. Her label might have
been spit from a machine and stuck on an envelope inadvertently. Or
perhaps Corrado had mailed the invitation on his own, against Rina's
wishes. Whatever the case, Honey didn't RSVP.

Still, she kept the card on her desk, propped up against the reading
lamp. Occasionally she traced a finger over the embossed cradle, above
which floated a golden cross, like the sword of Damocles. This was, after
all, a child born to powerful men; there'd always be danger.

And it was a boy, no less. Of course it was. Even as Honey shook her
head at this, she wished the best for the kid—a kid she'd never get to
know. The age difference alone prevented it.

Vittorio Carlo, his parents had named him (so it said on the invitation). Honey found it curious that he'd been given the same middle
name as Michael. Certainly, it couldn't have been Peter's idea; he, more
than anyone, seemed to despise his brother. Honey didn't attempt to
figure it out. Every family had its own magic for dealing with its skele-
tons—so who knew what these people were up to, what act of erasure or
rehabilitation this Carlo implied? At least it was a mellifluous appella-
tion. *Vittorio Carlo.* Hopefully they wouldn't end up calling him *Victor*
or *Vito,* neither of which Honey cared for.

Well, maybe she'd leave him something in her will. There were other beneficiaries she wanted to add, as well. For example, she wanted all of Florence's dresses to go to the grandson—that albino child Edgar, the angel of Florie's life. Of course, she still planned to leave most of her money to Mica.

It was an interesting moment for Honey. Some days, she was almost happy—not inappropriately so, but with a sense that her life had reached a pleasing balance, the lighting perfect, the relationship of foreground to background deftly handled. Often, for no reason, she found herself smiling.

Recently, Teena had shared more of Mica's music. One of the videos had over two hundred thousand views. That Honey knew anything about her grandnephew's life was solely by virtue of Teena. The women lunched together frequently, and always at Dante's. Honey felt she'd finally found a mature female friendship—something she'd not had since her days with Lara and Suzanne. Jocelyn was more of a child. But Teena was a peer, and at times an excellent sparring partner. The two women shared a perspective on life that was both compassionate and sardonic. And despite the pair of them being somewhat jaded, they could easily be seduced by wonder. They laughed often, occasionally to tears, and Teena was a fabulous gossip. The most delicious news, of late, was that Mica was in love—though Honey had already suspected as much. The songs hid nothing.

*　*　*

On the morning of the christening, Honey got dressed for her appointment earlier than was necessary. She chose a pumpkin-colored blazer and an upbeat tweedy skirt with flecks of pink. It seemed a good choice for the day, which was bright and cloudless, the sky a flawless cabochon of azurite. It might be nice to take a little drive before her noontime commitment. Maybe stop at that new café that had opened next to Mabel's, enjoy one of the potent espressos they served in those charming Le Creuset cups. A surprisingly stylish place for Ferryfield. No doubt its proximity to the gay bar was its raison d'être. That sort liked a fancy cup.

When she was in the car, though, she didn't head toward Mabel's.

Chopin was on the radio, one of the nocturnes she'd played repetitively during her soul sickness this past spring. The music exerted a mesmeric influence, and Honey found herself driving in another direction. Chopin, it seemed, wasn't in the mood for coffee.

Listening to the bright cold notes, Honey realized that beneath her fluffy mood there remained a heavy stone of sadness. It felt good, in a way—like justice. An all-encompassing happiness was not what she deserved. Often she recalled her moment with Lee. What she'd done to him. Even more: what Corrado may have done. Whatever had happened to Mr. Czernik after he'd been escorted from the closet, all the blame lay on Honey.

"Take him to Connecticut," she'd told her nephew. It was something her father used to say when he meant something quite different from New England. Had she forgotten that? In the car, under the spell of Chopin, Honey wondered if she'd been avoiding Corrado as a way of avoiding herself—which was to say, her guilt. Surely it was time to confront it.

She drove to St. Margaret's and parked across the street—not planning to enter the church, but merely to spy on the comings and goings. Perhaps, as penance, she'd be subjected to a glimpse of the baby.

And then, somehow—either through an error in time or her own judgment—Honey was inside the place, sitting in the last pew, not far from the statue of the patron saint. This area of the church was drenched in shadow, and it was unlikely that anyone other than the saint would see her.

The service had already begun, and apparently the family was going whole hog, with a full baptismal mass. Scripture, hymns, Communion, all the bells and whistles. In the air the festive reek of frankincense. It had been ages since Honey had attended a Catholic mass, yet it was so familiar—the drone of the priest, the liturgical phrases etched so deeply into her being, it was as if the man in the pulpit were stealing Honey's innermost words.

But it was the sound of the congregation that she found the most hypnotic. The communal responses, half mumbled, achieved the lonesome din of animals. And then the bang and creak and rustle, every time the worshipers kneeled or stood or sat. It was like a depressing square dance, in which no one touched. Honey danced along, feeling like an impostor. She'd always felt like that here. Even when she was young, at six or seven—when she'd been an absolute ray of innocence—she was filled with terror, waiting for the Almighty to find something wrong with her. As a child, she could never stop fidgeting during mass. She was doing the same thing now, glancing around in an effort to spot her family.

When, finally, it came time to perform the sacrament, the parents got up and approached the altar—Addie in a pale blue dress, carrying the child. Honey couldn't see it very well from the back. The best she could make out was a squirmy blur wearing a pint-size gown. It was a very tiny baby. Even more shocking was its coloring. That, Honey *could* see. The child was fair-skinned, the hair on his head diabolically blond. In this regard, he looked nothing like his parents, both of whom were brunettes. He looked more, in fact, like Michael—which was to say, more like the Great Pietro. Honey, too, had once had hair like that.

She wondered if the young father, standing at the altar, could see the various faces implied by the creature he'd created; if he could see his brother there. Genetics was nothing if not a spook show. The ghosts waited in the blood. Then pounced.

A moment later, another young couple ascended to the stage. The godparents, no doubt. They stood beside Peter and Addie, all of them behind what looked like a rococo birdbath. The squirming child was absolutely quiet as they prepared to drown him. The priest adjusted his microphone and then, with the fervor of McCarthy, began to interrogate the godparents.

"Do you renounce Satan and all his works?"

"Do you believe in God, the Father Almighty, Creator of Heaven and Earth?"

"Do you believe in Jesus Christ, His only son, our Lord, who was born into this world and suffered for us?"

"And do you believe in the Holy Ghost, the Holy Catholic Church, the communion of Saints, the forgiveness of sins, the resurrection of the body, and life everlasting?"

"I do," said Honey, as the priest poured the water over the child's head. The poor thing wriggled desperately, then opened his mouth, as if to wail.

But he only closed his eyes and yawned.

* * *

Honey glanced at her watch. If she didn't leave immediately, she'd be late for her appointment. And yet she stayed in the ill-lit pew as the congregation exited the church.

Not a single person turned to look at her. It was as if she were invisible. Even Corrado and Rina went blithely by. The godparents followed, heads bowed over the celestial glow of their cell phones. When Addie and Peter approached, they walked slowly, Addie smiling at the baby, and Peter lost in thought, looking as he often did: twitchy and pensive. A selfish man, thought Honey, not to mention a dishonest one. But it turned out it was he who noticed the old woman sitting in the shadows.

"*Aunt Honey?* Is that you?"

"Yes," she said. "I'm sorry."

"About what?"

"I should have told you I was coming."

Addie offered a warm hello as Peter shouted toward the exit. "Mom! Dad!"

"No, that's all right." Honey stood. "Please don't make a fuss. I just wanted to congratulate the two of you. I can't stay for long."

It was too late, though. Rina and Corrado had already turned around, and then they were beside Peter and Addie, the whole group peering awkwardly at Honey.

"You're here," said Corrado.

Rina's greeting was only a nod.

"I wasn't feeling well," fibbed Honey. "But then I decided to come at the last minute." She was babbling, feeling tossed around by her own ambivalence. To steady herself, she focused on the child.

"He's beautiful," she said to Addie.

"Would you like to hold him?" the girl asked.

"Oh, no," said Honey. "He looks so peaceful with you."

Peter encouraged her. "You gotta hold him. He smells *amazing.*"
Addie was already extending the tiny creature in the white gown.

Honey reached out nervously. "What if I drop him?"

"You've got him—don't worry. Just put your hand under his head.
There you go."

Honey could hardly bear to look at the child, but she did so, in order
to avoid looking at her family.

It was all too much. The boy had green eyes—as if the blond hair
wasn't enough!

Michael's eyes. Her father's. Her own.

"Hello," she said to the baby, in a ridiculously formal voice.

Vittorio Carlo only stared, blinking. Honey could tell, from the pu-
rity of the child's gaze, that half of him still existed on the astral plane,
the source of all wonder and possibility. Honey rather wished she could
send him back there, where it was so much safer, and where surely there
existed a more perfect communion of souls. It was harder here on earth,
after being assigned a name, a body. These things were sometimes pris-
ons; often they didn't fit. Part of Honey wanted to take the child and
run. Take him into the Lexus and drive away.

But where would they go? That was the rub. The possibilities, as she
saw them, were mere poetics. Still, they seemed compelling. To take
the little thing to Toms River, wrap him in the buried blanket, say *I'm
sorry.* A long overdue apology to the child she'd given away. In her time-
traveling mind, she imagined, as well, giving the child to her mother—if
only she could manage to arrive just after Enzo's death. If nothing else,
she could simply take Vittorio home, hide him in her closet, among the
dresses.

The baby stared at her, reading her mind. Then he lifted a tiny fist, as
if to sock her in the face.

Peter laughed. "He's a bruiser already."

"Yes," said Honey, handing him back to Addie.

For a moment, everyone was quiet. Honey was aware of the mud-
puddle of her heart. Nothing was clear.

"We should really get to the restaurant," Rina said. "People are probably waiting."

"Do you want to drive with us?" asked Corrado, reaching out to take Honey's arm.

"No," she said. "But thank you, dear. I just . . . as I said, I just wanted to come to the church to wish you all the best. Unfortunately, I have an appointment, so I won't be able to come to the party."

Once more, she could hear the formality of her voice, and she felt disgusted with herself. But there was nothing to be done about it. It was too late to break free from the armor of decorum.

"Congratulations," she said again to Peter and Addie. "I'm very happy for you."

Kisses were dutifully applied. Corrado, looking hurt, turned away. His clan followed.

"Who invited her?" whispered Rina, apparently forgetting the excellent acoustics.

"I did," said Addie, after which she turned around to glance at Honey. The girl offered a beseeching smile, as if to say, *I know—but you have to forgive them.*

Honey returned the smile, though it felt more like a defense, a dam to restrain her tears. A moment later, she shouted out: "Corrado!"

Rina mumbled something into her husband's ear. Honey suspected it was an admonition, telling him to ignore the old woman. But Corrado told Rina to wait outside. Then he turned and walked back toward Honey.

Uncertain what to say, she stood there mute, her mouth hanging open.

Corrado filled the gap.

"So what kind of appointment do you have on a Sunday?"

"Oh, it's a minor medical thing," Honey said, with a dismissive flick. "Nothing to worry about."

"You have a doctor's appointment?"

"It's complicated," she replied. "But I'm fine. Honestly."

"If you're meeting a doctor on a Sunday, it must be pretty serious."

Oh God, she wished she hadn't gone down this path.

"Really, Corrado—I'm not about to croak."

"Well, that's good, I guess."

"Is it?"

Neither of their voices was particularly warm—the tone was more argumentative. Honey desperately wanted to ask her nephew: *Did you take that man to Connecticut?* But this wasn't the time, and it definitely wasn't the place, what with St. Margaret looming behind them.

Instead, Honey said something even worse. She said, "I'd really like to have you and Rina—and the children—over for dinner sometime."

Corrado regarded her coolly, as if he didn't trust her pleasantries, her smooth generalities. "*Sometime?*"

"I mean it," she said. "Why don't you all come over next weekend?"

When her nephew didn't respond, Honey pushed on. "Really, Corrado. I want to try. For Michael's sake."

"What does Michael have to do with it?"

Honey admitted that she'd had news of him. "He's doing well," she said. "And he was curious how you and Rina were doing."

Corrado seemed not to know how to process this information. Unbelievably, he didn't ask about his son. As for coming to dinner, he said he'd need to talk to Rina first. "With Vittorio around, she's been pretty busy."

"Well, you just let me know . . ."

"Listen, I better get out there, before . . ."

"Of course."

Corrado leaned forward and kissed her—in the old way, on both cheeks. It felt a bit perfunctory, but then his arms surrounded her, and she could smell the insistent cologne, whose only purpose seemed a will to dominate. Honey didn't pull away, though. She breathed her nephew in, eager to unravel him.

After drawing away from each other, they lingered in the aisle.

"Amazing hair on that kid," Honey finally said.

"Yeah," Corrado agreed. "Second chance, I guess."

Honey felt a chill. "I'm not sure it works like that," she said. It didn't seem right to let her nephew off the hook so easily. She told him she didn't necessarily believe in second chances. And though she tried to express this kindly, Corrado stiffened.

"Of course, the same goes for me," she added quickly, not wishing to let herself off so easily, either. "I've hurt people, too."

Corrado's smile matched her own—a grimace to stifle tears. Honey patted her nephew's arm. "They're waiting for you."

"I'll let you know about dinner," he said.

It did not sound promising.

ecrets can be fortifying. Honey had said this to Jocelyn, just the other night. They'd both been tipsy, and the girl was talking too much about Lee, particularly about those last moments with him. Honey sensed that, eventually, Joss might forget herself and speak about it to others. She was a blabber by nature. It had seemed prudent to educate the girl about the various ways to organize a life—about the art of silence, the power of negative space. What should be said and what was best left unspoken. She'd told the girl that a woman's public and private selves needn't be bosom buddies. After a half-bottle of Barolo, this had all sounded quite reasonable.

But now, as Honey drove away from St. Margaret's, she wondered if her little lecture on secrets was nothing more than drunken blather. Because the more she thought about it, the more she had to face a very simple fact: secrets were inseparable from lies. For two people to keep a secret with each other, it was often necessary that they lie to others.

A minor medical thing, she'd said to Corrado. It wasn't *minor* at all. It was her heart, for heaven's sake. And no exaggeration to say, a matter of life and death.

Honey parked in the filthy alley, wondering what she'd got herself into. Jocelyn wasn't the only person with whom she shared a secret.

* * *

"Ilaria," he said, opening the metal door.

"I'm sorry I'm late, dear. I got caught up with some family business. Where is everyone?" Honey was inside now, and the room was strangely empty. A large fold-up table, featuring a generous offering of wine and sparkling water, looked untouched. Nathan was having an open studio today, in an effort to drum up business. It had actually been Honey's idea.

"Only one person showed up," the painter said with a frown. "Guy stayed for less than thirty seconds."

"Well, people often arrive late for these things. Look at me. I'm sure you'll have a crowd before long."

"If not, the two of us have a lot of work to do." Nathan gestured toward the chorus line of wine bottles.

Honey demurred. "I think I'll stick to mineral water, for the time being." She suddenly felt nervous. She'd been counting on the buffer of other people. Even though she'd been alone with the painter quite a few times since they'd reconnected, today felt different. Perhaps because she hadn't *expected* to be alone with him; she hadn't prepared her mind for it. Also, having just come from a church, she sensed a pernicious cloud of judgment floating above her—a fat gray menace with a belly full of lightning bolts.

Honey was more than just nervous; she felt vulnerable, and slightly sad. Possibly because she'd held the baby. Now she was half in love with the little thing, and that didn't seem an option.

"You all right?" Nathan asked.

Nothing got past him. It was what she adored about the young man; also what she feared.

"My family has a way of stirring me up," she admitted.

"Are you still at odds with them?"

"How can I not be?"

Honey had actually spoken to Nathan about the Fazzingas. She hadn't told him everything, of course, though she'd talked quite a bit about Mica. Several times, over dinner—always at a restaurant, since she avoided having Nathan to the house—she spoke at length about her grandnephew and his parents. She spoke plainly, without dressing things up. She rambled, she sighed, she contradicted herself. Often, she feared, she made little sense. Still, these conversations had given her a chance to unburden her heart—something she hadn't been able to do with Corrado and Rina, neither of whom could speak honestly about their son.

With Nathan, though, no matter what she said to him, however outrageous or outlandish, he never blinked. Never looked surprised or uncomfortable, never looked as if he wished he were somewhere else. He seemed genuinely content, even grateful, to be with an old woman babbling like a confused teenybopper.

And it was more than just politeness, or chivalry. Nathan listened with uncanny intensity, as if her problems were his own. At times, this intensity disoriented Honey. The young man seemed a pool of water, into which everything she said fell like a pebble, and created an expanding multitude of rings. It was hypnotic, and Honey was often afraid that not just her words but she herself might fall into the pool. It had been a while since someone had attended to her so completely. Even Nicky, God rest his soul, had never been the best of listeners. There were a few nights with the painter when she'd spoken with him more intimately than she'd ever spoken with anyone—at least not since Kleinerman, or Mr. Hal. And in some ways, even more than with those men. Her effortless rapport with the painter was a mystery, and though it was a beguiling and warmish one, it somehow seemed wrong.

Just last week, at a sneakily lit restaurant with smoky mirrors in which a person might be tempted to forget her age, the young man's face had come quite close to hers, and for a desperate moment she'd wished it had come even closer.

But Nathan had remained on his best behavior. Ever since Honey had upbraided him for his senseless attraction to her, he'd made no further overtures in this regard. They were simply friends—and that was enough, she assured herself. More than enough.

She was glad she'd mustered the courage to call him again, after so many months. That day when she was driving home from the cemetery and saw the snarling dogs at the side of the road, she had known what she had to do. There was no denying that she'd mistreated Nathan, especially the morning after they'd fallen asleep at her house, exhausted from their long conversation about Redon.

The dogfight on the sidewalk reminded her not only of the young man's paintings but also of her unkindness toward him. She'd been horribly rude, closing a door in his face. Even worse: she'd evicted him unfairly, less because of his inappropriate desire than because she'd been afraid of her own.

In the studio now, he poured her a glass of mineral water. She sipped excessively, pretending she was parched. Then she told him about the christening, how tiny the child was, how much he looked like Michael.

"Such a beautiful baby. Well, I suppose they all are—but he was just so perfectly made."

When Nathan smiled in a way that seemed wistful, she asked him if he hoped to have children one day.

He said he wasn't sure. "Did you ever want them?"

"No," she said. "Maybe that makes me a monster—but, no, I never wanted children. Though sometimes I've thought that I might have made a good mother." Perhaps one day she'd tell him the whole story. She sensed that such a telling was possible, and even this possibility seemed a miracle.

That was the ironic thing about being with the painter: though she lied to get here, when she was with him she spoke only the truth, or at least more of it than usual. Certain things, of course, she'd never speak of. Certain secrets, she knew, would die with her.

Honey sipped her water pensively. When Nathan asked if she planned to see Corrado again, she shrugged. "I have trouble letting go of certain things."

Nathan nodded. "I get it. I have people, too, that I can't make peace with. Just give it time, I guess."

"Yes," she said, as if his advice were sound.

Give it time. It was a phrase for a young person, one who had the elixir in spades. For Honey, there was a limited supply; she knew that not everything could be worked out in the time she had left.

"Enough about me." Honey put down her water, ready to turn this around—to ask Nathan about the people he'd alluded to, the ones *he* couldn't forgive.

But surely it wasn't the right moment to have such a conversation, especially in a room where the young man was attempting to invent his future.

"Let's see what you've got here," she said, glancing at the walls, chockablock with paintings.

* * *

They didn't speak as she looked at the work. Three of the walls were consumed by Nathan's larger pieces, most of which Honey had seen.

They were dramatically lit, with well-aimed spots that accentuated their chiaroscuro. The canvas Honey had coveted months ago at the gallery was prominently displayed, and still unsold. It looked even better here in the studio. Again, Honey was struck by its beauty. Despite the gruesome subject matter, the painting was brilliantly done. Those raging dogs, the gleaming fur, the teeth, the blood—and then behind the beasts that O-mouthed child on the verge of screaming. Horrible, and yet ecstatic. She mumbled some praise—though it was mostly to herself, a rosary. Nathan's talent was a balm, in the same way that her grand-nephew's was. It calmed her to be in the presence of someone who took the raw chaos of life and transformed it into poetry.

As Honey looked at the other paintings, she noticed that in every one there was a child in the background, watching. She hadn't realized this before, because the figure was sometimes hard to see. In one painting, the child was sitting in a tree, obscured by leaves; and, in another piece, only half his face appeared at the shadowy edge of the canvas.

"No one's ever looked at my work this long," Nathan said, with a nervous laugh.

Honey continued to stare in silence, and a few moments later the young man begged her to tell him what she was thinking about.

She murmured vaguely, wondering how to begin. "It's just that the work is so . . . I feel like you're being so honest in these paintings that it makes me want to do the same. Makes me want to confess things."

"I can't imagine you'd have anything that terrible to confess."

How sweet, she thought, that he should see her as a kind old lady.

Keeping her eyes on the dogs, she asked him if he thought there were people in the world who were despicable, by nature.

When Nathan didn't respond right away, she refined the question. "I guess I'm asking if you believe in evil. If you believe that such a thing exists."

"Okay, wow—you sure you don't want some wine?" Again, the nervous laugh.

"I'm serious," said Honey. "Because I look at these paintings, and I wonder what you've seen."

Maybe she had no right to ask him, and only did so because she hoped that, someday, someone might ask her the same question. Nathan was standing beside her now, and together they stared at the piece from the gallery.

"I don't know," he said. "I don't think I've seen more than what anyone's seen. Anyone who has his eyes open, that is."

Honey realized she was trembling, though whether this was from the violence of the art, or the nearness of the young man's body, she wasn't sure.

"I don't see the dogs as necessarily *evil*," he continued. "I mean, I don't even see them as actually *there*, or like analogous to flesh-and-blood animals. I mean, the kid is obviously watching them, but none of the other people in the background ever notices the dogs—do you see that?" He pointed out the other figures. "So it's more like the animals are fighting *inside* the kid."

"Yes," said Honey. "I can certainly understand that. A lot of great art, I think, comes from an artist having an argument with himself. In fact, the art itself is often a depiction of that argument."

They kept their attention on the painting, and Honey was glad for that. She was afraid that if Nathan looked at her, he would notice the tears. Even more disastrously, he might notice the effort she'd made with her appearance—the deceptive shimmer of her skin, due to a new facial powder she'd recently purchased. The salesgirl claimed it was nothing less than miraculous, the way it reflected light away from one's flaws. Honey realized only at this very moment that she'd bought the powder with the painter in mind. She was nothing if not a fool, keeping secrets even from herself.

When Nathan took her hand, she didn't move. The two of them continued talking, philosophizing about art, their outsized words a distraction from what their hands were doing. Still, Honey could feel the shame: of old age, of greed, of wanting more life after so much death.

It seemed important that they keep speaking. If they fell silent again, there'd be no safety net—and who knew to what depth they might sink. Honey asked the painter if she could tell him a story. She said it was a rather long one, and might take some time.

"I'm all ears," he said.

Honey had no idea what she was going to say. Maybe she'd share a secret. But before she could open her mouth, the metal door swung open and a small crowd burst into the room.

"Sorry," one of them said. "Didn't mean to scare you! Is this the open studio for Nathan Flores?"

Honey noted that the visitors were all women, quite young, in high heels and flimsy jackets unsuited to the season. Their faces were flushed from the pink cocktails they'd no doubt imbibed with brunch. They looked very much like brunchers.

The painter pulled his hand away. "Yes, hi—I'm Nathan. Come on in."

And then he whispered to Honey: "To be continued."

She nodded. "Of course." Gave him a smile.

To be continued. It was another phrase fit only for the young.

Honey stepped back, leaving Nathan to his guests.

At first she thought he was a boy she'd known at Bryn Mawr. But, no, the hair was the wrong color.

Maybe it was her brother?

Honey had been in the hospital for weeks now, and they were giving her something that prevented her from thinking straight, a drug whose purpose seemed to be to prepare her for the illogic of the world to come.

"You didn't have to visit," she said to the painter, because she recognized him now.

"Are you going to say that every day?" he asked.

"Well, I don't want you to trouble yourself," she told him, though she didn't really mean it.

Today he sat on the bed, instead of the chair. The latest prognosis wasn't good—it was terrible, in fact—and he wanted to discuss it. He looked very serious, as if he were about to deliver a speech. But, ultimately, he had little success.

"Sweet boy, don't cry."

And then she told him, "Go ahead, let it out," because clearly he couldn't stop, and she didn't want him to feel ashamed for it.

Finally, he dried his eyes. "You know, they're only letting family members in at this point."

When she asked how he'd managed to get through, he smiled. "I told the nurse you were my mother."

Honey nodded blandly, attempting to hide her disappointment. Even the prospect of death hadn't eradicated vanity.

"Of course, I never thought of you that way," Nathan added, in a whisper.

Honey squeezed his hand, said she was very glad to hear it. She was smiling now too, though it felt crooked, like a smirk.

"I must look awful," she groaned—to which the young man said all the right things.

Then they sat for a while in their favorite mode—silence. She wanted the painter to crawl under the sheets and lie beside her. But since this was a Christian hospital, she didn't propose the idea.

"I wish you could smuggle me out of here," she said.

"Where would you like to go?"

She told him to take a guess.

* * *

For several years, they'd lain together in other beds, sometimes his, sometimes hers. Naked, and nearly without shame.

The first time it happened was the night of the open studio. Honey had tried to slip away, but the painter was adamant she stay. When he saw her putting on her coat, he separated himself from the young ladies he was chatting with and suggested that, after everyone was gone, the two of them might grab some dinner. She told him not to be silly—"You have lots of friends here." She was nearly at the door when Nathan's shocking reply stunned her into submission.

"I only want you."

He hadn't been this bold since the exhibition at the gallery. Why choose now to speak his mind? Honey blamed the facial powder. After the painter returned to his guests, she excused herself to the studio's tiny bathroom and stayed in there for nearly fifteen minutes, staring into a decomposing mirror losing its silver. Even in the spotty glass she didn't look half bad.

She was torn, to say the least. Complimented by the attraction, insulted by the depravity. To be fair, the painter's infatuation with her was not *entirely* abnormal. This was because it wasn't just physical now; they'd become friends. And for a person Nathan's age, platonic closeness was easily confused for something else. Young people ran on sex; it was their fuel. Honey herself had been a racecar once. In L.A., people often said she looked as good as Jane Fonda—even better, less overtly puffed and pulled. Leaning toward the mirror, she puckered her rose-toned lips.

Jesus H. Christ—what the hell was she doing?

An hour later they were at an Indian place in West Mill, where mercifully the lighting, though eccentric, was forgiving. Strands of plastic

Christmas-tree bulbs hung from the ceiling—strands that nearly brushed their heads as they made their way to a table. What a ridiculous place—a candy-colored jungle, in which the reflections on the white plates made every entrée look as if it were garnished with jelly beans. The illumination alone would have had an intoxicating effect, though they added to it with several glasses of strong beer.

Nathan was in a good mood; he'd sold a piece to one of those young women—a friend of a friend from college. Honey learned that the painter had gone to the Rhode Island School of Design—"Risdy," he called it. Under the fairy lights, she realized how little she knew about Nathan. Over the last few months, they'd talked mostly about art—and even when they spoke of themselves, the discussions were brief and quickly brought back to the larger project of aesthetics. But that night, eating curry, they made a good-sized dent in their unknowing of each other.

Nathan told her, adorably, about his hopes and dreams. Sadly, in the H and D department, Honey had little to contribute. Like many people her age, she made do, conversationally, by mining the past. The invigorating food—they'd ordered a four on a heat scale of one to five—permitted no somber confessions. Honey reminisced a bit about her move from New York City to L.A., a story of which she was proud: a middle-aged woman driving a rented sedan, with shitty AC and a Morandi in the trunk; driving carelessly in sleeveless dresses through red states, with no man at her side. She crowed about landing a fantastic job within a week of arriving, a triumph, she said, for a woman of forty-five.

When Nathan asked why she'd left New York, Honey didn't speak about her brother or Mr. Hal, but resorted to clichés that were in no way untrue. *I wanted to start again. I was dying for sunshine.*

"As I may have mentioned," she said, finessing the subject, "I still have some professional contacts out there, with some galleries, and I'd love to show them your work." She said there was one venue in particular that would go mad for what she referred to as the young man's "moody epics."

"I'd be grateful," he said. "But you really don't have to do this."

Honey replied that it would make her happy to do it. "Why don't you send me some images by email. I'll write down my address before we go."

"I'll just put your email on my phone—that way I won't lose it."

Somehow the politeness of their exchange only seemed to remind them of all the things they weren't saying, things they were afraid to admit. Honey's mouth was burning from the spices, and it suddenly felt like punishment. But she spooned up more, as did the painter.

When he was paying the check (he insisted, and Honey let him do it), she said something that caused her to blush.

"I don't know if I mentioned it, but I moved the Redon out of my bedroom into the living room. I have to find something else to put in there now—in the vacancy."

Dear God, it was as if some demon inside her were speaking. It was like asking the young man if he wanted to come upstairs and see her etchings.

When he said that he'd be willing to help her decide, Honey, unable to control herself, replied that she wouldn't mind an extra eye, especially an artist's.

Donning her coat, she wondered if there was a circle of hell dedicated to recalcitrant flirters. Maybe they went along with the lustful, to be buffeted by ceaseless winds. Or, more likely, they were chucked in with the flatterers and buried in excrement.

"Namaste!" cried the hostess, handing Honey some mints as she exited the restaurant. Outside, she got into her car, and Nathan followed, the vintage Thunderbird trailing the youthful Lexus, like some absurd, time-warped caravan. Luckily, when they arrived at the house, Jocelyn wasn't on her porch, and Honey and Nathan were able to make it inside without incident. He kissed her almost immediately, as if forgiveness would be easier than permission. He required neither. After catching her breath, she simply said, "I'm very confused."

"Ditto," he replied.

It seemed the only way through their mutual stupefaction was another kiss. By that point, Honey was so beside herself that she seriously wondered if there were hidden cameras in the house, if this ill-advised passion in the foyer were part of some elaborate setup or scheme, perhaps some kind of prank being filmed for television. Or possibly Nathan was conducting a conceptual art project, in which he wished to portray, by extremes, the grotesquerie of human desire.

Whatever it was, it did not end in the foyer.

But as for what happened in the bedroom—why be explicit? Suffice it to say that, while it was the old hibbity-jibbity, it was not a thoughtless tumble; it was rather like one of those breathing exercises Honey had learned at that ashram in Encinitas. Pleasure reduced to prayer. From start to finish, the act was surprisingly gentle. In fact, more gentle than Honey had ever experienced. It was as if the guiding star above the young man's powerful body was a pulse of kindness. Nathan took his time, which in itself was a revelation. The only other person who'd ever been this patient was Hal—and Nathan was even more sublimely studious. Ever the artist, he seemed to like the process as much as the destination.

In her younger days, Honey had imagined sex as something that would change her—that, in having it, she would pass through some kind of magical door, at the other side of which both parties would be transformed, mainly by their deeper understanding of each other.

But of course this had proved largely untrue. While it was accurate to say that sex was a door upon which you and your partner rattled and banged, and through which you eventually gained entry, the problem was that beyond this door was not a place of perfect union. It often turned out that what you perceived as a single door was actually two, and that ultimately each lover ended up in a different spot. Ended up alone, in fact. A disconcerting contradiction, especially when you remained in the arms of the man you'd had sex with.

With Nathan it was different. It didn't seem necessary to break through a door, but only to make a camp on this side of it. Lying together on the doorstep was comfort enough. Which isn't to say they failed to arrive at bliss. They did.

If Honey was teary afterward, it was only because of the exorcism the young man had performed. As if the last bit of terror had been pulled from her body. Such astonishing grace. To begin with a rapist, and end with an angel.

* * *

When she woke again in the hospital, the boy was gone, but the girl was there—and, like him, she was noticeably distraught. For goodness sake,

was everyone who entered this dreadful room going to turn on the
waterworks? Joss was making an unnecessary fuss, crying her cocker-
spaniel eyes out. Finally she looked up and said, "*Oh*—you're awake!"

"Of course I'm awake," replied Honey. "How do you expect me to
sleep with all your blubbering?"

"Sorry. But I just talked to the doctor, and he said—"

"I know what he said. Please don't remind me. And how did you get in
here, anyway? I was told that it was only family members at this point."

"Yeah, I kinda lied. I said I was your daughter."

It hurt to laugh, but Honey did more than that—she *guffawed*. "The
two of you!"

When she touched the girl's hair, pushed a wayward wiggle behind
her ears, the poor thing succumbed to another squall of tears. After it
passed, Joss set her face for cheer and retreated into mundanities. She
was taking care of Honey's house, and she dutifully reported on her
activities—mail collected, garden watered. "Our tree's doing really well,"
she said. "There's lots of buds."

The flowering cherry, yes. Honey had forgotten it was spring. Such a
brilliant idea, spring; it never made sense why the human world hadn't
copied it. Dead for half the year, alive for the remainder—an eternal to
and fro. After a while, death would seem merely a vacation. *See you in
March!* we'd all yell at each other in the fall, a bunch of waving Perse-
phones.

"Sorry, what did you say?" asked Joss.

"Did I say something?"

"You were sorta mumbling."

"*Ucch*—it's the stupid drugs. Like being on a goddam hot air balloon.
Up, up, and away!"

"Oh, that reminds me," said Joss. "You're never gonna believe who I
got a postcard from. Try to guess."

"Jimmy Hoffa?"

"Who? No." The girl leaned forward and whispered ferociously. "*Lee*."

The name sounded familiar. "Do I know her?"

"*Lee Czernik*. That guy I dated years ago." Again, the militant whisper: "The guy in the closet."

"Was he a homosexual?"

"*No.* In *your* closet."

Honey blinked, trying to jump-start the computer. The first thing that came to mind was a Taster's Choice container—and then, slowly, the man's bloody face appeared before her. At which point, she feared that Jocelyn's postcard had come from the underworld.

"Are you sure it was from him?" Honey had a distinct memory of her nephew taking this Lee person to "Connecticut."

"It was definitely him. I mean, he signed his name."

"What did he say?"

"Not much. It was only a postcard. Wait, I might have it in my bag."

The girl picked up something from the floor that looked like a burlap bucket, and after rummaging through it she pulled out a battered rectangle with an image of polar bears on it. "Okay, here it is." She offered the card to Honey.

"No, dear, I don't have my glasses. Why don't you read it to me?"

"Sure. All he says is: 'Hi J, I don't know if you're still at this address but if you are I wanted to say I was thinking of you and I'm sorry. I'm not just saying it because I'm supposed to for the program but because I mean it, even if I think you were misled.' And then he signs it, with his full name."

"*Misled?*" said Honey. "What does that mean? Misled by whom? Is he talking about me?"

"I don't know what he means—it doesn't make a whole lot of sense. But that was nice of him, though, wasn't it?"

Nice? Honey stifled herself from commenting on the girl's laissez-faire attitude, not to mention her lazy vocabulary. All she said to Joss was: "Don't you dare contact him. Do you hear me?"

"Of course not. Are you crazy? Besides, there's no return address."

"And what's with the polar bears? Where the hell is he?"

"It's postmarked Alaska. Maybe he's working at a cannery. I remember him saying he'd done that once before."

After Jocelyn put the card back inside her bucket, Honey closed her eyes. Anger faded quickly, and was replaced by a profound, almost exhilarating, relief. *So the man wasn't dead. How extraordinary.*

"I was worried for a while," Joss said, as if reading Honey's mind—"you know, that maybe something happened to him. After he left your house."

Honey feigned outrage. "Don't be absurd. As I told you, years ago, my nephew only drove him away. He's in the garbage business. Recycling, actually. Gets rid of trash, that's all."

"Lee was definitely that," agreed Jocelyn. "And I can't believe you'd think I'd want to see him again. It's not like I learned *nothing* from you."

Honey harrumphed. "Well, I'm glad to hear it."

"Plus," Joss said with a loopy grin, "I'm actually dating someone right now."

"Really? You didn't meet him on the internet, I hope."

"No, I'm done with that. He's just another hygienist from the office."

"*Just?*"

"Yeah—I mean, he's kinda boring. But that's good for me. Because it turns out I'm boring too."

"You're not boring."

"No, I am. I think, with Lee, I was just, like, getting some crazy shit out of my system."

"Yes, well, it's a lifelong process."

"But I'm feeling really good now," the girl insisted. "I'm doing a lot of baking, which I love. And Brad's a big guy, so he doesn't mind that I'm so . . ." Here, the girl puffed up her cheeks, as if to imply she were some kind of pig, or glutton.

"Don't do that," scolded Honey. "Why sell yourself short? You're very attractive."

"That's what Brad thinks too. He says I still look like a teenager."

It was true. The girl must have been in her early thirties by now, but her face was completely unlined. Honey hoped that this Brad fellow would be a good fit, a good companion. There remained a sadness in Jocelyn. Maybe it was in all girls, at some point in their lives. Unfortunately, Joss had it more than most. In order to thrive, she'd require someone to soothe away the loneliness, the fear. She was not built for solitude.

"If he's a good egg," Honey said, "try to make it work."

"You know me—I always do."

Late-afternoon light was cutting through the window, and Honey studied the girl's precious and pale, rosacea-flared skin. She also noted the fingernails bitten to the quick, and the ferrety fidget of the hands. Honey sensed that if this girl didn't get a sufficient stream of affection in her life, she might end up like one of those women who collect antique dolls and keep them in the bedroom, porcelain legs dangling from dusty shelves. Honey had known a few oddball matrons like this, who buried their love in inanimate things. Honey had often done it herself. Taken too far, though, it could destroy one's capacity for intimacy.

So when Jocelyn said, "Brad and I are actually talking about moving in together," Honey was delighted.

"Besides," the girl added, "the landlord's raising my rent, so it just makes sense. And Brad's a renter, too—and this way we can both save a little money, and eventually make some plans or whatever."

"Sweetheart, let me tell you something..."

But then Honey paused, deciding not to share the news. The girl would only make another fuss.

The fact was, Honey had recently done a final revision to her will, and she'd left the house to Jocelyn.

"What did you want to tell me?"

"Oh, nothing—I just want you to promise that you'll keep watering my plants."

"Absolutely. But then, you know, when you get home . . . " the girl soldiered on, with a tremor in her voice.

Honey eyeballed her sternly, putting an end to such willful fancy.

"*What?* You'll come home."

"Darling..."

"No," Joss said, scrunching up her face, then covering it. "What'll I do without you?"

Oh, sweet Jesus—the waterworks again.

"You'll be fine, dear. Come on, now—just hold my hand and be quiet."

The girl nodded, obeyed—though after a moment she squeaked, "I love you."

"Yes, that's nice. Same here. Let's just stay like this, shall we? *Mmm,* your hand's so nice and warm. Lucky lucky lucky," mumbled Honey, closing her eyes.

* * *

Lucky, indeed.

Though, for a time, Honey had wondered about the nature of this luck. In regard to Jocelyn, the question was always the same. *Do I deserve to have a daughter?*

With Nathan, the issue was a bit more theological. Honey wondered if it was a sin—a perversion—to have slept with a man so much younger. It certainly wasn't her worst sin, but since it was the most recent, it had assumed a certain importance.

After their first night together, Honey was sometimes tortured when she thought about it. At the center of this torture lay an awful number. *Forty-seven.* Which was the number of years between Nathan's age and her own. For a while, this number had obsessed Honey. It seemed significant, like the year of some terrible disaster. The Great Fire of '47. The Great Flood.

Of course, this wasn't the first time she'd been swept away by a number. Mr. Hal was the precedent. He'd had decades on Honey, though not quite as much as she had on Nathan. Also, with Hal, there was a very important difference. *He* was the older one. And since he was the man, this had somehow made it acceptable.

After that first tumble with Nathan, Honey promised herself that it wouldn't happen again. A promise she'd broken countless times, over many years. At a certain point, of course, the lovemaking had tapered off. Still, Nathan had continued to share her bed—though he began to provide simpler comforts. Just the closeness of his body had been a balm. And such wonderful conversations they'd had, lying in the dark, holding hands. Even now, the thought of it can make her weep. The only word she can find is kindness—though the painter never liked it when she said this. To borrow his argument: "You make it sound like charity—and it's not."

The why of it still troubles her, the why of his wanting her. The why of him—as if, before she goes, she's required to unravel not only her own mysteries but his, too. She knows a fair amount about Nathan's life—about his parents, his childhood—but none of it's particularly telling, none of it explains his desire for her. And she feels she needs such explanations to defend herself. Perhaps it's something in the air at this Christian hospital, a miasma of judgment and morality.

Sometimes, late at night, her questions evaporate, and she feels at peace. But then, out of nowhere, that word comes back. *Perversion.*

Yet isn't it all perversion, she wonders—all of life?

A man striking his own son. Another man striking a woman. Not to mention a woman with a gun, raging and ready to kill.

A father asking his daughter to take a drive with the man who's raped her.

Everything goes against the grain of goodness. Or perhaps there is no goodness.

The man at the bottom of the stairs. A girl in a forest, giving her child to a stranger. Even more: that Honey had once *been* that girl. Time itself was a perversion—perhaps the greatest one of all.

In the end, everything got broken. Everyone was wounded. Why, then, did some part of her wish to remain here, on this violent planet?

And then she remembered. *Beauty.*

Aunt Honey? Can we come in?"

When she opened her eyes, she saw the last person she expected. The last two, in fact.

It was Corrado and his grandson.

"Goodness—have you been standing there long?"

"It looked like you were napping."

"No, I was just . . ." Honey smoothed her hair. For the first time in ages, she longed for the imposture of a wig. "Come in, come in."

The visitors entered slowly, as if testing the ice on a lake. Her nephew attempted a smile, but the boy's face remained circumspect. Vittorio was five now, maybe six. He wasn't a stranger. Honey knew him from the Sunday dinners she'd occasionally shared with the Fazzingas. Over the last few years, she'd seen them at least a dozen times. It hadn't been a matter of forgiveness, but rather the irresistible call of blood.

Honey had actually been hoping that Corrado might visit, especially after what she'd learned from Jocelyn.

But, in accordance with the old rules, she and Corrado never spoke of such things. Over the years of their reconciliation—though perhaps that was too strong a word—the two of them had made no real effort to excavate the past. And it was far too late to begin. Nonetheless, it was a relief to know that her nephew hadn't taken Lee Czernik to Connecticut.

"Just the two of you?" asked Honey, propping herself up before the unlikely duo—the large dark man running to fat, and the slight boy whittled from a paler branch of the family tree.

"Yeah, just us," Corrado said. "Rina sends her best."

Honey wasn't surprised that Rina hadn't come. For Rina, it *was* a matter of forgiveness; it seemed that she could never look at Honey without seeing something she couldn't forgive in herself. Their relationship was complicated—but they'd made do, on the occasional Sunday, with wine and small talk. At the hospital, over plastic cups of water, it would have been harder to keep the truth at bay. The Sunday dinners were a bid toward civility, a well-mannered truce—but the soil was too shallow for any real intimacy to grow.

Besides, Honey had attended those dinners more to see Vittorio than for anything else. He was very bright, and as was often the case with bright children, slightly odd. Rather like me, she often thought.

Corrado shepherded the boy into the room—the little face wary, eye contact withheld. Honey knew him well enough to understand it was necessary that she make the first move toward conversation.

"Have you missed me, dear?"

Vittorio made a noncommittal shrug, his indifference belied by the fact that he took a few steps forward, stopping just shy of the bed.

"I'm glad you're here," she said.

When at last he looked up, his words were bold. "How come you're alone?"

"I'm not alone," replied Honey. "You're here. And your grandfather's here."

The boy pursed his lips, unsatisfied. "But I mean, who else is saying goodbye to you?"

Corrado suddenly looked embarrassed, almost stricken; no doubt he'd said something to Vittorio about coming to the hospital to say goodbye. "Don't be rude," he told the kid.

"No, it's fine," said Honey. "It's a perfectly legitimate question." She looked at Vittorio and told him that she had other friends who'd stopped by. "But now it's your turn."

The child glanced toward Corrado, and then back at Honey. Surely, this was his first encounter with death, and she wanted to make it easy on him. She had no intention of making declamatory speeches, or pressing tidbits of wisdom into the little boy's fist. Their last conversation should be jovial—and it should be about him, not her.

"How are things in school?" she asked.

"Fine," he said. "I wrote a story."

"Did you?"

"It won a prize."

"Really? What was it about?"

"Cows," he replied, as if talking to someone slightly dim—as if there could be no other subject suitable for a story. And now that he'd exposed this literary vein, his words began to flow more easily. "It was the longest story of anyone in my class. It was, like, *twenty* sentences."

"Very impressive," said Honey.

He shrugged again—at which point Corrado came over and put his hand on Vittorio's shoulder. It gave Honey pleasure to see how kindly her nephew treated the boy. It caused her heart to ache, as well. Strangely, the two feelings were not that different.

As Honey continued to chat with the kid about cows, she noted the positions of the bodies in the room—how Vittorio stood almost exactly equidistant between Corrado and herself. It seemed to illustrate something she'd sensed over the last few years, but had never really articulated. Which was that the child was a kind of bridge. All the complicated feelings she had about Corrado, and which no doubt he had about her, moved back and forth across Vittorio's tiny body. Moved through it, to be precise—more of a tunnel than a bridge, and inside of which there occurred a mysterious translation. It was almost as if, without the boy, communication between her and her nephew wouldn't be possible.

In some ways, they were using him. Well, not exactly *using*. Both of them adored the boy and would never do anything to harm him. Still, they relied on the child to conduct the secret business of their agonized affection.

Vittorio seemed vaguely aware of this, evidenced by the way he kept glancing back and forth, from one adult to the other. Honey wondered if the silent negotiations between her and Corrado caused the boy any pain, if he could feel the strain of their heavy hearts shuttling through him, that dark and weary traffic.

Despite these worries, she was glad the boy was here, and felt quite ready to ask him a thousand questions about his fictional bovines. But, before she could get back to the prizewinning story, Vittorio abruptly changed the subject.

"Are you going to stay in the little house?" he asked her.

Honey assumed he was talking about the fort, the one he'd made in his grandparents' backyard last summer. Sticks and leaves and worn-out sheets. He'd done a bang-up job. Honey recalled how proud he'd been of his accomplishment, and how he'd encouraged her to crawl inside. But her knee had been acting up that day, so she'd only admired the fort from the outside. Vittorio had been disappointed.

"Well, I'd like to stay there," she said now, in answer to his question. "But I'm not sure it's big enough for me."

The boy narrowed his eyes, as if confused. "It's small," he said, "but it's not *that* small. There's room for twelve people."

Honey was confused now, too. She asked Vittorio if he'd made a bigger one.

"I didn't make it," he said. "It was made before I was born."

The lights in the room seemed to blink, and Honey wondered if the drugs were kicking in. For the life of her, she couldn't make heads or tails of this conversation.

"You're talking about your fort in the backyard?" she asked.

"No," he said, sounding almost annoyed. "I'm talking about where we go to see my great-grandpa."

Honey wondered if the boy was referring to her brother.

Corrado appeared flustered. "We took him to the cemetery, and now he's obsessed with it."

"I'm not *obsessed*," he said to his grandfather—and then, looking back at Honey: "I was just interested because the house has our name on it."

The boy, it seemed, was talking about the mausoleum. What a peculiar creature. "No, dear," she told him. "I don't believe I'll be staying there."

"Why not? It's your name, too."

"Yes, it is—you're right. But . . ." What could she tell him? She explained that she'd made other plans.

"What plans?"

"Victor!" Corrado scolded—"*Basta* with the questions!" And then to Honey: "He gets like this, sorry."

Why was the man apologizing? Honey wasn't troubled in the least by the child's morbidity. In fact, she found it refreshing. No one else had had the guts to speak of such things.

What was also delightful was Vittorio's willfulness, how comfortable he seemed resisting his grandfather. The gods had fun, didn't they? Putting Mica's delicate features and pale coloring into the boy, while also giving him the classic Fazzinga swagger.

When, after a moment, Vittorio spoke again, insisting that his questions were important, Corrado told him it wasn't the time or the place. "Just ignore him," he said to Honey.

"Actually," she said, "I'd like to speak to him honestly, if I may."

"You may," the boy said, taking matters into his own hands. At which point, Corrado rolled his eyes in capitulation.

"The reason I'm not going to stay in the little house," Honey explained to Vittorio, "is because I'm going to be cremated."

Corrado winced, clearly uncomfortable with such specifics, but the boy remained doggedly curious.

"What's cremated?"

"It's a kind of magic," Honey said. "It's taking one thing and turning it into another. I'll become a kind of dust, and then some people I know—the friends I mentioned to you earlier—will scatter me over a very pretty place."

"Where?"

"California. On a particular beach I'm very fond of."

"There are beaches in New Jersey," the boy said.

"Yes, that's true," agreed Honey, unexpectedly laughing.

"Like, have you ever been to Lavallette?" the boy asked. "We have a house there, right on the beach. If you wanted, *we* could scatter you."

When Honey glanced at Corrado, she saw that he was crying. Vittorio noticed it, too.

"What's wrong, Grandpa?"

He shook his head, pulled himself together. "Why don't you give Aunt Honey a kiss, all right? And then go wait for me outside, in the hall."

"Why?" the boy asked—"Are you having secrets?"

"None of your business, buster."

Vittorio sighed, accepting his fate. He moved closer to the bed, then leaned forward, placing his entire upper body against Honey's. She could feel the shocking warmth bleeding through the sheet. He offered no kiss, only lay there, as if trying to leave an impression, or take one of her.

Honey placed her hand lightly on Vittorio's head, though what she wanted was to grab him, drag him away to where she was going.

"*Lavallette*," he whispered, as if trying to hypnotize her. And then he lifted his body, said, "Bye, Aunt Honey," and left the room.

After he was gone, Corrado closed the door slightly. "I don't think he understands."

Honey wiped her eyes. "Children understand more than we give them credit for."

Corrado's face was aflush, strangely burning, as if there were something he wished to confess. But now that they were alone, he seemed to have forgotten how to speak. Honey, too, struggled to find more words. She clutched her fists against the void.

Finally, when her nephew sat beside the bed, she remembered some things she needed to discuss with him. For instance, she needed to explain why she was leaving the house to Jocelyn. It wasn't beyond reason that the Fazzingas would try to contest her wishes. As it stood, the only Fazzingas named in her will were Mica and Vittorio.

The most important thing, though, was to make sure Corrado understood that she had nothing to do with his father's death. She'd never been disloyal, only disheartened; she needed to make that clear.

But she only sat in the bed, propped up like a doll, and said nothing. The room was unbearably white, as if designed to erase all meaning. Corrado took her hand, but the gesture failed to bind her. A buzzing filled her ears. The light grew stranger. Honey found herself thinking about the little house. Was it too late to change her mind? What would it mean to join her parents and brother in that pink marble monstrosity? Something about Corrado's hand suggested she consider it.

She closed her eyes, to get her thoughts in order, and when she looked back at Corrado, he was crying again. Tears of love, of accusation. Honey felt the same.

"It doesn't matter where I'm going," she finally said. "Wherever I go, I won't forget." How could she? They were family, for heaven's sake. She squeezed her nephew's hand and told him, as kindly as possible, that she'd never forget anything.

I n her dreams she often feels drunk. She feels herself drawing closer to those strands of light she witnessed as a girl while tripping on LSD. Sometimes, though, she confuses these lights for others she's seen at an Indian restaurant.

She hopes the painter will come back soon. Next month, he's having another exhibition in Los Angeles, and she wants to remind him about that chocolate shop, with the truffles that taste like tears. She wants to tell him, too, about the painting she's left him. That winged creature standing on a cliff, looking up at a tawny blur—a feathered woman flying toward the sun.

Then, as if to grant her wish, there's a rapping at the door.

But for some reason, she's unable to speak, and when she opens her eyes there are only shadows. A pulsing darkness hovers above her head.

Not death, but Teena Novak, the orange-nailed proprietress. The woman runs her fingers through Honey's hair.

"Jesus Christ! Have the nurses never heard of a brush?"

If Honey could smile, she would. But her face is under the icy dictate of some foreign power. It's been like that for days now, her will completely overruled. She mumbles incoherently, when what she wants is to fill the room with *darlings*, with knockabout camaraderie. There's only her heartbeat, though. Only the labor of her breath.

"I've brought a friend," Teena says, as another dark form emerges from the doorway. This one's taller, slimmer, moving with such surety of purpose that Honey wonders if Teena has invited in the inevitable.

Honey isn't frightened, though. She's ready.

The second shadow sits beside the bed and takes her hand. When it leans forward to kiss her, there's a curtain of scented hair. Cloves and oranges, a tang of autumn leaves—possibly tobacco.

"Aunt Honey," the shadow calls her.

It says other things, too, that don't make sense. Things about gratitude and time and music. When the shadow apologizes for "breaking it," Honey wants to say, it's not important. Besides, if he's talking about the vase, it's hopeless. Impossible to repair, the restorers said.

"Do you recognize me, Aunt Honey?"

She nods, or tries to nod. His name won't come to her, but she knows it's broken too, a piece of something else. In her mind the only name that comes is *mother-father*.

Even as the shadow grips her hand, she hopes he won't stay long. He needs to get away, return to the light he came from.

Don't go home, she wants to tell him, though whether this is good or bad advice she isn't certain. Still, she knows there's something within her that has some value. And so when her blood leans down again to kiss her, Honey acts quickly.

She bleeds her entire life into him. Into them.

She does it as easily as singing. And she does it in silence.

Acknowledgments

I have carried this story in my heart a long time, and the translation to the page was often difficult. I'm very grateful to the people and organizations who supported and encouraged me, and who, at times, pushed me to a deeper understanding of my own life, which is to say, this book. Among these friends and allies, I wish to publicly thank: Bill Clegg, Millicent Bennett, Chris Rush, Adam Geary, John Johnson (and Henry), Liz Velez, Daniel Mahar, Rebecca Laursen, Eric Laursen, Richard Lodato, Janet Neipris, Polly Pen, Karson Liegh, Michele Conway, the Corporation of Yaddo, and the Civitella Ranieri Foundation.

Writing this novel was in many ways a collaboration with the dead, and so I feel compelled to thank, as well, those who have passed on, particularly the spirited women in my family, without whom I would not have survived: Sophie Lodato, Theresa Coari, Josephine Lodato, Teresa D'Auria, Susan D'Auria, Janet Lewis, and Austin Brayfield.

Chi si volta, e chi si gira, sempre a casa va finire.

–V.L.

About the Author

VICTOR LODATO is a playwright and the author of the novels *Edgar and Lucy* and *Mathilda Savitch*, winner of the PEN USA Award for Fiction. The recipient of fellowships from the Guggenheim Foundation and the National Endowment for the Arts, his stories and essays regularly appear in the *New Yorker*, the *New York Times*, *Granta*, and elsewhere. His novels and plays have been translated into eighteen languages. Born and raised in New Jersey, he now lives in Oregon and Arizona.